WOVEN

MICHAEL JENSEN
DAVID POWERS KING

SCHOLASTIC INC.

ISBN 978-0-545-83117-8

10 9 8 7 6 5 4 3 2 1   15 16 17 18 19

Printed in the U.S.A.   40
First printing, January 2015
Book design by Nina Goffi

FOR
NICHOLAS
AND
JOANNA

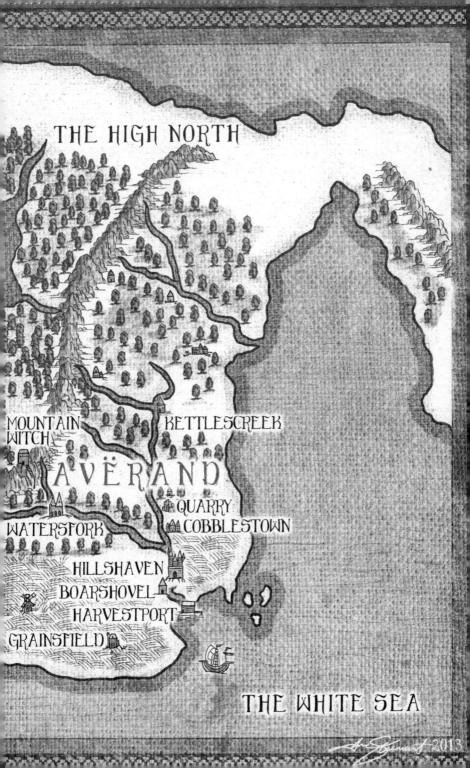

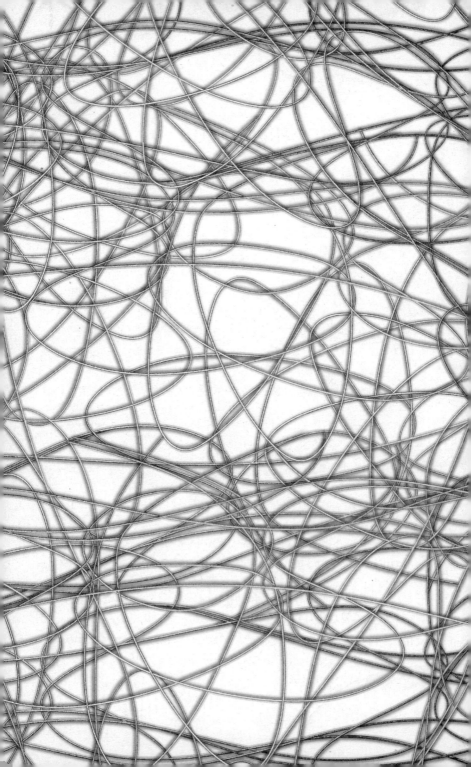

PROLOGUE

THE TRAVELER'S SECRET

Dust tickled the side of Kettle's nose, but he did not bother to scratch it. The torchlit outline of Castle Avërand loomed ahead in the moonless night, like a candle against the stars. He cared little for the grand edifice that stood over Hillshaven, but he traveled toward it anyway.

What lay within its walls was far more important.

It's been a long time. Not much farther now.

Kettle strolled down the wide country road, carrying a small knapsack over his shoulder, a dim lantern in one hand, and a short walking stick in the other. The weight on his shoulder was light but tiresome. Beads of sweat formed on his brow, appropriate for the warm summer night.

Torches lined the granite walls that surrounded the city, revealing moss and thick ivies on the old stones. The smell of fresh dew enveloped Kettle's senses and the trickling of a small brook met his ears, followed by the sight of a bridge. Making his way over the water, he saw a shadow move alongside the base of the southern tower. Kettle smothered his light, crept into the grasses, and peeked through the blades, hoping to catch another glimpse of the shadow before he approached. He waited and watched as torchlight illuminated the figure. It was a young maiden with long golden hair, dressed in a fine summer gown.

What's a pretty thing like her doing out in the middle of the night?

She made her way to the front gate, looking around cautiously. A guard stood from his chair as she neared. "Feeling better, Your Highness?"

The maiden shook her head. "These insects are awfully loud tonight."

"There's no moon. How else will they find each other?"

"Open the door — and speak of my leaving to no one."

The man frowned as he let her pass and then he locked the door behind her. Intrigued, Kettle reached out his hand to grasp the maiden's *thread*. The girl had a strong will, and noble blood flowed through her veins, just like his old friend.

Could it be?

Yes. He had no doubt. She was the daughter of his friend, the prince. When he had seen her last, she was nothing more than a babe in a bundle of cloth. Not anymore. She had grown into a striking young woman, a maiden of virtue and fair beauty, as Kettle would have expected from the prince's bloodline. He would surely see her soon enough, but, for now, he had to introduce himself at the gate and make his way inside. Kettle emerged from the grass.

"Who's there?" said the gatekeeper. "What do you want?'"

"I am a lone traveler," Kettle answered. "No one of consequence."

"It's much too late to be traveling alone, old man. What do you want?"

"A night's lodging within your walls, if you would accommodate?"

"You're too late to lodge here, stranger. Try the inn at Boarshovel, just down the road."

Kettle pressed his back against the wall. "I have come from Harvestport and would rather not retrace my steps. I will wait here, if you don't mind. I have business inside."

"You carry a light load for business . . ."

Smiling, Kettle lowered his knapsack and lantern.

The gatekeeper grunted as he sat down in his chair. "You'll have to move along."

"Would you like some company? I would imagine your job must be quite dull."

"Dull? Ha! Frightfully so . . ." The gatekeeper sighed and then smiled. "Fine — I suppose you can stay. Just don't try anything. I may not be young anymore, but I can still take you."

Kettle chuckled. "So it would appear."

"What's your name then, stranger?"

"You may call me Kettle."

This made the man laugh. "Like Kettlescreek, north of here?"

"Why, yes," he said, joining in the laughter. "Just like that."

"Curious name for an old goat — mine's Dyre."

Kettle smiled without allowing the remark to insult him. The gatekeeper had judged him only by what he could see. "Thank you for allowing me to rest here. It will give me a chance to study you."

Dyre raised his brow. "*Study* me?"

"I am an artist, my good man. Inspiration comes best while I watch people. I study their faces, observe the way they move and speak. Every subtle difference fascinates me."

Dyre rocked his chair back. "I'd rather not have you stare at me all night."

"If you would prefer conversation, there is much I would like to know. It's been years since I last visited Averand. Your crops are the healthiest I've seen since my youth."

"I could oblige that. What would you like to know?"

"That maiden who entered the gate — who is she?"

The man hesitated. "Oh, um . . . I'm afraid I can't talk about that."

Kettle dabbed his finger into a pocket within his sleeve and secretly flicked a drop of blue dye at the gatekeeper. It landed on the man's hand, unnoticed, and seeped into his skin.

That should do the trick. "You can tell me; I will not say a word."

"She's King Lennart's daughter," the man said without hesitation. His voice, throat, mind, and body had completely relaxed. Blue dye: subtle, yet effective. "She's not allowed outside this late, but it makes her happy, mostly. I'm not supposed to tell anyone."

"Of course, and neither will I. Prince Lennart has assumed the throne, then?"

"Not that he does much with it — he hasn't done much of anything since his father was murdered."

Kettle nodded his sympathies. "Yalva. I knew him well. Such a tragedy."

"Indeed, it was." Dyre coughed. "We don't like to talk of it, even though it happened ages ago — rumors and such. Some say a wizard killed him, if you believe such nonsense."

"Right," Kettle agreed. "Utter nonsense."

The gatekeeper cleared his throat. "What else would you like to know?"

"Much." Kettle had a long list of questions with hours left before dawn. He decided to save his more delicate questions for later. "What is it like to be the gatekeeper here?"

Dyre beamed. "Easy, with plenty of perks, the best being this sweet scullery maid who brings me cherry tarts — they're my favorite!" The man leaned forward and stretched his legs.

"I manage the outs and ins from here; three night watches and four day watches a week."

Kettle looked at the wooden lever beside Dyre's chair as the gatekeeper succinctly laid out his occupation. All of this was good to know. "Why do you sit out here and not inside the gate?"

"The night air is peaceful," the man said. "I've had no problem at this post for years. And besides, the most I would have to do is pull this lever if danger should ever come this way."

"I take it you've seen *everyone* who comes and goes this way?"

Dyre laughed. "I've seen every last soul in Averand."

"Then you know Lady Katharina and her boy, Lief?"

The gatekeeper furrowed his brow. "I haven't heard their names in years." Dyre sat up, placing his hands on his knees. "How do you know of them?"

"I knew them long ago," Kettle said. "Are they no longer among the nobility?"

"They vanished from the castle shortly after King Yalva's death."

Kettle's smile thinned and then faded. "Do they remain in this land?"

Dyre frowned as he shook his head. "How should I know?"

This news made Kettle clench his teeth.

The boy can't be gone. He has to be here! She wouldn't leave . . .

All had gone according to plan, but now he would have to improvise.

"Will he come for the princess?" Kettle asked.

"Come for . . . *who*?" The gatekeeper rubbed his eyes. The dye had worn off.

Since Kettle's business no longer resided in the castle, he would have to look elsewhere for the boy; but where else would he be? He had to find him. Kettle's return to Avërand would be pointless otherwise. He reached out his hand to grasp the boy's thread, to sense his presence in the land . . . but he felt nothing.

If I am to find him, I must stay close to the princess . . .

He had no other choice. Kettle focused his eyes on the gatekeeper and studied him. Chin, cheeks, forehead, then ears, eyes, nose. In seconds, Kettle memorized Dyre's face.

The gatekeeper squinted as he raised his hand for the lever. "Who are you *really*?"

Instantly, Kettle pushed off the wall and shoved Dyre away from the lever. He then covered the gatekeeper's mouth with one hand, brandished a knife in the other, and grazed its fine edge along the man's throat. Dyre's eyes widened as Kettle's face unraveled and coiled in the air like a spool of fleshy thread — and wove back as a mirror image of the gate-keeper himself.

"For now," he said, using Dyre's voice, "I will be *you*."

1

THE KNIGHT OF COBBLESTOWN

Nels did not like the taste of dirt.

An unrelenting hand pressed down on his head. "Do you give?" Wallin jeered.

Clenching his jaw, Nels twisted his leg free and rolled Wallin to his side. "Never!"

The boys around them cheered as the two seventeen-year-old grapplers leaped back to their feet and watched for the other to make his next move. Nels held out his arms, waiting for Wallin's counterattack. A layer of dust, bonded by sweat, caked their skin — and Wallin had removed his shirt, making it even more difficult for Nels to gain a firm hold. Nels smiled confidently as he eyed the steps of his opponent. He had never lost a match to Wallin before — he wasn't about to let Wallin win now.

Nels let go of his breath as a summer breeze touched his sandy-brown hair. He had only a short time to finish his chores, so it was unwise of him to use the last of the day's light to accept this challenge — but it wasn't like Nels to turn down a match with Wallin in front of an audience. Wallin had something to prove, apparently; otherwise he wouldn't have come all this way or stayed so late. Nels watched him. Timing and strategy were Nels's strongest assets — although his height and strength were certainly helpful as well.

Go for his leg?

No. Wallin would expect that.

Fake a grab and then go for his leg?

That might work.

Making his move, Nels jumped to the side, ducked for Wallin's leg, and quickly threw him off-balance. He then tossed his weight and rolled Wallin onto his stomach, leaped for his head, and planted his face deep into the upturned soil. No matter how hard he struggled, Wallin would never escape this hold.

The boys counted: "One — two — three!"

And the match was over.

"Enough!" Wallin spat as he tapped the ground. "I give!"

Releasing his grasp on Wallin, Nels reached out his hand and helped his friend to his feet, all while the young spectators clapped. Nels remained their champion, and he planned to keep it that way.

"How'd you know I was coming after you like that?" Wallin asked.

Nels laughed. "Knights always anticipate the moves of their opponents."

"Yeah . . ." Wallin mustered a sore smile. "We're not exactly knights yet."

"Nels!" A woman called to him from the cottage at the south end of the field. "What are you doing? Stop fooling around and finish your furrows. Go on home, you lot — all of you!"

Wallin chuckled as he shook his red head and patted the dust from his trousers. "I'll get you yet," he promised. "One of these days, I'll get you — unless that old nag beats me to it."

Nels readied his fists. "That's my mother you're talking about."

"With all this work, she's more like a slave master!"

Nels threw a playful punch, one that Wallin avoided with ease. Wallin threw the next fist, also easy to dodge. One of the young boys stepped in to prevent a third. No — it was a girl. Jilia's boyish, short, dark-brown hair had misled Nels again. The girl scowled at the shirtless Wallin. "Knock it off, you ruffian!" she said with childish formality. "You've lost this day."

Wallin glanced down at her and laughed. Picking up his shirt, he ran toward Cobblestown with the others, leaving Jilia and Nels alone.

"You didn't have to do that," Nels said. "We weren't serious, you know."

"I know." Jilia picked up a stone and chucked it at Wallin. The projectile bounced off a tree's trunk instead. "But they should respect the Knight of Cobblestown . . . and your squire . . ."

"*My* squire?" Nels said. "Is *that* why you keep following me?"

The girl crossed her arms, a blush rising in her cheeks. "It's my duty."

"Then fetch me that spade, milady; I have a field to vanquish!"

Jilia dashed straight for the tool and placed the handle in his hand.

Nels could not contain his smile. "You didn't have to do that, either."

"Well, until you become a squire, you'll just have to deal with it."

"Guess that means I better hurry up then." Nels winked.

The girl furrowed her thick brow. "When will that be?"

"When will I ask you to go fetch something else?"

"No, you dolt! When will *you* become a squire?"

Nels glanced at the cottage and the white clouds beyond. He did not have a ready answer for her question, one that he had asked himself many times. The knighthood chose their squires once each year, an event that Nels had yet to experience firsthand. Tomorrow was the big day.

"You'll have to take that up with my mother. Knowing her, it's out of the question."

"What's with your mother? She's so prim and proper — she never lets you do anything." Jilia scrunched her small nose. "My father lets me do whatever I want, and I turned out fine!"

Nels smirked as he looked at the torn sleeve of her hand-me-down shirt. Patches covered her trousers, frayed shoes barely fit her feet, and her ankles drowned in oversized stockings. Her round cheeks had splotches of dirt on them, all but hidden by her small, charming smile. Unlike Nels, she had no mother, raised with her five brothers on a pear orchard on the other side of town.

Inversely, Nels had no father — none that he knew of, anyway. "I'm all my mother has."

"Not if you get married!" The girl slugged him in the shoulder.

"Hey!" Nels rubbed at the smart. "What was that for?"

"That's what'll happen if you marry someone other than me."

Nels raised his brow, his deep-green eyes at home among the oak leaves that surrounded them. He hadn't expected their conversation to suddenly veer down this thorny path. Nothing so bold had ever come out of the thirteen-year-old's mouth. Nels had to keep his tone light if he wanted to come out of this unscathed. "Marriage? Aren't you a little young to be thinking such a thing, Jilia?"

The girl shrugged and spat phlegm over her shoulder. "If things keep going the way they are, you'll still be living here, and then" — a soft pink rose to Jilia's cheeks, making her small freckles stand out more — "I'll be old enough . . ."

Nels tried his best to laugh subtly. "I think I'll keep you as my squire for now."

"Sure." Her voice fell flat. "Well, I'd better go, but you will come to the festival, won't you?"

"We'll see what happens," Nels said. "I'll ask my mother over supper."

"Good, because you may not have another chance. Please, *please* come!"

"I'll do my best," he answered, with a more sincere smile.

"You always do." She winked back. "See you then!"

The girl ran across the field, stepping clumsily over the furrows. Nels shook his head, smiling as he watched her go. His friends were interesting; Jilia followed Nels whenever he went into town — not that he went to town often — and Wallin turned every encounter between them, from eating pies to shaking hands, into a competition. Still, they were his friends. And they believed in his dream.

It would be dark in a few minutes — not enough time left to sow the barley seeds and other vegetables that needed planting. A thick forest of white oak trees surrounded their land, hiding their little cottage from the world. Their shrouded path traveled east into Cobblestown, not more than a half-hour's journey on foot, half that on horseback. Not that Nels would know; his mother forbade him from riding horses after Old Brown had — just once — bucked him off.

Nels leaned forward and dug another furrow.

"Some knight I am . . ."

Despite his efforts to talk himself out of it, he could not surrender his desire to become a knight of Avërand. Everyone in the village approved, and many were surprised that Nels was not already among their ranks. He was old enough and strong enough, and plenty had vouched for his bravery. When the townsfolk saw him save a half-buried man from a rockslide last summer, they hailed Nels as their hero. And after he jumped into the river to rescue the locksmith's daughter from drowning, they called him "The Knight of Cobblestown."

Nels was no knight, though. He could not leave his easily frightened mother. Doing so would throw her into a panic. If Nels earned so much as a scratch, she would always assume the worst. Tonight, the village was preparing for the summer festival, and he was stuck at home, laboring for their winter stores — since his mother had again forgotten to get the seeds until it was nearly too late in the season.

With a disappointed sigh, Nels watched the sun lower behind the treetops.

I can't blame her. What would she do without me? She needs me here.

He knew becoming a knight would never happen as long as his mother had her way. She hated all knights, the royalty, *anything* that had to do with authority or nobility in the land of Avërand. No one else seemed to mind the royals. They were quite generous to the people; they kept taxes at a reasonable rate, and they made sure to visit the villages each year.

What they *did* was not the problem. It was what they *did not* do.

An apathetic monarch held the throne — a king who moped inside his castle, convinced that he was cursed. By what, no one knew for sure. But whatever was haunting the king caused him to ignore relations with other lands. If it were not for the sea town of Harvestport, the world would have forgotten about the minuscule country, a directionless kingdom with a languishing knighthood. Nels had never seen the king, but he knew if he were a knight, he could help — just as he helped everyone else. Mother forbade him from going to Hillshaven, home of Castle Avërand. In fact, she forbade him from going anywhere, especially to the summer festival.

"I could do so much more. If only I could convince her . . ."

The inviting smell of asparagus stew reached his nose. Tired from tilling and sore from wrestling in the dirt, Nels gathered his tools and headed, sluggishly, for the old cottage.

"Did you enjoy wallowing in the dirt like a sow?" Mother asked.

Sporting a cheerful grin, Nels strolled over the cottage threshold. "I sure did!"

The woman stirred her pot. "Be glad I am not cooking you up like one."

"*You* should be glad." Nels laughed. "I'd taste horrible, don't you think?"

With a sweet harrumph, Mother went back to her stewing.

Their quaint cottage was a small, homey place, crowded, but organized. Tapestries made by his mother hung on the walls, and heaps of fabric, spools of thread, and piles of linens occupied every shelf and corner, filling the entire cottage with color. His mother was a seamstress. Her ability to make any textile, be it napkins or fancy gowns, was extraordinary. Nels couldn't complain, really; few people in Cobblestown had a wardrobe as neatly fashioned as his.

Mother kept busy most days, earning enough money to buy what they needed. Buying what they *wanted*, however, was a matter they hardly spoke of. This added to Nels's confusion, because she had fashioned a number of stunning outfits — suits fit for kings and dresses worthy of queens — but she never sold them or showed them. Instead, she had them locked up in a wardrobe.

We could be rich. Why won't she do more than patch jobs?

Nels changed out of his filthy clothes. The taste of dirt still lingered in his mouth.

"Wash thoroughly," Mother commanded. "I cannot afford to soil the fabric when I lay it out for measuring." She spooned a few helpings of asparagus stew into two bowls and daintily placed them on the table. "Such a ragged thing, that girl, but she may look lovely with age."

"You mean Jilia?" Nels slipped on a fresh shirt. "Why would you say that?"

"Time has a way of changing a girl . . . and the way a man thinks of her."

Nels walked to the table and sat down. "She's not the kind of girl I have in mind."

Mother snickered as she returned the pot to the hearth. "No, no, not *that* little thing. You deserve someone better, someone calm and refined, a girl who will appreciate your character." Her warm smile almost taunted him. "I understand several in the village have an eye on you."

He shrugged. "I suppose. They're nice, but . . . none of them seem right."

Mother finally sat herself down, soft and gentle like a feather. "That may be for the best. I let you try working with Lars the blacksmith, after all," she reminded him. "That work did not impress you, and the same goes for the quarry. Not even tailoring holds your interest. If you do not take up and master a trade soon, you will have nothing to offer a young bride."

"There's one trade you haven't let me try yet, Mother."

She reached for a pinch of pepper, obviously ignoring him.

Nels let his chin rest on his knuckles. "I need to tell you something."

"Elbows."

He heeded the reprimand by lowering his hands. "It's about the festival —"

"I will not hear of it." Mother reached for her spoon. "Imagine what could happen if I were left alone. What if thieves should come? No. Now stop slouching and eat your supper."

Nels sat upright with a groan as a fragrant steam rose from the bowl of stew in front of him. His mother's unconvincing response to his incomplete question had made him lose his appetite. What sort of knight fails to stand up to his own mother? Nels glanced at her; she did not look back. She had a thin frame, and her vibrant red hair curled around her ears. Her eyes revealed a hint of blue that sparkled whenever she laughed. No other woman in the region could match her striking looks. Suitors from the village knew this, and she had refused every single one.

Mother dabbed her chin with a napkin. "Eat, before it cools."

"I'm going to the festival, Mother."

"You may not. Festivals do not finish work. Frivolity after drudgery."

Nels clutched his chair and took a calming breath. "Why don't we set up a stand at the festival? We could afford to buy our stores for winter if you sold the dresses in your wardrobe."

"You have no business in my things," Mother warned. "And why would I do that? We have all the seed we need. Why buy what we can grow? Are you looking to weasel out of your chores again?"

"I don't see the need for it, and you always give me extra chores right before the festival."

The woman fidgeted. "Summer is our busiest season, Nels. You know that."

"Then why buy the seed so late? Everyone had their crops set *weeks* ago." His mother glanced away, resisting his question, so Nels placed his hands on the table — more forcefully than he meant to — and stood up. "I want to become a knight, Mother," he said. "Why won't you let me?"

"Nels." Mother shot him a reproving look. "I will not have this. Those villagers have filled your head with these dangerous aspirations for too long. Do you believe saving a man from a rockslide is merit enough to affiliate yourself with *that* wretched horde of crooks and merrymakers? Sampling wine is all the knights of Averand are good for!"

Nels shook his head. He did not enjoy arguing with his mother. He knew she loved him — and he loved her — but there was nothing to love about her outlandish excuses. Past arguments told him that debate was useless, but he had to do something. Going to the festival was the only way he could fulfill his dream. "All the more reason to join them. I could do something!"

"Must a parent explain herself when protecting her child?"

"Protecting me?" Nels stared into her eyes. "From *what*?"

"From making a fool of yourself. Why do you *really* want to be a knight?"

"I want to make a difference," he said. "I want to be of help to the kingdom."

"Helping me is not enough? Is that what you are telling me?"

Nels had no answer. Of course he wanted to help her, but she didn't understand. What was so wrong about lending a hand to others?

"We are finished with this discussion," Mother continued. "Sit down and eat your stew."

Before he did, Nels had one last thing to ask: "Mother, why are we hiding out here?"

"Hiding out here?" She raised a hand to her mouth. "What makes you say that?"

"We don't fit in, Mother. If you went outside more, you'd see what I mean. Everyone thinks we're strange for living in the woods, and you hardly let me leave your sight. Why?"

He waited for her to speak. She raised her other hand and covered her face. "It is not a matter of hiding; I simply do not like strangers."

"You're afraid of something. I've known it for a while. I know you hate the royals and the knights, but it's more than that. Does it have to do with Father? Every time I ask about him, all you say is, 'I will not hear of it.'"

His mother turned away from the table, assuring Nels that his assumption was right. At long last, a lifetime's worth of questions and secrets were out in the open, all because she wouldn't let him go to the festival. Nels should have put his foot down sooner.

"If you can't tell me why I shouldn't go, then I have no reason to stay."

Tears filled the woman's eyes as she lowered her head and sobbed. Nels's heart sank; he did not mean to make her cry, but he had run out of options.

I've done it this time.

He clasped his hands over hers. "I'm sorry, Mother."

"He was murdered."

Nels looked up. "What?"

"Your father was murdered." Mother dabbed her nose, trying to compose herself.

After years of speculation, she had finally answered him. Father hadn't deserted them. He was *taken* from them.

"Who murdered him? Someone from the castle?!"

"I cannot — I *will* not say," she said. "But that is why you will not go to the festival."

The cottage fell silent, her decision final.

Nels sat back. "May I be excused?"

Without looking up, Mother nodded. "Night is upon us. Do not go far."

Feeling betrayed and sick to his empty stomach, Nels

stepped out the door and went around back. If he had stayed much longer, he would have said something he would later regret.

Nels did not bother to watch for the chickens as he walked, and each of them ran out of his way, clucking frightfully. At the end of the slope behind the cottage lay a small pond. An inlet trickled freshwater into it, and its calm surface had a way of quieting his rare temper. When Nels reached the marshy edge, he picked up a small rock and threw it — hard. It skipped over the surface, cracked against a boulder, and plopped into the water. Ripples spread back, lapping the bank at his feet.

My father was murdered . . .

Nels sat by the pond, allowing new questions about his father to surface. Nels knew very little about him — next to nothing — as did all the people of Cobblestown. But surely *someone* knew about their coming here. With the sky's remaining twilight, Nels looked at his frowning reflection. Maybe he should've felt more content; at least his mother had finally confided in him.

It was not enough, though. He had to know the rest of the story.

If someone murdered him, why would she keep that from me? Is Mother hiding from his killer?

Nels had spent many hours trying to understand his mother's plight: jumpy at night, her guard up with every new customer. Now he knew why. It was still unfair; all he wanted was a chance — one chance — to prove his worth to the kingdom. Had he already compromised that chance? A knight's duty is to ensure the welfare of all, a selfless charge for life, but what kind of knight makes his mother cry? For her sake, perhaps it was best if he deserted his dream altogether. After all, the older he became, the less likely it was to happen.

"I want to be a knight, but not like this. I have to be *better* than this."

Nels lay beside the pond and closed his eyes for a moment. A frog croaked on the other side before it jumped into the water. Seeing the ripples calmed him further. Feeling defeated and tired, Nels stood up and walked back to the cottage.

Nels found his mother drying a plate as he entered. She looked at him, her expression fallen more than it was when he left. His big bowl of cold stew remained on the otherwise empty table.

He stared at the bowl. "I want to know more. Will you please tell me?"

Mother hung up her rag. "When the time is right, I will tell you."

I've heard that before.

Thinking it best to end the subject for now, Nels turned for his bed.

"We need to discuss a small errand," Mother said suddenly. "I have run out of turquoise dye. I cannot finish Magdalene's tablecloths without it, so I need to fetch some in the morning."

Nels turned back, surprised by this news. "We're going to Cobblestown?"

"Of course not — not during the festival. I will have to go to Kettlescreek."

"Kettlescreek?" Nels sighed. "That's a three-hour journey each way!"

Mother removed her apron. After she hung it up, she left the kitchen and walked to her loom around the corner. "I bought the dyes from Agen. If the tablecloths are going to match, I will have to go to him in Kettlescreek. As you said, I need to get outside more."

Her journey to avoid the festival was a foolish one, but Nels held his tongue. He had an idea that renewed his hope. "I'll finish the chores," he said, "while you're away . . ."

"I should hope so," Mother said. "We're behind enough as it is. I will go to Kettlescreek for dyes and other supplies while you finish up here. If I return and see you are not finished —"

"Don't worry," Nels said. "It will take me all day."

Mother nodded as she proceeded to weave.

"I didn't mean what I said," Nels apologized. "I love you."

"I love you, too, Nels — my perfect son."

Hiding a smile, Nels slipped into his nook and lay on his wool mattress.

She never said I couldn't go if I finished my chores first . . .

All he had to do was wake up early, finish everything, and see what he could of the festival before she came back. The plan was foolproof!

Nels closed his eyes, imagining what the festival would be like. His friends had told him of games and races, pies and tarts, and merchants who visited from Harvestport to sell their wares. This time — for the first time — he would see it all for himself. This time, he would have his chance to become a knight, even if he had to bend the rules to do it. He refused to spend the rest of his life in the shadow of his mother's fear.

Mother hummed as she wove, the mild tune lulling Nels to sleep.

Nels slept in. He felt like a fool.

Scrambling out of bed, he barged out the back door to gather every tool he needed. The morning sun was high, hard at work baking the ground. Noon would arrive in a few short hours, meaning his chores would carry him into the evening. Old Brown and the wagon were gone.

"She left me asleep on purpose!"

No matter. He didn't have time to stew over it.

I have to finish this!

Nels fed the chickens first. They would never stop clucking if he ignored them. He then ran into the field and shoved a spade into the dirt. He rushed through the first and second hour, digging and planting, setting up the crops faster than he ever had in his life, but he still had so much to do. The barn needed a sweep and he had to fix the fence — he needed wood for that.

Nels charged to the back, grabbed the old ax, and began chopping branches off his latest felled tree. But it wasn't long before the iron head flung off the handle and plonked into the pond. Nels collapsed by the stump. Hot sweat stung his eyes. It was no use.

Even if he skipped the fence, he would never make it in time.

"Maybe this is for the best," he muttered to himself.

Exhausted and out of breath, Nels staggered to his feet, removing his shirt. His body teemed with sweat. He dunked his face into the trough, feeling instant relief in the cool water.

"You work yourself like an ox, young man."

Nels spun around, water dripping down his face. By the corner, an old gentleman stood holding a cane with a metal grip — like the hook of a large crochet needle. Curly hair ringed his bald head and his short beard matched his gray robe. Even his eyes seemed worn and gray, like beads of unpolished steel. Nels looked over his shoulder, making sure they were alone.

He held his hand up, the bright sun forcing him to squint. "May I help you?"

"I am a friend of your mother's," the old man answered, his voice warm and cordial. "No one answered the door, so I thought I would look around back, and lo, here you are!"

Nels shrugged. "Here I am," he said halfheartedly. This man was much too cheerful for Nels's present mood. "But my mother isn't here. She left for Kettlescreek early this morning."

The old man leveled his lips. "Pity. I had hoped to see her before the festival."

Nels stopped mid reach for his shirt. "You've come for the festival?"

"Why else?" he said, taking a few steps closer. "Cobblestown is colorful, and the smells in the air are delicious. The king and his family will arrive soon, including fair Princess Tyra, the most beautiful maiden Avërand has ever known." The old man looked Nels up and down. "Have you seen her before? If not, you should, and I could use an escort back to town."

Nels let out an envious sigh. "I must finish these chores before I go anywhere."

"Pity," the man said again. "Though I see your mother has raised an obedient young man."

Laughing at that, Nels patted the old fellow on the back. "By all means, if you want to help me finish my chores, I will gladly walk with you to the other side of the world!"

The man tilted his cane. "That is unnecessary — but what have you left to do?"

Nels blinked, thinking the old man had taken him for a fool. "I wasn't serious."

"I am sincere, dear boy," he said, following Nels to the front of the cottage.

"Well," Nels said slowly, "the fence needs fixing, and the barn needs sweeping, and the field needs —" Nels froze in his tracks, his eyes staring at the repaired fence, the swept barn, and the watered field. He could not believe it. Every single one of his chores was finished. "But . . . when did —?"

The old man chuckled and winked mischievously. "Some youth labor so hard, they do not know what they accomplish." He reached into his pocket. "I came to give this to your mother." He placed a spool of white thread in Nels's hand. "I commend your obedience, but if you should change your mind about the festival . . ." He then placed a small brass thimble in Nels's other hand. It was cool to the touch. "Good afternoon to you."

Nels watched the old man leave for the road before he looked at his chores again. He could not have finished them all. Had the sun gone to his head? Was something else at work here? For now, there was no time to find answers — only enough time to get ready.

He ran inside, washed his face, and slipped on the shirt and green vest he saved for going into the village. Good thing he had wet his hair outside; his loose locks were now tamed across his forehead. Nels laid the thimble and spool of thread on the counter and started for the door, only to hear a chime at his feet. He spun around. The thimble had rolled toward the threshold and had come to a stop in front of him. Rather than retrace his steps, Nels shoved the bit of brass into his pocket and opened the door.

The bright sun lingered just beyond the middle of the sky as Nels stepped outside. Their field was perfect. Never before had their property looked so well tended. Mother would not be home for three hours, at least. If he timed this right, she would never know he left. At long last, he was about to have his chance. Nels ran after the old man without bothering to look back.

He should have.

One by one, every chore unraveled to the way it was before.

2

THE FESTIVAL

A cool breeze rustled the dark leaves over Nels's head as he sprinted to catch up with the old stranger, who had already reached the divide where the shrouded path unfolded into a grassy meadow. Either Nels had taken a long time to get ready, or he had greatly underestimated the old man.

The man's weathered cheeks cupped a wide smile. "Changed your mind?"

Nels nodded as he paused to catch his breath.

"Good. Squirrels are less likely to pounce with you here."

"Squirrels?" Nels glanced up, catching a serious look in the man's eye.

"Indeed. Vicious little hoarders. They always go after my spools and batting!"

Releasing a wary laugh, Nels pressed on beside the man. The dirt road arched eastward with the rolling hills before them, away from the tall white oaks. The first hill lay just ahead, lush and green, with thick grasses and drooping purple flowers that basked in the summer sun. It was a beautiful day — and a mysterious one.

Nels studied the stranger and his cane. "How do you know my mother?"

The old man glanced at Nels, his brow slightly beaded with sweat. His lips thinned as the same wide smile spread over his face again. "She was one of my better pupils some years ago. I taught her everything about her trade. I see she has done well for herself . . . with your help, of course."

"I do what I can," Nels said, "but she never mentioned you before."

"She may prefer not to. I work in the castle, you see."

Nels stared him in the face. "You do?"

"I do. I am the tailor of Avërand."

Something about his answer made Nels stop. He had heard of this man. The tailor was the greatest cloth maker in the kingdom, an artisan who attended to the royals' fabric needs. "Wait — you're *the* tailor of Avërand?" Nels said. "It's a pleasure to meet you!"

"And you, dear boy. Are you sure your mother never mentioned me?"

Nels shook his head. "Never."

"Well, Katharina should have told you by now."

"Katharina?" Nels had never heard that name before. "Who's that?"

"Why, your mother, of course."

That wasn't her name at all. Nels's suspicion returned. What kind of friend was this man if he did not even remember her name? "You're mistaken; my mother's name is Norell."

"Ah," the man said. "Thank you for correcting me. My memory is not what it once was."

"Right," Nels replied, still a bit suspicious. "So what should she have told me?"

"That is Norell's responsibility to answer."

Nels kicked a small rock off the road. Maybe the tailor's mistake was just that. The man was old, after all. Many men

25

his age could not tell the difference between breakfast and supper, let alone remember names from long ago. "She doesn't tell me much," Nels said.

"Then we had better acquaint ourselves." The tailor bowed. "I am Ickabosh, but you may call me Bosh, as your mother once did. If I remember right, your name is Lief, correct?"

"Lief?" Nels could not help but laugh. "Wrong again — I'm Nels."

Bosh chuckled. "See what I did? I said the first name that came to mind and you corrected me with your *proper* name — it's a clever trick."

"Uh-huh," Nels said. "You're an odd old man, you know that?"

"A few weaves short of a basket, perhaps — but still useful."

A minute later, the two reached the top of a quarry just outside Cobblestown. They could see much of the vast kingdom from the final hill's summit, and a boisterous noise reached their ears from the village below. Excitement filled the air. Fiddles played. Horns blared. The festival was well underway.

"Let us hurry!" Bosh motioned. "The princess will be here soon."

"Why are you excited about that? Don't you see her all the time?"

"Naturally — but I want to see *your* reaction when she arrives."

That seemed an odd thing to want. Why would he care? Nels shoved his hand into his pocket and felt the thimble against his knuckles. It surprised him how cool it felt.

"She turned sixteen not long ago," Bosh said. "I believe you share the age."

"I'm seventeen."

"Are you really? My, how time passes."

"I'm sure she's nice, but what does it matter? I'm a commoner."

"Then why do you wish to see the festival?"

Nels hesitated before he answered. "To become a knight."

"A knight, you say?" Bosh squinted at him. "Just like your father."

"My father?" Nels stumbled a little. "Wait — he was a knight?"

"Slipping seams!" Bosh cursed. "I meant he *aspired* to be a knight . . . like you."

"My mother told me he was murdered. Do you know anything about that?"

Bosh eyed him carefully. "That is for your mother to discuss with you."

"Please," Nels said. "If you have any information, I deserve to know."

Bosh shook his head. "My lips are stitched."

Glaring at the old man, Nels again fiddled with the thimble in his pocket. The piece of brass still felt cool in his warm hand. "Why did you give me this thimble, anyway?"

"It is for luck," Bosh said craftily.

"Like a rabbit's foot?"

"Better. You might even say it has magic! Hold it when you need it most."

Nels shook his head, trying not to laugh. *Magic.* He wasn't one for superstition, nor did he think highly of lucky trinkets, but Nels smirked and gave the old man credit for being unique. A lucky thimble was at least different. This Bosh fellow was eccentric, but he was certainly amusing.

The village had no wall around its close assortment of houses and shops, each bearing roofs of packed yellow straw. Before they reached the edge of the village, Nels could see that everyone was outdoors and moving cheerfully about the decorated lanes. Small blue flags dangled on strings, connecting the numerous booths that filled both sides of the crowded main road. Local vendors and merchants sold their fruits, jewelries, and simmering meats. Children ran through the crowd, chased by playful dogs, begging the merchants for a taste of honeysuckle candies.

All Nels could do was smile. He'd never seen the village so jovial!

"Well, well!" cried Dungus, the cobbler. "The Knight of Cobblestown is here!"

Heads turned and faces smiled. A few girls admired him shyly while others waved. Nels returned their welcomes as he swallowed his embarrassment.

"Why do they call you the Knight of Cobblestown?" Bosh asked.

"Well," Nels began, "they know how much I want to be a knight —"

"Sausages!" interrupted Klen, the butcher. "He saved the locksmith's girl from the river!"

"And pulled my husband from a rockslide," Hilga added from another direction. The burly woman neared and tousled Nels's hair. "Thanks to him, my children have their father."

Bosh scratched his beard as she left. "You did all that?"

Nels was about to explain how much the villagers exaggerated when someone jumped onto his back. "You're here!" Jilia wrapped her arms around his neck. "I can't believe it!"

A sharp blow struck Nels in the shoulder. "I can't believe it, either," said Wallin.

Nels rubbed his arm and adjusted the weight on his back. "You can let go, Jilia."

The girl slid off, grinning impishly. Somewhere in the last several hours, her trousers had found a new hole. "I can't believe your mother let you come. I will be your escort all day long!"

"Lucky you," Wallin teased Nels. "You guys hungry? Gamel's got a spit going."

Before Nels could answer, Jilia gestured at the old man. "Who's your friend?"

Bosh's smile seemed to reach his ears now. "No one of consequence, and I have a small errand to attend to before Their Majesties arrive, anyway. Thank you for accompanying me, Nels. The squirrels know better than to mess with the brave Knight of Cobblestown. Enjoy the festival!"

With that, the old man strode off into the throng.

Wallin knitted his thick brow. "Squirrels?"

Nels nodded. "That's what *I* said."

"Who was he?" Jilia asked.

"A friend of my mother's," Nels answered, thinking it best not to mention that he had escorted the tailor of Avërand — his friends would have fewer questions that way. He peered down at Jilia and extended his elbow. The girl looked back with a raised eyebrow. "Show me what a festival's all about, milady!"

Her face filling with glee, Jilia locked her arm with his.

The three set off into the bustle, sampling fresh pies, playing games, and running races. It did not take long for Nels to feel dizzy amidst all the excitement. Men slapped his back, and girls flirted with him despite Jilia's warning glares — everyone wanted his attention. The three friends had such a good time that Nels wondered why the village held this event only once a year. He brushed at his hair and glanced up at the sun to make sure he would have enough time to run home.

Just after they browsed the trinkets available at the busy market, a group of people dressed in unusual clothing caught his eye. They wore shirts with bagged sleeves and colorful vests, and skirts embroidered with golden flowers, metallic moons, and crystal stars. They were not from the village, nor even from Avërand. Nels could tell by the unique tailoring of their clothes, their raven hair, and their silvery eyes. They had to be the Vagas, a free-roaming people who lived in the forests on the other side of the Westerly Mountains. He'd never had the opportunity to see them up close, let alone meet them, considering the things that he'd heard about them.

Some of the villagers assembled to watch their cartwheels and other tumbling tricks. A few knights stood by as well, also watching. But apprehensively, with hands on their hilts.

"Can't trust these Vagas," one of them muttered.

"Keep watching, or they'll steal right from under you," said another.

"If not for Arek," said a third, "they'd have already run off with the king's crown!"

"Right you are," said the first. "They had better leave before Arek shows up."

Did they mean *Sir* Arek, the favored knight of Avërand? Nels looked again at the graceful dancers and musicians. The few times he had heard the village people speak of the Vagas, they had done so with disdain. Now that he had seen the Vagas, Nels couldn't understand the villagers' contempt. The Vagas resonated with warmth and they played well-rehearsed music, a rare sound for Nels.

The Vaga men strummed instruments and played tambourines while the women twirled about in their long skirts, but the reverie came to an abrupt end when one of the girls fell, thumped in the head by a putrid turnip. The music stopped, and the villagers yelled, booed, and urged the foreign people to leave the village at once as they threw more vegetables. Nels couldn't believe what they were doing.

He waited for the knights to step in, to keep the peace, but they laughed instead.

The Vagas gathered their belongings and rushed to leave, but the fallen girl struggled to get up. Nels stepped in, blocked another turnip, and helped the girl to her feet. Her silvery eyes gazed back at him through long strands of dark hair. She could have been the same age as Jilia, but her appearance was far more defined. A sapphire stone dangled around her neck. Suddenly, she gasped as she pulled away from his touch. "You are not supposed to be here," she said, a soft accent on her small lips. "I am sorry." She gathered her skirt and dashed off with her people.

Her words ran a chill down Nels's neck. *What did she mean by that?*

The angry crowd dispersed, and the festival continued as if nothing had happened.

"They'll be back," Wallin said. "And we'll just have to kick 'em out again."

Shocked by his friend, Nels faced him. "Why would you say that?"

"The knights say they can't be trusted," said a strong voice. It belonged to Lars, the blacksmith, his brown hair shorter than usual, making his broad shoulders look even broader. "They tried to steal the crown a few years back. Once thieves, always thieves, those people."

"Come off it," Nels said. "You can't blame a whole people for one crime."

Wallin thumped him on the shoulder. "Yeah, you can, if it runs in their blood."

Lars chuckled. "That's right, Wallin. You remember the story of King Hilvar, the man who ruled the forested Valley of Westmine?" Nels nodded, but the blacksmith carried on. "The Vagas stole a mound of treasure from him hundreds of years ago. Hilvar searched for the rest of his days, but he never found it. The Vagas have decimated that land with witchcraft ever since, summoning demons and keeping the dead from leaving our world. Some say Hilvar searches for his treasures to this day. No one goes to Westmine anymore; they fear the wrath of his ghost."

"Ghost?" Wallin laughed. "You don't believe stuff like that, do you?"

"What nonsense," Nels said. "That happened centuries ago."

Lars shrugged. "It's in their blood, that's all I need to know." He waved his hand as he left. "The shop's not the same without you, Nels. Visit more, and say hello to your mother for me."

Nels frowned as he faced his friends. "They didn't do anything." Wallin looked indifferent, and though Jilia didn't seem to enjoy what had happened, she hadn't said anything to protest.

"It's a sly cover," Wallin said. "They draw in the crowd with entertainment while their little rat children pick our pockets and raid the shops. Living in the woods has made you too trusting."

"At least I don't treat people like rubbish!"

Wallin clenched his teeth and rolled up his sleeves.

Jilia thrust herself between them and pointed at the square. "The royals are coming!"

Nels let the argument slide as the girl dragged him to the village square. He could not believe what Wallin had said about the Vagas, or how the knights stood by and laughed as the Vagas were accosted. He felt sorry for the mysterious girl, too. No one deserved such treatment, even if they were criminals. And the girl's unique and mysterious voice continued to haunt him.

You are not supposed to be here . . .

She was right — but how did she know?

Onlookers filled the square as a team of horses trotted into the village. Nels was tall enough to see without having to peer around the heads in front of him. Stewards blew horns as the knights entered, wearing black coats of leather armor. The largest of them was a burly man with dark hair and hazel eyes. Two squires followed him on foot, holding tall banners. Davin and Alvil were the squires' names, boys from the villages of Kettlescreek and Watersfork. Nels knew them well, having heard of their appointments last year. They were younger than Nels — by a few years.

"That's Sir Arek," Jilia pointed. "He's the *favored* knight of Avërand."

"And the *biggest*," Nels replied. "I'd hate to have a go with him."

Jilia almost sneered at the knight as a couple entered on white horses.

Everyone but Nels knelt as they arrived. Wallin tugged at Nels's sleeve, urging him to do the same. He did not understand why until he noticed the couple's fine clothing and golden crowns — King Lennart and Queen Carin. The red-haired king looked side to side and waved halfheartedly, his gaze vacant and dispassionate. In contrast, the queen beamed a bright smile and blew sincere kisses, her blond bun shiny in the sunlight.

Nels admired their attire. Even his mother would appreciate such excellent tailoring.

He looked to the sky again, using the sun to gauge how much time he had left.

When will they select their squires? I shouldn't stay much longer.

Jilia peeked over the shoulders in front of her, trying to catch a glimpse of the royalty, as a white mare entered the village next. A young maiden rode on its back. She looked around and waved to the people as well, but there was something more to her — something truly striking about her. It wasn't the beautiful teal dress and bodice that accentuated her slender frame; nor her perfect, blushing lips. Not even her clear blue eyes or the radiant shine of her flowing golden hair adequately explained the warmth that spread through Nels when he looked at her.

Bosh was right; Tyra was the most stunning maiden he had ever seen.

Nels rose to his feet, as if her presence enchanted him to do so. She noticed him immediately, and her blue eyes pierced into his as a curious expression appeared on her face. She then tugged at her horse's reins, urging the mare to step forward. Nels's blood stilled as she neared him.

A sharp pain shot through his foot.

Cringing, he found Jilia's heel pressing into his boot. Realizing he was the only one standing, Nels dropped to one knee again. The princess shook her head, looking flustered, and rode on.

Nels pulled his foot back. "Thanks, Jilia. I don't know what I was thinking."

"Dunderhead." The girl glared at him. "You're supposed to kneel, not gawk!"

"I gawked?" As transfixed as he was, Nels knew he must have looked like an idiot.

The knights dismounted at the other end of the square before they assisted the royals down from their own steeds. Nels's attention stayed focused on the princess. She smiled at the touch of Sir Arek's hand as he helped her down. They then whispered in each other's ears before joining her parents on the stands. By the looks of their informal interaction, they seemed to be very close.

"People of Cobblestown!" Everyone quieted down to give the queen their full attention. "Thank you for your affectionate welcome; we are most pleased and delighted to see you again. Spring has been good to our fair Avërand, and we should expect yet another prosperous harvest!"

When the new cheers settled, everyone waited to hear from the king.

Lennart simply waved his hand, beckoning the festivities to proceed.

Cobblestown bloomed into a bustle again. People mingled in the streets, returned to their carts, and continued their fun — but Nels did not. He was much too captivated by the princess to think of anything else. Of all the girls that he had met in Avërand, he had to be smitten with *her*.

The knight who sat by the princess was a giant in comparison to her, and considerably older, too. The queen looked at them frequently with disapproving eyes, and the king did not seem too happy about their flirtations, either. Nels had heard of the king's melancholy, but he'd never imagined that it was this bad; King Lennart looked as if he wanted nothing to do with the festival.

Jilia tried to divert Nels's attention, suggesting he should participate in a meatball-eating contest. He did not want to, nor was he in the mood to glut himself. That did not stop Wallin, who finished first, his stout chin dripping with grease. Whenever he could, Nels glanced over his shoulder to catch a glimpse of the royals and their beautiful daughter. Each royal yawned in turn.

"May I have your attention, please?" The people looked to the square. Arek was on his feet, summoning the villagers. This was it; time for the selections to begin! Every boy of age made their way to the front. The favored knight revealed an awkward smile before he cleared his throat. "I regret to inform you all that we have no need for new squires this year."

All the gathered boys let out disappointed moans.

And like a stone hurled into a vast ocean, Nels's heart sank.

"We will recruit next year, but this means our visit will end sooner than we would like."

The crowd muttered with disappointment.

"Come now," said the queen. "Surely we could find some way to entertain ourselves."

From out of nowhere, a voice shouted, "How about a match?"

Ickabosh? Nels searched, but he couldn't find the old man. No one could pinpoint the location of the voice, either.

More people gathered, curious about the knight's response: "A match?"

"I'd like to see that," Lars said. "Your best against *our* best."

Sir Arek nodded. "A fitting challenge!" The knight removed his leather vest. A pair of black trousers and a thin shirt remained. "If it pleases His Majesty, may I be your champion?"

The king nodded without looking at Arek.

"Now, who among you will challenge me?"

The square fell silent. No one volunteered.

"Come, now. Surely one of you would like a friendly spar with me?" The knight's eyes fell upon the blacksmith. "You are clearly an even match for me. What do you say?"

Lars held up his hand. "My sparring days are done, young'n."

"Is there a prize?" Wallin asked.

The knight laughed. "I suppose we could have one. What should it be?"

The voice boomed again: "A kiss from the princess!"

Nels knew the voice had to be Bosh's, and he sounded much closer now. The suggestion stirred a commotion as all eyes turned to the king's daughter.

Her thin brow rose as she smiled at the knight. "Agreed," she declared. "I will kiss the winner!"

The king glared at the princess, but the crowd was delighted by the suggestion. Nels hoped she would speak more; even her voice was beautiful. It held a confidence that sent warmth through his whole chest. How sweet would it sound if she spoke directly to him?

A sinking feeling in his gut suddenly yanked the idea from his head.

Like I would have a chance like that . . .

"Who will turn down such a rare opportunity?" Arek asked. "It will make a legend of any man!"

Several men squirmed, including all five of Jilia's brothers. A few hoots came from the crowd, trying to encourage a volunteer to come forward. No one accepted, but that changed when someone from behind pushed Nels into the square. "How about the Knight of Cobblestown?"

Nels's heart seized with panic as the villagers cheered their instant approval.

The voice belonged to Bosh, as did the hand that shoved Nels forward.

What is that old man thinking?!

He was a decent wrestler, sure, but Nels had never faced a real knight before. When the king raised his head and stared at Nels, a startling change occurred on his face. He examined from head to toe the attractive young man before him, and then looked at his daughter with an unexpected smile.

She returned the look, her eyes widened with surprise.

"Let him compete!" the king answered.

Astounded by the king's active participation, the villagers roared into an ovation. Nels glanced at Jilia and Wallin, who were as speechless as he was. He then looked over at Bosh, standing where Nels once stood, grinning at him with dimpled cheeks, his weathered hands resting on the hook of his cane. Bosh had landed him in this mess, and if he refused, Nels would look like a coward.

I won't be a coward.

Nels caught Tyra's eye. She was already staring at him.

Their eyes locked for a moment before she turned her head away.

And if I win this, she'll kiss me . . .

The very thought of it made him nervous — but, kiss or no kiss, he had to make a choice, for this could be his only chance to prove his worth as a knight of Averand.

Nels removed his vest. "I accept!"

The people cheered even more as they formed a circle around the perimeter of the square. A pair of knights ordered their squires to carry a chest to a bench in front of the stands. Nels wondered what the chest was for, but only for a moment. He was preoccupied with thoughts of all that was at stake. A kiss from the princess was certainly a fine prize — but if he won the match and proved himself a real knight, it would be worth a sound bruising.

The squires moved aside as Arek kicked the chest open. "Choose your weapon, boy."

Nels paused. "*Weapon?*"

"This is a match," Arek said. "So what will it be? Swords? Maces?"

"He's never held a *real* weapon in his life!" cried Tessan, the baker.

The others laughed as the man's words spread among the spectators.

The king rubbed his chin. "What *do* you know, lad?"

"Wrestling!" Jilia shouted. "He'll take on anyone with his bare hands!"

"Jilia!" Nels cried, but the mixture of laughter and cheers muted him.

"Wrestle?" Arek laughed. "Are you serious? That is a sport for children!"

"Then you should have no problem," the king jested. "Carry on!"

The princess scowled at her father, more severely than before.

"Very well." Arek stretched his neck as he readied his stance. The knight grabbed the hem of his shirt and pulled it over his head, revealing his massive chest. The men seemed impressed, and the women fawned as Arek threw the shirt aside. His muscles bulged. "Let's do this — quickly."

Nels knew what he had to do if he was going to stand a chance against this much bigger, stronger, and older knight. He handed his vest to Jilia and removed his shirt, too, which made the villagers shout even louder. The boys applauded thunderously as several girls screamed his name. Nels stretched his arms in a defensive stance, as he had with Wallin on numerous occasions, and then stepped forward.

The princess watched them, her eyes darting back and forth between the two.

Nels concentrated, smirking at his opponent. Arek was a good foot taller, with broader shoulders and thicker biceps. Doubting himself for a second, Nels formed a staggered stance and waited for the knight to make the slightest twitch. The first move was essential, but Arek seemed to know this rule as well. They faced off, sizing each other up for quite a time . . . but Nels could wait.

"I said *quickly*," Arek sneered. "Do you wrestle with snails, boy?"

"Not before now."

The crowd threw a fit. Even the king joined their laughter.

Growling, Arek raised his arms and bolted for Nels.

Nels dodged to the right as the knight reached out and caught only the air.

"The *Knight* of Cobblestown, are you?" Arek grinned. "Not for long!"

The knight sprang forward again. Nels dug his heels into the ground and wrapped his arms around the advancing knight's torso. As he dug his head into Arek's formidable chest, the knight grabbed Nels by the shoulder. Their hold was tight, their resistance intense, but Arek could not throw Nels off his feet and the knight was much too thick for Nels to push down. He slipped out of Arek's grasp to plan a new approach.

Nels jumped to the right, feinted left, and grabbed Arek's arm, yanking the knight over his leg with a hard tug. Arek fumbled and rolled onto the ground, long enough for Nels to slip in and hold the knight down. Excitement thundered about the square. But the cheers faded as Arek slipped away and returned to his feet. Adrenaline surged through Nels's body. His ears rang.

This won't be easy.

Closing in for the offensive, Arek caught Nels off guard and seized his thigh. The square turned into a blur as Nels landed on the dusty ground — he still did not like the taste of dirt. Gasps ensued as Arek jumped over and pinned him down. Nels countered, shoving his head into Arek's elbow to collapse the hold long enough to escape. Applause erupted as Nels leaped to his feet.

He could not allow the knight to hold him like that again.

That was too close!

"Go for his legs!" Jilia hollered. "Knock him off his high horse!"

Nels glanced at her for a second, distracted, as a fist struck him in the face. The villagers cried out as Nels fell. A dull numbness throbbed around his eye as he sat up. Arek stood over him, his fists clenched. Sweat dripped down his livid face.

"Whoa!" Wallin yelled. "What was that? You can't just clout him!"

"He struck the first blow," Arek said. "Elbow *me* in the ribs, will you?"

"What?" Nels said. "I didn't —"

The knight didn't give Nels a chance to speak.

Arek grabbed him and socked him in the gut. Winded, Nels tried to get up, but Arek kicked him back to the ground. Boos and hisses sounded, and even the other knights appeared to disapprove. Nels rolled to the other side of the circle, oblivious to the concern that filled the villagers' faces. A delighted smirk blossomed on the princess, as if she were enjoying the match — more than before.

A kiss isn't worth this trouble!

"We should stop this," he heard the queen say.

"Not yet," the king answered. "I wish to see this through."

Arek pressed his foot on Nels's back and twisted it, as if he were smashing a bug. Nels clenched his jaw. The pain was extreme. He couldn't escape. He was in no position to even think of defeating this knight.

How will I get out of this?

A blinding flash of sunlight flickered into his eye from the middle of the circle, reflected by his tiny, brass thimble. It must have fallen out of his pocket when he handed his vest to Jilia.

Nels caught sight of Bosh staring at him from the crowd. The old tailor's eyes flicked to the thimble, reminding Nels of what he'd said on the road:

Hold it when you need it most . . .

41

Nels didn't know why, but he needed the thimble — now!

Gathering his strength, Nels slid out from under the knight's foot, twisting Arek's ankle and knocking him to the ground. The cheering returned as Nels grabbed the thimble. The knight rebounded and leaped at Nels. But instead of catching him, Arek flew over Nels's back and rammed headlong into the iron chest on the bench. Everybody cringed, except for Nels, who was trying to figure out what had happened.

"What the . . . ?" The knight stood, teetering a little on his feet. "I had you!"

"You . . . missed?"

Snarling, Arek charged again, but this time Nels stepped aside with ease and tripped the knight. Laughter filled the square as Nels dodged the knight's next attack, too. For some odd reason, the knight could not lay a finger on him. Nels looked at the thimble as Arek passed him a third time. The tired knight lunged again, with momentum that Nels could use.

Let's see how well you fly.

Nels rolled onto his back, pressed his feet into Arek's approaching gut, and launched him straight into the air. Arek crashed into the stands and smashed the railing at the royals' feet. He raised his head, a perplexed look on his face, groaned, and collapsed. One of the other knights stepped forward and declared that Arek was out cold. The roar of the crowd exploded with pride; Nels, a commoner, had bested the favored knight of Averand! He pocketed the thimble. Maybe there was such a thing as magic, after all.

Lars patted him hard on the back. "Three cheers for our knight!"

A chorus sounded as the knights hauled Arek to a tent behind the stands. The villagers carried Nels to the front, where King Lennart beamed. "What is your name, young man?"

"I'm" — Nels could not believe it; he was speaking to the king — "Nels, Your Majesty."

"Hooray!" some of the people shouted. Others cried, "Nels! The Knight of Cobblestown!"

The queen smiled. "The knighthood could use a man of such bravery."

Nels tried not to shake as he bowed. If the queen herself suggested it, Nels didn't have to speculate his chances anymore. After this day, he would be a knight. He wanted to dance on the spot, but he resisted and turned to look at the princess. She was shorter than he expected, but no less lovely, her lashes long and dark. Aside from the smattering of freckles high on her cheeks, she was free of blemish. There was a calm surprise about her — along with sheer disbelief — as she looked at Nels.

"Here is your champion," the king said. "You may reward him."

The crowd hushed and Nels stood still, doing his best to remain composed. Tyra stepped forward. Her lips parted as her face neared his. The smell of pear blossoms from her hair filled the dimishing space between them. Not knowing what else to do, Nels held his ground and closed his eyes, waiting to feel the touch of a girl's lips on his for the first time.

It never came. Nels opened his eyes, just as the beautiful maiden was stepping back.

The princess glared at him, disgust painting her face. "I will *never* kiss this . . . *peasant*!"

3

THE AX

Before Nels could speak, Tyra stormed off after the knights who had carried Sir Arek behind the stands. The villagers made their disapprovals known through mutterings and abrasive glares as she passed. Releasing a great sigh, the king left the stands to pursue her.

"Pardon my daughter," the flustered queen said as she departed, too. "She's not feeling well."

The people quieted once the royals left, leaving Nels to stare at the crowd. The jovial mood was unquestionably dead; the festival was over. He stood alone, dumbfounded, eye throbbing, all because the most enchanting girl he had ever seen decided to make a public spectacle of him. What really surprised him, though, was that he cared. He came to the festival to be a knight, not to be mocked by some spoiled princess. Still, he felt drawn to her, and he had wanted her to kiss him. He stepped down from the stands and looked around for the old man who had started the whole fiasco.

But the tailor was nowhere in sight. "Where did he go?"

Jilia ran to Nels and handed him his shirt without saying a word — for once. Neither did Wallin. He was about to, but Lars pulled him aside to help clean the square. No one asked Nels to do anything, giving him space and trying not to make things worse. When Nels slipped his arms through his vest, a redheaded merchant in a well-made cape walked up to him quickly.

"You are quite the grappler, boy," he said. "Come — you deserve a prize."

Not feeling like he deserved a prize, Nels followed the stranger. The merchant guided Nels to a cart shaded by a thick red-and-lavender tarpaulin. The cart contained bows, swords, daggers, and a few axes, but in their unsavory condition — rusted and porous — they amounted to only useless junk, not that Nels was particularly fascinated by the man's offerings in the first place.

"Now then," said the merchant. "What would you fancy?"

Nels forced a smile as he considered the dented, old blades.

"Take your time; choose whatever you'd like."

Although he wasn't interested in foraging through a pile of shoddy weapons, Nels did spot an unused swing ax under a pair of crusted maces. It had a long, finished handle of hard oak, and the forged head shone like obsidian. Nels took up the shiny new ax and weighed it in his hands. Glancing again at the decrepit swords, the choice was obvious. He needed a new ax anyway.

"Oh," the merchant said, frowning, "I forgot that was there."

Nels raised it back to the cart. "If you'd rather not —"

"No!" The merchant held up his hand and laughed boisterously. "Please, keep it, my young friend . . . so you will always remember the day when Princess Tyra gave you the ax!"

Cocking his brow, Nels glared at the man. He then seized the ax, held the handle tightly, and walked away with it, his jaw clenched because of the merchant's jest. It was bad enough to have the princess humiliate him in front of the villagers; now a complete stranger had to go and pour salt into his fresh wound. Nels's emotions peaked, his eyes burning. The glare of the late afternoon sun was of no help, nor was the pain in his side or the crusted dirt on his face.

Someone tugged on his vest. "Cheer up, Nels. I thought you were brilliant!"

The knot in Nels's throat made it impossible for him to speak to Jilia.

"Why'd you take an ax? Why not a sword? He had some nice ones."

Some nice ones? Nels did not know how to respond. Every old sword that he inspected on that cart would have snapped midswing. It took all his will to not take the ax back and see how well it could chop up the merchant's lackluster cart, but Jilia's words kept him at bay.

"How's your head?" she asked. "Whoa — your eye!"

He didn't want to hear that, but she was right. The area around his right eye had swollen like a ripe plum, each passing second made it more difficult for him to see.

"You're banged up a bit. How are you going to explain this to your mother?"

The shock of the situation had made him forget about that. His finished chores would not explain the condition of his pummeled body. Nels sighed, and his head began to swim.

"Old Brown!" Jilia said. "You blame everything on that horse, anyway."

Nels gritted his teeth. Her voice grated on his nerves.

"I'm glad you didn't kiss that princess; she's a real witch."

"Leave me alone!"

"N-Nels," Jilia sputtered. "I . . . I didn't mean . . ."

He took a deep breath and cut her off with a glance, doing his best to keep his face calm. He had a hard time of it.

"Don't let her get to you," Jilia hesitantly continued. "Or that louse of a knight, or that crummy old merchant."

"It's not them, Jilia." Nels grasped his ax. "I'm never going to be a knight."

"Yes, you will," she said. "The queen said they needed you!"

"No, Jilia. I don't *want* to be a knight anymore!"

The girl's voice caught in her throat. "You can't mean that!"

But he did. Nels looked at the empty streets, now lacking the festive music and cheer that once filled them. Even the weapons merchant had packed up his pitiful cart and headed toward the west. Nels could hardly look Jilia in the eye. Never had a silence lasted this long between them.

"You can't desert your dream, Nels. It's my dream, too!"

Nels stared at her as seriously as he could. "Then you'd better wake up."

Jilia's lip quivered as she glared at him. "Go then! Go home and quit — lousy *quitter*!"

She punched him dead in the arm and ran off. After a brief chance to cool her hot head, she would be fine. Brushing away her sting, Nels let the ax rest on his shoulder as he turned to leave. He had barely passed the cobbler's shop when Wallin blocked his way and stared at him angrily.

"If you weren't already all roughed up, I'd smash your other eye," he said.

Wallin chased after Jilia, ramming into Nels as he passed.

Nels left the village then, paying no heed to those who had overheard his declaration of defeat. Some gestured with disappointed headshakes. He didn't care; he was done. They could think whatever they wanted. The Knight of Cobblestown. Someone else could have the meaningless title.

I don't want it. I never wanted it.

The sun fell fast toward the west as he climbed up the quarry's steep hill. He had lost track of time. Mother would be home soon, if she wasn't already. He should have listened to her. The festival and the royals *were* nothing but a headache, and those knights — they were the worst of it.

Who in their right mind would want to stand among their egotistical ranks?

Not Nels. Not anymore.

Trying to weed the princess from his mind, Nels jogged back into the woods.

An aged squirrel scampered down a branch as Nels slowed to a walk. He lumbered along the road, looking at the evening sun through the oak leaves. Mulling over what happened to him at the festival only slowed him further, his thoughts occupied by the pompous knights, the cold princess, and the outcast Vagas. But what haunted him most was the Vaga girl's warning.

You are not supposed to be here . . .

"Did she know my day would end like this?"

There was a light in the cottage window. Mother was home.

Great. She'll never forgive me for this . . .

He slowed his pace, no longer seeing the need to return as quickly as he had planned. But then, as he neared, he stopped, mouth gaping open, and dropped his ax by the edge of the field. He stared with his good eye at the incomplete fence, the unswept barn, the bone-dry field, and his tools lying haphazardly in the dirt. Aside from the planted field, he had never finished his chores.

Nels pocketed his hand. The lucky brass thimble rubbed against his fingers. The magic sewing implement had helped him defeat the knight, but it didn't matter now.

"Luck," he scoffed. "That *tailor* did this . . ."

For now, the old man was the least of his worries. Going to the festival would make his mother angry; but going to the festival without finishing his chores would make her furious.

Taking a deep breath, Nels picked up his ax and headed for the inevitable.

The floor groaned as he stepped inside, the noise drowned out by the clicks and clacks of his mother's loom. He closed the door and stood near the table. The spool of thread was still on the counter, unmoved. No meal was cooking and no fire was burning. He placed the new ax on the table and waited for his mother to scold him. But she said nothing. Not a single word.

Tension filled the room as the minutes rolled on. The new tablecloth Mother was making was quite exquisite — the first of a dozen left to be woven.

"We have no wood for a fire," she said. "Will you chop some for us?"

Nels had been expecting the greatest reprimand of his life, but now he assumed she was waiting until later, when she was done weaving and could focus on his punishment. He picked up his ax and walked through the back of the house. His ribs ached from where Arek had kicked him. He hoped nothing was broken; he would find out for sure with his first swing. Nels chopped at a felled tree and split a few decent logs in half the time that it normally took. The new blade was sharp. Although his time at the festival had turned out to be a nightmare, at least his consolation prize was useful. He raised the blade over his head and buried the ax into the chopping block before gathering up the wood and walking inside.

Mother said nothing as he built the fire. The flames rose high and hot, casting shadows around the room. If Mother refused to speak, he would have to. "I'm sorry, Mother."

The woman finished her edging. "How was the festival?"

Nels sat up straight, struck by her pleasant voice. She blinked at the sight of the bruises on his face, but there was no anger in her eyes, nor did Nels see a smile on her lips.

This is unlike her. Why is she so calm?

She breathed a deep sigh and returned to her work. "I see you learned your lesson."

Nels could only stare at her. That was it? She was letting him off that easily?

"I don't want to be a knight," he said. "You were right. I should've listened."

"A parent's word is not enough," she said. "Children have to learn for themselves. You are home and safe now, and that is what matters most at the end of the day."

"You're really not mad at me?"

"I was furious, but who is to say I have no fault in this, cooping you up in this cottage?" She touched his hand. "I never want to see you hurt, Nels. I could not bear to lose you."

"I see that now," Nels said, pointing at his swollen eye.

"And wherever did you find that ax? Did you buy it?"

"I won it," he said. "It's okay, though. We needed a new one."

"Won it? Wrestling, no doubt. Is that how you blackened your eye, as well?"

Nels nodded, grateful that she was no longer angry with him. "I'll wash up."

"You must finish your chores tomorrow. You are behind enough as it is."

"Lars said hello," Nels added quickly, hoping it would lighten the mood.

Instead, Mother's eyes suddenly widened. "What is that?" She was pointing at the spool of thread on the counter.

"It was left for you," Nels said.

She stood and slowly picked up the spool. "*Who* left it?"

"Some old man . . . Ickabosh. He said you and he were friends."

"What?!" she cried. "He knows better than to come here when I am gone!"

A knock rapped at the door before Nels could ask further. His mother held the spool of thread in her hand as she marched to answer it. Beyond the doorframe was a young man wearing a brimmed hat with a white feather. Draped over his shoulders was a bold banner of the royal crest, embossed with a golden seal. Mother grabbed her chest, backing away with a start.

"Is this the home of Norell, the seamstress?"

"What are *you* doing here?" she answered.

"I, uh, brought you a message," he said, surprised by her reaction. He unrolled a piece of thin parchment and read from it. "'His Majesty desires an audience with Norell, the seamstress, and her son, Nels, known as the Knight of Cobblestown. Give your consent to the messenger' — that's me — 'and arrive at the castle by midday tomorrow,' signed, Lennart, King of Avërand."

"No!" Mother answered without hesitation. "We will *never* go there."

The man clutched the parchment. "Begging your pardon?"

Nels felt like a cornered mouse. The man had already said too much.

"We will *never* set foot in that castle," Mother said. "Go!"

"But — but the king wants —"

"I do not care what he wants. He has no right to want anything from me!"

"Good lady, be sensible!" the messenger pleaded. "You should have seen your son this afternoon. The favored knight of our land was no match for him. It was amazing to watch!"

"Serve His Majesty these words," Mother said. "'I will *never* forgive you!'"

She pushed the man over the threshold and out of their cottage, slamming the door as the speechless messenger scuttled away.

"Mother?" Nels asked. "Are you all right?"

"Oh, Nels!" She braced the door with her back. "What have you done?"

Without waiting for an answer, she shot past Nels, gathered a burlap sack, and frantically searched the cottage. Nels did not understand what she was doing until she started to raid the pantry and dumped all of their food into the sack. She was packing their things.

"What are you doing, Mother? What do you mean you'll never forgive the king?"

"There is no time to explain. We must leave at once!"

"Leave?" She could not be serious. "Why?"

"Confound it, Nels!" Mother cursed. "I brought us here to protect *you*! If the king knows where you are, so will *he*." She collected a few blankets and bundled them under her arms after she doused the fire. "We must get you out of here before he finds you . . . and kills you, too!"

"*Kills* me?" Terror sheered through his body, causing him to tremble. "What are you talking about?"

She refused to answer as she carried the sack out the door. Nels followed her to the barn, completely baffled.

Why would someone want to kill me?

"Will you tell me what's going on?"

"What happened at the festival?" Mother asked. "How did the king find you?"

"I wrestled with his knight, and I won," Nels said proudly, "and the prize was a kiss from the princess, but she refused. Maybe that's why the king wants to see us — to apologize?"

"*The princess* refused you?" Mother stared at Nels, her lips pressed tightly together. "That girl is mad if she thinks she can do better than you." She proceeded to load the cart when she cursed again. "Not even a *slip stitch* can save us now."

"Slip stitch?" Nels had no idea what she was talking about. "What's a slip stitch?"

The woman turned around and looked Nels directly in the eyes. "I cannot explain right now, my son. You must go back inside and get your things. Bring only what you absolutely need."

She really meant this. Nels could see the urgency in her eyes, but how could he up and leave without saying good-bye to anyone? No more secrets. "Tell me what's going on first."

"I lost your father to *him*. I will not lose you, too. Now hurry!"

"I'm not going anywhere until you tell me!"

Mother stopped and looked him squarely in the eyes again. "Get your things."

His anger rising, Nels left the barn and headed back to the cottage.

"Hurry," Mother called. "We must not waste a second!"

Nels kicked the door open. Never had he felt so furious, so untrusted. Mother had always had paranoid fits in the past, but this instance was unlike all the others. He did not want to leave his life in Cobblestown — or his friends — without knowing why. Then again, the extreme way she was acting was reason enough to pause; this was not the time to rebel. Mother had never created a fuss like this before, never in his life. If she was speaking the truth, they were in real danger.

She may have kept secrets from him, but she'd never lie to him.

Someone could be after us.

Nels grabbed some of his clothing and a few things that might come in handy on their journey to . . . wherever they were going. They would also need something for protection. The ax. He had left it outside. Opening the back door once more, Nels dashed out to the chopping block, pried his ax free, and turned back to the cottage to gather up the rest of his belongings.

"Did you think you could hide from me, Lief?"

Nels stopped in his tracks. A man's voice whispered all around him, using the name Ickabosh had called him earlier. He turned to see a caped man leaning against the largest oak — not the tailor — someone else. The stranger entered the clearing. Pale twilight revealed dark hair and equally dark eyes.

Mother was right. Someone *was* after them — and he had found them.

Nels held his ax up to his chest, ready to strike. "Who are you?"

Without a word, the man raised his arm and threw a knife.

Nels held up his ax and deflected it. When he saw a second knife, he knocked it down, too. It surprised him how powerful these throws were, and also that he managed to evade the knives with ease. Nels still had the thimble with him, so that probably had something to do with it. A third knife flew at him. This time, it rose high and wavered in the air before it came down to strike.

Before he could think of how such a throw was even possible, Nels swung the ax and struck the blade. His blow sent the knife back to the villain, finding a home in the tree behind him. Their confrontation was at a standstill.

"Leave us alone!" Nels warned. "You're outmatched here!"

The man raised his hand.

A sudden chill ran through Nels's body, and then he couldn't move. The man jerked one hand and Nels fell, pulled by something unseen. The man's other hand slammed downward toward the ground. Nels wanted to get up and fight, but he was flat on his back — he couldn't budge. The thimble — on its own — slid out of his pocket. The shiny piece of brass hovered over his head before it drifted out of reach and fell to the ground nearby.

"Now that you're without protection," said the dark stranger, "you will die."

"Nels?" his mother called from the cottage. "Where are you?"

Growling, the man stepped back to the edge of the woods, grabbed his knife, and pulled it from the oak. The trunk burst like thunder, sending splinters up the hill. "Farewell, *Nels*."

With a twirl of his cape, the stranger vanished into the shadows.

Unable to move or shout, Nels watched as the oak fell toward him.

A half-moon hovered in the reddening sky as Nels sat up by the edge of the pond, gasping for breath. Surprisingly rejuvenated, he looked around and searched for the dark stranger. Strangely enough, his face even felt better. He touched it; the skin around his right eye felt normal.

Nothing had happened, nothing at all. Nels exhaled a long sigh of relief.

The festival; the dark, caped stranger; the tree — it was all a dream.

I can't believe I fell asleep out here.

Nels jumped to his feet and ran back to the cottage. The back door was open and the kitchen was dark, with all the dishes put away. Mother was not at her loom, nor was she in her bed.

"Mother?" No answer.

He called again. No response.

Why was the back door open?

He stepped outside, back into the dusk, watching the wind tousle the treetops.

Strangely, he couldn't feel the wind.

A mournful wail reached his ears from the edge of the woods. Nels went to investigate. The cries intensified as he approached a felled oak, the same oak from his dream.

Is this really happening? I'm not dreaming now, am I?

He found his mother at the base of the tree, her face buried in her hands.

"What's wrong, Mother?" he asked. "I'm here."

She did not answer him. All she did was cry.

Nels jumped over the fallen tree. "Mother, what's wrong?"

"Oh, Nels!" She sobbed into her hands. "It's all my fault."

"What's your fault?"

Again, she didn't respond — when Nels looked down, he understood why.

Beside her lay a pale body, crushed beneath the oak. She picked up the thimble lying nearby and carefully placed it into the palm of the body's lifeless hand. "My perfect son . . ."

Nels stared at his own body on the ground. He trembled and reached for his mother's shoulder, to comfort her, but his hand passed right through her instead.

The woman shivered as he backed away.

4

A KNIGHT IN THE WOODS

Long strands of golden hair brushed Tyra's shoulders as she
guided her mare along a path lined by tall white oaks. She
never imagined going this far from the castle in the middle of
the night, or riding into the woods on her own . . . but to be
alone with Arek was worth the risk.

Why did he send the old tailor to fetch me?

Riding through a shadowed thicket was not how Tyra
planned to spend her midsummer evening. Her secret walk
outside the city was interrupted when she found the tailor by
the bridge, holding the bridle of her mare in his weathered
hand. Tyra reprimanded him for saddling Brooklet — no one
could touch the mare without her consent — but when he
told her that Sir Arek was waiting for her in a clearing within
the white oaks, she mounted her horse and rode off into
the night.

A meeting in the woods was such a spontaneous and
romantic idea, even if the location was rather inconvenient.
Why would he pick such a distant place? Tyra had heard
rumors, of course — rumors about a question he wanted to
ask her, and she had a good idea of what that question was.
A late summer night, a full moon, a secret tryst in the
woods. This fueled her excitement about the possibility that

she'd entertained — and embraced — ever since the end of last summer.

He was going to propose to her.

How did he obtain my father's blessing?

She had no idea. Her father, the king, hardly showed an interest in anything — except to oppose her desire to be with Arek. Regardless, Tyra rode on, peering between the trees for her love. Arek's conduct had changed somewhat since the festival, thanks to that arrogant peasant who bruised more than her beloved's face. She shuddered at the thought of almost kissing him.

Hundreds of thick trees surrounded her the farther she journeyed into the woods. The full moon shed enough light through the high branches to guide Brooklet along the road. Some commoners spoke of the full moon as though it was a terrible omen, but that was silly. There was no better time to go out at night than during a full moon — and nothing was more romantic than a proposal beneath one.

Still, Tyra could not understand why Arek had sent the tailor to fetch her . . . that strange, old man who wove fabrics in a dingy cellar within the castle's foundation. Tyra had to admit that the tailor's abilities were praiseworthy. His skilled hand provided her with comfortable, extravagant dresses. Some in the castle claimed that he could do more than weave beautiful fabrics, that he had gifts of a magical nature, and that he knew of things that no one else knew. And the most peculiar thing about him was that he never took measurements.

With a deep sigh, Tyra let go of her thoughts about the tailor.

As the daughter of Avërand, she had everything she wanted.

Well . . . *almost* everything.

What she truly wished for, even more than Sir Arek's hand, was her freedom.

There was no doubt that she was fortunate. She had a good life, with obedient servants to cater to her every whim. Beyond that, she could only guess what it would be like when her parents left the world, leaving her to rule the kingdom. Govern the people all by herself? She couldn't stand the thought of it. No tutor was competent enough to give her the knowledge she needed — or the courage — and Father's constant gloom caused him to overlook her worry. Mother's attention to his woes was of no help, either. It was no surprise to the Court that Tyra had sought out a strong, worthy man to be at her side, to admire her, and love her.

If not for Arek, Tyra would be lost.

But Brooklet, her faithful mare, was the only creature that seemed to truly understand her plight. When, as a child, Tyra went to select a horse for herself, she found the smallest foal standing by a dribbling brook. The creature trotted to her and pressed its nose against her arm with a gentle nudge. She connected with the filly instantly, both of them smaller and more vulnerable than they wanted to admit. From then on, she and Brooklet were bonded. If only Tyra's parents felt as strongly about their daughter. Another memory invaded her thoughts as the princess recalled the most genuine smile that had ever graced her father's face, all because of that insolent peasant.

If I should ever see him again . . .

What troubled her more than anything was that she had actually considered kissing him.

It had been a week, and she was still thinking about it.

Never had she seen green eyes like his before, deep enough that she could see reflections in them. Of all his features, she remembered his eyes most. She'd caught him glancing at her that day, more times than she could count. Aside from the dust in his hair, he was actually rather attractive, although the thought of a commoner defeating her perfect knight was infuriating.

Rewarding the peasant would've completely undone her.

Tyra shook her head and focused on the path in front of her. The woods grew darker as she rode deeper. Arek was waiting for her in a clearing somewhere, but she did not know where.

Shouldn't I be there by now?

The tailor had instructed her to follow the wooded path west to find the clearing, but she'd been traveling for nearly an hour with no sign of her Arek. Frustrated, but not wanting to become lost in the shaded group of dense oaks, Tyra kept to the path. An owl hooted. The sound startled her, but only for a moment. She spotted a lone figure walking on the path in front of her.

Maybe this person knows where the clearing is.

Tyra hooded her head and tightened the sash on her cloak before reaching the stranger. She then encouraged her mare to follow his pace before she spoke. "Excuse me."

The stranger came to a stop and raised his head.

It was too dark to see his face.

"I'm looking for a clearing along this path. Would you happen to know where it is?"

He said nothing. He just stared at her. His eyes made Tyra shiver.

"I assume you can speak . . . or do I assume too much?"

"You . . . you can *see* me?" he asked.

Tyra cinched her brow. "Should I *not* see you?"

"No one else can see me. Are you dead, too?"

Shocked by the outrageous question, Tyra could only blink in response. Perhaps a full moon *could* drive people to madness. "My apologies, sir. You are in no condition to help me."

"Wait!" He dashed in front of her. "*I* need help."

"You are beyond my help. You are quite mad."

"I swear I'm not. Please, miss, you —"

"Quite. Mad." Tyra guided Brooklet's reins. "Come on, girl!"

She urged the mare to take off in a sprint, but the simpleton ran ahead and spread his arms wide. Tyra pulled back, but she was too late to stop Brooklet in time. The mare trampled right over the stranger. Spooked, Brooklet reared her legs and tossed Tyra from the saddle. The princess let out a shriek before she hit the road. The mare took off toward Cobblestown. With the wind knocked out of her, Tyra rolled to her side and gasped several times before producing a solid breath. She was unharmed, but could tell her rear end was going to be sore in the morning. Tyra rose to her knees. The sash around her waist was loose, and her hood had fallen from her head. The young man stood over her, his body and clothing untarnished.

How is he not hurt?

Brooklet had run right over him. There was no chance that he dodged her in time. But then, to her surprise, with his sandy-brown hair and his deep-green eyes, she recognized the young man,

He was the peasant from the festival!

"*You!*" Their voices sounded as one.

Tyra jumped up and ran to the side of the road, wanting to be anywhere but here.

"What are you doing out here?" he asked.

"Stay back!" she warned. "Don't even think of touching me!"

The boy raised his hands, surrendering. "Don't worry. I can't."

Tyra gave him a hard stare before she shook the dust off her dress.

"Are you hurt?" he asked.

"No," she said, "but how are you *not* hurt? What fool runs in front of a horse?"

"Well . . . nothing can hurt me. Not anymore." His eyes met hers. "I'm dead."

Her heart pounding, Tyra looked for something with which to defend herself. She grabbed a long fallen stick and swung it at him. "Get away from me!"

The peasant shook his head. "What are you going to do with that? Swat me?"

Pressing against the bark of a rotted oak, Tyra held her stick at the ready, but the peasant refused to yield. She swung at his head, but her blow failed to strike him. She swung again, hard this time, right at his chest, but her stick passed through him, hit the ground, and snapped in half.

"You see?" said the peasant. "I'm dead."

"Stop that!" Tyra demanded, even though she was starting to believe him.

Her blows had not missed him — they had gone right *through* him. She couldn't decide whether she wanted to scream or run, so she took a few long breaths and tried to calm down.

"You're, uh, um . . . Explain yourself!"

There was a dull shine of moonlight in the peasant's eyes. "What's to explain?"

"Well, you were . . . *alive* when I last saw you. What happened to you?"

He shrugged his shoulders. "You wouldn't believe me if I told you."

"Wouldn't believe? Either I've lost my mind, or I'm talking to a ghost."

"You haven't lost your mind," he said.

Tyra exhaled a deep breath. "That's comforting." She stepped a little closer and extended her hand, enough to poke his chest. Her finger sunk into him — where his heart would have been — and she felt nothing there. The sight sent a chill through her body. "You really *are* dead!"

The peasant cocked his brow. "You don't have to be insensitive about it."

"Sorry. I just didn't expect . . . you don't *look* like a ghost."

"What are ghosts supposed to look like?"

"I — I don't know. See-throughish?"

He chuckled. "I thought that, although I never believed in ghosts until I became one."

This was incredible. Here she was, talking with a ghost. It might not have bothered her so much if it had been someone else, but, despite her disdain for him, she marveled at this unexpected wonder. She crossed her arms, actually feeling a bit sorry for the poor boy. "What happened to you?"

"I was crushed by a tree," he answered.

Tyra shivered at the thought. "How did *that* happen?"

"A man attacked me with magic. I couldn't move. The next thing I knew . . ." He paused. "I've searched everywhere for help, and you're the only one who's been able to see me."

Tyra chortled. She didn't mean to, but she couldn't believe the situation or the conversation she was having.

The peasant glared at her. "I'm glad you find this amusing."

"I'm sorry, but — you must admit how odd this is."

His glare persisted.

"Look, I'm sorry for what happened to you," she said. "Truly, I am."

"You should be, after what you've done." He crossed his arms and stepped closer.

Tyra had to tilt her head back as he neared. His height made her uncomfortable. She stood her ground and slowed her breath. "What have *I* done? I'm not responsible for this!"

"No," he said, "but you made a fool of me at the festival."

Oh . . . that . . .

The memory had completely escaped her mind; how pathetic, holding on to a grudge like that. "*I* made a fool out of *you*? You have no idea what you put *me* through!"

"Forgive me if I can't sympathize," said the peasant. "I'm sure whatever you've been through is *much* worse than death."

She looked into his eyes with a knifelike stare. It did nothing to him. Not a trace of fear showed in him, when anyone else would have groveled at her feet. No one else would dare act like this, or make offensive accusations, in her presence. Dead or alive, this peasant should be no different. "I am sorry for your loss, but what do you expect me to do?"

Without waiting for an answer, she headed down the road to find Brooklet.

"I guess my friend was right," he said. "You *are* a witch."

Tyra paused in her stride. "A witch, am I?" She turned back and found the peasant where she had left him, looking frustrated and miserable. "A witch? Is that really the best you can do?"

He lowered his head, ashamed that he'd used the childish insult. It served him right.

"Just as I thought. I must go now. If I don't return home, they will worry."

"Will you speak to my mother first? She's down the road in a clearing."

Clearing? Tyra's interest was piqued. "What clearing?"

"If you follow me, I'll show you."

Could this be the same clearing where Arek wanted to meet her? The idea warmed Tyra's chest and settled her nerves. "If I speak to your mother, will I be finished with you?"

"I swear on my grave."

Imagining his buried corpse made her quiver, but if he promised to leave her alone on the condition of her help, it was worth a short detour, if only to see if this was the same clearing where Arek had intended them to meet. "I will hold you to that, ghost. Take me to your mother."

He smiled, pleased that she accepted his terms. "This won't take long. Thank you!"

Tyra tailed behind him, begrudging a smile of her own.

It had better not . . .

5

THE PEASANT'S MOTHER

A quaint little cottage sat in the center of a plowed clearing, its front shadowed from the full moon. Soft candlelight danced along the sills of two sturdy windows. There was also a barn to the left, and several chickens walked freely about, but there was no sign of Arek anywhere.

Tyra could not believe she was helping a ghost — the ghost of a peasant who had the nerve to humiliate her, no less. She jabbed him in the back, just to be sure — again — that he was a ghost. And again, she felt nothing. His presence went against everything she had ever heard about ghosts. He did not glow, nor was he transparent. He seemed normal, like any healthy person. Despite the illusion, he was dead. Not that it was a tremendous loss, in her opinion. She hadn't heard of his death, something the royal scribe would have mentioned at the morning meal. Mother liked to know of Avërand's new births; Father, on the other hand, preferred news about the deceased.

Pushing the morbid thought from her mind, Tyra surveyed the clearing and smelled the air, catching a tinge of smoke. The ground was soft, too, but free of moisture, since it had not rained all week. They walked by a grave mound, not far from the road.

"That's where they buried me," said the peasant.

At the head of the grave was a stone with the inscription, *Nels: The Knight of Cobblestown*. Flowers and wreaths adorned either side of the plot, along with a few burned-out candles. The collection of flora was the greatest that Tyra had ever seen for a deceased commoner.

"Once I speak to your mother, I am going home."

"You'll want to put on your hood," he warned.

Tyra did so without knowing why. "Whatever for?"

"My mother hates royalty. If she knows you're the princess —"

"Why would anyone hate royalty?"

The peasant raised his brow with a conspicuous stare. She glared back as his eyes turned to the cottage. In spite of the peasant's insolence, Tyra was intrigued and curious about him — if only a little. He annoyed her, most definitely, but she also remembered him being rather nimble during his spar with Arek — beguiling, even — and Tyra did have a tendency to find tall men attractive. But not this one; no, she couldn't stand this peasant in the least. Then again, it would one day become her duty to settle the kingdom's affairs, to resolve disputes and help the people. Fulfilling the request of a dead peasant was a memorable way to start.

"I'm glad you found me. You have no idea what it's like to go unnoticed."

Tyra sighed. "Actually, I *do* know what that's like."

"Isn't ignoring the princess a high offense?"

"Not if you're my father."

Nels was silent, a look of curiosity on his face.

"Look," Tyra said. "All I want is to speak to your mother and be done with this."

"You didn't come here to apologize, then?" he replied. "Why are you out here?"

"I came here to practice *witchy* spells. Do you want me to speak to your mother or not?"

Again, the peasant said nothing. He just smiled with a nod and pressed for the cottage.

When they reached the door, Tyra gave it a knock. No answer. "Is she home?"

"Give her a moment," he said.

"Wait," Tyra said, panicking. "What should I say to her?"

The door opened a crack. Standing on the other side of the threshold was a middle-aged woman with red hair, her face glazed with sorrow. She looked lovely, aside from her puffy, bloodshot eyes. She stared at Tyra with a suspicious frown, stooping to see more of what lay beneath her hood. "Do I know you, young lady?"

"We, uh, have never met," Tyra answered, "but I have come to tell you . . ."

The peasant stood beside her. The woman did not seem to notice. "What is it?"

Tyra looked to the peasant, unsure of what to say, as the woman waited.

I can't just say her son is a ghost. "It's . . . sensitive. Can we talk inside?"

"I have no idea who you are," the woman said "but I see by the dress beneath your cloak that you are a Lady of the Court. You are not welcome in my home. Good night."

Without giving Tyra a chance to speak, the woman closed the door.

Tyra glanced at the peasant. "She can tell by the hem of my dress?"

"She knows a lot about nobility," said the peasant.

Tyra shrugged. "So what now?"

"Try again?"

"And what should I say to her? 'Your son is a ghost. He has a message for you'?"

"Not like that. Just . . . let her know I love her, and that she shouldn't blame herself."

Easier said than done. "I'll think of something." Tyra knocked on the door again.

"Her name is Norell, if that helps."

The door eased open again, enough for the woman to reveal her left eye and a portion of her annoyed frown. "Young lady," she said brusquely, "I insist you harass me no further!"

"Your son," Tyra uttered. "This is about your son."

Norell widened the door. "You knew my son?"

"Well." Tyra tried not to shift her eyes at him. "Sort of."

"Come in, milady. You should not be out there alone."

Tyra entered, surprised by the woman's quick insistence. The peasant followed as the door closed. A few lit candles revealed a cluttered room with cloth strewn about. A loom sat in the corner, its heddles laced with thread. Norell pulled up a chair and encouraged Tyra to sit down.

"Mind your voice. I have a guest asleep in the back. I thought her mouth would never stop." She walked into the kitchen and raised a kettle from the hearth. "Care for tea?"

The peasant nodded at the princess. "A sip would be fine," Tyra answered.

Norell eyed her as she searched through a cupboard.

"I don't get it," said the peasant. "She's being *nice* to you."

Tyra waited for Norell to tip her kettle, and then she whispered, "Is that uncommon?"

"Did you say something, dear?" the woman asked.

"I — I, uh," Tyra stuttered, trying to keep track of them both. "I like your tapestries!"

"Why, thank you, child." Norell carried two cups of steaming tea to the table, their brims lined with silver. Tyra quickly raised hers and sipped, surprised by the strong taste of honey and angelica root. The concoction was more delicious than she was expecting. "I am sorry for being so affront with you, my dear," Norell said, taking a seat across from her. "I have not been myself since my son . . . passed . . ."

Tyra lowered her cup. "I am sorry for your loss. It came as a shock to me."

"As it did for many," Norell added. "How did you know my son?"

"I met him in the village," Tyra said. "Last week."

"At the festival, I take it. Would you remove your hood, please?"

Tyra knew it was impolite to remain hooded in another's household, but the peasant shook his head, insisting that she keep it on. She removed it anyway, exposing her yellow hair and soft complexion. The woman leaned forward, astonished, as Tyra's strands settled.

"Such a pretty girl. He made no mention of you. Were you fond of him?"

"Oh — no, no," Tyra said, blushing. "It's nothing like that."

The woman nodded as she turned to the fire. "He was such a picky boy when it came to girls," Norell said. "I never knew of him meeting you, a young noble girl. He must have been scared to death to say anything; I thank you for your condolences." She closed her eyes and sipped from her cup. "I severed my ties with the Court many years ago. Perhaps the nobility is not as conceited as I remember."

The peasant backed away a step, as if startled by what the woman had said. "Severed ties with the Court?" He snapped his fingers. "I knew it! Her manners, the gowns in her wardrobe, the way she always knew so much about the nobility . . . Why didn't she ever tell me about this?"

Tyra studied Norell, finding it hard to accept the unlikely herself. "You're a Lady?"

"I *was* a Lady — of the Court, that is," Norell said. "Perhaps I am saying too much, but I must make up for years of silence. If I had told him sooner, Nels may still be with us."

The woman raised a hand to her eyes while Tyra caught a shattered look on the peasant's face, as if he refused to believe his mother's words. Tyra had a hard time believing them, too. Why would this woman voluntarily leave the Court and live the life of a peasant? Tyra would rather die first than be a commoner. "Why would you renounce your title and live out here?" she asked.

"I doubt you know what happened to my husband," Norell continued. "He was murdered before the entire Court. Because of Lennart, my husband's life was taken by a madman."

Tyra blinked. This was news to her. "No," she said. "I've never heard of this."

"Lennart never had the backbone to confront his problems, after all my husband did for him. Now all he does is sulk in his castle like a coward, while my son is murdered by the man who killed his father." Norell began to sob, softly. "It was a clear night. It was not lightning that brought down that tree!" The woman quickly composed herself. "My apologies," she said, changing the subject. "Please tell me, young lady. Who are your parents? If they are native to this area, surely I would remember them."

Tyra didn't know what to do. Telling the woman that she was the king's daughter would be a terrible idea. Luckily, before Tyra could speak, a thump sounded on the other side of the cottage. A scrawny young girl appeared in the kitchen, her brown hair unkempt and her clothing tattered.

This had to be the guest that Norell mentioned. The girl rubbed the sleep from her eyes and looked at them. "Who's there?"

The peasant winced. "Oh, great . . ."

Tyra shot him a glance, wondering what the matter was. She watched the girl wander to the fireplace and sniff the warm kettle. "Company," Norell said, releasing a deep sigh. "This is Jilia. She has been kind enough to help me these last few days. I honestly do not know what I would do without her. She and Nels were such good friends. You never did tell me your name, milady?"

"I . . ." The situation had officially overwhelmed Tyra. "I'd better go."

"But," Norell insisted, "you had something to say about my son?"

"What about Nels?" The mousy girl ran closer to the table and stopped suddenly. Her brown eyes widened like huge apricots as she pointed at Tyra. "What's the princess doing here?"

Norell whipped her head back and locked her eyes with Tyra's. "*Princess*?"

With a groan, the peasant raised a hand to his forehead.

"Yes," Tyra admitted with a gulp. "I am the princess."

"Princess *Tyra*?" Norell's kindly face changed to one of astonishment. "Carin's girl?" She then placed a hand over her heart. "I never expected. In *my* house. Why are *you* here?"

Tyra didn't know how to explain, but she tried. "This will sound . . . strange." She closed her eyes, knowing how absurd she might sound. "I saw Nels in the woods. He is a ghost now."

His mouth gaping open, the peasant stared at her. "What are you doing?"

"I don't know. What am I *supposed* to say?" she responded.

When silence followed, Tyra's eyes drifted to the girl and the woman. Both of them stared at her with horror in their eyes. An ember popped out of the hearth, making Norell jump.

"Nels — a ghost?" Jilia said. "A *ghost*? Are you mad?"

"I will not hear this." Norell's jaw clenched. "Leave my house at once!"

Tyra caught her breath, stunned by their contempt. Even the look on the peasant's face was exasperated. "I knew they wouldn't believe me," she said, glaring at him. She then stood up and turned to the woman, ready to leave. "He loves you and he doesn't want you to blame yourself." After that, she turned to the peasant and folded her arms. "There," she muttered. "I said it."

"You have said *enough*!" the woman cried. "You humiliated my son, and now you insult my grief. You wicked, shameful girl — you and your entire family are nothing but a disgrace!"

"How dare you!" Tyra cried back. "I could have you imprisoned!"

"Leave my house!" Norell shouted. "*Get out!*"

"Who are you to order me about, *peasant*?"

The woman stormed around the table and seized Tyra by the arm. She yanked the princess to the door and cast her out. The door slammed before Tyra landed on the ground. A loud bawling sounded within the cottage. The door opened a crack, just enough for the girl to poke her head out.

"You're a vile, wicked trollop!" she said. "If you come back, I'll make you sorry!"

Again, the door slammed. Tyra dusted herself off, storming past the grave.

The nerve of that woman, handling me like that!

She should have left the moment she couldn't find Arek in the clearing. The peasant started to call after her, but she went on. She had given into his plea once already, yielding to assist his problem, but she wouldn't make the same mistake twice. She should not have come here.

The peasant caught up with her. "Will you stop and listen to me?"

"I did what you asked," she said. "I did my best and it only made a mess of things. Are you happy now?" She kept marching. "I fulfilled my agreement; now you fulfill yours!"

"If you won't stop, I'll —"

"What will you do, ghost? Walk through me?"

"I'll . . . I'll *haunt* you. That's what ghosts do. I'll haunt you for the rest of your life!"

Scoffing at him, Tyra proceeded into the woods, hoping to find Brooklet in Cobblestown. The peasant persisted, walking in front of her with every step. She refused to acknowledge him, and she refused to think of him haunting her, following her wherever she went, so she hoped his threat was an empty one. As they reached the edge of the woods, he ran ahead and stuck his leg out in front of her. Unhindered, she walked right through it.

"What were you doing?" she asked, finally acknowledging him.

The peasant grumbled back.

"I can't hear you, ghost."

"I was trying to trip you."

Tyra laughed. "There's a problem with that — you're *dead*!"

Without looking back, she walked over the quarry hill and finally descended into the village. The peasant didn't follow her this time. Perhaps the edge of the woods was as far as he could go. Master Wussen, one of her instructors trained in ghost lore, mentioned how ghosts can only go to certain places. The peasant could stay in the woods. She would not have it any other way, even if the thought of leaving him gave her no comfort.

She had tried to help, and she had failed — miserably.

How can anyone expect me to rule? I can't even help a dead peasant.

Tyra figured it was midnight by now. The moon was still high and bright. Upon entering the village, Tyra found her mare drinking from a trough. The princess approached Brooklet, stroked her mane, mounted, and guided her toward the castle. They rode for a while and then stopped. At the east end of the village, Tyra turned to see the silhouetted hill once more — for the last time.

"I will never again go into those woods."

Slipping quietly into her soft bed and feeling the down of her countless pillows, Tyra blew out her candle, pulled the long silk sheets up to her chin, and closed her eyes for the night. Her thoughts lingered on Arek as she listened to the quiet.

The silence was rather comforting.

"Excuse me, I'm looking for a 'witchy' princess."

Tyra sat up with a start, her eyes peering into the darkness.

A tall figure stood in the center of her room, staring back with dark eyes. Moonlight bled through the windows behind him and reached the foot of her bed. He should have cast a shadow on her sheets, but there was none. Master Wussen was mistaken. Ghosts could go anywhere — and *he* had found her.

He stepped closer. Tyra clutched her pillow. Her heart raced.

She wanted to scream, but what good would that do?

No one else could see him.

6

THE TERRACE

Tyra wanted to lay her head on the table the moment she sat down for breakfast — not a comfortable place to rest, but if given a moment, she would have fallen asleep effortlessly. Sunlight bled through the stained-glass windows, splashing color on the bland stone walls.

"My goodness," her mother said. "Are you still in your nightclothes?"

Moaning, Tyra sat upright.

So much for that idea . . .

Wrinkles covered her beige robe, and dark circles drooped beneath her tired eyes. She had brushed her hair some, but Tyra refused to slip into a dress with unwanted eyes watching her every move. The peasant had proved himself a complete nuisance by keeping her awake all night. No matter how many pillows she threw at him, he would not stop. The peasant didn't sleep, so neither could she, and Tyra's back ached terribly. Falling off Brooklet had certainly not helped, but being forced to endure the peasant's voice for hours had proved far worse. She couldn't tolerate his pestering for much longer.

If this goes on for another night, I will lose my mind.

Father tapped a shelled egg with his silver spoon. Mother had one, too.

Tyra stared at it. "You know I don't eat eggs."

"We expected as much," said her mother, signaling for Tyra's meal to come.

From the side door emerged a fat scullion wearing a white apron that draped over his protrusive belly. Tyra simpered. He walked to her chair, placed a dainty platter on the table, and removed the cover. An inviting aroma wafted into her nose — an assortment of sliced fruits and a fresh pastry. Her empty stomach grumbled. Such a lovely spread. If she hadn't skipped out on her last meal, she wouldn't be starving now. Tyra reached for a fork and held it delicately.

"Enjoy your breakfast, Your Highness," said the scullion.

Just then, from below the table, a head jutted up — right through her platter. "There you are!" said the peasant. Tyra let out a shriek and her fork slipped from her fingers. He then belted a laugh and turned to the startled scullion. "What . . . No sour custard?"

"Go away!" Tyra slammed the cover over her platter. "Meddlesome spook!"

With a flabbergasted frown, the scullion reclaimed the meal and dashed back into the kitchens. Tyra cried for him to stop, but he was too quick, and she watched as her beautiful meal vanished behind the swinging door. She stared at the peasant with a look of severe contempt.

"What are you doing now," she cried. "Trying to starve me to death?"

The room fell silent. Tyra looked at her father and mother. Both of them stared back, their brows creased. Father's mouth hung open, while Mother had a goblet pressed to her lips. The queen lowered it slowly. "Was something wrong with your meal, darling?"

Tyra bit on her lip as she sank deeper into her chair.

"Honestly, Tyra." Mother shook her head. "What has come over you?"

"She went out last night," Father said. "Longer than usual."

"On the full moon, Tyra? What an absurd thing to do!"

"The guards also told me you conversed with yourself in your room all night." Father resumed eating his egg. "I would advise against going outside on the full moon, Tyra."

The peasant laughed again. "You should tell them who you were *really* talking to."

Tyra felt her face turn red. "I couldn't sleep."

"Well," said Mother. "That explains your mood. It is bad enough having to repair the damage you caused in Cobblestown. No one will take your word seriously if you break it."

"I know I won't," the peasant chimed in. He walked behind the king and queen and stood between them. "What do you think would happen if they knew a peasant had tossed you on your arse?"

Tyra slammed her fist on the table. Having suffered embarrassment from his mother the night before was enough. "Bite your tongue!"

Mother pressed a hand over her heart. "*What* did you say to me?"

Feeling like a buffoon, Tyra closed her eyes, wishing to disappear. *Idiot. No one can see him but you!* Speaking to him in front of others surely made her look strange. "I — I didn't mean —"

"Enough," Father said. "You obviously do not feel well. Take rest today."

Tyra sat up straight again. "I will be fine, Father. I don't want to miss archery."

"I wish you would. I would rather not have you spending time with *him*."

The peasant shot Tyra a curious look. "Who's *him*?" he asked nosily. "Arek?"

"Really," Mother continued. "What I have done to deserve such a resentful —" The royal scribe entered the room, carrying under his arm a thin book that contained the daily report of the kingdom's affairs. His entrance saved Tyra from having to explain further — an appreciated distraction. Mother's stormy mood instantly became sunny. "What news do you bring today?"

"Much, Your Majesties. First, there is a couple who wish to wed."

"Wonderful! How wonderful," Mother said. "Grant them our blessing."

The man nodded. "I have disturbing news as well. There was a death."

It was Father who looked up this time. "What of it?"

The ghost anxiously glanced at Tyra. She scowled back as the scribe cleared his throat and opened his book. "An accident claimed the life of a young man of seventeen years from the outskirts of Cobblestown. The villagers say an oak crushed him after it was struck by lightning."

A sullen expression washed over the peasant's face as Tyra glimpsed at him. What would it feel like, having someone speak of her death in such a casual way? A knot wrenched inside Tyra's stomach, but not from hunger.

"Cobblestown," said Father. "Did this lad have a name?"

"His name, uh . . . here it is! His name was Nels."

Unlike his usual slump during other reports, Father sat up. "The lad from the match?"

"How dreadfully careless," Mother said, tsk-tsking. "Letting a tree fall on himself."

"I didn't let anything fall on me!" the peasant cried. "I was murdered!"

Tyra smirked at the peasant before she turned to her mother. "Indeed."

"I have some sensitive news, as well," the scribe added.

Father abandoned his egg. "How sensitive?"

"A murder was reported."

Everyone turned to the scribe, especially the peasant.

"*Murder?*" Mother cried. "Are you absolutely sure?"

"A farmer from Boarshovel found a man buried in his field, a knife wound in his back," the scribe explained. "All we know is that he was a weapon's merchant from Harvestport. His cart was found beyond Cobblestown." The scribe searched through his papers and notes, urgently seeking more information. "Witnesses claim to have seen him and his cart at the festival, but our investigation has led us to believe that he was murdered within a day *before* the festival."

"Two deaths at the same time?" Tyra piped in. "Quite a coincidence."

The scribe adjusted his stance, as if his feet were uncomfortable. "Yes, Your Highness, and the lad's mother swears her son was also murdered, but we have no evidence to support that."

Tyra's mother, looking terrified, glanced at the king. "Do you suppose —?"

The king stood. "Look into this matter. Send for the knights. I want to know their findings immediately. Please excuse me." He left the room, the tail of his mantle flying behind him.

Tyra didn't understand what was happening. She had never seen her father so focused and motivated — or disturbed. Granted, these were the first murders Tyra had ever heard of; such things did not happen in Avërand. Or if they did, she was unaware. The weapon merchant's death was unfortunate, but it validated everything the peasant had said throughout the night.

Who is this murderer? "May I be excused, too?" Tyra asked.

Mother squeezed a napkin as she consented. "Be mindful of your conduct, dearest. And until further notice, I do not want you to leave this castle. Is that understood?"

Checking on the distraught peasant first, Tyra hastened to the nearest corridor without giving her mother an answer. Suits of armor were mounted evenly along the limestone walls of the hallway. She paid little attention to them. All she wanted was to outrun the ghost while he was lost in his own wallowing. She hoped the terrace would provide the solitude she needed.

Morning sunlight glistened over the polished granite landing as Tyra stepped outside. A wide stair led to a grand terrace below. Mother hosted parties and dances here for the residing nobility whenever the weather permitted. Tyra stepped down the stairs, strolled to the far side, and looked over the edge of a short wall of stone, garlanded by overgrown ivies. A pauper walked through the main gate below — although he looked more like a large rodent from her perch on the terrace.

She leaned on the trellis, wondering why Sir Arek never arrived in the woods as he'd promised. The only way to find out was to ask him, but she wouldn't have the chance to see him until noon. Until then, she would have to wade through another long set of grueling lessons.

"I can see the quarry from here!"

Tyra rolled her eyes and blew a strand of hair from her face as the peasant emerged onto the landing. The central tower rose high above him, anchored by eight buttresses that supported the outer walls. Beyond that, a second wall had been added years ago, when the castle became more than just a storehouse for annual crops. A small city surrounded the castle, with mansions in the upper district, cottages in the lower district, and a busy market for those who did not go to Harvestport.

Hillshaven was just that, a small haven on a hill, overlooking the kingdom.

The peasant stood by her. "So the merchant was killed *before* the festival?"

Tyra shrugged. "I guess."

"The merchant I saw . . . he didn't look anything like the man who killed me."

She shrugged again. "I guess."

Together, they gazed at the lush land of rolling hills. The grassy fields moved with the breeze, spreading like thin waves over a shore. Tyra was too exhausted to appreciate the view, and she was used to it, anyway. The wind blew at her hair, making each golden strand dance behind her back. The peasant's hair was darker than hers, like sheaves of wheat.

Strangely, it didn't move in the wind.

"How did I end up in this mess?" she wondered aloud. "Must *I* suffer because of *your* problem?"

"I think it's *our* problem," said the peasant.

"*Our* problem? Why must *I* be involved?"

"You can probably see me because you refused to kiss me."

She glowered at him. "That's absurd!"

"Think about it. You made a promise and never fulfilled it."

"Promise? Ha! You swore on your grave to leave me alone, yet here you are!"

"I was hoping you'd fulfill my request with a bit more tact."

Tyra ignored him. "I find it hard to believe that *you* are a ghost because *I* withheld a kiss."

"Me too, but I can't think of a better reason why only *you* can see me. Can you?"

"Yes! You're punishing me because I didn't kiss you and you can't get over it."

"Believe me, I wish I could show myself to someone else — *anyone* else."

Tyra shook her head, wanting nothing more than to see his wish come true so he could be someone else's problem. There had to be a reasonable explanation for this. "My instructor once told me that ghosts exist because of some injustice, or because of some important business that they never had a chance to finish, or for completely selfish reasons — like haunting *me*."

The peasant snapped his fingers. "That's it!"

Tyra leaned her hands on the trellis. "*What* is it?"

"The reason you can see me — *you* have to help me!"

"Help you? Ha! I've already tried that, remember?"

"If I'm to be at peace, then you have to bring the man who killed me to justice."

"Find your killer?" Tyra laughed at the thought. "What do you suppose I should do if we find him? Let him kill me? No. I bet the merchant's ghost may know something. Go ask him."

"I would," he said, leaning against the trellis, "but I'm the only ghost I've seen."

"Well then, I'm rather sorry for you, but I refuse to chase after a killer."

"But you can order the kingdom to comb the entire land for him."

"On the grounds that a dead peasant told me so? I'd rather not."

He stepped closer, making Tyra tilt her head back. Daylight intensified the green in his eyes. "This isn't just about me, Your *Highness*. What if he kills again? What if he keeps hiding in your kingdom and murders more of your people? You *have* to stop him."

He spoke the truth, but she had no idea where to start or how to deal with a villain — and if she did summon a search party, who would believe her story? "This is not my responsibility, especially after what you did to me at breakfast."

"I didn't tell that man to take your food away. You did."

Tyra turned on him, her hands pressed on her hips. "Just stop haunting me, all right? I have no idea who your killer is, and I cannot help you find him."

"Ickabosh might know," the peasant said. "Do you know where he is?"

"I doubt that cooped-up old man will be helpful."

"He might know what's going on. I know he used some kind of illusion on me. He even mentioned something about my father — perhaps he knows something about our killer."

"I don't care about *your* killer." Tyra stood her ground. "I want to be left alone!"

"Have it your way." The peasant placed his hands on the trellis and hoisted himself up. He let his legs dangle as he sat. "Until my murderer is brought to justice, you will never be rid of me."

Tyra could hardly keep her tears back. If this was to be her fate, haunted for the rest of her days — no, she couldn't bear to imagine it. She was already distraught from having to accept the fact that this boy was indeed dead, even if he looked and acted like a normal person, as if he were still alive.

As he glanced up, their eyes met. "What if you kissed me now?" he asked.

A shiver ran up Tyra's spine, making her cough. "What was that?"

"Maybe if you kissed me now, that's all you'd need to do."

"How would I accomplish that? You don't have a body!"

"I have a soul. Maybe it would work if *you* had one?"

She glared at him. "I'd rather search for your killer."

"Just as I thought." The peasant laughed. "No soul."

Balling her hands into fists, Tyra charged at him. "You . . . !

84

Insufferable . . . !" The peasant leaned back to avoid her wrath. "I don't care about you or what you plan to do, but I will not have you embarrass me in front of anyone, especially my mother and father!" She moved right into his face, forcing him to lean back farther. "You will never convince me to help you. Am I clear?"

"Whoa!" The peasant flailed his arms back as his body angled over the side.

"Watch it!" Tyra shouted as she sprang for him, but her hands passed through his ankle.

She stood on the terrace, completely useless, as the peasant fell toward a group of knights on horseback in the courtyard below. But before he struck the cobblestones, he looked up at her and laughed again. No one else saw or heard him as he jumped to his feet and ran inside the castle.

He had fallen on purpose.

Tyra clasped her hand over her eyes and released a long, frustrated scream. A terrible silence followed her tantrum — not one utterance came from the normally busy courtyard. Tyra peered over the trellis to see why. Many eyes stared at her, followed by a few residents clearing their throats uncomfortably. A man had dropped his vegetable basket, and a few knights looked about the castle grounds for danger. Even the gatekeeper gazed at her, looking especially puzzled.

"Uh," she said. "Carry on!"

The everyday commotion resumed as she disappeared from their sight.

"Insolent apparition . . . He's trying to make me look mad!"

From what she could tell, the ploy worked. Two servants ran by the stairs. When Tyra saw them, they scurried across the terrace as fast as they could until they were out of her sight.

The morning bells rang. The hour tolled nine.

Tyra sighed. It was going to be a long day.

7

THE MAD PRINCESS

Whispers.

Whispers.

Whispers.

No matter where she went, Tyra heard nothing else.

Her ears perked at the sound of every quiet voice, and her eyes darted to every concealed mouth. The entire morning was made worse by the peasant's constant interruptions. She could do nothing. No one else could see the peasant or perceive the irritating songs that he sang — purposefully off-key. Tyra tried her best to pay him no heed all morning, but in the end, his attempts to divert her attention were more than successful.

Lady Candise invited Tyra to leave her etiquette session because the princess refused to display a suitable introduction to a group of noblemen. It wasn't her fault; the peasant stepped in front of them whenever she tried to give them a curtsy. Even Master Wussen seemed thoroughly baffled during geography because she would not answer questions about the disaster that decimated the land of Mendarch in the northwest. She wanted to participate, but the peasant's antics distracted her from hearing the questions. Then, when Wussen changed the subject to history and the fall of

Westmine, the kingdom beyond the Westerly Mountains, Tyra was too exhausted to listen. But when he brought up the legend of King Hilvar's ghost, she couldn't help but ask a few questions of her own. "How do you stop a ghost from haunting you?"

Wussen raised his white head. "Why?" he asked. "Are you being haunted?" Tyra gave a reluctant nod, hoping he wouldn't dismiss her. If there was anyone who would believe her story, it was he. "How very fascinating," Wussen said. "When did this haunting begin?"

"A ghost followed me home after a ride in the woods."

The old tutor glanced about the room. "Is it here now?"

"Yes," she said, relieved that someone finally believed her.

"Where?" Wussen continued. "What does it look like?"

"He's right there." She pointed at the table next to her, where the peasant sat, perched like a hunting hawk. Master Wussen looked in her direction, but he did not appear to see anyone there. Tyra expected no less. "He looks like an ordinary peasant, until my hand goes through him . . ."

Her instructor shook his head. "If you had seen an actual ghost, he would be transparent, like a pane of glass," he explained, "but thank you for humoring an old man."

"You didn't give him much to go on," said the peasant. "What about my good looks?"

Tyra scowled at him. "Exactly how many ghosts have you seen, Master Wussen?"

"I have not actually seen one, but I had the strangest experience in Westmine . . ."

Crossing her arms, Tyra stopped listening to him. Some ghost expert. She knew more about ghosts after one night than her teacher did after a lifetime of hunting them.

The peasant heaved a bored sigh. "I'd do myself in if I had to go through *this* every day."

For once, Tyra felt inclined to agree — not that killing herself would necessarily improve her situation. She couldn't bear the thought of ending up like the peasant.

When it came time for the midday meal, Tyra ran for the banquet hall, decorated for one of her mother's many social gatherings. She sat at her place at the table, and — without heeding her guests — gorged herself on a selection of jelly tarts. A single laugh filled the hall, unnoticed by everyone but her. The peasant sat cross-legged on the table.

"Slow down," he said. "You don't want to swallow your napkin."

"At least *I'm* not sitting on the table!"

Food flew from Tyra's full mouth.

Everyone stared at her. Several nobles gave indignant huffs, while another leaned back in her chair to fan her face in disgust. Understanding the spectacle she had made of herself, Tyra swallowed and left the dining hall with a few tarts in hand. Although she had embarrassed herself, Tyra didn't give the people a second thought. She had somewhere else to go, an important place to be.

It was time for archery practice.

Arek had better be there . . .

Dodging her usual route, she made a pass through the kitchens and lost the peasant before she hurried to her room. She then changed into her archery dress, sewn with a fine indigo fabric. She covered her arms with silver bracers, slipped a leather strap over her shoulder, and buckled it to a belt around her waist. The strap was useful if ever she wanted to carry a quiver.

"That's a new look for you," said the peasant. "Sporting!"

Tyra slipped on her gloves. "Were you watching me change?!"

He seemed pleased by her distress. "Did you want me to?"

It was no use speaking to him. Tyra grabbed her bow and a quiver of arrows. "At least I can change my clothes. You're still wearing the same shirt and trousers from the festival."

"Would you have me remove them?"

Ignoring his attempt to rile her, Tyra passed through the peasant and proceeded out the door. "Come if you must. I will not even bother telling you to go away, since I know you won't."

He followed her with an amused smirk. "You catch on quick, Your Highness."

A few flights of marble stairs later, Tyra was in the grounds behind the castle. Beyond the courtyard, near the inner wall, lay a sheltered pavilion. A few hunters stood by, holding readied bows. Their behavior was rather unusual this afternoon; they were providing more space for Tyra than usual. She tightened her bow, nocked an arrow, and let it fly at a bale of hay. The arrow soared through the afternoon air and pierced the center of a burlap target. The other archers clapped.

Thirty yards. Despite her lack of sleep, at least her aim remained true.

"Splendid shot, Your Highness!" Arek entered the shade of the pavilion.

"Arek!" She was so happy to see her knight, more than could be contained. The swelling in his eye had improved some. "Can we speak in private, before Master Niklaus arrives?"

"Certainly." He turned to the others. "It seems I have misplaced my armguard. Fetch it for me, lads, and do take your time." Arek crossed his arms as he watched the hunters depart. "I was hoping to speak with you myself," he continued, once they were alone. "How do you feel?"

"I'm fine." Tyra rubbed at the twitch in her left eye. "Why do you ask?"

"There are few flattering things being said about you this day."

I'm well aware of that. "What have you heard, exactly?"

"That you speak to yourself and scream for no reason, as if you were mad."

Tyra tucked her lower lip some. "What do you make of these rumors?"

"I do not believe them, but believe me when I say that I am mad about you."

In her ear, the peasant burst out laughing. "No man in his right mind would like *you* . . ." He was standing behind her, leaning right over her shoulder, like the nosy simpleton that he was.

Tyra closed her eyes. "Sir Arek, where were you last night?"

The knight brushed a hair behind his ear. "Training my squire. Why do you ask?"

"You weren't waiting for me in a clearing in the woods, outside Cobblestown?"

"Waiting for you . . . in a clearing in the woods . . . on a *full* moon?" He laughed. "Why would I do that?"

"That's it?" the peasant cried. "You came to *my* woods last night to meet *him*?" Tyra refused to answer, so he threw his hands up in disbelief. "The Princess of Avërand really *is* a trollop!"

Tyra couldn't endure this torture any longer. Anger surged inside her veins, making her hot enough to sweat. Even her cheeks felt as if they had caught on fire. "Shut your impudent mouth!"

Arek's smile fell. "Whatever have I said to offend you?"

"I — I, uh, uh," Tyra stammered. "I didn't mean to say that, Arek."

"But you did," he replied. "Maybe you should go inside and rest."

"I can't rest!" Tyra pointed at the peasant. "*He* won't stop pestering me!"

Arek looked to where she pointed. "Who are you talking about, Princess?"

"You can't see him because he's *dead*." Tyra winced as she said it. She knew this would make her look mad, but she couldn't take it anymore. "I went out to meet you in the woods last night, but when I arrived, I found this meddling *ghost* instead. Now he won't leave me alone!"

Realizing that she had spoken louder then she meant, Tyra sensed a new awkward silence in the courtyard, worse than before. Arek's shoulders trembled as the returning hunters came to a halt. The gardeners stopped clipping their hedges, and a group of squires turned their heads.

She had caused yet another scene.

"Maybe we should go inside and consult the physician?" Arek suggested.

"I don't need a physician," Tyra cried. "I need *you*!"

"Stay here, Princess, and I will fetch the physician for you."

Sir Arek turned and left, leaving Tyra alone with the ghost. "You make this haunting business easy," said the peasant. "Shall we keep this up? I still have a few good ideas left in me."

Instead of answering, Tyra threw down her bow and headed for the castle.

"Hey," said the peasant. "Where are you off to now?"

This was the final straw. She was more than disappointed that Arek didn't believe her — he didn't even listen to her. She feared what he thought of her now. Had she scared him away forever? Tyra hoped not. It was time for drastic measures. If she was to have any success in removing the peasant from her life, she had to look into her final option. "The tailor sent me into your woods, and he is going to tell me why."

"Didn't I say that this morning?" The peasant smiled. "You've decided to help me then?"

"Help *you*?" Tyra spun around and jabbed her finger through his chest with each word she spoke. "Who said I was helping you? Nothing in this world could *ever* make me help you!"

"That's too bad. I'd hate to see how you'd handle *two* sleepless nights."

Ignoring the threat, Tyra stormed off to find the cellar — the darkest, most disgusting place in the castle. She had to know why the tailor had sent her into the woods, and why he had lied to her about Sir Arek. She desperately hoped that he would have all the answers.

"By the way," the peasant said, following after her, "you're quite good with a bow."

She already knew that, but she welcomed the compliment. Even if it came from him.

Dim torches guided their descent into the castle's deep foundation. As they went, Nels wondered when they would reach the bottom of the dark, grimy place — not that it bothered him very much. It was the tailor that concerned him. He may have the answers that Nels was searching for, certainly, but he wasn't sure if Bosh could be trusted. Nels had to stay alert. Observing was all he could do. Ever since his death, Nels felt nothing, not even the air.

What about that smell?

The most curious thing about death was the constant aroma that followed him. No matter where he went, a stale, sugary smell accompanied him. He tried to ignore the scent by thinking of another — Tyra's hair came to mind. As they walked, he remembered his first impression of her at the festival and how his heart and mind battled over her status and beauty, but he hadn't accounted for her selfishness. His method of haunting her was cruel — he knew that — but maybe she deserved it; her parents took no initiative in putting her in her place. Then again, no one deserved the ruthlessness that he had put her through. Nels didn't like his actions and wondered if he had gone too far.

"I can't believe it's come to this," Tyra said. "This place is so dismal."

"I prefer this over that knight of yours." She didn't respond, but that didn't keep Nels from asking further. "Why do you like Arek so much? The guy can't even wrestle."

"He wrestles just fine."

Nels laughed. "Do you know this from experience?"

A touch of pink surfaced on her cheeks. Again, she would not answer him. Nels only meant to tease her, but the awkward silence made him question her all the more.

"You've had other meetings besides the woods?"

"What he and I do is of no concern to you."

"Is that why you wouldn't kiss me?"

"Stop bringing that up!"

Disappointed, Nels let it go. "If that's what you want."

"That *is* what I want," she said through gritted teeth. "Stop your babbling."

Another minute passed before they reached the bottom of the castle. Its damp walls spread deep into shadowed corridors. Their eyes focused on an oak door in front of them. They stepped up to it and Tyra knocked, long and hard. No one answered. She tugged at the handle.

The door was locked. "It wouldn't surprise me if he's hiding," she muttered.

"If you were coming after me, I know I would."

A loud clack echoed down the corridor, followed by the grating of an iron hinge. Tyra backed through Nels as the door opened. A figure stood in the frame, a soft light beside him.

Bosh held up a lantern. "Why hello, Princess Tyra. I have been expecting you."

"Have you? I mean, yes . . . I'm sure you have . . . after what you did."

Bosh puckered his aged lips. "*Did*, Your Highness?"

"Last night at the bridge. Do you remember that?"

"Oh, *that*! Yes, I do. Did you find your knight?"

"I didn't find my knight. I found something else."

"You found the boy who was killed by a tree?"

Nels and Tyra shared a glance. "How do you know —"

Bosh stepped aside from the doorframe and waved his hand between them. "Tension," he said slowly. "There is a great deal of tension between you two. That will complicate things."

"What do you mean?" Tyra asked. "You can see him, too?"

"No, I cannot," said Bosh, "but I can *sense* him."

"You can tell he's with us, then? How?"

"Come inside," Bosh said, ignoring her question. "Be mindful of what you touch."

Nels went first. Lanterns hung from brass hooks in the ceiling, filling the tailor's chamber with ample light. Tables filled the room, heaped with stacks of fabric. His mother had organized her materials like this, but Bosh's collection was far more extensive. Shelves lined the walls, stocked with countless rolls of fabric and spools of thread in every color imaginable.

In the center of the chamber was a loom, the largest Nels

had ever seen. On an adjacent table was a small cage with an old squirrel inside it.

"Please pardon my clutter. I was tending to my little friend here." Bosh motioned to the caged creature. "It's dying, you see. I happened upon it as I was coming back from the festival." The old tailor turned to Nels. "Turns out I was wrong, young man. They are not at all vicious. Immensely tame, if treated right." Bosh reached into a pocket and gave the small creature an acorn.

Tyra glanced at Nels with her most incredulous glare yet.

"Now," Bosh said. "There is a place to sit in the back —"

"Arek never waited for me," Tyra snapped. "You lied to me!"

"Finger pricks!" Bosh patted his robes, as if feeling for something. "I believe you misunderstood me, Princess. I said you would find your *knight*. I said nothing about Sir Arek."

"He can't be talking about me," Nels said. "How does he even know I'm here?"

"Are you suggesting that this *peasant* is the knight you are speaking of?"

The tailor chuckled. "Knights. Peasants. What does it matter, really?"

"It matters the world to me!" Tyra cried. "This peasant is ruining my life!"

"I highly doubt that," Bosh said. "Nels is a knight among his neighbors, eager to help in any way he can. He won the match, and you refused the kiss that you had agreed to give."

The very mention of her refusal caused Nels to question what a kiss had to do with anything. He meant only to taunt Tyra over the kiss they never shared — to convince her to help him — but maybe they were onto something. The old man asked Nels to go to the festival. He'd suggested the match —

and the kiss. Was this done by his design? "He wanted us to kiss!" Nels blurted out.

"You *wanted* us to kiss each other?" Tyra suddenly cried at the tailor. "Why?"

"I will tell you," Bosh said, "although I am not exactly sure where to begin."

"Begin as all stories do," Tyra said, "at the beginning."

"That would take too long. Perhaps it is best if I *show* you."

The tailor shuffled to a closet, opened it, and reached inside. He bumbled through a collection of metallic rods until he found a long wooden handle affixed to a sharp blade. He drew it out and held the handle in both hands. Nels's eyes widened. All at once, he understood. With some kind of magic, the tailor had created the illusion that his chores were finished, to trick Nels into escorting him to the festival. And then, when the match ended, Bosh vanished. In like manner, the merchant had emerged from out of nowhere with only the single ax in good condition.

If the tailor could create an illusion, could he change his own appearance?

"That's my ax!" Nels turned to Tyra. "Get out of here!"

She turned to the peasant with a bewildered stare.

"*He's* the one who killed me. Run, Tyra!"

Without wavering, Tyra backed away. Her hip rammed into the corner of the table where the squirrel's cage sat, making it topple over. The tailor stood still, surprised, the ax in hand as Tyra gasped and bolted for the door — but she never reached it. As if yanked by an unseen cord, something pulled her back, and she slammed against the back wall. Her impact opened a secret passage and she tumbled into a dark room.

Nels ran after her, light on his feet, but cursing that he could do nothing to help. The room was small and damp. The tailor stood in the doorframe with the ax in his hands, blocking Tyra's escape. The princess cowered in the farthest corner, looked at Nels, and pointed to the middle of the room — her arm trembling. On a makeshift bed of white sheets, a gauze-wrapped body had been laid to rest.

Beneath a thin layer of amber goop, Nels could see his own dead face.

8

UNWOVEN

Nels didn't move, nor could he speak.

He stared at himself as Tyra caught her breath.

What is my body doing here?

Increasing his surprise, Nels saw a hint of color within his amber-coated cheeks, as if blood still flowed beneath his skin. Many of his bruises and scratches appeared healed, and his body's brow glistened with fresh sweat. The sticky matter that smothered his pores puzzled him the most.

"Wait a second." Nels raised his hand to Tyra. "Maybe Bosh didn't kill me."

She held a hand over her chest, looking from Nels to his body and back. Her lips squirmed with unease. "Then why did you tell me to run?"

"Rusted rippers!" The old man lowered Nels's ax and leaned it against the wall. "That was rather unwise of me. Forgive me, Your Highness. I did not mean to startle you."

"Explain yourself, tailor," she said. "Why did you come after me with that?"

"I only meant to show you this tool, which has been traced with Fabrication by the same man who tried to murder Nels." Bosh stepped away from the ax and interlocked his fingers.

"He placed a stitch on this ax so that he could use it to follow Nels home and lie in wait for him."

"What is he talking about?" Nels asked. "What's a stitch?" He had an idea of what the old man meant, and he'd obviously known something was *unnatural* about his death. The voice he heard, the way his murderer had made him freeze, and the tree's trunk exploding: Magic was the only explanation. Everything Bosh said related to weaving and sewing in one form or another, but not always in a normal weaving and sewing way. "Is Fabrication some kind of magic?"

"I haven't the slightest idea," Tyra said, her eyes still wide with fear. Her body shook. "Is that how you pulled me into this room?" she asked Bosh. "With some kind of magic?"

"Such an observant girl you are," he answered. "I wanted to keep you from leaving, so I do apologize. The hook I applied to your thread was stronger than I intended."

"My *what*?" Tyra turned to Nels. "My *thread*? What does he mean by that?" She twisted her torso around, searching her dress for loose fibers.

Nels looked at Tyra's slender back and shrugged. He saw the laces of her bodice, but no sign of a hook or a tethered cord. "I don't know," he said, "but I want to know how my body got here. The villagers buried me."

"Did you steal his body?" Tyra asked Bosh. "Why would you do such a thing?"

The tailor folded his arms and stood firm in the doorway. "I never really stole his body, Princess. I replaced it. Not with another human body, of course, but with something I *altered* so it would look like his body. If I had not, Nels would be under the earth now, buried alive."

"Alive?" Tyra stared at Nels again. "You mean he's —"

"Slightly," Bosh added. "I implemented some alterations that will delay his decay. This beeswax, for example, is preserving his body."

"Beeswax?" Nels thought of the strange odor. "Is *that* what I smell?"

Tyra shuddered as she rubbed her arms. It was hard to imagine what she was thinking, but Nels was not about to interrupt. She had more to say. "Are you saying he's *not* dead?"

"Touch his face," Bosh invited. "Feel the truth."

"Touch his face?" Tyra recoiled at first, but then she stepped toward the body, reached out a finger, and hesitantly poked his cheek. She pulled away with a start. "Your skin is warm!"

Nels wished he could feel it to believe it. "How come I'm not in my body, then?"

The body's chest rose suddenly, causing them both to jump back. Nels heard an unearthly groan, an undead sigh exhaling from his nose. The body relaxed and lay motionless again.

"Speak plainly, tailor," Tyra demanded. "If he's *not* dead, why is his ghost roaming about?"

A smile creased Bosh's cheeks. "Because Nels is *unwoven*, Your Highness."

"Unwoven?" Nels didn't know what to make of this. Tyra seemed just as confused.

"Everyone is a thread," Bosh said, "woven into the Great Tapestry."

"Woven?" Nels asked. "What's a Great Tapestry?"

Tyra shushed him. "Go on, tailor."

"The Great Tapestry is the record of our world, the actions of our reality pressed by the very reeds of time." Bosh paused for a second. "Do you know my trade, Your Highness?"

She knitted her brow. "You make my dresses."

"Yes, like the one you wear now. But is that all I do?"

"Don't answer me with questions, tailor."

Bosh breathed deeply. "Making dresses and lining the halls with tapestries is my *second* trade. My first is a rare form of magic called Fabrication. I am a tailor. I maintain the Great Tapestry."

Nels and Tyra stared at each other, equally confounded. Magic based on the fundamentals of sewing and weaving? Nels never would have imagined such a thing.

At the same time, it made a great deal of sense.

"Would you understand if I called myself a sorcerer?"

Tyra scoffed as she folded her arms. "And everyone's calling *me* mad." She looked at each of them in turn. "First a ghost, and now a sorcerer. How do I find you people?"

"We often find what we seek when we do not search for it," Bosh said.

With a short laugh, Tyra walked to the body and knelt beside it. She laid her hand on its arm and tenderly clenched its bicep. To Nels's surprise, he could almost feel her touch. "Suppose I believe in your magic," she said seriously. "How is it keeping him alive?"

"Patience," Bosh said. "Fabrication is a tenacious art that requires meticulous attention." The man lowered his hands into his inner pockets and removed a tiny spool of thread from one and then a pair of scissors from the other. "As I have said, *everyone* is a thread, invaluable to the Great Tapestry's design, regardless of how insignificant they may seem. Their choices weave it, and time presses it." Bosh pulled thread from the spool and cut it with his scissors. "When a life ends, that individual's thread is severed, and they have left behind a pattern that has been permanently *woven* into the Great Tapestry throughout their life." His gray eyes rose, staring at Tyra. "Although his thread is unwoven, something keeps Nels bound to us."

"Then" — Tyra glanced at Nels — "you say he is not severed completely?"

"Without me, he would be. For now, he is like a loose thread dangling from the tapestry."

The princess nodded. "And what if he remains loose?"

"An astute question, Your Highness." As Bosh spoke, Nels couldn't help but wonder why Tyra had touched his arm. Did she actually care? "If a thread remains loose, it will cause a snag in the Great Tapestry, which can warp the very fabric of reality itself." A weighty silence followed his words. Aside from the breathing body, the room was quiet. "If Nels's thread is not woven back into our reality, his thread must be severed, and his pattern in the Tapestry will end."

Nels stood speechless. The inevitable had only been delayed; but why would Bosh go to all this trouble to keep him alive?

"Are you saying he can come back?" Tyra asked, gesturing at Nels.

Bosh rubbed his beard, a look of concentration etched on his face. "There are two options that may work," Bosh said. "One way is simple, and the other is not . . . and it's possibly even deadly. Either of these choices will require your involvement, Your Highness."

Tyra rose to her feet and left Nels's body. "What is the simple way?"

Impressed by her willingness, Nels smiled at the princess, his dampened spirit relieved by her sudden change of heart.

The tailor pointed at the body on the bed. "You must kiss him, Your Highness."

"*What?*" Tyra's cry rebounded off the walls. "He's practically a corpse!"

"I know you think little of him," Bosh said, "but a kiss has a strong way of drawing forth another's thread. Your living lips should tug his soul together enough that I can weave him.

I would have brought you together sooner, if I had known my other methods would not work."

Nels pondered this. *That's why he sent Tyra into the woods . . .*

She peeked at his body. "Can I have someone else do it?"

"No," Bosh answered.

"Why not?"

"Only you can see him. Only *your* thread can mend his."

The princess said nothing, her face skewed with concentration. This was a lot to ask. However impossible the idea seemed, she looked to be deep in thought, as if she were actually giving serious consideration to Bosh's theory. Nels hoped so.

A quick kiss was certainly worth a try.

Finally, she looked up, her face serious. "And what is the difficult option?"

Nels held his tongue. *So much for that . . .*

"The difficult option is an item, long lost from history," Bosh said. "A tool that can restore him. If it still exists."

Tyra's eyes brightened with hope. "What tool is this?"

"The Needle of Gailner," Bosh said in a whisper.

Nels's thoughts brightened. "A needle?"

"All we need is a *needle*?" Tyra echoed.

"Not an ordinary needle. This particular needle was personally fashioned by Gailner, the first tailor who wove Fabrication. The Needle provides anyone who uses it with the power to alter the fabric of reality. No living soul has seen the Needle, and few know of it — it has been lost for centuries. But someone west of us may know its location. Visiting her is risky, however, and you may not come back as a human."

Tyra scoffed. "Are you referring to the Mountain Witch?"

"Mountain Witch?" It had been ages since Nels had heard that story.

"It's a foolish myth," Tyra explained. "A scarecrow story. She is said to reside in a mansion on top of the Westerly Pass before you descend into the Valley of Westmine."

"Astute again, Your Highness," Bosh said. "Very astute. But I must warn you: The Mountain Witch is very real. She's not a scarecrow. She is known to turn humans into animals."

The tailor seemed gloomy as he spoke of this. Nels wondered why.

Tyra sighed. "I'd rather take my chances with a ghost."

"Which means . . . you're going to kiss me?" Nels asked.

Tyra opened her mouth, said nothing, and closed it again.

"If we are to save him," Bosh said, "you *must* kiss him."

"Neither of you understand," she said, squirming. "It's not that I *don't* want to — I mean, I don't — I just —" She stared desperately into Nels's eyes, as if her own life were at stake. Tyra sighed again as she closed her eyes. "If this works, you will leave and never come back."

"Good." Bosh motioned them to the bed. "Lie within your body, Nels."

Without further encouragement, Nels sat on the bed, leaned back, and allowed his spirit to seep into his body. A stiff coldness stirred within his chest as Tyra's face hovered over his. This was the closest they had ever been.

What if she can't bring herself to do this?

"Your Highness?" Bosh encouraged her to proceed.

Tyra closed her eyes again and lunged for Nels's lips. As their lips began to touch, the smell of her hair — pear blossoms — overcame the stench of stale beeswax — and then he felt it. A twinge crept through Nels, followed by nothingness as Tyra flung herself back. She wiped her mouth, having grazed his lips for merely a second.

Nels sat up and glimpsed down over his shoulder.

His body remained on the bed.

"It didn't work?" Tyra cried. "Why didn't it work?"

"You cannot mend an unwoven thread with just a needle stick," Bosh said. "You must *weave* it. Let your lips linger, firm like a reed. Focus on bringing him back to us. Try once more."

"How can I focus? I'm being forced to kiss . . . him!"

"No one is forcing you." Bosh assured her. "This choice is entirely yours to make."

A sob sprung from Tyra's throat. "Lie down, peasant!"

Nels did. When she pressed her lips on his again, longer this time, warmth replaced the cold. A new rush shot through his body, head to toe. Tyra's hair intoxicated him. He wanted so much to raise his hand and hold the back of her head. The more her lips caressed, the more Nels could feel his arms and legs. It was working. If they kept this up, he would live again.

A tear lined Tyra's cheek as they parted. "I was saving that kiss."

His warmth dissipated. She'd never kissed Arek before?

On second thought, had she ever kissed anyone? Nels swallowed the rising pang of guilt.

Am I her first?

"Much better," Bosh said. "Now, try to sit up, Nels."

He swung his legs over the side and sat up, but the more Nels moved, the less he could feel. It was no use. He turned to look, disappointed that his body was still on the makeshift bed.

"Why isn't this working?" Tyra asked, her frustration obvious.

"I was afraid of this," Bosh said. "There was no love behind your kiss."

"Love?" Tyra jumped away. "You said nothing about *love*!"

"I do not mean intimacy," Bosh clarified. "I mean the love one feels for their fellow man — or the love you feel for your

105

people. *That* would be enough. Do you not have even that, Your Highness?"

"I did what you asked of me!" Tyra's jaw quivered. "What else am I to do?"

"Unless you kiss him as an equal, you will share the weight of his death."

"*You* kiss him!"

Darting for the doorframe, Tyra sobbed into her hands as she fled the room. Nels was about to run after her when he heard a small, metallic chime at his feet. His body convulsed. Its arm flailed. Its hand opened. Bosh lunged for the floor. What had happened? For a moment, his body was alive. Tyra had to come back — she had to try again.

"Do not follow her!"

Nels stopped at the door and turned around. "How do you know I'm still here?"

Bosh didn't respond. He was crawling on his hands and knees, searching the stone floor beneath the makeshift bed. Nels wondered what Bosh was doing until he noticed that he could see the floor *through* the flesh of his spectral hands. And not just his hands, but his feet and lower legs, too. His arms and his waist were the next to become translucent. He was no longer an opaque ghost — suddenly, the whole room began to change, the contrast between light and dark becoming more extreme.

Like a vapor, he was disappearing. "What's happening to me?!"

The tailor stretched his hand under the bed, sat up with a groan, and shoved something into the body's open palm. Nels gulped, and his ghost body turned back to normal — opaque again. The tailor had placed a small, metallic object into his body's nearly lifeless hand.

The thimble.

"That was close," Bosh said. "A few seconds more and you would have left us." The old man wrapped the hand with a cloth and tied it over the body's chest to secure the thimble in place. "We are fortunate that your mother knew what to do with the thimble when she found you under the tree. Ordinary thimbles are made to protect fingers, but a Fabrication *thimble*, laced with magic, protects much more than that." Bosh made quick work of adjusting the body's position and then knelt beside it. "I have done all I can to stay death's hand. The beeswax will keep your body from decay." Tousling the body's hair, the tailor stood and moved to the door. "I thought her kiss would be sufficient," he said.

It would have been, Nels was sure, if Tyra had placed more effort into it.

"I must bring her back," Nels said. "She has to try again."

He began to move toward the door.

"Stay with me," Bosh said, as if he could sense that Nels was leaving. "She will only refuse you."

Nels headed for the door anyway.

"The time has come for you to know the truth, Nels."

Nels stopped at the exit and turned around. "What truth?"

The tailor righted the squirrel's cage and muttered to himself as he shoved another acorn through the bars. Bosh gathered an armful of thread spools. Nels couldn't tell what the tailor was doing as he placed the spools on a table by the loom. Even if he couldn't hear Nels, Bosh had certainly felt his presence.

"*What* truth?" Nels asked again, though he knew the old man could not hear him.

Surprisingly, Bosh looked right where Nels stood. "It is time you learned the truth about your father."

9

THE LOOM

The tailor's words lured Nels away from the door. "The truth . . . about my father?"

"Stand by me," Bosh invited. "Once my thread is exhausted, I will explain further."

Nels approached, and they faced the loom's shed — the space where threads pass back and forth between the pressing of a reed. This loom had no such reed. No heddles or hooks lined the tops or bottoms of it, either. The components necessary for weaving were missing. The loom was worthless, nothing more than a frame with a hundred dowels around it, each dowel holding a spool of thread. There was a sparkle in the dowels that glistened like gemstones. Nels looked closer. They *were* gemstones.

Bosh rummaged through a drawer and retrieved a shuttle, the tool for weaving threads so they could pass through the shed without getting entangled with the others. There was no thread on this shuttle, but Bosh fiddled with it anyway. He pinched and pulled at the groove.

"Ready yourself," he warned Nels. "You have seen nothing like this."

The old man threw the shuttle into the center of the loom. The shuttle stopped in the middle of the shed and hovered like a feather. Nels stared at the tool, amazed that it didn't fall. Even more amazing was the unraveling of every spool of thread on the dowels. Each thread reached inside the loom. They wove in, through and around one another until the shuttle was hidden from view. A colorful pattern emerged — in blues, reds, greens, and several other colors.

Observing the threads move on their own mesmerized Nels. They created a fabric that slowly revealed an image of a place that Nels had seen before: the terrace where he and Tyra had spoken — and from where he had fallen that morning. The pattern was quite different now. It was dark. Several guards surrounded a single man in the middle of the terrace. Like watching a scene unfold through a knitted window, Nels waited to see what would happen in this animated tapestry.

A young Lennart appeared on the landing; the surrounded man held a bloodstained knife in his hand. It was raining on the terrace. Heavy drops fell in shimmering lines across the loom. Voices sprang from the fabric, surprising Nels even more.

"What have you done, Rasmus?" Lennart asked.

This man — Rasmus, apparently — shifted his weight to one side as he shivered with a smile. Like a pulled skein of yarn, his appearance unraveled . . . and then wove back into a *different* man, his hair and eyes dark. Rasmus wore a violet vest with a matching lined cape and black gloves, all soaked in the pouring rain.

Right away, Nels recognized Rasmus as the man who had killed him.

A couple of guards looked over the trellis. In the courtyard below lay a man with a broken crown by his body. "He's dead," one of the guards cried. "King Yalva is dead!"

The other guards closed in on Rasmus, their spears pointed at his heart.

"R-Rasmus!" Lennart stammered. "What have you done?"

"I did it for you," he answered. "You deserve to be king."

"He was my father!" Lennart cried. "How could you?!"

"Fathers get in the way. He's dead and now you're free!"

"Enough!" A new voice sounded from the loom. The threads rustled as a new figure appeared — a tall, handsome knight with sandy-brown hair and deep-green eyes. Nels had never seen his father before, but he knew this was him. "Stand down, Rasmus," Nels's father ordered, bold and strong. "It's over. Your treason ends here!"

"Me?" Rasmus glared at him with a smirk, followed by a spiteful laugh. "*I'm* guilty of treason when *you* are the one purveying deception among us? Your existence has already destroyed us!"

Nels furrowed his brow. "Destroyed us?"

The violet-clad villain twitched; his fingers curled as they pinched the air.

"I know what you think of me, Rasmus," said Nels's father. "If I am what you believe me to be, why not come for *me*? Why not kill me instead?"

"I will kill you, Ulrich!" Rasmus said. "Our late king was blinded by his love for you — just as you have blinded everyone!" His fists tightened. "Because of you, Yalva banished me and I lost everything."

"Seize the traitor!" Lennart ordered.

As the guards moved in, Rasmus closed his eyes, raised his fists, and then thrust them down toward the floor. Every guard stopped. Their feet were stuck fast to the terrace floor, just as Nels had been frozen beneath the falling tree.

Rasmus withdrew a knife. "You should have accepted my gift of freedom, Lennart."

The weapon flew through the air, heading directly toward Ulrich's chest. Lennart dashed in front of Nels's father, attempting to use his body as a shield. Suddenly, Ulrich grabbed Lennart and they spun around together on the rain-slicked terrace. The knife found its mark in Ulrich's back, and the knight fell at Lennart's feet. Blood spread from the wound.

"Wait your turn, Lennart!" Rasmus shouted as he threw a second knife.

The blade hurtled for the prince's throat, but suddenly the knife flipped, darted back, and sheared through Rasmus's cape. A new figure emerged on the landing, his fingers also pinched.

"What have you done?" a younger Bosh cried. "Your severing will tear the Great Tapestry!"

Rasmus held out his hands. His fingers skittered. "You taught me to uphold the tapestry, but then you brought Ulrich to our land — you have done far more damage than I ever could!"

"Surrender, Rasmus," Bosh said. "You cannot mend anything this way."

"It is too late, Ickabosh. The rendt has already begun!"

Both men raised their arms, but the young Bosh dodged to the right and Rasmus's sopping cape flew up from behind and wrapped itself around him. Bosh motioned with his fists, and the actions sent the newly bound Rasmus into the air like a jostled cocoon. When Bosh opened his hand again, Rasmus crashed to the floor. Rasmus snarled as he tore off his cape and threw it over the trellis. "The worst is over, tailor, but I will return to sever what is left of Ulrich's thread!"

Rasmus raised one arm across his chest, turned, and vanished into the night. Nels found it difficult to keep track of what he had just witnessed.

Why would anyone do such a terrible deed?

What is the rendt?

"Why?" Ulrich reached out for Lennart. "Why did you step in front of me?"

The prince sobbed. "You are my friend, Ulrich. I would do anything for you . . ."

"You are the king now. Give your life *to* your subjects, not *for* them . . ."

Nels's father drew his last breath. His blood mixed with the rain. Lennart fell to his knees, his eyes racked with horror. A woman ran to them: Nels's mother, younger as well. She knelt by the knight and raised Ulrich's head to her chest while she wept.

"Ulrich, please," she cried. "Please stay with me!"

As quickly as it had started, every thread in the loom wound back onto their respective spools, leaving the shed empty. Heaving, Bosh retrieved the floating shuttle from the loom. "What you saw was the past, a moment in time . . . A segment of the Great Tapestry."

Bosh was right; nothing could have prepared Nels for this. He wanted to cry, but no tears came. Learning the truth was worth witnessing his own father's murder. Finally, Nels understood.

"Rasmus was my apprentice," Bosh said. "Instead of upholding the Great Tapestry, he fell into jealousy and madness, even more so when he learned of your betrothal."

"Betrothal?" Nels repeated the word before it had a chance to sink in.

"Perhaps it is best that Tyra has left us; she may not be ready to hear this."

"Betrothed? To Tyra?" For the first time in his afterlife, Nels felt as if he was going to be sick. Having witnessed his father's death was gut-wrenching enough. "I was betrothed to *her*?"

The tailor remained at the table. His eyes moved to the far corner of the cloth-ridden chamber. "You must feel all tangled up inside. So would I, if I had learned such a truth."

"How can this be?" Nels asked. "I *can't* — not to *her*!"

"I have a story for you, Nels." Bosh pointed at the loom. "I wish I could show you, but age has caught up with me." The tailor reached for a patch of cloth on the table and dabbed his forehead. "Before you were born, there were three friends. The first was Lennart, a shy prince who thought himself cursed because his mother had died during his birth. The second man was Rasmus, a boy among the wealthiest of our nobility. Rasmus was a charismatic young man, and it did not take long for him to win Lennart's friendship. Then, one day, I felt something more in Rasmus. Those who can influence the fabric of reality are rare, so I took him as my apprentice." The tailor released a sad sigh. "If I had known his twisted mind . . . I would have reconsidered."

A draft stirred the stagnant air around them, causing the lanterns to flicker. Nels waited for the lights to burn steadily again. "And the third friend was my father?"

Bosh continued. "I found the third friend — Ulrich — and cared for him from a young age. He had no home or memory to his name." Bosh rubbed his temples with his fingers. "King Yalva allowed the child to reside in the castle. Even as a boy, Ulrich insisted on earning his keep — and he did, from stable hand to becoming the favored knight of Avërand."

Nels sat up, both astonished and affirmed. "He *was* a knight? The *favored* knight!"

"Your father fell into the good graces of everyone he met. Rasmus was drawn to him, as well, hoping to use Ulrich to increase his own standing in the Court — and it worked for a while. For years, Lennart, Rasmus, and Ulrich were rarely apart, but time has a way of changing people."

Nels remembered how his mother had said the same thing, but about Jilia.

"They each grew into men with a broadened interest in women. Two such maidens caught their affections: Lady Carin, a bright, lively girl whose family owned the most successful shipping enterprise in Harvestport; and Katharina, your mother."

That name — Bosh had said it on their way to the festival.

"Carin's family cared for your mother after an illness took your grandparents."

Nels lowered his head. Mother had never spoken of her parents.

"Rasmus once fancied your mother, but so did your father. She chose the latter. Not only did Ulrich win your mother's heart, but he won the confidence of Prince Lennart, as well." Ickabosh sighed. "Rasmus was troubled on the day your parents married. By then, he had fully mastered the fundamentals of Fabrication — he had picked up *threading* particularly easily"

The tailor straightened his posture and explained: "Threading is like an illusion: You weave the fabric of reality around you to temporarily change your surroundings. It is the same trick I used to make you think you had finished your chores so you would escort me to the festival."

Bosh paused and looked contemplative, then continued his story. "As Rasmus's obsession grew, he was no longer content with his status among the nobility. He wanted more. He wanted to *rule* the kingdom through Lennart — who was not eager, anyway, to take on the responsibility that would be required once his father left him the crown."

114

"When the day came that Yalva died, Rasmus planned to become his friend's mouthpiece and rule the kingdom for him. But your father stepped in and encouraged Lennart to enthusiastically accept his birthright as Averand's future king. Lennart married, as did your father, and when Rasmus learned of Ulrich and Lennart's intent to betroth their children, it sent him over the hem. Hoping to thwart this alliance, he set out to find the Needle of Gailner."

"The needle that can save me?" Nels asked. "Why would Rasmus want that?"

"I never should have told him of it. Rasmus wanted to use it to alter his fate and regain Lennart's loyalty, which he thought your father had taken from him. Fortunately, he never found the Needle, but it was clear that something in him had changed in the search. When he returned, he was convinced that your father would cause the end of our world — the rendt, as we fabricators call it. Rasmus vowed that he would not be satisfied until Ulrich — and his newborn son — were dead. Yalva heeded Ulrich's counsel and had Rasmus banished, which forfeited Rasmus's title and fortunes. I expected Rasmus to seek vengeance — and obviously, he did."

Nels stared at the limestone floor. "He murdered my father for revenge?"

"Fearing Rasmus's continued threat to you, your mother renounced her title, altered your names, and fled with you into the woods."

Nels swallowed. "That's why you called me Lief," he whispered.

Bosh crossed his arms and pressed his elbows on the table. "I sometimes visited your mother in secret to supply her with a special thread that would allow her to sew a *slip stitch* into your clothing. But with that *traced* ax, Rasmus was able to follow you and wait for an opportune moment to kill." The weary tailor cleared his throat and prepared to stand. "The merchant at the festival was Rasmus, threaded in a clever disguise. I felt something amiss in the crowd, but I could not trace him." Bosh stifled a cough. "There is only one reason for his return: He believes he has finally grown more powerful than I am . . . and I fear he may be right."

"I don't even know this man. Why would Rasmus want to kill me?"

Bosh stopped speaking. Waiting in the silence, Nels's thoughts returned to the weapon's merchant. Rasmus had killed him; that explained Averand's other recent murder.

Standing up, Bosh moved to a stack of fabric. "Forgive me if I am confusing you with strange words; Fabrication is full of them. Every aspect of sewing and weaving has a part in the magic. A *stitch*, you see, is another way of saying *spell*." Bosh grunted as he hauled a roll of green satin onto the table. He reached for a drawer, grabbed a pair of sheers, and began to cut. "What you and I call *reality* is nothing more than the never-ending fibers that make up the fabric of our world. Fabrication allows us to mend the fabric so it can weave on without obstruction."

Nels watched the tailor work. In no time at all, Bosh had cut a few pieces of fabric: a front, a back, interfacing, and some sleeves and extensions. By the cuts, it seemed that he was making a dress. Bosh laid the pieces on the table and began to embroider them with a golden thread.

"I never meant to put you in harm's way. I am truly sorry for what happened to you. You are free to blame me, if you like. It was my intention to lure you to the festival so you could hasten your reunion with Tyra."

Nels scrunched his lips; he still had mixed feelings about that.

"Broken bobbins!" Bosh cursed. "What if that was Rasmus's intention and I led you to him? Clever rogue. I can only hope that Rasmus is still ignorant of your *basted thread*."

The tailor's way of saying things puzzled Nels. He knew what a basted seam was, of course: a loose stitch for connecting two pieces of fabric prior to sewing them. But what was a basted thread according to Fabrication? Nels figured it out quickly: "If we were betrothed, then Tyra and I are *stitched together*?!"

"Pardon the phrase," Bosh said. "It is a complicated piece of magic. I was not the only one to question Rasmus. Your parents wanted protection for you both — more than a thimble could offer. On the night of your betrothal, before King Yalva was murdered, I took you and Tyra in my arms and I basted your threads together. This would allow you both to find each other — even in death." Bosh rearranged the pieces he cut. "That is why Tyra can see you, but no one else can."

That was the most logical explanation Nels had heard yet — strange as it still was.

Finishing the collar and sleeves with a hem, Bosh reached for a white thread, much like the thread that he had given Nels for his mother. He picked up another needle and began to assemble the dress. "Your pattern is not mine to design. There is friction between you and the princess, so the Needle of Gailner is your best hope. But in your unwoven state, you cannot retrieve the Needle on your own. You will need mortal help; Tyra is the key to reuniting you with your body. How much longer will the thimble sustain you? By the strength of my thread, I judge you have a week — before the next half-moon wanes, at best. And if Rasmus learns that you are not dead, he will trace you and seek to finish you for good." With his first seam sewn onto the bodice, Bosh moved to sew another. "Your body will be safe with me, as long as your thread is slip-stitched."

It was making more sense; if fabricators had the ability to sense people from far away, wearing clothes sewn with the white thread Bosh was using would keep that person hidden. Now the old tailor was making a dress with a similar white thread.

Did Bosh suspect Tyra was in danger, too?

"You may be a ghost, but the world is more tangible than you realize," Bosh said. "That is the advantage of being unwoven. You can do what no one else can — pass through walls, or spy on others. But I suspect you can do even more than that. So long as your thread is in our world — and you believe that you are still a part of it — you may be unlike any ghost we have ever known."

Though he wasn't exactly sure what the tailor meant by that, Nels nodded anyway.

"Before you go, give heed to what I have to say," Bosh said. "The Mountain Witch is the only one who might be able to lead you to the Needle. You and Tyra must find the witch's shadowed book and learn everything you can. But be cautious — I do not know if she is alive or dead — or sane."

"That sounds . . . splendid," Nels said, fully aware that the tailor couldn't hear him.

"I have told King Lennart of Rasmus's return, so you can expect Tyra to have escorts at all times. It will be necessary for you both to leave them out of this; otherwise, you will draw Rasmus's attention."

"What if I can't convince Tyra to go?"

"I have said enough," Bosh finished. "And I have work to do. Tell Her Highness what you have learned and convince her to go on this journey. She must, if you are to live."

Nels couldn't help but sigh. His fate depended on a fabled needle and a selfish princess.

"Many have failed to find the Needle," Bosh said, "but then, none of them had a ghost."

The tailor walked to a spinning wheel and sat before it. He pressed his foot to the pedal and the wheel spun. Bosh moved his hands as if to spin thread, but Nels didn't see any — there were no fibers to work from. Was the tailor producing an invisible thread? Quietly, the tailor hummed a soft melody, reminding Nels of his mother.

The wheel spun. The pedal creaked.

The tailor had nothing more to say.

10

REFLECTION

Nels left through the closed door and climbed up the spiral stairwell.

He was still absorbing everything that the tailor had said and showed him. He knew why his mother hid them in a cottage in a clearing in the woods, and why she never spoke of his father: She was trying to save him from Rasmus. And that's why she'd kept him from becoming a knight — so no one would recognize him as the son of Ulrich.

He knew the truth, even if a few pieces of the riddle were still missing.

Why does Rasmus want me dead? I've done nothing to him.

Nels had no idea how Fabrication worked, how it could mask his chores, fell a tree, or paralyze his body — there had to be more to this magic than Bosh had told him. But it didn't matter. Understanding Fabrication wouldn't help him regain his life. Finding the Needle would.

His mind was filled with questions, more than anyone could answer, except maybe the Mountain Witch. But getting her shadowed book was only half the problem; the other half was Tyra. He couldn't visit the witch alone, nor could he pick up the Needle — if he were to find it.

"Surely you can convince Their Majesties that *I* will keep her safe!"

The moment Nels reached the top of the stairs, Arek's voice sounded from the antechamber across the hall. He had seen the room earlier, a gallery filled with prominent statues.

"Your request will be made in the morning, Sir Arek," said the royal scribe.

What are they up to?

Nels watched the knight meander behind the scribe. They both had wide cups in their hands. His curiosity piqued, Nels followed them. They stopped at the base of a grand staircase lined with carpet. At the end of each stone banister was a carved bust. One depicted a king, the other a queen. A large portrait of Lennart, Carin, and Tyra hung high above the landing.

"I consulted the royal physician," Arek said. "He thought it would be good for her to be distracted from her current stresses. An afternoon picnic should do it." The knight placed a few silver coins into the scribe's waiting palm. "I am in no way opposed to the company of an escort."

"That is for His Highness to decide" — the scribe pocketed the money — "but I will state your proposal — your *request* — and send word if he agrees to your little excursion. Good evening."

Excursion? Nels furrowed his brow.

The scribe turned and headed up the stairs. Nels was almost at Arek's side when the knight hiccupped, leaned on the banister, and stared at the queen's bust.

"Worry not, my queen. I will wed your daughter's hand, even if she is madder than a rabid dog." Arek belched into the statue's face. "I will manage your kingdom while she seeks sanity — I just have to convince that worthless husband of yours. Stealing and returning his crown should have worked."

He peered into his cup and frowned. "Where did that cask wench go?"

The knight exited the hall, leaving Nels alone with clenched fists.

Arek was more than a cheater; he was a pompous clod of dirt! He only cared about Tyra so he could have the throne. He had even stolen King Lennart's crown and framed the Vagas for the crime. Nels couldn't understand how Arek became the favored knight of Avërand — let alone why Tyra liked him. There was nothing noble about Arek, but if she fancied him, she was more than welcome to him. Nels took a deep breath. Her relationships were none of his concern.

I need to persuade her to help me . . . but how?

Nels ran up the grand stair and stopped at the landing. The painted blue eyes of Tyra's childhood stared at him, solemn, beseeching, like the loneliest girl in the world.

He had an idea, though there was no guarantee it would work.

A cat meowed on the balcony outside as Nels sat in a beam of moonlight. Still wearing the clothes she wore for archery, Tyra lay asleep on top of her quilts, her head nestled on a tear-stained pillow.

Nels wanted to wake her, but he didn't have the heart. He even felt sorry for causing her distress that day — although it was terribly fun. If he was going to convince her to help him, he would have to try something more sincere. Pestering her hadn't worked; perhaps being nice to her would.

Letting her sleep for a few hours was a good way to start.

As she lay in her bed, questions raced through Nels's head. The segment of the Great Tapestry that he saw in the loom had upset everything he thought he knew about himself; but at the same time, he had gained an even greater understanding of who he was. His father was a knight. His parents used to be nobles. Nels smirked. Would he have enjoyed a life of nobility? He couldn't see himself raised around Tyra or others like her. He never would have known the good people of Cobblestown as he did if he had lived as a noble.

His betrothal to the princess, however, was more than he could shake off.

I'd better not tell her about that; she wouldn't understand.

Tyra rubbed her chin into her pillow, her soft breath like music. Nels faced her decorated vanity, a tall mirror mounted in the center of an iron frame. He couldn't see his reflection, but he could see Tyra's. She looked so peaceful in her sleep, like a rosebud waiting for the sun. She breathed quietly — beautifully.

Tyra may have been a pain, but she was much too good for Arek.

I should tell her — will she listen to me?

For now, being frustrated over Arek wasn't worth the effort. When Bosh had reached for the ax, Nels realized something: He was a ghost — he could do nothing to stop Bosh. If Tyra were in real danger, he was useless to help her. And if Tyra refused to help him, he could do nothing to save himself. He was totally helpless. His frustration mounting, Nels thrust his fist on the vanity, and a hollowed bang thundered through the chamber. Tyra stirred. A high note rose in her throat before she turned to her side.

Nels stared at the vanity. *Did I just hit that?*

He reached for its surface and watched his hand pass through the polished top.

He *had* touched it . . . but how?

No longer worried about disturbing Tyra, Nels tightened his fist and tried to think of everything that made him angry:

his mother keeping the past from him, Tyra's refusal to help him, and the fact that he was a ghost that only Tyra could see. Winding together his mustered frustration, Nels threw his fist at the vanity. He fell through the furniture and landed on the floor. Nope — not that. Nels pondered. How else could he have touched the vanity?

He then remembered something that Bosh had said to him earlier.

The world is more tangible than I realize. What did he mean?

On the edge of the vanity sat a silver candlestick with a layer of hard wax on its shaft. Nels reached for it, wrapped his fingers around the coated handle, and raised his arm.

The candlestick remained on the vanity.

Nels walked to a nearby chair, sat down, and pressed his shoulders into its padding. Just then, as he was leaning his elbows on the armrests, he realized what he was doing.

I'm sitting in this chair!

He fell through the chair immediately. As he stood again, the answer dawned on him. He could walk on this floor. What kept him from sinking through it? All this time, he sat in chairs and stood on tables. He could interact with objects!

He *was* a part of this world. He was alive.

He just had to believe it.

Nels reached for the candlestick, focused, and grabbed it. "I am alive," he whispered, his grip tightening. "I *am* alive!" When Nels raised his arm, the candlestick hovered in the mirror.

"You will never leave me alone, will you?"

Startled, Nels saw Tyra staring at him in the mirror, where his reflection should have been. The candlestick fell through his hand and crashed to the floor.

Tyra jumped to the sound. "What was that?"

"Uh . . . candlestick." Nels pointed. "It fell."

She flopped back onto her bed. "What is it now? Are you some kind of draug?"

Nels looked at her with a vacant stare. "I . . . I don't even know what that is."

"Of course you wouldn't. Draugs are tormentors. They like to move things and haunt treasures, and they are said to cast a most terrible smell — you have spared me that, at least."

"If a draug can move things, can they pick things up too?"

"If it's not too heavy, like a quill or parchment. But what would I know? Wussen likes that kind of supernatural rubbish. I would rather study history than hear more of his nonsense."

"Right." Nels smiled at the candlestick. "Nonsense."

"You let me sleep," Tyra said, slightly surprised. "Was it not your plan to make me miserable?"

Nels turned from the princess and leaned his elbow on the vanity. It didn't seep through until his concentration waned. "What good is haunting you if you won't help me?"

Tyra tilted her head to the side. "Are you giving up?" She clapped her hands and cheered, and then paused. "If you're not going to haunt me anymore, why are you still here?"

"You're the only one who can see me." Nels expected cold and derisive words from her lips, but there was only silence. Tyra had cast her eyes toward the hem of her matted dress, deep in thought, like she'd been before they kissed. "The magic Bosh is using to keep me alive won't last much longer," Nels added. "When the next half-moon wanes, I will go. You will be free of me."

"Will I?"

Nels turned to her. She was already staring at him, her eyes somber.

"I think not," she said. "The tailor was right about everything. How can I be free of you, knowing I could have done something to —" She paused. "You win, ghost. I will help you."

125

Nels jumped to his feet. He could not believe his ears. "You will?"

"If I must," Tyra answered quickly. "I cannot promise that I will find this *needle* or whatever it is that will bring you back, but I will search for it — instead of leaving you to die."

"You'd feel guilty if I died, you mean?"

"Responsible — and nothing more." Tyra slid out of bed, put on a pair of slippers, and walked to him. "If you want my help, you must do as I say. I expect no less from my *living* subjects."

"Can do!" Nels beamed as he nearly hugged her. "Thank you, Princess!"

Tyra arched her neck back. "You're rather close."

"Oh." Nels stepped away. "Is that better?"

"Much." In the moonlight, Nels saw something new in her blue eyes — her change of heart. Tyra slowly walked to a divided screen in the far corner of the room, stopping to pick up a silk evening gown draped over the foot of her bed. "Please turn around? I want to change."

"Into a nightgown?" Nels asked. "Why?"

"It's the middle of the night. I'm going back to bed."

"Or you'll sneak off on me again. I'm not falling for it."

"Are you giving me a reason to change my mind?"

Nels turned to look through the dark windows instead. "There are a couple of guards stationed outside your door. How are we going to ditch your escorts and leave the castle?"

"I'm not sure. They do pose a problem. Maybe they should come with us."

The suggestion tempted Nels to look at her. "*With* us?"

"If we are to comb every haystack in the kingdom for a needle, the more hands the better. Plus I have questions for the tailor, and maybe Sir Arek will give us a hand!"

"Oh," Nels mumbled. "I'm sure he will . . ."

"What was that, ghost?" she hummed. "Don't mumble."

It was clear that she had her heart set on Arek, even though Nels knew perfectly well where the knight's true intentions resided. Such ignorance was not fair to her. He had to say something.

"Tyra —"

"*Princess*. Helping you does not make us friends."

"Look . . ." Nels turned away from the windows. "I need to warn you —"

His words fumbled at the sight of a man standing in Tyra's room. Wearing a lavish suit and a rich mantle, he looked terribly pale — so pale that Nels could see the chamber door behind him.

"Beg your pardon," said the stranger. "I did not know Her Highness had company."

He turned and walked *through* the locked door.

"Warn me about *what*?" Tyra asked.

Nels shook his head as the princess emerged from behind the divide, wearing a slender, pearly nightgown. The fabric shimmered in the moonlight, hugging the curves of her frame.

She looked wonderful.

Tyra crossed her arms. "What's wrong? You look like you've seen a ghost."

Nels turned to the door, almost forgetting what he *had* seen. "Wait here."

Leaving the princess behind, he walked through the door and saw the guards still stationed on the other side. Nels looked down the hall and called out to the stranger. He heard no response. Apparently, Nels was *not* the only ghost in Avërand after all.

"What's going on?" Tyra asked through the door. "Who are you shouting at?"

The two guards glanced at each other and laughed quietly.

11

PICKING PANSIES

Tyra batted her eyelashes for Arek. He smiled back as they reached the shaded ashen hills. With a cool breeze and no clouds above, it was the perfect afternoon for a picnic.

She felt much better after a good night's sleep. She had also apologized to the scullion for her behavior the day before. Father did not come to eat with them, but her mother was impressed — impressed enough to grant Arek his request to share the afternoon with Tyra, on the condition that they bring an escort. Tyra would have preferred to be alone on this outing with Arek, but if she was going to help the peasant find his needle, they would have to set off on their journey regardless. Arek had provided the perfect excuse for them to leave the castle.

Tyra had a new dress for the occasion: green satin embroidered with a bright gold thread that matched her flowing hair. Much like the dress she wore for archery, it had pockets sewn within her bodice, which laced up the front. Beneath it all, she wore a flattering flax chemise. The tailor had made them especially for hard travel. But when did he have time? And how did he know she had agreed to go? Strangest of all was what he had given her: a small cedar box, filled with beeswax and sewing tools. When she tried to ask about these items, Bosh gave her a cryptic answer: "There are dangers in the wilderness, so mind your dress. It will serve you well."

She accepted both gifts, finding his response rather peculiar and unhelpful.

He never answered my question.

Tyra knew the peasant would be more direct. She wanted to ask him, but at present, it was best to say nothing. Maintaining the appearance of sanity was far more important.

So far, everything was going according to plan.

"How do you plan to sneak off with all these guards watching?" the peasant asked.

"Relax," Tyra spoke through her smile. "Everything is going the way I want it."

He stared doubtfully at her. "Bosh said we have to make this journey alone."

"Stop worrying so much," Tyra said. "Let me deal with the living, all right?"

Arek dismounted as the caravan arrived at the summit. The prominent view of a noon horizon stretched out before them. Castle Avërand lay to the southeast. The distant shore lay beyond. Her home looked so small from here, but Tyra needed to be this far away if they stood a chance of leaving. If their escort refused to help, evading them here would be easier than evading the entire castle host.

"What a sight," Arek said, standing by Brooklet. "May I assist you down?"

Tyra smiled. "You needn't ask."

Blushing at the knight's hands around her waist, Tyra held on to Arek's broad shoulders. He raised her from the saddle and lowered her to the ground, lush with shin-high grass. He offered her his arm, took Brooklet's bridle in the other, and tied the mare next to his stallion. Tyra guided them to a shaded spot by the edge of a thicket, where two servants stretched a blanket over the cool grass. Two more servants followed, carrying a basket from the carriage that had accompanied them.

Skipping onto the blanket, Tyra sat herself down. "This is such a gorgeous day."

"Indeed, it is," said Arek. "You look mighty comfortable. Might I join you?"

Tyra giggled. "Is that not why we are here?"

"No. It's not," the peasant grumbled.

"Please," Tyra said, having found it easier to ignore the ghost after a good night's sleep. "Sit with me."

The knight obeyed after he removed the sheathed sword from his belt. He crossed his thick legs and lay on his back, sinking into the grass-cushioned blanket. Clad in brown trousers and a cream shirt, Arek had dressed well for the occasion. He placed his hands behind his dark hair, putting his muscular arms on display. He was a vision of perfection, a man Tyra dreamed of having all to herself. If they had been alone, there was no telling what she would've done.

"I was thrilled when you accepted my invitation this morning," Arek said.

Tyra urged the men with the basket to finish their serving. "I'm glad you thought of me. I do enjoy this place." She stopped to think. "I'm terribly sorry for what I said yesterday. I don't know what came over me." She glanced at the peasant, who yawned. "I'm better now."

"Glad to hear it. You gave me a start." Arek stretched his neck. "I wished to be alone with you, to be honest, but with this talk about a murderer roaming the land and all . . ."

"You're referring to the man who killed the Harvestport merchant?" Tyra asked.

The knight nodded. "I helped reclaim the body. Stabbed in the back, terrible sight." Arek leaned on his side and supported his head with his hand. "How did you know about this?"

"The scribe brought it up yesterday during breakfast."

"Not an easy story to digest first thing in the morning," Arek said. "I had no idea you were privy to that kind of information. It was meant for the king alone — a royal secret."

"I am *royalty*, Sir Arek," she said, smiling. "I will be privy to all affairs one day."

"Yes," he said, placing his hand over hers, "with a man to shoulder that burden with you."

Never before had Tyra felt their fingers entwine. Her breath stilled as she returned his tender grasp, until a foot entered her view and stomped through both of their hands. The peasant was glaring down at them, his arms crossed impatiently. Tyra swallowed and pulled her hand away.

"Will you need anything else, Your Highness?" asked one of the servants.

"Flowers!" she answered. "Some bluebells and pansies will do nicely."

Arek snapped his fingers. "I should have thought of that! Sir Canis!"

One of the older knights emerged from among the escorts. "Sir Arek?"

"Take a few men below the hill and gather flowers."

"Send them all," Tyra said into his ear. "I must ask you something."

He smiled at her and whispered back, "So must I."

Sir Canis restrained a frown. "You want us to gather flowers?"

"Send everyone. Make the largest bouquet Her Highness has ever seen."

"Your Highness." Sir Canis's tone was perturbed — clearly not amused by the request. "Our mandate is to protect you, not leave you alone while we make floral arrangements."

"I insist," Tyra said. "Check the grounds, but start at the bottom of the hill."

"And as I live," Arek added, "no harm will come to her."

Canis grumbled as he turned. "Ready your feet, lads. We're pickin' pansies!"

Excited and nervous, Tyra waited for them to go before she spoke. If she could make Arek realize her problem and convince him to come, it would be a cinch to persuade the others.

"I see what you're doing," the peasant said, looking at the knight. "What about him?"

She glared at the ghost before she mouthed, "Be quiet."

"Now that we are . . . alone," Arek started, "may I speak my mind?"

Tossing her hair over her shoulder, Tyra focused all of her attention on the knight. This was it. Time to make her move. "Do not think me prudish, Sir Arek, but I must ask you —"

"Tyra." The knight moved close, his finger suddenly pressed against her lips. "I can no longer hide my feelings for you, Tyra. You and I know that we are meant for each other."

He leaned forward. His bruised lips neared her face, ready to kiss her.

Startled, Tyra pulled away. "What are you doing?"

"I love you, and I know you feel the same." A frown appeared on the peasant's face as Arek stared longingly into Tyra's eyes. "Am I too forward? Please, forgive me."

"No, Arek," Tyra said. "I mean, I feel the same, but —"

Reaching for her hand, the knight rose to his knee. "Your father still disapproves? Why does he not trust me? I serve him well, and I returned his crown that the Vagas stole. Am I not the favored Knight of Averand?" He took her by the hand. "What must I do, Tyra?"

"Oh, brother . . ." The peasant sighed. "He's a better thief than they are."

Choosing to ignore his words, Tyra grasped Arek's hand back. "Leave with me."

Arek jumped back this time. "*Leave* with you? You want to elope?"

Tyra's cheeks flushed at the thought. "No, but I need your help with something, a special task that only we can accomplish, together. If we do not find it, I will be haunted forever."

"Haunted?" Arek asked. "What do you mean?"

"*This* is your plan?" The peasant groaned. "You want *him* to come with us?"

She didn't respond to Nels, nor did she look at him. An awkward silence hung over the picnic, but then, without warning, the peasant stormed into the thicket and vanished among the trees.

"Tyra?" Arek's eyes locked with hers.

"I'm sorry. I —"

"What is the matter? You can tell me anything."

Tyra slinked out of his grasp and started to worry. She had worked hard all morning to maintain her appearance, to ensure a sane demeanor. If she were to speak about ghosts, she could ruin everything, but what else was she supposed to say? "You would not understand."

"I want to understand, Tyra. But more important, I want you to marry me."

Stealing the breath from her chest, Tyra stared at him. "What did you say?"

"Marry me," Arek said, bolder this time. "I will be yours forever."

She could not believe it; the rumors of his proposal were true. "Oh, Arek!" Tyra cried. "Of course I will!"

She surveyed the scene — a picturesque, romantic place — wanting to capture a memory of this moment with Arek. The knight suddenly pressed his lips against hers. Tyra's eyes flashed open before she returned the kiss. The touch of his warm breath on her skin sent a newfound elation through her body, like the fluttering of a thousand butterflies — far better than kissing a corpse. But something was amiss, her excitement short-lived. Where was the peasant?

What if he's watching us?

"No," she said as they parted. "I can't. Not yet."

The knight's joy changed to a wounded stupor. "Why?"

"I . . ." She hesitated. "I must see the Mountain Witch."

"The *who?*" Arek raised his chin. "Whatever for?"

"Because she may know where a magic needle is."

Arek scooted back. "Are you delirious? You cannot visit her!"

"I'm *not* delirious, Arek," she said. "And if you love me, you must believe me. I need your help." Tyra realized how ridiculous she was sounding. Talk of witches and magic needles was just as bad as ghosts. "Please," she said, closing her eyes. "I don't know who else to —"

Thwack!

A loud crack, like the splitting of a tree branch, sounded behind Arek. Tyra watched as the knight's hazel eyes rolled back. He slumped forward and fell on top of her. Shrieking, Tyra struggled to free herself. Their picnic basket tipped on its side, spilling its contents onto the blanket. Her heart quivering, she stood up and looked over her love, lying unconscious on the ground.

A thick stick entered her view.

"Hold this," said the peasant.

Tyra complied, still in shock, and took hold of the wooden stick as the peasant darted for the packhorses. When she examined what she was holding, she made the connection. "*What* have you done?"

The peasant reemerged, holding supplies in each hand. "We can't wait any longer." A waterskin slipped through his wrist. "Help me. I don't want to spook your mare again."

"Wait." She pointed at the waterskin. "Since when are you capable of carrying things?"

"I'll tell you after we go." He winked at her and left for another load.

Hoping that Arek was not seriously hurt, Tyra knelt beside him and touched his face. She could feel his breath passing through his nose with her fingers. He was alive, only unconscious, but that was more than enough to boil her blood. "Why did you do this to Sir Arek?"

"This is *our* journey," the peasant said, shrugging as he came back, "and I'd hate to see what the knights will think when they see you standing over him with a club in your hand."

Tyra threw the stick on the grass. "You conniving —"

"Make it quick, Your Highness. They're coming back."

Frightened, she looked at Arek again. "They'll blame *me*!"

With that, the peasant smiled, as if that was his plan.

Caught in his trap and knowing that she could never explain what happened, she ran to the carriage, grabbed her bow and quiver, and her dagger in its sheath. She seized a traveling cloak and her personal knapsack. Brooklet whickered as Tyra approached. She didn't return the salutation. As soon as they loaded the mare with the additional supplies, the peasant hoisted himself up and sat behind her.

"After we bring you back to life, run as fast as you can, before *I* kill you!"

135

"Remind me after we find the Needle."

"*If* we find the Needle, you mean."

"We will. Just don't ride too fast; I'm not good with horses."

From the concerned look on his face, Tyra could tell that he was speaking the truth. Shaking her head, Tyra handled the reins of her mare and guided Brooklet into the thicket as fast as she could ride. Tyra looked around the peasant's arm and caught a glimpse of her knight sitting up and rubbing his head. She didn't want to leave Arek like this, but she had no choice.

Dyre took his place under the stone arch between the outer and inner doors. The shade was cool here, a pleasant perk from the summer heat. He crossed his arms and leaned back — something the *real* Dyre would have done.

I wish I'd had more time to study him, but this will do for now.

"You're late," said Jarvis, one of the other gatekeepers. He was impatiently waiting for Dyre to end his shift, no doubt. "I was about to have the guard search for you."

"No need," Dyre replied. "I had to run an errand. Have I missed much?"

"Princess Tyra and Sir Arek left with a caravan. A picnic, I gather."

"Did they?" Dyre asked. "I hope they enjoy themselves."

"Just keep an eye out for anyone suspicious. King's orders."

Raising his hands behind his head, Dyre leaned farther back as he watched the eldest of the gatekeepers leave. The tone of Jarvis's voice rubbed Dyre the wrong way, but he let it slide. The man was a glorified peasant, a weakling with no connection to the castle other than keeping the gate. If Jarvis were more than this, taking his life and assuming his face would be worth Dyre's while.

Such was the fate of those who crossed him.

Having played gatekeeper for over a fortnight, Dyre's patience had begun to wear thin. He did not anticipate his plan would take so long, but he knew that one false move would expose him. It was safer this way, taking it slow, waiting for an opportunity to strike — and he had found the boy. If any other part of his plan should fail, at least the world would be safe.

Dyre saluted a new patrol as they marched by.

Ickabosh knows I'm here. It won't be easy to find him now.

The old tailor was the only man alive who could stand against him — or at least he was once, many years ago. If he could find the tailor and be done with him, no one could stop Dyre from seizing Avërand. Because of Lennart's father, his life was stolen. Only the kingdom could remedy that crime — the whole of it. Lennart's family would make fitting slaves. The lovely princess would make a particularly special one.

Dyre's fantasy was broken by the smell of fresh pastry. He sensed the scullery maid coming his way with a cherry tart in her basket. He opened his eyes and smiled weakly at her. She had let down her graying hair. "Lovely afternoon," he said. "Wouldn't you agree?"

"Oh, yes, very much," she answered quickly. "I saved this one for you." She held out a cloth-covered basket for him. "You missed breakfast again. I know these are your favorite."

Dyre gave her a grateful laugh as he uncovered the basket, reached for the pastry, and cringed as he took a bite. He despised the sweet and sticky sensation in his mouth. He ate it anyway, for it was the *real* Dyre's favorite. The things he had to endure to maintain his character. "Thank you much. Now, tell me: Have you any plans this evening?"

The woman's eyes widened. "None at all, why do you ask?"

"You're so kind . . . and I've grown fond of you."

Her face reddened. "I was beginning to think —"

"I hadn't noticed you?" Dyre's smile broadened. "Meet me here tonight."

The overjoyed woman nodded before she returned to the kitchens. Dyre leaned back again as he reconsidered his plans. Since the maid worked inside the kitchens, assuming the bothersome woman's appearance would substantially shorten his wait. No one would miss the scullery wench or her homely looks. By using her face, he could more easily infiltrate the castle.

Outside, a man was riding hard toward the city gate.

It was Sir Canis — and he looked terrified.

"Summon the Order!" he cried. "Have Sir Arek's squire ready to ride!"

Finding it easy to appear surprised, Dyre stepped back. "What's happened, Sire?"

"We've not a moment to waste. Find Alvil and have him pack his horse. I'll round up the other knights and inform the king. We must follow them before the trail runs cold!"

Dyre looked outside the gate and saw no one. He reached for the blue dye in his sleeve and flung a drop at Canis. It landed directly on his head. "Where's the princess?" Dyre asked.

"The Vagas have her," Canis replied without resistance. "Arek says they used magic on him, and that Her Highness spoke nonsense about a witch and a needle before he was attacked." Canis took a deep breath. "He was struck from behind. I could hardly tell what he was saying."

Dyre's cherry tart slipped from his fingers. "Needle?"

"Hurry now! We must catch up if we are to find her."

"I'll do as you say," Dyre said, "straightaway!"

Canis nodded before he charged for the castle.

Dyre reached out his hand to touch Tyra's thread.

He felt nothing. *Is she using a slip stitch?*

Abandoning his post, Dyre ran for the squire's quarters, conjuring a new plan. If the princess had spoken of the Needle of Gailner, how did she know of it? He had taken that road many years before, and he returned with nothing except the knowledge that led to his banishment. To know the truth, he had to find the princess. He had to accompany Arek, the knight she favored most.

I know what to do.

When Dyre reached Alvil's quarters, he knocked and reached for a knife.

***

"There's a good spot," Nels said. "We'll camp here tonight."

Crickets chirped as Brooklet neared a covered glen. Tyra hadn't said a word since they made their escape into the woods. Nels tried to coax something out of her, but she would not yield. The mare brushed the branches of a willow tree as they found a place where aspen leaves covered the ground. A large rock sat on the other side of the knoll, near a circle of ash. Someone had camped here recently.

When the mare stopped, Tyra threw her bag on the ground and dismounted as fast as she could, leaving Nels on the saddle. He jumped off next, but his hand slipped through Brooklet as he descended. The mare hollered and darted to the other side of the tall rock.

"She really doesn't like it when I touch her."

Tyra unrolled a quilt and sat on it.

"Should we take her saddle off?"

She turned her back on him.

Nels sighed. *How long is she going to keep this up?*

He walked to Brooklet, unfastened her girth, and slipped the saddle from her back. The mare whickered and adjusted her jaw before she wandered to the bank of the nearby river.

"So long as I don't go through her, she doesn't mind."

Tyra pulled an apple from her knapsack and bit into it.

"Bosh told us to go on this journey alone, remember?"

The princess remained silent, except for her munching.

"Are you angry with me?" He waited for her to speak, but she refused to acknowledge him. "If we're going to do this, let's have it out; otherwise, this is going to be a long journey."

"*Anger* isn't the word I would use, ghost." Tyra repositioned herself and looked at him with utmost contempt. "How about abhorrence? Or disdain? *Hate!* That's a good one."

"Listen," Nels said. "I didn't mean to —"

"Loathing!" Tyra threw her apple core at him. It passed through his chest. "I *loathe* you!"

Nels crossed his arms, his jaw clenched. "Are you done, or do you have more?"

"Oh, I have *plenty* more," Tyra hissed. "Not that I should expect you to comprehend." Her eyes thinned so much that Nels couldn't see the blue in them anymore. "You coerced me into coming here!" She choked back a sob. "And you harmed my Arek — he could have helped us!"

Nels shook his head. "He had it coming. Why do you like Sir Arek, anyway?"

"He is strong and brave and . . . and he is everything a princess could want."

"I hate to tell you this, but he doesn't care about you."

She glowered at him. "What would you know?"

"I heard him last night. He only wants you for the throne."

"You stay out of my affairs!" she cried, glaring fiercely. "Listen to me, half-wit! Once we find the Needle and end this nonsense, you will leave me alone forever, and I will marry Arek!"

"Marry." Nels hated saying the word. "You're going to marry him?"

"You're dead, ghost," she said. "Not deaf."

He shrugged. "Marry him, then. It's not like I care."

She stared back at him, her brow rising. "You do!"

"What?" Her sudden accusation flustered Nels.

"Of course you do! It all makes sense. You're jealous of Arek!" She hunched over and laughed hard. "This is too much. Did you really think you and I could ever —?"

"You tell me," Nels said. "I saw the way you looked at me during the festival."

Tyra's cheeks flushed red. "I would never! You are a peasant — a *dead* one!"

"Titles and status mean nothing. At the end of the day, we're all the same."

The girl snickered. "Where did you hear such nonsense? Your mother?"

Complacently, Nels crossed his arms. "So what if I did?"

"Then she is a great fool, raising a worthless son like you."

"Better a fool for a mother than a coward for a father!"

Tyra suddenly turned away and curled up on her side.

"I didn't mean —"

"Go away!"

Stepping through the log, Nels headed to the river, frustrated and discontent. He sat by the bank, searched for a rock, and skipped it on the water. So much for a seamless start, but he was glad to have told the truth about Arek. The night was not so dark — the moon had risen. It looked full, but he knew it was waning. In less than a week, a half-moon would dominate the night sky.

We don't have much time.

Nels threw a second rock. It plinked into the river. The hollow tromping of a horse's hooves drew near as he searched for a third. Brooklet came close and drank from the bank.

Nels smacked his lips. He missed the taste of water. "How do you put up with her?"

The mare shook her mane and snorted before she took another drink.

"Right." He laughed. "Don't stroke her the wrong way. I know."

Nels reached for another rock, just as a foot stepped *through* it.

"Good evening, young man."

Nels jumped back, passing through the mare's underside. Brooklet screamed and ran to the glen where Tyra lay. A man wearing royal attire stood before Nels. White hair came to his ears, and he wore a blue vest on his chest.

It was the man that Nels had seen in Tyra's chamber.

12

THE KING'S CHARGE

"Mindless half-wit!" Tyra cried from the willow glen. "Quit spooking Brooklet!"

The transparent man turned back to Nels, wincing. "I hope you will be patient with my precious granddaughter. She has a good heart, whether she chooses to show it or not." The phantom approached the riverbank and tossed his mantle back before he sat down; an excited look beamed from his eyes. "You find solace in the water, I take it?"

Nels stared at him as the crickets resumed their song.

"As do I." The ghost motioned his hand to the space beside him. "Have a seat with me. I have been without conversation for years. What better place to have one than by this ford?"

Not sure how to conduct himself, Nels complied and nearly laughed. Nothing could be sillier than a ghost acting skittish around another ghost. "You're really Tyra's grandfather?"

"*Was* her grandfather, fifteen years ago. It pains me to see you like this, Lief."

That name again.

Nels was grateful for the change his mother had made to his name after they fled the castle. This man — this ghost — was the murdered king that Nels had seen in the loom, the ghost of King Yalva. So there were other ghosts after all; it made Nels wonder what other myths were real.

"Call me Nels," he said. "It's an honor to meet you, Your Majesty."

"The honor is mine, Nels." Yalva turned to the water. "It is good to be seen."

Nels moved his eyes to the water as well. "Did you come to check on her?"

"The kingdom believes Tyra was kidnapped by the Vagas."

Why would they draw a conclusion like that? "She's not kidnapped."

"I can see that, but that is what Sir Canis told them. It is clear that Sir Arek's story never happened as he told it, but she *did* disappear." The king shifted his pale eyes, waiting for Nels to look at him. "Her escorts would not allow her to ride off alone. How did she escape them?"

"Tyra ordered everyone away" — Nels smiled — "and I clubbed Arek."

Yalva's thick brow rose. "You did? I have never known a ghost to do such a thing."

"I'm not like other ghosts." Picking up a rock, Nels chucked it across the river. It skipped off the water's surface, reached the opposite bank, and skidded to a stop in the grass. "See?"

Yalva harrumphed. "I suppose you are." There was envy in his voice. "This confirms that Arek's story about the Vagas is false — and rightly so. They are a peaceful people."

A wave of guilt washed over Nels as his thoughts returned to the mysterious girl with the silvery eyes wearing a sapphire stone. Now Arek believed the Vagas had taken Tyra. Nels never meant to bring the Vagas into this. He should have swung that stick a little harder. "When did you hear this?" Nels asked.

"I heard it from Sir Canis while spying on the gatekeeper."

"The gatekeeper? Why would you do that?"

"Because he is the man who killed me."

Nels gawked at the ghost. "Rasmus?"

Yalva nodded. "The Master Threader. He returned a fortnight ago and overpowered the night gatekeeper. I watched Rasmus use his deceptive art to trick the gatekeeper into letting his guard down, as Rasmus did to me. It takes little time for the Master Threader to study a man and learn everything there is to know about him before he takes on their appearance. He assumed the appearance of a merchant from Harvestport, and many others. Even now he rides with Sir Arek as a trusted companion, hoping to catch up with Tyra."

Nels thought of Arek's squire. "You mean Alvil?"

Yalva bowed his head.

Nels refused to believe it. He knew Alvil — not especially well — but enough, from the few times he visited Cobblestown. He was a bright lad with a strong future, and he always spoke with admiration of his service to the knighthood. Nels dug his fingers into the bank. His anger rose. So did his fear. If Rasmus could turn himself into anyone, no one was safe.

"When you knew I could see you, why didn't you tell me?"

"I have had no one to talk to in sixteen years." Yalva looked up to the sky. "I suppose I have become shy, and to find a young man in my granddaughter's chamber took me by surprise. But I tell you this now" — he breathed deeply — "I fear my granddaughter is in terrible danger."

"I'd better wake her, then."

King Yalva stuck his feet through a patch of dandelions. None of the seedlings broke from their stems. "Arek and his company made camp a few hours south. There is no need."

"I'd rather not take any chances." Nels stood up and faced their camp.

"This quest *is* a chance!" Yalva bellowed. "It is an enormous risk."

"You think I'll let harm come to her?"

"Of course not, but if she dies, you and the entire kingdom of Avërand may be lost."

The old ghost's urgent voice caused Nels to tremble. "Neither of us want that."

Yalva rose to his feet, a strange sight to see: He looked so old, yet he moved so quickly. "I came to warn you about Rasmus, but even more than that, I came to ensure that I could trust you with my granddaughter's life. She needs to see a strong spirit if she is to make this journey."

Nels laughed, though he tried his best not to. "All she sees is a peasant."

"That is what she *will* see if you keep presenting yourself like one." Yalva raised his hand and clasped it on Nels's shoulder. The grip surprised Nels. He could feel the king's firm, solid hold. He never imagined that ghosts could interact with one another. "I have been a ghost long enough to know what has bound me to this world and what keeps me from passing on. I thrust my whole soul into the welfare of this kingdom — so much so that I cannot leave its borders. Until my rule is upheld by a worthy heir, I cannot rest in peace."

"But your son is king," Nels said.

"In his heart, Lennart never accepted the crown. I fear his example has caused Tyra to think she has failed already." The king released his grip. "Your father was a great man. Ulrich feared nothing. He desired nothing more than the welfare of others. Perhaps if you can be an example to my granddaughter — as your father was to my son — there may be hope."

Nels looked at the ground, allowing the idea to settle in his mind. *Be an example?* How could he, having already made a mess of things? Tyra had every reason to refuse him. He had made a fool out of her and haunted her and clubbed the man she loved. "I will try."

"Not good enough. I must know that you will ensure her safety, above all else, even at the cost of your life. Only through the living can a ghost's matters be resolved. My granddaughter must accept her duty. Until then, you need her, but, unlike me, you are an exception."

"How am I an exception?" Nels asked.

"The same reason you can throw rocks across a river. Do you not see? She can help you, but only if you protect her." Yalva looked Nels squarely in the eyes. "I have a charge for you."

"What kind of charge?"

"Kneel."

Nels didn't understand the request. "Why?"

The ghost said nothing. He only stood there, waiting for Nels to obey. Hesitantly, Nels lowered himself to one knee, not knowing what Yalva had in mind. The ghost king's hand came to rest on his shoulder again. "Nels, son of Ulrich and Lady Katharina, I charge you with the protection of Tyra. Let your courage and wisdom shine, so she will come to know and respect the woman that she is." Yalva's grip tightened. "Arise, Sir Nels, Knight of Avërand!"

When the ghost removed his hand, his touch still lingered.

"You knighted me?" Nels asked. "But, if you're dead —"

"I am no more a king than you are a knight, but it is the thought of the honor that defines us, and I saw how honorably you fought during your match with Sir Arek at the festival." Yalva bowed his head. He was a king; dead or alive, he could knight whomever he wanted. "You have the heart of your father. Even if no one else sees that, know that you are a knight to me."

Nels rose to his feet, overcome with emotion. He had waited his whole life for someone to say these words to him. And in the eyes of a king, Nels was more than worthy.

If only Wallin and Jilia could've seen this.

"Thank you." Nels's voice caught in his throat. "You have no idea what this means to me."

"You are quite welcome." Yalva turned to face the willow tree, clasping his hands behind his back. "Since you kidnapped my granddaughter, where do you plan on taking her?"

"To the Mountain Witch, for the Needle of Gailner."

"Ah, yes — I have heard of such a needle, and I know the woman you speak of; she is a conjurer, different from fabricators." Yalva shook his head. "I would come with you if I could."

Nels understood. If Yalva was tied to his land, he couldn't leave it. "If you can't come, can you tell me anything that will help us?"

A smile dimpled Yalva's cheek. "I will do more than that." The king jumped from the ground and rose higher than Nels's head, but he stayed in the air, buoyant, like a feather. He floated and curved with the wind, then gently settled back to the ground. The ghost king could fly.

"How did you do that?" Nels asked.

Yalva chuckled. "Humor an old specter and share a conversation with me. I will teach you everything I know about the nature of ghosts — and of witches — if you have time for it."

Nels smiled back. "I've got all night."

A golden line buffered the edge of the horizon as dawn drew near.

Tyra heard birds chirping.

Sunlight spilled through the willow branches that draped over their camp like a curtain. Rubbing the sleep from her eyes, Tyra searched the grounds. The peasant was gone, and so was her mare. She was about to stand up when galloping hooves, heavier than Brooklet's, came from beyond the curtain of leaves. It parted, moved by a dark horse, ridden by a man in a suit of metal armor. Before she could speak, the man lowered his shield and removed his helmet.

Arek had found her.

"You came for me!"

"I can fly!" he said.

Tyra opened her mouth, but she didn't immediately know what to say. "You can *what*?"

The knight jumped off his saddle and floated into the air. He glided to her, like a drifting dandelion seed, and swept Tyra off her feet. They fell together onto a patch of grass.

"You have to see this!" Arek's voice changed. "Wake up!"

Her dream broken, Tyra opened her eyes.

The peasant hovered above the ground, right over her.

He *was* flying.

She jumped away with a scream. "What are you doing?"

He returned to the ground with a laugh. "Sorry. I got a little carried away."

Tyra scrunched her nose. "Not funny." Even so, she was surprised. The peasant had never flown before. "Your face isn't what I want to wake up to. Since when can you do that?"

"I could all along. I just didn't know it. How'd you sleep?"

"Well enough," she said, eyeing him, "I suppose."

He pointed at the log beside her. "I made you something."

Looking to her right, Tyra saw one of her handkerchiefs spread over the log's surface. A ripe apple sat on top of it next to a torn lump of rye bread and a heaping pile of brambleberries. She glanced around their camp. Everything was packed away with no trace they had camped there.

"Is there anything else I can get for you, Your Highness?"

"What are you doing?"

He looked around and shrugged. "What do you mean?"

"You're acting like a gentleman — and I don't like it!" She frowned. "I said some rather terrible things to you last night. And I meant every word, so why are you being so nice to me?"

"Shouldn't I? I'm a subject of yours, after all. If anyone should apologize, it's me."

Tyra stared at the leaves on the ground as she mulled over the peasant's sudden manners and formalities. They had shared a heated row last night — their worst one yet — but he was acting as though nothing happened. And by the sound of his voice, he meant every word.

"No, really," she said. "What has come over you?"

The peasant said nothing. He hitched the last strap of Brooklet's saddle before he stepped toward Tyra. It made her timid, the closer he neared. Those eyes of his, green as the grass, made him look more alive than he really was. "I know my place now, thanks to your grandfather."

"My grandfather?" Tyra had never known her grandfather — or any of her grandparents. They were long dead. "Which grandfather? Are you telling me that he is a ghost?"

"King Yalva, yes," the peasant answered. "We talked last night. He was all see-throughish, just as your instructor described. He also knighted me, and he charged me with protecting you."

Tyra flinched. "It doesn't count if you're dead, does it?"

"It's the thought of the honor that defines us," he said.

Tyra scoffed. "My grandfather, knighting you? I find that hard to believe."

"You don't have to, but then, how believable am I? This magic is unbelievable, but you know it's real." He stepped right in front of her. The confidence in his eyes left her no choice but to take his word for it. "When this is over, you won't see me again. You have my word."

Does he really mean that? "Well, that's . . . comforting."

The peasant smiled. "Let's get going. The sooner the better, right?"

"If you say so."

Tyra sat up, slipped on her boots, and ate quickly, but she could barely digest what the ghost had told her, much less chew on her dried-out bread. In a way, she'd thought his lack of formality was refreshing — how he treated her like anyone else — but now he was like any of her predictable servants.

Beyond that, the words he had spoken last night troubled her. Perhaps he meant nothing by saying he caught her looking at him during the festival. In truth, he had intrigued her. But Tyra refused to entertain the thought: She had given her heart to Arek. And in that regard the peasant's *other* words concerned her. Did Arek truly love her? Was he merely interested in the throne? She never saw it that way. The idea of him using her — she could not think of it.

He will prove his love by tracking me down.

When Tyra finished her breakfast, she wadded the handkerchief in her hand, mounted Brooklet, and gathered her reins. "We should reach the Westerly Pass before nightfall." The peasant nodded as he jumped into the air and glided along Brooklet's side. His supernatural ability continued to surprise her. "Let me know what else you can do, before you startle me."

He bowed graciously in midair. "Yes, Your Highness."

Thrown by his subservient attitude, Tyra smiled as she guided her mare along the westward path. It was muddy enough to leave behind a noticeable trail. "Let's go this way."

"We should walk in the river for a little while, in case we're being followed."

"Oh," she said. "Well, I suppose we can," but she did not want to. Arek was a champion when it came to tracking. If they left nothing behind, how would he follow them?

I should be planning our wedding, not hiding from him.

"Just for a little while," Tyra conceded. "Brooklet doesn't like to have her hooves wet."

The peasant's mouth curled at the corners as he smiled, as if to keep from laughing. As he walked ahead, Tyra thought up a plan and tossed her handkerchief at the nearest bush.

The white linen caught hold of a branch. It waved with the wind.

Tyra hoped it would linger there for Arek to find.

Arek pointed at the ground by a fallen log. An aged willow glen kept the abandoned camp cool from the sun. "She slept here, but her captors left no markings — not one sign of rest."

"As I have said," Sir Canis replied, "I don't believe she was kidnapped."

"How can you say that? They struck me over the head!"

"Or maybe a branch fell and hit you. I wager she ran away."

"No!" Arek bellowed. "She was *taken*. You know these Vagas. They conjured up some spell to hide their tracks, I am sure of it, just like when they attempted to steal the crown."

Alvil tried his best to keep himself from glaring at the knight. Riding beside the boorish likes of him, it was nearly impossible to stay in character. He had never taken the life of one so young, or changed to a body much smaller than his own. It required some getting used to.

Vagas don't have that kind of magic.

He knew this, having studied magic abroad. He could tell the knight was lying. He could sense in the knight's thread what the truth was. Arek was anxious about having once used the crown to frame the Vagas so he could gain favor in the eyes of the king — ambitious, but futile. Alvil scanned the ground as the *real* Alvil would. Aside from the horse's markings, he saw nothing. "Maybe there's only one captor?"

"Just as I thought," Arek said. "Her mare was guided north, led to the river!"

The knight jumped onto his stallion and steered the animal to the water.

Canis turned to the squire. "This madness is spreading."

Alvil smirked. He couldn't agree more. Although Arek was a fool, Alvil needed the knight if he stood a chance of finding the princess. Thanks to Ickabosh, he could no longer trace her.

Why would he use his magic on her?

Since she had mentioned the Needle, Alvil had an idea of where she was headed.

The Mountain Witch . . .

He had tried to visit her once, many years ago, but the woman refused to divulge what she knew about the Needle. They shared a duel and she died as a result. He never did find her secret book or learn where he could find the lost Needle. He did, however, learn the truth.

"Nothing here either," Arek said. "Not a single print along this bank."

"What about that handkerchief?" Davin pointed. "Isn't that hers?"

Arek spurred his horse and retrieved the cloth. "It *is*!"

"See," Canis said. "A competent kidnapper wouldn't leave that behind."

"Maybe her kidnapper is *in*competent. She has obviously left a trail for us."

"Sir Arek!" Canis insisted. "There's nothing to suggest she was taken. You may have only imagined the Vagas, for all we know. Let us find her. You should head back and rest."

Alvil was not about to waste the moment. Besides, if Arek found the king's daughter, how much more favor could he earn? "Perhaps we should split up. We can cover more ground."

"I like your suggestion." Arek glanced at Canis. "I will head up the river."

"Come, Davin," Canis said, walking toward the others. "We better inform the king. If word spreads that Her Highness was taken by the Vagas, everyone would take up arms."

Alvil watched them and popped his neck before he turned his horse upstream, away from the departing company of knights. It was better this way, leaving them alone. Bringing too many on the search would complicate his scheme. "He's using the river to hide their tracks. So would I."

The knight cocked his mighty brow. "Good thinking. I knew I could count on you. They are headed for the mountains — the Westerly Pass, perhaps. But why would they go there?"

"Is that not where the Mountain Witch lives?"

"So they say." Arek spoke as if the idea made him nervous. They glanced at the graying clouds rolling overhead. "A storm is coming. We had better press for that mountain before it arrives."

The knight spurred his stallion, and they galloped up the shallow river. Alvil sneered as he struggled to keep up with the knight, but it was the princess who remained in his thoughts.

Ickabosh told her about the Needle. What does she want with it?

The only way to find out was to ask her.

13

THE WESTERLY MANSION

Tyra pulled her dripping hair back once she had found an alcove to rest under. After traveling all day and hiking up the mountain until dusk, she was exhausted. They should have made camp at the base of the mountain, but the peasant insisted that they should move on. Now they were stuck in a downpour. When Brooklet could no longer handle the weight, Tyra dismounted and walked the rest of the way.

Her hair and clothing were wet. She had blisters on her feet. Her legs ached terribly. It was enough to make Tyra regret her decision to help.

"How can a mansion be up here?"

The peasant stood on the edge of the trail and glanced over his shoulder playfully. "I was just thinking that. Imagine hauling lumber and stone up here, back and forth."

"It . . . would take . . . forever," Tyra puffed.

He whistled. "The trail's too steep here. We'll have to go on without Brooklet."

As much as Tyra hated to admit it, he was right. The tailor warned them that their climb would be long and dangerous, but she did not anticipate ascending the Westerly Mountain after sunset, and in the rain. Tyra tightened her cloak and looked up the short cliff that ended their trail. Was there really a mansion at the top? Her thoughts turned to the shadowed book, hoping it would tell them where to find the Needle. Like the peasant had said: the sooner, the better.

She placed more faith in Arek. He had to have found her handkerchief by now.

I will find the Needle and show it to him. That will prove to him that I'm not mad. I hope he will still marry me.

"Not much longer." The peasant leaned over the trail. "We'll be there in —"

"Baaaah!"

A sudden bleating interrupted him.

They both looked up. Standing on top of the rock wall was a creature with curled horns and a long face, silhouetted before the clouds. Lightning flashes revealed its gray coat.

"A goat?" The peasant scratched his head. "Look at the horns on him."

"I have never seen a wild one," Tyra said. "What an odd little thing."

The animal jumped onto the alcove above them.

"Would you like to rest awhile?" the peasant asked.

Tyra grabbed Brooklet's bridle. "She needs it more." Finding a sturdy branch, she tied the mare's reins to it. "You be good while we're gone, Brooklet. This shouldn't take long."

The mare shook her mane, as if to protest their absence.

Before Tyra turned around, the peasant had already reached the top of the wall.

"That wasn't so bad," he said. "You'd better take it slow."

Tyra pulled on her hood as she stepped into the rain, shivering as she left her bow behind. There was no need for it, but she decided to keep her dagger, just in case. When she made it to the wall that ended the trail, she saw the peasant's hand reaching for her. "What are you doing?"

His eyes shifted. "Helping you up."

"I've climbed rock faces before."

"It's slick here. I'm just trying to —"

"Hold my hand? Not on your life."

Finding a solid foothold, Tyra reached for a groove and hoisted herself up. She repeated her motions once, and then twice, until she neared the top. She then stepped onto a protruding rock and shrieked as it shifted under her weight. Her grasp slipped. Tyra's breath escaped her as she reached for something — anything — to hold on to, when someone grabbed her wrist. Wincing at the thought, Tyra saw the peasant smiling above her. There was a calming assurance lurking behind that crafty smile of his. It made her feel uneasy, yet also safe.

He easily pulled her up the rest of the way, as if she were weightless. Tyra avoided his eyes as she slumped against the wet mountainside, gasping for breath. Hooves clicked against rock. The goat stopped and stared at her with its shining gold eyes.

"That felt strange," she said. "Your hand, it was so —"

"I know. It was like grabbing the air. I couldn't feel you."

"I could." Tyra rubbed her wrist. "Don't do that again, if you can help it."

The peasant bobbed his head with another smile. "Shall we continue?"

"You lead on. It's better if you slip over the edge than me."

The peasant walked on, as though he were pleased with himself for having caught her. For all she knew, she could have broken something or plummeted to her death. Tyra looked at the back of his head and shuddered. He really had saved her life.

Good thing he learned that trick.

She trailed behind him, her boots trampling mud. She knew she should thank him, but she didn't want to give him the satisfaction. That charming smile of his was of no help.

The Needle was hers to find. It was her task to complete. *Ruling a kingdom should be easy next to this.*

"Baaack!"

Tyra heard a voice behind her. She spun around to investigate.

All she saw was the goat. "Baaack! Turrrrnnn baaack!"

Startled, Tyra dashed to catch up. "Did you hear that animal speak?"

The peasant raised his brow. "It's just the storm."

She didn't agree. A voice *did* come out of the creature — a warning. Tyra tried to hold on to the peasant's arm for reassurance, but her hands slipped through him like a cold vapor. "This is not a good idea," she said. "I think we should turn back."

"It's too dark now," said the peasant, "and we're here."

Tyra glanced over his shoulder, amazed by the sterling mansion in the middle of a small meadow. Dark clouds rolled over it, grazing its dilapidated shingles. She couldn't believe her eyes. The mansion was like those within the walls of Hillshaven, except for its menacing gargoyles. All of them sat like sentinels, their talons curled beneath each sill.

No light shone from within the windows, but the front door was open.

"Not exactly an inviting place . . ." the peasant said. "Let's have a look!"

Tyra shivered. The rising mountain winds had chilled her skin. Rain pelted against her hood, making her ears ring. This was no place for her. This was no place for anyone. She wanted to go back home. The idea of facing a witch had finally dawned on her. "Must I go in there?"

"I suppose not, but we may not have another chance."

A blinding flash crossed the sky as Tyra shook her head. A loud crash followed the sound of tumbling rocks. In this weather, standing on top of a mountain was not the safest place to be. They needed shelter from the escalating storm — or at least *she* did.

Until the storm passed, the mansion was their only option.

"You have a look," she said. "I will stay by the door."

"It doesn't look like anyone's home. I'll see what I can find."

Tyra walked by his side to the mansion's front door. An eerie feeling overcame her, like someone, or *something*, was watching her every move. She glanced over her shoulder again. The goat had followed them. This time, it had a cautious, curious look in its unblinking eyes.

Tyra pondered what the tailor had said about the witch.

Could she really turn travelers into animals?

Is that goat one of her victims?

Tyra turned around and dared herself not to look again.

Get a hold of yourself.

They ascended a short flight of stone steps that stopped at a covered porch. Each new burst of lightning revealed carefully laden stonework. The granite walls reflected the light. They peeked inside the door and saw nothing remarkable about the mansion's interior. It was spacious, wide, and terribly quiet. White sheets covered abandoned furniture, the linens grayed with settled dust. A few burning embers in a tall, spacious hearth caught Tyra's attention. Fires weren't known for building or lighting themselves.

Someone had to be in there.

"Where would we find such a book in here?" Tyra asked.

"Maybe this place has a library. I'll start upstairs."

The peasant jumped inside, crossed the floor, and glided into the house. Tyra thought it would be best if they stayed together, but she had no intention of going inside unless she absolutely had to. The porch was good enough at keeping the rain off. The hem of her cloak whipped her boots as Tyra leaned on the door, silencing its noisy hinge. She folded her arms to keep herself warm against the cold wind. Only a moment had passed, but it felt more like hours.

Why did I agree to this?

Hoping to keep the storm and the darkness from disturbing her thoughts, Tyra tried focusing on something else. It was useless. Was seeking after a Needle worth all of this trouble, risking blisters, a cold, or a tragic metamorphosis into a goat at the hands of an evil witch? She thought not. She prayed that the storm hadn't washed away their trail.

I hope Arek finds this place. I'd feel much better if he were with us.

"Baaack!"

Tyra jumped and looked back. The old goat stood at the base of the steps, staring at her with unyielding eyes. It then hopped onto the first step and ascended toward her.

"Tuuurrrn baaack!"

Gasping, Tyra ran inside, grabbed the iron handle, and slammed the door shut. She found a thick wooden latch hanging on the wall to her left, so she pulled it down and secured the door against the wind and the creature. Hooves scratched at the other side as she backed away.

Tyra laughed nervously to herself. "What's with that goat?" she muttered.

A moot question. She had no desire to know, just a desire to keep the goat away.

She caught her breath and searched the darkness. The struggling embers in the fireplace provided little light. Someone had lit that fire, but the mansion felt deserted. A chandelier dangled above; the stirred air clinked its crystals. Lightning revealed parts of an expansive room with a marble hearth and a flight of stairs guarded by two carved gargoyles. A thick layer of dust buried their stony faces. Tyra waited for her eyes to adjust as her drenched cloak left grimy streaks on the floor. She walked on, gingerly stepping onto a plush rug.

"Ghost?" she called out. "Where are you?"

The house groaned with the storm. The peasant didn't answer.

Anxious and annoyed, Tyra removed her cloak and draped the soggy heap over a chair by the hearth. She tried to warm her arms, but the fire was too faint. If she had a candle, she could look around and be of more use. Just as she thought it, she saw several long candlesticks on top of the high mantle. She stood on her toes and knocked a few of the candles down. She snatched one off the floor and prodded its wick into the ashes. A small light flickered to life.

When she looked up, a pair of eyes glared at her.

Not one pair — three.

Tyra stopped short in the middle of the room and waited for the lightning. Brief flashes revealed a fine portrait of a bearded man and two girls. Their clothing depicted the loftier style of the old Averand era, before Tyra or her father's time. Both of the girls had braided hair. Curled locks framed their faces, their dresses fashioned with black satin.

Such a dismal color. "Who would wear such a thing?"

Just then, as Tyra moved, so did their eyes.

All three pairs followed her every step.

It's my imagination. The storm. That's all.

A sudden crash sounded behind Tyra. She spun around in time to see dozens of books on a tall shelf. Numerous thuds hit the floor, as if the volumes had fallen there — but none of them had. She then heard a terrible scream, like the shriek of a murdered woman. Tyra turned back around and heard another thud on the rug at the base of the stairs.

This mansion was haunted.

"Ghost?" she cried. "Wherever you are, come back here!"

All of a sudden, the front door latch shattered to splinters and the door burst open. A fierce wind entered the hall, fanning the embers in the fireplace and blowing out Tyra's candle. She stumbled backward in the dark, tripped over the rug, and landed on her back.

The goat was standing under the doorframe. Even at this distance, Tyra saw anger in its eyes. A new flame burst in the hearth as the creature placed a hoof over the threshold.

Before her very eyes, the hoof twisted into a human hand.

The goat's front legs morphed into arms, the joints curling and stretching with sickening cracks. Its back hoofs swelled into human feet while its front femurs extended, bursting out into thin legs. In a few short seconds, the creature turned into an old woman with hunched shoulders. She wore a tattered black dress, her head covered in white-gray strands of hair. Her cold eyes chilled Tyra to the bone.

With nowhere else to run, Tyra bolted for the stairs.

"Stop her!"

When Tyra reached the first step, something knocked the wind out of her. A stony fist, belonging to one of the coarsely chiseled gargoyles, had blocked her escape. Both turned their heads and blinked dust from their eyes. Terrified, Tyra skittered back and pulled out her dagger.

"Seize her!"

Something caught hold of Tyra's ankle. The rug's thick, wool fibers had woven around her boots, anchoring her feet to the floor. Slashing to free herself, Tyra lost her balance and fell on her hands and knees. Her dagger slipped out of reach. Several new fibers rose up and tied down her wrists. The woman laughed and rubbed her old hands together.

"I warned you to turn back, child. Why did you not listen?"

Tyra searched for a scream as the witch drew near.

14

THE MOUNTAIN WITCH

The dark hallways made it difficult for Nels to see.

Like the entryway, dust, cobwebs, and more dust covered everything he saw, be it tables or lofty chairs. Green paper lined the walls, etched with fancy floral designs that had a silvery sheen, even in the dark. Nels walked along, door to door, poking his head into each room in the left wing, only to find more dusty furniture. The house held no sign of life, much less a shadowed book.

A dark figure caught the corner of his eye as he strolled down the next hall. Nels flew around the corner, but saw no one. He could have sworn there was a woman in a black dress.

A light bled through the space beneath a closed door ahead. Returning to the floor, Nels approached and took a breath before he passed through. On the other side, Nels thought he had stepped into a dream. Lit candles were everywhere, a fire was burning in the hearth, and not a speck of dust tarnished the colorful walls, the floor, or the four-poster bed with its deep red curtains. Compared to the rest of the unkempt house, this bedroom was immaculate — clean enough for someone to sleep in.

"Is someone here?" he asked, not that he expected anyone to hear him.

After a brief look around, Nels saw for himself that no one was inside the room. Above the mantle hung a huge portrait of a young woman sitting in a garden. The woman in the portrait had long ebony hair and a lovely smile, and the walls of Castle Avërand were behind her. She wore the same dress as the figure he had seen, or thought he had seen. Suddenly, the fire in the hearth billowed, and when he looked up again, the woman in the portrait had a knife stuck in her chest.

Her eyes flew open, and she unleashed a blood-curdling scream. Startled, Nels stepped back. When he looked again, the portrait had returned to normal. If he had a heart, it would be pounding.

That woman — was she a ghost?

If so, she wasn't like him or Yalva; she was more of a presence than a person.

Another scream seized him, coming from below. "Tyra?"

He heard it again. It *was* her scream. She was in trouble!

Without thinking twice, Nels dived into the floorboards as if they were the waters of a placid lake. He sunk through wooden supports, iron bracers, and ceiling plaster until he reached the main hall. It was much brighter than before, more than when he'd first entered.

Tyra was bound on all fours, kneeling before an old woman.

The Mountain Witch!

Nels swooped down and crouched in front of Tyra. When he glanced up, the woman was still closing in, her weathered face shrouded by gray and white hair. Tyra's dagger lay on the floor. Nels picked it up and waved it in front of the witch. The old woman jumped back as she stared at the floating knife, her blue eyes widening. When she was far enough away, Nels saw Tyra's wrists — both tied to the rug, its threads slithering over her skin like woolen snakes. He cut them off and pulled Tyra free; the threads wove quickly back into their old seams. He then shielded Tyra and brandished her dagger at the witch, ready to use it if he had to.

"Where were you?" Tyra asked, quivering behind him.

"I shouldn't have gone off alone. I'm sorry."

"Don't ever leave me like that again!"

Trembling, the witch took a step back. "What are you muttering, child?" Before Tyra could say anything, the woman's eyes widened. "What have I done?" The witch threw herself to the floor. She bowed her head so low that they could no longer see her face. "Do not cast a spell. I beg you!"

At a loss for words, Nels glanced at Tyra. Her puzzled expression told him their confusion was mutual. "M-Miss . . . W-Witch?" Tyra stuttered. "What are you talking about?"

The witch pointed a shaky finger at the floating knife. Nels returned the dagger to Tyra, who grasped it without taking her eyes off the old woman.

"What are you doing in my home?" the witch asked, looking miserable on her knees. "I thought all the conjurers returned to Cravélle, beyond the White Sea?"

"But you're a conjurer," Tyra said, "are you not?"

"No," the woman answered. "You are the only witch here."

Reminded of a similar comment he had made to Tyra on the first night they spoke, Nels snorted. Tyra glared at him. Straightening his stance, Nels cleared his throat and kept his guard up. This woman had given them a start. She could still do something terrible to Tyra if she wanted to.

"But you were a goat a moment ago," Tyra said. "How are you *not* a witch?"

"It is a curse," the woman answered. "I change whenever I leave this house."

Nels focused on the woman. Was what she said even possible? He should have taken Tyra's concerns a bit more seriously when she complained about the talking goat.

"But that rug," Tyra pointed, "and those statues —"

"This mansion does whatever I wish," said the woman.

Tyra shook back her tousled hair. "You're *not* the Mountain Witch?"

"I am Gleesel. The *witch* you speak of is Sibylla." The woman pointed at the youngest girl in the portrait above the fireplace. The man sitting between the two girls must have been their father. Sadness and anger prevailed in her voice when she said the girl's name. "She is my sister."

"Oh," Tyra said. "Is she home? I need her help."

Gleesel frowned. "She . . . she cannot help you."

Tyra looked at Nels for a second. "Why not?"

"Why do you need her help, conjuress? Will you lift my curse?"

"I can't," Tyra confessed. "I'm not what you think I am."

The woman stared at her. "You're not a conjurer?"

Tyra shook her head. "I'm Tyra, the Princess of Avërand."

Gleesel stood up. Astonishment washed over her. "A princess? In my house?" She glanced at the fireplace and walked to it. "Clear out," she said. "Her Highness and I need a place to sit."

The moment she said this, two white sheets flung into the air and exposed two comfortable-looking chairs with tall backs. Gleesel sat in one and invited Tyra to have the other. Tyra bit her lip and looked at Nels before she accepted. "The Princess of Avërand in my home. This is an unexpected surprise!" The woman pressed her hands against each other before she raised her fingers to touch the end of her nose. "If you have no magic, how did your dagger protect you?"

"You won't believe this" — that same embarrassed expression appeared on her face again, the one that manifested whenever she tried to tell someone about him — "it was held by a ghost."

"A ghost, you say?" Gleesel laughed. "I suppose I should believe you."

Her reaction surprised Tyra and Nels both. "You should?" Tyra asked.

"It explains why you spoke to yourself. Ghosts are all too real — I should know." Gleesel reached for something around her neck. Nels hadn't seen it before: a bronze trinket, bell-shaped with dimples, fastened to a chain. It was a thimble, just like the one Bosh had given to him.

Why does she have one?

"What I have a hard time believing is you, here, in the middle of a storm." Gleesel ran her fingers through her hair, taking several strands of it with each stroke. It looked more like goat hair than human hair. "I'm curious, Princess. Why would you come all this way with a ghost?"

"I was told you have a shadowed book," Tyra answered.

The woman heaved a wry sigh. "I knew someone would come for that. Even if I were to show you, you cannot read the book. Only a skilled conjurer can see what is written."

"Can your sister read it for us?" Tyra asked.

Gleesel stared at her. "My sister is dead."

Dead? Nels looked at the portrait again. Gleesel was clearly the older of the two girls. Sibylla resembled the young woman in the portrait upstairs. Her ghost was somewhere in the house — he knew it. If they could find her, she could give them the information they were searching for.

"I'm sorry," Tyra said. "It must have been a terrible loss."

"More than that," Gleesel said. "She was the only one capable of lifting my curse. I can only be human inside this

168

house." She held up her thimble and dangled it from her chain like a tiny bell. "Answer me, Princess. What information could that book possibly hold for you?"

"I don't want it," she answered. "It's not for me."

"Not for you?" The woman scoffed. "Then whom is it for?"

"It's rather complicated . . . You see, we were told your book can tell us where to find a Needle that can sew a ghost back to life." She glanced down. "I'm trying to save him."

Her sincerity surprised Nels. He liked the way she'd said that. The storm outside had quieted down. The fire crackled and popped. Gleesel gazed into the hot flames. "You're looking for *that*, are you? I have heard of it, this Needle. It is a tool for Fabrication, said to hold powers beyond imagination." She laughed. "My father went in search for it . . . and he never came back. Who told you about this Needle?"

"My tailor," Tyra answered. "He told us to start here."

Gleesel glanced at Tyra's dress. "What is his name?"

"Bosh, I believe."

The firelight reflected in the woman's eyes as she held her thimble tightly. "Ickabosh?" Gleesel leaped to her feet and grabbed Tyra by the shoulders. "He's alive?" Surprised by the woman's speed, Nels seized Gleesel's wrists and pulled her away from Tyra with a yank. She let go of the princess the moment he touched her. Silence divided them. Gleesel rubbed her wrist and looked at Tyra with a hopeful glimmer in her eye. "Your ghost is rather protective of you."

Tyra blushed. Nels couldn't help but notice. "How does she know Bosh?"

"How do you know Bosh?" Tyra asked for him.

Gleesel sighed. "He was Threadbare's apprentice — and the love of my life."

"He was?!" Tyra and Nels asked in unity, Tyra leaning forward in her chair.

The woman nodded. "My father went to help Threadbare with some crisis in the land of Mendarch. The journey changed him. Whatever the crisis was, he was never the same after that. He whisked us to this place, made it our home, and forbade us from ever going to Avërand. But I had to see Ickabosh, so I disobeyed him. When my father found out, he cursed me."

Nels understood. Her thimble was a gift. "How come Bosh never mentioned her?"

"Bosh never mentioned you," Tyra said. "Did something happen between you?"

"While my father and sister were away, Ickabosh came to the house to convince me to run away with him, but I could not — because of the curse. I was too embarrassed to tell him. And I knew what my father would do if he learned of Ickabosh's trespass. There was only one thing I could do to protect him. I lied. I told him to leave and never return. I told him I did not love him. He left me, his heart undoubtedly as broken as mine. I have regretted that lie ever since." The woman cupped her cheek with her hand. "My father was certain he knew where the Needle was. He went to find it and left me with a curse that my sister could not undo. My father vanished and my sister died. Everyone I loved has left me."

Nels was captivated by the woman's tragic story. Tyra, resting her own chin on her cupped hands, seemed to be even more captivated. No one spoke. Only the draft and the fire drew breath.

"I'm glad you're here, Princess. It's been a long time since I've had company. I'm sorry that I cannot be of more help to you, but there is no way I can read that book."

"If you can't read it, do you think a ghost can?" Tyra asked.

Nels liked the suggestion. He was quite good at seeing in the dark now.

"Ghosts are said to see what mortals cannot, so it is possible." Gleesel raised her head. "I will show you, if you promise to see Ickabosh for me. Will you tell him I'm sorry?"

Tyra glanced at Nels, her brow raised. "I certainly will!"

Gleesel stood from her chair. She picked up a candle and a flame lit on its wick as she held it upright. "The book is in the east wing; this way." She strolled over to the stairs, still blocked by the two hulking gargoyles. They had massive, powerful shoulders and beast-like faces. "Back to yourselves." Like shifting millstones, their arms moved and their hands clasped over their knees. Gleesel reached for the banister to steady herself. "Come."

Relieved, Nels followed Tyra as she reached the stairs and ascended with the woman. The steps creaked, but only for Tyra and Gleesel. Ornate decorations greeted their eyes as they mounted the landing, but they didn't stop long enough to admire them. They continued on, deep into the mansion, every corner piled with dust. A grand clock and countless paintings covered the richly colored walls, depicting places different from the kingdom of Avërand. They turned a corner into another hall.

"How did your sister die?" Tyra asked suddenly.

Nels turned to the princess. "Let her take us to the book first."

Tyra swatted at him.

The woman stopped and spoke without turning around. "It's too terrible. I don't wish to discuss it." Before they could say anything more, she continued. "There's nothing we can do for her. I will show you the book, but I ask that you not bring this up again." Gleesel sighed as she pressed on.

Nels and Tyra followed her. "What was that about?" he asked.

"She's not telling us everything," Tyra whispered. By the suspicious frown on her face and the sound of her voice, Nels could tell something was troubling her. "When I was alone, I heard a struggle and a scream, but I couldn't see it. I think something terrible happened in this place."

"I saw something before you screamed," Nels said. "Let Gleesel show us this book before you ask her anything else." She flashed him a look, and he shrugged. "Just a suggestion."

Gleesel paused before a narrow flight of stairs, the steps thin and steep. Only one person could go up them at a time. "Light up, candles! Light up, lanterns!" Small flames effloresced onto the wicks of various candles in mounted holders, brightening the ascending stairs.

"I wish my candles could do that," Tyra said.

Nels laughed. "Your servants don't light your candles at your command?"

She smirked back. "Not *that* fast."

"Let me go first, Princess," Gleesel said. "I'm not so young anymore. Many years have gone since I last went up these steps. I may need your help if I am to reach the top."

Tyra peered up the dark stairs. "Well, go on and have a look, ghost."

Complying with her wish, Nels floated through the trap door. A small room caught his eye, the only trace of light coming through a window on the other side when the lightning flashed. The ceiling was low and angled, like the attic of a textile shop he once explored as a child.

Before the rain-streaked window was an old desk.

A thick book lay on its dusty surface.

15

THE SHADOWED BOOK

A thick layer of dust slid over the trapdoor's hinges as it opened behind Nels. Candlelight spilled into the attic, throwing the shadows aside. Not a single rafter was without spiderwebs, their eight-legged inhabitants, or the dried remains of flies, beneath them. Brittle and discolored candles lay on the desk, their rancid wax nibbled on by rodents. No one had set foot in this room for years.

"Light up," Gleesel commanded. "All of you, light up!"

Wicks sparked to life in the lanterns above Nels, giving the room enough light to reveal the grime he had missed. The woman struggled out of the hatch, fanning the dusty air with her hand.

Tyra's head popped up next. Her eyes explored the room.

"There's the book." Gleesel pointed at the desk. "Take your time."

Tyra coughed as she neared the desk and pinched the cloth jacket with her fingers. "This is what we came for," she said, looking at Nels. "You want me to open it?" When he nodded, she carefully parted the volume. She leafed through the first few pages, but none of them contained any writing, not a single line. "Gleesel's right. I don't see a thing. What about you?"

Nels looked over her shoulder and scanned the next page. It, too, was blank. He reached over Tyra's arm and leafed to the next one. He turned to another page, and then another, frantically searching the book for a scribble, a blotch of ink, anything — but there was nothing.

Nels's hand trembled as he turned another page. "I see nothing."

Tyra heaved a sigh. "So we climbed this mountain for nothing, you mean."

Flipping through the rest of the volume, Nels reached the back of the book. There were hundreds of pages, but not a single one had writing. Nels faced Tyra, ready to admit defeat, when a young girl appeared next to Tyra, right before his eyes. She materialized out of nothing, as though a mix of vapor and moonlight. She ran right up to Nels, like a memory from the past.

"Sing Mother's lullaby," she said, and then she was gone.

Nels swallowed, amazed by what he had seen. "Did you see that?"

Tyra perked her head up and scanned the room. "See what?"

"Another ghost; a child — I think it was Sibylla."

"Really? Where is she?"

"She's gone now, but she told me to me to sing Mother's lullaby."

"Sing Mother's lullaby? What does that mean?"

"What did you say?" Gleesel gasped behind them.

Tyra looked at her. "Does that mean something to you?"

The old woman's arms shook, as if she were terrified. "My sister often wanted me to sing a lullaby to her, after our mother passed away. I never had the heart to sing it again."

"My ghost just saw your sister," Tyra said. "I think she wants you to sing it."

Lowering her head, Gleesel turned away. "I cannot bring myself to."

"But this lullaby could mean something; you have to try."

The woman crossed her arms with a defiant glance.

"Please, Gleesel," Tyra begged. "Recite it for us?"

After a moment, Gleesel cleared her throat and raised her chin; a new resolve made her look slightly younger. "If it will bring peace to her soul, I will," she said. Then she started to sing:

> "Do not tremble, dear child.
> Trust in the darkness, now.
> Treasures await, dear child.
> Nothing there harms, I vow.

> "The sun is gone, dear child.
> Let the shadows take form.
> The moonlight glows, dear child,
> Beyond the coming storm.

> "Darkness abounds with no light,
> Magic roams beyond the sight.
> Like the gentle wings of a lark,
> You will find it in the dark . . ."

As she trailed to a stop, Tyra placed her hand on the woman's shoulder. Gleesel turned and embraced Tyra, gently reciprocating her touch. "Oh, Sibylla — why did you leave me?" Tyra's eyes shifted to Nels. All she could do was allow the woman to hold her, and all he could do was shrug. "Those verses have restored memories, locked away inside my mind for many, long years." Gleesel let Tyra go. "Forgive me, Sibylla. I know you tried. Please forgive me . . ."

A strong gust of wind splashed sheets of rain against the window.

"A riddle," Tyra said. "*You will find it in the dark . . .* I know!"

She left Gleesel, ran up to the nearest candle, and blew it out — but she did not stop there. She went to the next flame, and the one after that, and the ones after that, slowly vanquishing all the light in the room. Nels didn't know what she was doing, but the old woman nodded her head, as if she had come to an understanding of her own. "Be dark," Gleesel commanded. "All lights, all candles. Snuff yourselves out!"

Darkness ensued as the flames died — but only for a second. "Look!" Tyra cried. "The book!"

Nels spun around. Words appeared inside the book, spreading across the pages in small green letters. Each new sentence cast an emerald light into the room, emanating a soft glow with every word. Tyra flipped through the pages, where the same transformation was happening to all of them.

Tears welled in Gleesel's eyes. "*You will find it in the dark . . .* I understand now; who would think to read in the dark? Not I!" She neared Tyra and beamed gratefully at her. "Without you and your ghost, I never would have discovered the truth. Thank you. Thank you so much!"

As Nels glanced at Tyra, she gave him a warm, sincere smile.

"Now it's time for me to help you." Gleesel took up the book and held it firmly. "An account of the Needle should be here." She flipped a few pages back. "Here is my father's last entry."

They stared at the words as the woman read them:

I, Oyren, am set to embark on a task that may lay claim to my life, for I know the secret that ties us all. I have found and removed all signs that would lead one to the Needle of Gailner.

No one can find it now — as no one should — and only by these words can I contain the truth: Hidden deep in Westmine's treasury is the Weaver's Gate.

From there, I will enter. I will find and use the Needle to mend what was torn and return the thread that does not belong in our world.

Some secrets should never be found.

Some gates are meant to stay closed.

Nels stared at the passage, the words leaving him with more questions. "A Weaver's Gate . . . a thread that doesn't belong in our world . . . what do you think Oyren meant?"

Tyra shook her head. "I've never heard of any of this before."

"We'll have to go to Westmine to find out for ourselves."

"The Valley of Westmine? Are you telling me we have to travel to the other side of the mountain now?" Tyra let out another long sigh. "Must we really go there?"

Gleesel gasped. "Please reconsider, child. That place is unsafe."

"I have no choice," Tyra said. "Why is the valley unsafe?"

The woman waved her hand. Every lantern lit up again. "After King Hilvar's demise, he became a draug. His presence brought ruin upon the grand city of Westmine, and a great darkness came over his castle. No one dares to inhabit it, and my father never returned from it." Gleesel closed the book. "My room is the only clean one in this house. You are welcome to it, Princess."

"I can't take your room," Tyra declared. "Where will you sleep?"

"I couldn't possibly sleep!" Gleesel patted the book. "With this, I may lift my curse tonight. It might hold something useful for your journey, too. Help me downstairs, will you?"

Nels stood still, thinking about the Needle as Tyra left to assist the woman.

Is the Needle of Gailner in Westmine? Could it really be in Hilvar's treasury?

He didn't know for sure. Whatever this Weaver's Gate was, maybe it led to the Needle's whereabouts. Knowing that it lay somewhere else was a disappointment, given their short time to find it. And, according to Lars, the blacksmith, people did not go to Westmine anymore. They feared the wrath of Hilvar's ghost. Even Tyra's history lesson had affirmed that the haunting of Hilvar was responsible for Westmine's fall and desertion. Nels gathered his confidence. Draug or not, they would find the Needle, even if they had to search the entire Valley of Westmine.

"Put out those lights, will you, ghost?" Tyra asked as she ducked out of view.

Nels was about to carry out her request when an apparition materialized before him. Floating by the window was a woman wearing a black dress, the same woman from the dark hallway and from the portrait he had seen in the bedroom below. Gleesel's sister smiled at Nels.

Her eyes gleamed in the darkness. "Thank you."

She passed through the window and disappeared into the storm.

Gleesel's bed was like a cloud compared to what Tyra had slept on the night before, but still she woke early, troubled by a dream. She had seen her father walking in a forest, but no matter how loud she spoke or how hard she screamed, she remained invisible to him. The thought chilled her, despite the bed quilts that were almost *too* warm.

Before she met him, the peasant had experienced that same loneliness.

Tyra cast her eyes to the window; dawn was breaking. A fire danced in the hearth, casting enough light to define the red-and-gold walls of Gleesel's room. The evidence of Avërand's artisanship was noticeable in the molding, the rafters, and every cleft and corner.

A book lay open on a small table by the door, and there was a chair beside it. The peasant had been sitting there when she drifted off to sleep.

"Ghost?" she called out. No answer. *Where is he?*

Tyra stretched before she slipped out of bed. Her hair felt tangled in places, but then her nose caught a delightful aroma. It made her hungry. As Tyra stepped into the hall, the sun peeked over the horizon, barely illuminating luscious green-and-gold walls and a dark marble floor. To her amazement, the dilapidated state of the mansion had changed completely. All dust and every trace of grime was gone. Everything looked perfect, like any of the mansions she'd known at home.

Has Gleesel learned the secrets of her book already?

Something wonderful was baking downstairs.

Reminded of her reason for leaving, Tyra lifted her skirt and walked to the stairs. The steps were also spotless, just like the halls. The delicious scent was strongest at the bottom of the stairs.

She reached the rug and looked around. "Where is that smell coming from?"

The grinding sound of moving stone startled her, making her jump back. Without looking at her, one of the gargoyles at the base of the stairs raised its hand and pointed to the door at her left.

"Uh." Tyra wasn't sure if she should curtsy or not. "Thank you."

The statue returned to its post. Tyra left it alone and went through the side door.

Moving gargoyles — the mansion's magic continued to amaze her!

After a moment of searching, she finally heard Gleesel's laughter behind a swinging door. A kitchen lay beyond it. A hardwood table and a heaping platter of fruit, bread, and a bowl of steaming oatmeal caught her attention. The peasant was sitting across from Gleesel with a sheet of parchment before him and a quill in his hand. A drastic change had occurred in the woman, her face now cheerful — younger looking, even. Her eyes beamed with newfound hope.

Gleesel looked up at Tyra and smiled. "You're awake, sooner than I thought!"

Tyra grinned back as she eyed the parchment. "What's that?"

"What's what?" The peasant leaned over the writings.

"I hope you don't mind me borrowing your ghost," Gleesel said. "I read through the book and practiced all night, thinking I could find a remedy for you." The woman pushed her chair back and stood up. "Listen to me talk! Have a seat, Your Highness. Eat. You must be off soon."

Tyra hesitated before she accepted the chair and placed herself opposite the peasant. The woman had her back to them. With an oversized stick that looked more like an oar, she stirred the contents of a cauldron. Tyra turned to the peasant, who seemed rather nervous.

"I didn't know you could write," she said.

He smirked. "There's a lot you don't know about me."

"You could have written to your mother, or anyone else for that matter."

"That was before I could touch things. You're still the only one who can see me."

"I would very much like to know *why* I'm the only one who can see you." Even after her visit with the tailor, she still didn't understand. She stole a quick glance at the parchment. It read more like a conversation. The ghost had used it to communicate with Gleesel, his writing neat and pleasing to the eye — much too pleasing for the hand of a commoner. "Your mother taught you how to read and write?"

"And sew," he added, "but I can't do more than patch jobs."

A spoon tapped the cauldron's lip. Gleesel hummed, distracting Tyra from reading what the peasant had asked in his writings. He had questioned Gleesel about her dead sister and had asked if a man named Rasmus was the one who killed Sibylla. Noticing Tyra's prying eyes, the peasant crumpled the parchment and threw it to the embers in the hearth. It burst into flame.

If there was anything the peasant seriously lacked, it was subtlety.

"I didn't know your sister was murdered," Tyra said to Gleesel. "What happened?"

The peasant shook his head as the woman returned with a wooden bowl, her voice hesitant. "I was not in the house when she died. When I came back inside, I found her at the stairs with a knife in her heart. I do not wish to discuss it further." She placed the bowl in front of Tyra. A creamy green goop bubbled in the dish. "You should eat this."

Tyra nearly gagged. "May I ask what *this* is?"

"A cure," Gleesel answered, "for your cold."

"But I don't have a cold."

"You will if you refuse," she insisted. "Your exposure to that storm was more than enough to chill your bones."

Tyra looked doubtfully into her bowl. The ghost seemed just as unsure about the substance. Raising her spoon, Tyra dipped it into the ooze and placed it in the back of her mouth. She swallowed fast but was surprised by a sweet, creamy taste. Whatever the concoction was, it left her refreshed.

"I will pack you a flask," Gleesel said. "You'd best be prepared if caught in the rain again."

The woman left and began to search through a few cupboards.

Tyra filled her plate with food. "I cannot believe how good this is." The peasant's eyes shifted as she took a bite of a pear cobbler sitting on the table. "What are you keeping from me?" she asked suspiciously.

He gave her a blank stare. "What makes you say that?"

"People don't burn their writings unless they have something to hide."

"You should finish your breakfast," he said.

Tyra shook her head. "You can be such a headache."

Nels shrugged. "I've heard the high mountain air can do that to your head."

"Speaking of mountains, how are we going to get Brooklet? We left her on the trail."

"She is fine, Your Highness." As Gleesel turned around, she traced her finger along a line of ingredients. "I prepared a trough of oats for her. She will be ready to leave when you are."

Tyra's heart calmed, but her mind still wondered. How did the woman bring Brooklet up to the mansion? The wall at the end of the mountainous trail had to be a ten-foot climb. Had Gleesel gleaned some magic from her father's book? She must have. Now that she had the book, perhaps Gleesel could become a conjurer herself. Taking a deep breath, Tyra returned to her meal, then noticed a large bowl of fresh lingonberries, her favorite wild fruit.

She took the whole dish.

The peasant gave her an amused smile. "It's like you haven't eaten in a week."

"I've had nothing but a knapsack to live on for two days," Tyra countered as she rolled her eyes. "You *are* going to tell me what else you and Gleesel were talking about, right?"

"We talked about you, mostly. She told me things about her father, too."

Gleesel's hand touched the corner of the table, leaving a pouch next to Tyra.

The princess eyed it carefully, wondering what it could be. "You're not having me sample anything else, are you?"

"No, child." The woman chortled. "It's a special item that once belonged to my dear sister. It should bring you added clarity as you seek the lost Needle of Gailner."

Tyra unfastened the knot on the small, velvet pouch and plopped a small ring into her palm. There was nothing elegant or special about the ring; it was simple, made of iron, and within its setting it contained a green stone, speckled with red spots. It was one of the most ordinary pieces of jewelry that Tyra had ever seen, but she didn't want to be rude; that would be ignoble. "Oh, I couldn't take something so precious to you," she said.

"Nonsense!" Gleesel said. "I would like you to have it — I insist."

Tyra was moved by the old woman's gesture, plain as the old piece of jewelry was. "Thank you," she said. "I appreciate your thoughtfulness." Tyra swallowed her food, still annoyed by Nels's secrecy. If he refused to answer her questions, then perhaps Gleesel would oblige. "I saw what my ghost wrote, Gleesel. Who is Rasmus?"

The woman was about to answer when the peasant nudged Tyra's bowl of lingonberries off the table. Porcelain shattered and spread over the stone floor, making Gleesel jump back.

Tyra leaped to her feet as well. He had done this on purpose!

Why would he do such a thing? What is he hiding?

"You should be going, Princess." Gleesel stooped down to clean up the mess. "Nothing I can say will lead you closer to what you must find. I wish you well on your journey."

As Tyra's temper flared, she placed the ring on the table, walked by the peasant, and then paused at the door. The peasant eyed her apologetically, but Tyra wasn't convinced.

"You're not helpless anymore," she said. "Find the Needle yourself."

With a brief farewell to Gleesel, Tyra retrieved her dried cloak and placed it around her shoulders. She found Brooklet outside, contentedly feasting on oats in a trough at the base of the porch steps. After she brushed the mare's side, Tyra continued down the path until she reached the edge of the cliff and the path that would take her home. She stumbled a little, and her heart pounded as she took in the sights. They had climbed rather high in the middle of the storm.

The trail wound endlessly downward, back and forth, until the forest shrouded the path at the bottom. No wonder the trail was so hard on Brooklet; the path was much too steep for her.

From this height, as the sun rose in the sky, Tyra could see the ocean and the castle before it. The sun's rays touched the peaks behind her. In no time at all, the dawn had revealed a land of flowing waters, green hills, and ample forests. She had never before seen Avërand like this, from mountain to sea — her kingdom was vast and beautiful. Avërand had always seemed large from her bedroom window, but standing here had truly put the immense kingdom in scale.

One day, she would rule this land. The thought of it made her feel small and unprepared.

"You were right," the peasant said. "Rasmus killed Sibylla."

Taking a deep breath, Tyra turned around and awaited his explanation.

"He killed her in the main hall. That scream you heard was her — an echo." He came to Tyra's side, took her hand, and placed Sibylla's ring in her palm. "Because of her, we know where to go." He stepped forward, his toes aligned with the cliff's edge. "I should have told you sooner, but I thought you'd be safer not knowing."

"How can I trust you if you're keeping secrets from me?"

An apologetic look replaced his determined face. "You're right. I'm sorry," he said.

Tyra released the tension from her shoulders. "That's better. Will you tell me your secrets now?"

"Rasmus was the man who tried to kill me. He murdered my father, your grandfather, and who knows how many others." Nels looked at her nervously. "Bosh told me a few others things, too, after you left me alone with him."

"What exactly did he tell you?" Tyra asked, shocked by this new information.

"A lot, and I want to tell you, but I don't know if you can handle it."

"As the heir to the throne, I should be able to handle anything."

"Our parents betrothed us."

Tyra's stomach fell, her voice caught in her throat. She forgot how to speak.

The peasant gave her a light smile. "Handling that?"

"I'm betrothed to *you*?" She could not fathom the notion. Them? Married? A peasant and a princess — she'd never heard of such a thing. "That's impossible! Why should I believe you?"

"I couldn't believe it myself. That's why I didn't tell you."

Her thoughts numbing, all Tyra could do was breathe.

"My mother was a noblewoman," he added, "and my father was a friend to yours — when they were young. My father used to be the favored knight of Avërand, too. Should I go on?"

Tyra wanted nothing more than to remove his words from her mind, to forget she even heard them. "That's enough, thank you." She turned to the lowlands. The sun's light sparkled on the faraway ocean — a warm sight, contrary to the cold breeze she felt. She couldn't turn back now. He needed her. No one ever needed her. She couldn't leave him to die.

"I said I would help. I intend to keep my promise."

"Have you ever seen a view like this before?"

Tyra shook her head. "No. Not ever."

He glanced at her. "Neither have I."

She returned his glance and she didn't turn away. Something about his dark green eyes made her wonder what he was thinking — and what he thought of her. She looked deep into them. Really deep. She truly wanted to know. Tyra saw the ridge of his lips and how calm and serious the rest of him appeared. "If I am to journey with you any farther, tell me everything."

"Little by little," he half agreed. "It won't be such a shock that way."

"Right." Feeling the ring in her hand, Tyra decided to try it on. It fit her finger well, as if the iron band was made for her. "You can start by telling me about this Rasmus."

The peasant was about to speak when he looked over the

cliff. Curious, Tyra peered over the side with him. She saw two animals — two horses — making their way up the steep trail. It was hard to tell who was riding them, but they rode fast. They would reach the clearing in no time.

She recognized one of the animals — a black stallion.

"Arek!" Tyra cried. "He's caught up with us!"

The peasant grabbed her wrist. "We have to leave."

Tyra yanked back, trying to reclaim her hand. "Let go!"

He released her, clearly disturbed. "How did he catch up with us so fast?" The peasant suddenly turned away, his face intense, as though he were angry — and terrified.

Tyra shook her head. "What's wrong with you, ghost?"

"You have to trust me." He held her shoulders with a strong grip. "From now on, we can't trust anyone." The peasant let go of her as he ran for the mansion to untie Brooklet's bridle.

Tyra couldn't understand — why was he so afraid of her knight? If anything, he would help them find the Needle faster. "You're being ridiculous, ghost," she said. "There's nothing to worry about."

He continued with his work without heeding her. Fidgeting with the ring on her finger, Tyra saw something different about the stone. A black rock, dark as midnight, had replaced the olive-green gem with its dark red spots. Tyra examined it for a moment. Why had the stone changed?

"Odd," she said to herself.

Relieved as she was to see Arek, the peasant's urgency caused her more alarm than she expected. She wanted to run to Arek, but in her heart, she agreed with the ghost. If she waited for Arek to reach them, she knew what would happen: He would refuse to help. He would force her to go home.

She looked over the side of the ledge, her heart torn in two, then left to find Brooklet.

The false squire waited for the knight to emerge from the decrepit mansion. He knew the princess had long since left this place — searching the mansion was a waste of time — but he had no idea where she had gone. Other than along the path they had come, there was no way to leave the meadow except for the westward trail. But why would she enter the valley? Unless . . .

Is that where the Needle lies?

What stumped him even more was her horse. The wall at the end of the trail was too high for their steeds to climb, but her mare had come this way somehow. No horse could jump such a wall.

Has Ickabosh found himself a new apprentice?

Arek stepped out the front door, brushing dust from his shoulder. "This place is a wreck!" he bellowed. "Who in their right mind would build a mansion here and abandon it?"

"Someone who isn't in his right mind?" Alvil answered.

Arek smiled. "She was here, though. I just know it."

"Her captor may have taken her down the other side of the mountain."

"Yes." The knight looked to the trail with a slow nod. "Into Westmine."

"They can't be far," Alvil said. "We should press on."

"No. Take the horses back. I will go after her alone."

Alvil blinked. "She can't be more than an hour off!"

"Westmine is dangerous. One can slip in and out better than two."

"Without a horse? Our chances of finding her are better together!"

Arek turned his back on him. "As my squire, you will do as you are told!"

Until now, Rasmus — as Alvil — had barely tolerated Arek. The knight's voice, and the condescension behind his words, reminded Rasmus of a wealthy lord he once knew who had frequently satisfied himself with drink — and any woman he could lure with gold. Even as a child, Rasmus couldn't tolerate his father's infidelity, least of all the way he struck Rasmus at the whims of his short temper. The act of spilling his father's blood freed him then. Spilling the knight's blood would free him now.

With knife in hand, Alvil moved close to the knight and satisfied the urge that had lingered with him for far too long. Arek let out a sharp gasp as he stumbled and fell to his side by the trail's edge. He rolled onto his back, his hazel eyes staring in dismay as Alvil's face unraveled — and wove into his.

"I do as I wish," the boy said, using Arek's voice.

Struggling for breath, the knight fell to the ground, a pool of blood spreading beneath him. The imposter held out his arms and clapped his hands — a grassy mound slid over the knight like a blanket. He picked up Tyra's handkerchief and cleaned his knife.

"I need the princess to trust me. Your face will suffice."

The false Arek approached the top of the cliff wall and swayed his palms. With his hands, he wove both ends of the trail, moving the earth down until they joined together in a gradual slope. The stallions below whinnied, startled by the sudden movement of the earth. The false Arek had one horse too many now; he couldn't risk having anyone find them. He pinched his forefinger with the tip of his thumb, reached for the thread of Alvil's horse, and yanked it to the side.

The animal screamed as it flew over the edge of the trail and plummeted to the jagged rocks below.

"Baaah!"

A bleating above the false Arek made him jump. Peering

at him over a dangerous ledge was a woolly goat. The creature bleated again, lowered its chin, and nibbled on a weed.

Shaking his head, the imposter mounted the knight's stallion and gave chase. He could not sense the princess, but he knew she was headed for the valley.

Nothing could keep him from her now.

16

A STONY CONSCIENCE

By noon, the peasant had guided Tyra to the upper hills of the Valley of Westmine. The west side of the mountain was steeper than the east, making their descent a relatively quick one. Tyra remembered Gleesel's instructions for them to reach Westmine City — west, south, and then west again — but as they journeyed deeper into the pine forest, she began to question their path on the unkempt trail. Few people had traveled this region; the thick overgrowth served as proof.

Even Arek would have a hard time tracking them here.

The peasant picked up a branch every once in a while and used it to sweep their tracks. Tyra couldn't understand what he was so worried about, and he was too busy helping her mare down the mountain to answer. No matter what the peasant did, nothing would keep her knight from finding them. The thought relieved her. He was the favored knight of Avërand, ever faithful, the man she had always dreamed of. He was a lover who would scour the globe on her behalf.

"You're sure quiet," the peasant said. "What's on your mind?"

Tyra tightened her grip on Brooklet's rein. "Nothing." As she answered, she noticed the ring on her finger. Its stone had turned black when she put it on. What would have caused it to change?

The peasant smirked. "You're always thinking about something."

"I *was* thinking, but my thoughts don't concern you."

"If you say so." The peasant started to hum a pleasant song to himself. "I've never seen a forest quite like this. What does it smell like?"

Tyra raised her brow and sniffed the air. "Trees . . . and fungus . . ."

He laughed. "I'd rather smell that than another whiff of beeswax." Still smiling, he tried to steal a glance at her. "Did you know about Bosh's Fabrication magic before all this?"

"No," she said. "I didn't." Up until now, magic was something she had only heard about in stories. She never imagined that magic was real. Tyra went to gather up Brooklet's loosened reins when she noticed the stone on her ring had changed. The black had turned back to green. Red spots speckled the surface once more. "Oh!"

"What is it?" the peasant asked. "Did you see something?"

"Uh . . . n-nothing," Tyra stammered. "It's nothing." But it *was* something, and it was happening again. A dark cloud crossed over the stone, and again it was as black as the bottom of a well.

"Have it your way."

Tyra examined the ring again, wondering if the stone had reacted to something she had said. Was it lies that made the stone change? Is that what Gleesel meant by added clarity? To find out, she had to test the stone. "I eat eggs for breakfast every morning."

The peasant stopped in his tracks and turned around. "What was that?"

Tyra focused her attention on the ring. The stone remained black. "I hate eggs." The blackness cleared, revealing a green luster. She cupped her hand over the other to conceal the ring from the peasant. This iron band contained a stone that revealed truth and deceit.

The peasant stared at her, clearly confused. "What are you talking about eggs for?"

"My dress is blue," Tyra said, smiling, as she watched the stone go black.

His brow creased, the ghost kept staring. "Are you feeling all right?"

Tyra didn't heed him; this was all too exciting. She had a ring that could detect the truth. Would it change color only for the person wearing it, or was its power beyond its possessor? She would have to test it to be certain. "Do you want to be united with your body, ghost?"

He seemed hesitant to answer. "You already know . . ."

"Of course I do," she said. "Answer my question."

He shrugged. "That's why we're here, isn't it?"

Tyra moved her hand enough to see the stone. It was green again — as she expected. Not only could the stone expose her lies and reveal her truth, it could do the same for anyone, even if they were dead. Such a ring would be the most valuable tool in the world. No one could ever lie to her. "Tell me a lie, ghost."

He wouldn't speak.

"Go on," she said. "Any old lie will do."

"What kind of request is that?"

"Oh, come now. Peasants lie as often as the sparrows fly."

He scowled. "You don't care about your people, do you?"

As the stone remained green, Tyra stared back at him. "I *do* care about them!" The moment she said this, blackness devoured the stone. Apparently, the ring didn't agree. Tyra slumped into her saddle, shoving her hand angrily into the folds of her skirt.

"The people in Cobblestown are some of the most honest and hardworking people I have ever known," he continued. "Why would you even say something like that?"

"Forget it . . . Don't speak to me unless spoken to."

The peasant's jaw clenched as he turned back to the path ahead.

Tyra could not understand. She cared about her people. She was obligated to. How could *that* be a lie? No matter how she tried to justify it, the small stone had spoken otherwise. Annoyed, she pulled the ring off her hand and tossed it quickly into her knapsack hanging around Brooklet's neck.

The afternoon had grown late when Tyra and the peasant reached a fork in their trail. Neither of them spoke much, which gave her an opportunity to listen and look about. The farther they traveled into the forest, the denser the trees became. At first the sky had peeked through the branches overhead, but eventually the trees blocked out every trace of the horizon and its darkening dusk.

Tyra grew displeased with the gnats that pestered her relentlessly, but it wasn't the insects that bothered her most — it was the ring. If that stone had turned black because she only claimed to care about her people . . . what did that mean? She didn't want to admit it, but the ring had revealed a truth that stung deeply. She hardly spoke that truth, even to herself.

The stone hadn't turned black for the peasant, but it had for her.

"There's no path to the south," he said. "Did we miss a crossroad?"

Their trail came to an end at a junction with faded signs, the remaining paths leading everywhere but south. Tyra dismounted to stretch her legs and to give Brooklet a rest. "Are we lost?"

"West, south, and west again," the peasant recited. "There's no trail to the south."

Opening the knapsack around Brooklet's neck, Tyra rummaged for a helping of Gleesel's bread. Traveling was terrible on her stomach. "The way south is clear and looks wide enough."

"I wouldn't call that overgrowth a clear path. Should we go west some more?"

Feeling the cold ring brush against her hand, Tyra came up with an idea. She slipped the ring on her finger. "The way to Westmine Castle is south and west of here." It turned green. Tyra smiled as she mounted Brooklet. "Think of it — we're looking for Westmine Castle, right?"

The peasant's bottom lip shifted to the side. "Right . . ."

"You know the legend about that castle being haunted?"

"Yeah," the peasant answered.

"Most people tend to avoid such places, which can only mean one thing: The path with the *most* overgrowth *is* the clearest way to the castle."

"I think you're right!" The peasant pointed to a space between the trees. "That might've been a path once."

Tyra pulled Brooklet's reins to the south. "You catch on quick, ghost."

Laughing, the peasant presented an exaggerated bow. "I do my best."

With a soft tap on Brooklet's side, they set off again and headed south, with nothing but the thin spaces between the trees to guide them. The peasant found a new branch and began to sweep at the prints as Brooklet made them. Tyra had nothing to worry about — not anymore.

This journey wasn't about her; it was to prove that she cared about others.

Together, they would find their way to Westmine City.

The sun set just as they came to a river. They crossed over shallow foam that drifted from a churning waterfall nearby. Nels stood close to the mare, making sure she stayed clear of the edge of another fall downstream. The valley's basin lay a short distance down the river, which led to a lake that reflected the orange heavens. In spite of their progress, Hilvar's castle was nowhere to be seen, even from their elevation. With no clear path left for them to follow, judging where to go next was nearly impossible in the dark. But the princess seemed confident in her direction.

Her eyes, for some reason, frequently strayed to the ring on her hand.

Nels jumped out of the water and floated above the bank.

Since taking the southward path, the rest of the day had gone by without so much as the beginning of an argument. Tyra's insults and haughtiness had toned down considerably, and this change caused Nels some concern. He had grown accustomed to her snide remarks. This new manner was disconcerting.

"There's not much more we can do tonight," Nels said. "You should rest."

Tyra looked up from her hand again. "Find us a camp."

Nels led them to an area near the lake's shore; it was surrounded by dying birches and pines. A few small flowers grew around the tree trunks. Now that the sun had set, it was hard to make out their fair colors. Nels kicked a few rocks aside and laid Tyra's quilt on a patch of ground.

Tyra dismounted. "I would like a fire." She stroked Brooklet's neck and unfastened her saddle. "I didn't think we would travel this far. Some flint would have been useful."

"Maybe it's for the best. A fire might attract attention."

Tyra removed her knapsack and bow. "We are surrounded by trees in the middle of a deserted forest," she implored. "No one will see a fire with this much cover."

Nels nodded. Maybe he was being too cautious. "I'll make a small one."

With a little effort, he gathered some tinder and a couple of stones and sparked up a modest fire. Tyra looked comfortable as she feasted on provisions, while her mare meandered to the lake for a drink. She finished off the last drops from her waterskin and then tossed it at Nels.

"Fetch me more water, will you?"

Picking up the skin, Nels retraced their steps and filled it at the waterfall. A thick mist drifted around him like a fog, the roar of the water deafening. At least he could hear it. When he came back, he found Brooklet resting. The princess, however, had a hand over her stomach.

He carried the water to her. "Are you sick?"

Tyra moaned as she took the waterskin. "Maybe . . ."

"Did you eat too fast?"

She shook her head.

Is she still upset with me?

Nels faced a dead tree, picked up a stick, and swung it like a sword.

"Do you often fight with unarmed trees?" Tyra said.

Surprised by the question, Nels turned back to face her. "I used to," he said, laughing. He had often parried with the dead oaks near his cottage, pretending to be a knight fighting for the kingdom. "I meant to apologize for what I said earlier, but you told me not to speak unless spoken to."

With a small smile, Tyra nodded. "A request you are presently violating, ghost."

Nels laughed again as he thrust his stick forward and slashed down, knocking loose bark from the trunk. "You can call me by my name, you know. Or have you forgotten it?"

"You will have to earn it," she said in an almost playful tone. Nels swung his stick high and then low, whacking at the decaying tree with merciless blows. The sound of his blows echoed back from the forest as dull thuds. Tyra reached for a stick of her own and stood up. "Your form is ghastly." She stepped forward, her arm raised.

Nels gave her a slight smile. "You think you can handle a branch better than I can?"

Without any warning, she swung her stick and slashed it through him.

"Hey!" Surprised, Nels jumped back and blocked her next blow.

"Bend your arms," she said. "Keep your elbows close to your center."

She continued to advance on him, thrusting and slashing with intense focus, her eyes keen and gleaming in sport. Nels could do nothing except deflect her blows and step away from her — until he remembered that he was a ghost. Smiling, he jumped over her head and waited for her to turn around. The hem of Tyra's dress whipped at her ankles.

"What was that?" she cried.

"Are there any rules about flying during a match?"

"No," she said. "Strike when you can. Use your advantage!"

Nels was unsure why, but they continued to duel. Only twice was he able to extend his arm to strike her. Tyra drove her weapon through the center of his chest once more. She was good — Nels could not argue that. He never expected that she could spar so well, even if she was only doing this to spite him — or was she? She did appear to be having fun.

He welcomed this foreign, playful side of her.

She swung forward with an uppercut, an easy block — or so Nels thought. "Make use of your surroundings," she commanded. "Your stance is everything. Hold your ground or you will never advance!"

Nels took the advice to heart and lunged at her, but he missed, and she swung her weapon next. Their sticks clashed. They paused, and their eyes met. Her eyelashes fluttered. The beauty in her eyes surpassed all her previous stares. Smiling, she jabbed her stick directly through Nels's throat.

She'd won.

"And never," she panted, "*ever* let your guard down."

Nels grabbed her stick and pulled it away from his neck. While Tyra was clearly out of breath, Nels wasn't winded in the slightest. He'd never learned so much about swordplay in a single match. Judging by Tyra's practiced stance and the range of motion she employed, he could tell that she'd gone easy on him. He had a lot to learn if he was to become a real knight.

Tyra glanced at his hand, gripping her weapon. Her breathing slowed as she stared into his eyes. "Not half bad," she told him, "even if you can't hold your ground against a lady."

"You're better than my friend Wallin. You're amazing!"

She smiled. "I know."

"Don't let it go to your head; I'll be ready next time."

"Sure." Her smile faded as she glanced downward.

Something troubled her.

"Is something wrong?" Nels asked.

"At the festival, they called you the Knight of Cobblestown. The whole village knew you, but I'd never seen you before."

Curious as to why she had brought this up, Nels tried to think of an excuse that wouldn't embarrass him. "Mother never let me go. That was the first festival I'd ever attended."

Tyra held on to her stick with both hands, her finger tracing the knots and loose bark. "Why did you want to become a knight, anyway?"

"My mother asked me the same thing before I died." Nels thought his dream had died with him. Now that he had another chance at life, his answer was no different. "I want to make a difference. I've always had a knack for helping others and solving problems."

Tyra greeted his eyes with a new smile. "You hardly need to be a knight to do that."

"You don't really mean that, do you?"

She turned away at that question. "What do you mean?"

"Isn't that why you like Arek, because he's a knight?"

Tyra's eyes shifted to the green stone on her finger.

Why does she keep looking at that?

"The people love him. They listen to him. He would make a great king."

"I don't think people like him as much as he thinks they do." There was no way to say that without sounding jealous, so Nels left it there. "You're their rightful heir. You should rule."

"I know," she snapped. "I'm forced to live with that thought every day, in everything I do, but . . . How can I live up to their expectations? What will happen when I fail them?"

"What makes you think you will?" Nels asked. "You haven't failed anyone."

Her eyes glistened in the firelight. "How can I rule a people that I don't care about?"

The charred firewood shifted. Hot ashes floated into the air.

Nels sighed. "It was wrong of me to say that. I'm sorry."

"No. You spoke the truth. I should thank you for that — thank you, Nels."

He reached for her hand — still holding the stick — and wrapped his fingers around hers. There was no warmth from her hand, no texture, but his chest burned like the embers in the fire. Her hand moved through his when she tried to return the touch. Tyra raised her chin and her eyes connected with his, voiding Nels's mind of all other thoughts. "You're welcome."

Tyra averted her stare to the fire. "I think it's dying."

Nels nodded as he looked. "I could gather more wood."

"Yes," she said, clearing her throat. "That would be —"

Something rustled behind the trees. A fallen limb moved in the shadows, followed by a playful yelping. Tyra jumped back as Brooklet raised her head and snorted. Nels reached for his stick and Tyra removed her dagger as two furry animals, dark and clumsy, scurried into the clearing, chasing each other. They paused at the fire, their short round ears up, stiff and alert. Nels had heard of creatures like this before, but he had never seen one — let alone two.

"Ooh!" Tyra cooed. "Little bear cubs — how adorable!"

Adorable? Nels didn't think so. "Don't make a sound."

With their small black noses sniffing at the air, the two cubs lazily explored the camp and soon found Tyra's knapsack. It didn't take them long to dump everything out of it.

"Hey!" Tyra cried. "That's mine! Shoo. Go on — shoo!"

"Wait! You'll scare them!" But Nels was too late. The cubs raised their ears, saw Tyra, and with whimpers and cries, sprinted up the nearest birch. Although her provisions were now safe, the cubs continued to mewl, calling to the night.

A great roar returned their cry.

17

BEARS AND BEESWAX

A humongous bear lumbered into their camp from behind the shadowy trees, stomping its brown paws on the ground before it let out another roar. Nels had no reason to fear for his life, but the bear's massive claws and crushing jaws gave him plenty to fear for Tyra.

With thankful cries, the cubs descended from their sanctuary and scurried into the bushes. But the bear didn't leave, its fierce eyes glaring at the princess.

"Don't look at it," Nels warned. "Don't make a sound."

"What am I supposed to do, then?" she whispered.

The bear snorted and stood, taller than a castle's gate. Nels jumped back. Tyra did as well — that was a mistake. Ramming its paws into the dirt, the creature roared as it charged for the kill.

Brandishing his stick, Nels swung at it, but he missed his mark and stumbled through the bear's stomach. Dropping her dagger, Tyra cried out as she bolted for the rotted tree behind her. The bear caught up to her and swiped its paws. Chunks of bark flew as Tyra dodged the blow, her face turning white. She sprinted for the other side of the camp, where her bow lay.

Nels pointed at the branches where the cubs had hidden moments before. "This way!"

With her bow in one hand and an arrow in the other, Tyra ran toward Nels as the bear rebounded and charged again. Nels hurled his stick at its head. It bounced off, doing little more than upsetting the creature. An arrow whizzed through the air, right over Nels's shoulder, and found its mark in the bear's arm. The creature howled and paused, providing them more time.

"Here!" Nels stooped by the tree and cupped his hands. "I'll hoist you up!"

Placing her foot in his palms, Nels thrust her high, aware that the animal was behind them. Nels elbowed it in the gut, but this only angered it more. Snarling, the bear reached up and pawed at Tyra's middle. She gave a terrible cry. Blood dripped from her side and fell through Nels's arm.

"Tyra!"

Nels dashed for his stick again and swung it at the bear with all his might. The creature turned its head, caught the stick in its jaws, and snapped it in two. There was a loud crack. Then the tree leaned, its roots ripping from the soil. The bear rounded on the tree and pushed.

In a matter of seconds, Tyra's haven would crash down — and she with it.

Just then, Nels caught a glint of firelight.

The fire . . . "Hang on!"

He raced for it, seized a hot coal in his bare hand, and drove it into the bear's side. The creature yelped as it backed away and stared at the floating ember. The bear showed its teeth and clawed at the air, but Nels maintained his lure, waiting for the right moment to strike. He grabbed the bear's paw, yanked it hard, and tripped the creature onto the burning coals. The camp went dark as the bear's cry shook the air. The creature jumped up and retreated into the trees.

"Nels . . ." Tyra said, her voice shaky and weak.

He looked up at her. "Are you all right?"

She teetered. "I don't . . . think . . ."

Her eyes closed as her grip gave out.

Nels sprinted and caught her before she hit the ground. He laid her down on the quilt. Their camp was a complete mess, but Tyra was worse: her bodice mangled, her side torn. The bear's claw had ravaged her flesh, leaving deep slashes that had dyed her skirt red with blood.

She was losing too much; he had to stop it.

"Stay with me, Tyra!"

Nels looked for a cloth or a handkerchief. There were none. Their supplies and provisions were smashed in the dirt — except for a little box of cedar wood. Maybe something inside could help. Running to the box, he picked it up and returned to Tyra's side. She moaned and shook as he tried to open the latch.

Suddenly, he heard the hooves of a horse drawing near. Nels raised his head, surprised by a floating light in the distance, bobbing up and down like a drunken firefly.

A stranger with an excessively large stomach emerged from the thicket, followed by Brooklet. The man had a dense beard, and he wore a glowing lantern fastened to a metal hat on his head. Adorned with furs across his burly shoulders, the bearded man entered their camp while speaking to Brooklet. "A bear, you say'n," he said in deep voice. "Come'n from over here?"

Brooklet gave a gentle whinny. She didn't seem to mind this man.

"Girl might be hurt? Better have'n a look."

Nels couldn't trust this man, whoever he was. When the man approached the princess, Nels retrieved one of Tyra's arrows and held the tip inches away from the stranger's throat.

To his astonishment, the stranger merely smiled at the floating arrow.

"Ol' Hilvar?" the man asked. "Nah, Hilvar bothers no bears this late." He scratched his head, his eyes fixed on the floating object. "Well, best not be scare'n the cubs. Makes you not welcome." The stranger pointed a pudgy finger at Tyra. "Better if I help, or else'n she dies."

Nels lowered the arrow. Eccentric as the bearded man was, he was Tyra's only hope.

***

Tyra found herself in the midst of a strange dream.

There was a hill and, beyond it, a gentle river. She knew this river. It flowed from the mountains to the sandy shores of her kingdom. She had camped here under a willow tree on the first night of her journey. Then she saw two figures along the bank; one knelt before the other.

The man who stayed on his feet had a sword in his hand. He used it to tap the other man's shoulder — a peasant's shoulder. This mysterious king had knighted the peasant. To see the peasant obtain his lifelong dream brought her comfort. She was happy for him.

"Here is your champion." The king joined her hand with the peasant's. "You may reward him."

To Tyra's surprise, she tilted her head back, her lips ready. He leaned in for the kiss — and dissolved into a white mist.

"Nels?" she cried. "Don't leave me, Nels. Don't go!"

"It's all right," he said, his face returning. "I'm here."

"She be stir'n," said a husky voice. "Wax works!"

Tyra struggled to open her eyes. Her side was burning, and a streak of blood — her blood — had stained her skirt. A cold sweat added to her sudden wooziness. She felt dizzier than a whirlwind.

She must have fainted, but for how long? "Who . . . who is this man?" she asked.

"I don't know," Nels said, "but he knows about —"

"I be Fargut! Found your mare, saved your life — be right for a trade."

Her heart beating normally again, Tyra looked at her wound. A thick, custard-colored substance coated her side. The stranger moved away from her, grinning through his beard. Half of his teeth were missing. Little could be said about the stained nubs that remained. He had a sun-weathered face, his clothing smelled of skinned animals, and his breath was worse than a pig's trough.

Tyra inched closer to Nels as she eyed the stranger. "Who are you?"

"Said already I be Fargut," he grunted. "And you know'n why?" He stood and leaned back as he patted his protrusive belly with both hands. " 'Cause me gut be come'n out so far!"

Tyra smirked at Nels. "A rather curious name."

The man beamed. "Lucky girl, have'n Fabricat'n kit. Haven't seen one'n ages."

"Fabrication kit?" Tyra glanced at her feet. The cedar box that Ickabosh had given her was open. The inside, lined with red velvet, contained a torn lump of beeswax. She remembered the peasant's body down in the tailor's chamber, and the amber beeswax that Bosh had covered him with from head to toe. Fargut must have used it to coat her skin, too. The bear had clawed a deep gash in her side, but it hardly hurt anymore. Now there was no gash — not even a scratch. The substance had healed her. Tyra took note of the other items in the kit: a seam ripper, a vial of black dye, a spool of thread, and a thimble. She saw a golden inscription sewn inside the lid:

The world is your fabric, the people your thread.
Within are your tools. Mend us with care.

"How long have you had that?" Nels asked.

She met his eyes. "Since we left the castle."

"Trade'n for kit?" Fargut asked. "Knives, skins, cushion for pins? Currencies?"

He reached into his brown vest, pulled out a little sack, and dumped a heap of golden nuggets into his soiled hand. Tyra gasped. How could a wild man in a deserted forest carry such treasure, and why would he trade that much gold for a sewing kit? He seemed eager to exchange for it.

"Thank you," she said, "but I would like to keep it."

Fargut sighed as he stowed the gold back inside his vest. "What I'd give'n for a fancy Fabricate'n kit — be'n a wise girl, you keep'n it. Best I leave'n girl and her ghosty alone."

"Wait!" Tyra cried. "You know there's a ghost here?"

"Had'n arrow at me neck. Was think'n Ol' Hilvar come to take me."

"You know of Hilvar?" Tyra asked. "Do you know where his castle is?"

"Oye," Fargut said. "Not so far from 'ere."

"We're trying to find the castle. Will you show us the way?"

Fargut frowned as he poked at the fire. "I be look'n mad?"

"Are you sure we can trust him?" Nels asked Tyra.

She turned to face Nels. "Why not? He saved me."

Nels nodded at the stranger. "But he's kind of strange."

"Stranger things have happened to me in the last few days." She looked at Fargut again. "We seek the treasury of Westmine Castle. I would be grateful if you showed us the way."

"No treasures there," Fargut said. "They say Vagas take'n

treasures, but where's their place for hide'n such a treasures? No use for wealth, them diviners."

"Diviners?" Nels and Tyra asked together.

"Three magical folks there be: conjurers, diviners, and makers of seams!"

"I've heard of the Vagas' magic," Nels said.

"Magic or not, we *must* reach the castle." Tyra's mind was made up. "Will you guide us?"

Fargut closed his eyes and shook his head. "Nope."

"Please, Fargut. Will you make an exception for a princess?"

"A *princess*, you say'n?" Fargut gasped. "A *real* princess?" When Tyra nodded, Fargut jumped onto his feet, held out his hand, and posed daintily. "I be'n a princess, too!"

All Nels and Tyra could do was stare at the big-bellied man.

"I don't think he believes you," Nels said.

Tyra glared down at her lap, then suddenly held out her hand. "Do you know what this is?"

As Fargut looked, his eyes opened wide. "That be'n a conjure'n ring!"

"I eat eggs every morning." Tyra ignored Nels's confused stare as the stone turned black. "I *am* a princess," she followed quickly, and the stone returned to green.

"Your ring!" Nels said, astonished. "How did you do that?"

Fargut raised his chin. "It be'n dangerous here for a princess."

Tyra wasn't interested in avoiding danger — not anymore. She hadn't come all this way to be lost. She wondered if bartering would entice the man. She happened to be a particularly great barterer. "Listen, Fargut. If I give you something, will you please guide us to the castle?"

He blinked a few times. "Won't part with Fabricate'n kit. How about'n that ring?"

She looked at her hand. There was not enough light to see it clearly, now that the fire had started to burn low, but she could tell the stone was green. He'd helped her, a stranger, without a clue that she was a princess. At least he was an honest fellow. "I'd like to keep this as well."

"When did you know that ring could do that?" Nels asked.

"I'll tell you later," she whispered at him. She turned back to Fargut. "I'm afraid all I have is this dagger, a bow, and my horse, but . . . I wouldn't dream of giving those up . . ."

"What about tha' cloak?" Fargut pointed. "It be'n too warm for it."

"Done!" Tyra slipped off her cloak and handed it over.

The man traced his finger along its seams. "Edge of the city, no farther."

Tyra sighed, relieved in more ways than one. "Imagine our good fortune," she whispered to Nels. "We found a guide!"

"You should rest," Nels suggested. "We'll start again in the morning."

"Not when we're so close. You said you could sew, right?"

He nodded.

"Then . . . would you please patch this hole in my dress?"

It was a bold request, but it was better to ask than travel through the forest in a torn skirt. Nels reached for her sewing kit. The beeswax on her side was hard now, orange flakes beginning to shed off her skin. Her dress and bodice were shredded and bloodied. Neither of them could help that. As Nels searched the sewing kit, he looked confused.

"Is something wrong?"

"I don't think I can fix your dress."

Tyra frowned. "But I thought you could sew."

"I can sew fine," he said, "but not without a needle."

She rummaged through the kit. He was right — there was no needle, just the beeswax and four tools that she'd seen earlier. "How utterly pointless. What good is a sewing kit without a needle?"

"No *ordinary* kit," said Fargut, waiting at the edge of their camp. "Come'n?"

"I wish everything would stop being so *un*ordinary." Tyra got ready to stand. "For now, I will have to cover my side with my knapsack, I suppose. Will you fetch it for me?"

Nels complied. Since the cubs had ruined most of her provisions, there was nothing else to pick up. From now on, she would have to forage for food — something she had never done. Maybe the peasant would pick her more brambleberries, if they were to come across any.

"Here," Nels said, handing her the sack. "Keep that kit with you all the time, *especially* the thimble — it will protect you." Nels paused, a wistful look on his face. "At least," he continued, "it will protect you from *most* dangers. A thimble couldn't save me from Rasmus."

"If you insist, Nels," she said, wondering how much help a tiny thimble could be. She placed the strap over her head and let it rest on her shoulder. The peasant stared, unsettling her. "What?"

"You said my name. It sounded nice . . . coming from you."

"It doesn't mean anything," Tyra said. "Help me up."

Nels helped Tyra to her feet, gathered her dagger and belongings, and saddled Brooklet. The mare rubbed her nose into Tyra's hair, as if thankful for her safety. "Can you go a little farther tonight, Brooklet?" the princess asked gently. The mare whickered in response. Although Tyra's side ached like a beesting, she gathered her reins and mounted the mare. If the castle wasn't far, she could handle this. Perhaps the castle would offer a decent place to rest.

"A ghost, move'n about as the live'n," said Fargut. "Why you look'n for treasury?"

"I will explain on the way," Tyra insisted. "We mustn't waste moonlight."

Fargut laughed as he turned his back on them and started to walk. Tyra urged Brooklet to follow. Nels lumbered by her side, looking gloomy — almost brooding. "What's the matter?"

"I promised to protect you. You could've been killed."

"I could have, but thanks to you, I wasn't." As she smiled at him, a humorous thought caused her to laugh. "Sharing an afterlife with you . . . now *that* would be terrible."

The two shared a glance and started to laugh as they headed up the trail.

Without the moon's light, the false Arek would have missed the crossroad.

He had many directions to choose from, but which had the princess taken? She could have gone anywhere. Having driven his horse to exhaustion, Arek dismounted and searched the ground. He could not find anything, not even a hoof mark.

His path was the only one that led away from the mountains. She had come this way unless she jumped the trail and journeyed into the thick of the forest.

Without a thread to trace, finding her would be impossible now.

Then, just as he was about to abandon hope, Arek felt a stir in the air. A familiar strength surged near him — a passing thread was tying itself to the kingdom of Avërand.

Her thread . . . She's torn her slip stitch!

Reaching into his pocket, Arek pulled out a bodkin made from a boar's rib. He raised it over his head, laced her thread around it, and closed his eyes. He saw her on a horse in the distance, heading toward the ruined city of Westmine. She wasn't alone. A man walked ahead of her.

Someone *was* traveling with her.

Who in the Great Tapestry can this be?

Arek raced for his horse and guided the creature west.

Whoever the man was, Arek would deal with him soon enough.

18

WESTMINE CASTLE

A pair of foxes chased each other by the foundation of an abandoned cottage. They looked up suddenly and barked, running to a burrow beneath a tall pine. The clomping of Brooklet's hooves must have spooked them.

The night had grown late, but the waning moon shed enough light for the small company to see their way. Fargut had led Nels and Tyra through a modest village overrun by wild shrubbery, sharp thorns, and dense trees, which seemed to make the forest even darker. Each of the structures looked sound and sturdy, making Nels wonder why they were deserted. They soon crossed over a bridge and a parched ditch before they hiked up another gradual slope.

This place made Nels uncomfortable — not because of the rustling of leaves overhead or the foreboding sounds of owls and other nocturnal creatures. Rather, he felt an intrusive, lingering presence that stirred his core. Fargut appeared just as disquieted, but Tyra, on the other hand, seemed composed and thrilled about finding the castle sooner than expected. He sensed a hint of excitement from her, too, for reasons that certainly differed from his, or so he assumed. The way she presented herself had changed some since the bear attack.

"How long have you known about that ring?" he asked.

"Since this afternoon," she answered.

Although Fargut was pudgy, he had no problem trudging ahead, allowing Nels to converse with Tyra in private. She shared all she had learned about the ring, which explained her earlier, unexpected comments about eggs. She was testing the ring.

And me.

Before long, they reached the top of a bare summit that overlooked a shallow valley, the silhouettes of buildings below. A majestic castle sat on a high hill in the distance. Trees and roots had taken the streets, and a few branches had grown through the windows, but it wasn't the overgrown foliage that impressed Nels. He had never seen a settlement like this, with roads organized and paved with stone. A few bridges crossed over a forked river, and the buildings loomed high as they neared the castle. This was Westmine City, deserted for hundreds of years.

"Remarkable," Tyra said. "It's just as Master Wussen described."

"Be'n far enough," Fargut said, not at all winded from their walk. "Girly, be careful in that valley. Devil reside'n in there — he's take'n me once; he may take'n you, too!"

"I will be fine, Fargut," Tyra assured him. "I have a ghost with me, after all."

The man's gut shook as he laughed. "Best leave'n. Fair'n well, Princess." Their peculiar guide turned and left them, moving out of sight as he headed back down the path from where they had come.

"Unusual fellow," Nels muttered. "I'm glad he's gone."

"Give him some credit; he did save my life."

Tyra pressed on, descending into Westmine City without fear.

She was right. Fargut *had* saved her life, a task that Yalva had assigned to Nels. The ghost shook his head. Who had done what was inconsequential. They had found the forsaken city. Now they had to find the treasury.

A gentle breeze passed through the empty streets, swaying branches that had long ago bludgeoned through the brick walls of homes and shops. As they passed an old marketplace and a blacksmith, Nels felt uncomfortable again. The abandoned city reminded him, in a way, of Cobblestown. He missed the warmth of Lars's furnace, the smell of Tessan's cakes, the smart of Jilia's punches, and the fun of wrestling with Wallin. He missed the taste of hot asparagus stew, or any stew, for that matter. The more Nels thought about his life, the more he wanted it back.

A row of shops had all their grimy windows broken or completely missing. Brooklet hesitated when they rounded the corner of a general store. The door was gone, rotted away by time. Even in passing, Nels could see the floor was littered with shredded sacks, left by hungry scavengers. The most curious thing of all was what lined both sides of the streets: tall iron poles, each topped with a glass bowl.

"Light posts," Tyra explained, catching his upward glance. "I've heard of them. They gave light to this city."

"We have nothing like them in Avërand. Your father should have some made."

"My father?" Tyra laughed. "He would never take such initiative . . . nor refuse another's, I suppose."

Given what he knew about the king, and the tragedy that Lennart shared with Nels's father, Nels could see how this self-imposed curse of his had affected Tyra. "Is he really that indifferent about everything?"

"He's inconsolable! Mother coddles him all day long, which only makes it worse." She bowed her head and sighed. "He rarely talks to me. When he does, it's as if I am a burden."

"I wouldn't say that." Nels turned to her, smiling. "I'm sure he thinks the world of you."

"He doesn't care for me at all." Tyra's eyes thinned and her jaw clenched. "I hate him."

Flattered by her willingness to confide in him, Nels began to better understand the princess. Perhaps there was something he could say to change her perception. "I'm sure you don't mean that, Tyra."

She wiped a single tear from her cheek. "I simply can't stand gloomy people."

"You've done well enough around me, haven't you?" Nels laughed, his eyes falling back on the road ahead of them.

"True, and I'm glad the kingdom has someone like you."

He looked up, elated but confused. He had never expected her to say something like that, not in a hundred years. "I thought you were only doing this to get rid of me."

She returned his look and smirked. "Not entirely; you could be of use elsewhere."

For once, her remark didn't carry the same derision that others had in the past; it sounded more like a playful tease. Even her voice seemed lighter, filled more with hope than sadness. She also smiled at him more, a welcome change compared to her usual onslaught of icy glares.

"There is something else on my mind," Tyra said. "Back at the mansion, when we saw Arek and his squire climbing the trail, you said we couldn't trust anyone. Why is that?"

"Do you remember what I told you about Rasmus?"

She nodded.

"People call him the Master Threader. He can turn himself into anyone he wants. Rasmus went after the Needle himself once, hoping to change reality. Rasmus killed Arek's squire and took his place — that's what your grandfather warned me about."

"But I told Arek about the Needle!" Tyra raised a hand to her cheek. "What have I done?"

Her confession created a pit in Nels's stomach. "Good thing I covered our tracks."

"Yes . . ." she said, her voice shaking. "Good thing . . ."

She tapped Brooklet with her heels, urging the mare to quicken her pace.

Nels breathed deeply as he peered at the sky. The moon fell on the horizon, its shadow creeping farther along. If the thimble's magic could preserve him for only two weeks, then they had three nights remaining to find the Needle and return to Hillshaven. That wasn't much time. Nels hoped the Needle was in Hilvar's treasury — or, if not there, somewhere nearby.

"You must be exhausted," he said. "We can rest here and start in the morning."

"No," Tyra said, shaking her head. "I can rest after we find the treasury."

Before long, they reached an open gate that led into a courtyard overrun by dry weeds and vines. Tyra navigated through it without a problem, which made Nels smile. She was beginning to impress him in ways he never thought possible. He didn't know what to think of her now, or if he should even think of her at all.

Wild rosebushes and withered willows filled the gray courtyard, along with roots that had long since parted the stones in the path. A grand stair ascended to a large iron door. Tyra dismounted Brooklet and pulled on the door's handle. Nels tugged along with her. The door would not budge. The castle was greater than even Averand's. Maybe there was another entrance. They circled around the structure, searching, only to return without finding so much as a crumbling wall.

Tyra rummaged through her knapsack and retrieved the sewing kit.

"What do you plan to use that for?"

She was too busy opening the kit to answer. Moments later, she pulled out the small seam ripper and removed its tiny leather sheath. Tyra knelt down and started to pick the lock.

"Those are delicate; twist it wrong and you'll break it," Nels warned.

"Shh!" Tyra leaned in and twisted the ripper, as if her tinkering met no resistance. "I can't feel the mechanism." When she removed the ripper from the lock, metallic dust sifted through the keyhole. Little grains spilled onto the threshold like brown sand. "What is that?" she asked.

It wasn't brown sand — more like tiny bits of rusted iron. Nels pushed at the door, and it swung open without resistance. The lock came apart and fell onto the floor with a clatter, the latch severed in two.

"Let me see that seam ripper," Nels said. She handed Nels the tool as he looked through the doorframe. He stuck the tiny ripper into the nearest wall; the tip penetrated the stone with ease, validating his thought.

"Did you see that?" he asked. "I bet this seam ripper can cut anything!"

Tyra took the tool back. "I knew what I was doing."

Nels laughed. "You're telling me you expected that to happen?"

She turned her head away from him with a startled expression.

"What is it?"

"Would you look at this place — it's enormous!"

She had good reason to be astonished. Everything — the stone, the metal, the woodwork — was of the finest quality, hardly disturbed by time. There was a healthy amount of dust, reminding Nels of Gleesel's mansion, although no fire was burning. There were no cobwebs, either. The castle was cold and lifeless.

Something stirred the air, as if someone else was breathing it.

After Tyra fastened Brooklet to a statue, they went inside. The place reminded Nels of Castle Avërand, but on a much grander scale. Above their heads, several pillars supported arches, bearing the weight of a sharply angled roof. A few tapestries hung between tall windows, their colors faded by the sun. It was dark, but the moon still shone bright enough to see by.

As Tyra placed the ripper inside her kit, Nels wondered about the spool of thread and the black dye. What were they for? He knew the thimble would protect Tyra, so long as she carried it with her. To think they could have avoided the altercation with the bear — if only he had known.

They explored an extravagant gallery of ancient arts and statues to their left, and then a library to their right. Hundreds of books littered the floor; only a few remained on the towering shelves.

"Where do you think we should look?" Nels asked.

Tyra shrugged as they passed from the library. "Why are you asking me?"

"You're more familiar with castles than I am. Where would *you* keep a treasury?"

"Well, somewhere out of reach . . ."

"See!" He laughed. "I knew you would be helpful."

Tyra's smile widened. "Let's start upstairs —" She stopped and sniffed the air. "Do you smell that?" she asked. "It's terribly foul!"

Nels inhaled through his nose. "I can only smell beeswax, remember?"

She lifted her skirt and took a first step onto the grand stairs. Nels didn't trail behind her or fly ahead; he stayed at her side. His growing feelings for her — repressed ever since the festival — began to resurface. The memory of the pear blossom scent of her hair, the thought of touching her blushed lips — this wasn't an appropriate time or place to think of her like that.

"Is someone there?" Tyra asked, her eyes focusing on something ahead.

Ahead on the landing, Nels saw the outline of a woman.

Tyra quickened her ascent. "Hello?"

Nels wanted to hold her back until he realized that it was only a portrait. The frame stretched from the floor nearly to the ceiling. The painting depicted a woman in a red dress. She had black hair and silver eyes, and she wore a sapphire stone around her neck.

The Vaga girl at the festival had a necklace just like it.

"She's lovely," Tyra said. "Who do you suppose she is?"

"She looks like a Vaga," Nels answered.

Tyra looked at him, impressed. "You said that rather calmly. Most of the people I know hate or fear them. They brought this kingdom to ruin, they say."

Nels placed his arms in a fold. "The ones I met didn't act like thieves."

"What of the ones who stole my father's crown?" She walked across the landing without waiting for his answer. She reached out and grazed the painting with her fingers, touching the woman's skirt.

"What if I told you Arek stole the crown so he could gain your father's favor?"

Tyra stood still. She gave him no answer. The news must have shocked her.

"I knew you wouldn't believe me, but I heard him say it —"

Without warning, she spun around and punched him square in the jaw. Nels flew backward and floated to a stop in the middle of the stairs. "Why did you do that?!" And then he realized, "*How* did you do that?"

Something about her had changed. The locks of her hair floated in the air, waving like threads in water. The look in her eyes had turned vicious and desperate. Nels touched his face again. The blow didn't hurt, but it was too great for someone as small as Tyra to deliver.

"Get out!" Tyra commanded, cold and deep — in a voice that wasn't hers. "Leave us!"

Dumbfounded by the mannish timbre in her voice, Nels approached her again. "*Us?*"

Tyra swung, but this time Nels grabbed her fist and then ensnared her other hand with his free one. She bared her teeth as she thrashed to free herself. She possessed unnatural strength. "I have what I need!" Her tone clashed like thunder in his ears. "Do not interfere!"

Nels held fast until her wrists slipped through his grasp. Tyra tumbled down the stairs and came to rest on the floor, but Nels still felt something in his hands — the grip of another. He was not alone. A tall man sneered at him. The man was wearing epaulets on his broad shoulders and a golden vest on his chest. His square, almost transparent face supported a short, well-trimmed beard. If they were able to see each other — and touch each other — then this man was a ghost as well.

Tyra rolled onto her back with a soft moan, the distraction

causing Nels to drop his guard just long enough for the specter to slip away and go after her again. Nels knocked the other ghost aside before it could touch her. The ghost floated back to the ground, his ruthless expression giving way to a befuddled one. "How did you do that?" he cried. "None have resisted me before!"

Nels maintained his stance. "Have you ever faced another ghost before?"

"*Ghost*?" He laughed. "Be you ghost or phantom, I will have her!"

Bracing himself for the unexpected, Nels charged at the man.

The ghost tried to run around him, but Nels grabbed the hem of his vest and tossed him across the hall. Their fight carried them into the armory, where Nels ducked a punch that landed on a suit of armor, bending it in half. In the dining hall, the ghost hurled dusty porcelain cups and saucers at Nels. Nels tried to catch one of the saucers while flying in the air, but the dish passed through his grip. Nels looked at his hand, bewildered. He had never tried to hold something and fly at the same time. Perhaps he couldn't.

Taking advantage of Nels's distraction, the ghost soared back to where Tyra lay. Jumping to intercept, Nels rammed his shoulder into the ghost before he could possess her again.

Before the ghost inhabited Tyra the first time, she complained of a terrible smell, reminding Nels of what she had said in her bedchamber. And he could grasp objects and throw them, just as Nels could. Unlike Yalva and Sibylla, this infuriated specter was a draug.

Nels grappled with the draug and they rolled into the scullery, where they tumbled down a well. They landed in an underground lake without a splash; droplets fell through their heads from long stalactites. The draug tried to fly away, but

Nels jumped into the air to pursue him and grabbed him by his ankle. Their struggle sent them crashing to the nearest shore. They battled a moment longer before the draug pushed Nels through a stone wall — into a room of reflected moonlight. Heaps of gold and mounds of jewels surrounded him. Nels waited for the draug, tripped him as he entered, and pinned him down.

"Release me," the draug ordered. "I yield!"

"Promise to leave Tyra alone first!"

"If that be the girl's name, I swear it. Now release me!"

Nels consented, but continued to watch the draug closely.

The defeated phantom sat against a wooden chest, a look of amusement on his face. "Ages have passed since I last combated a foe. Fine display, lad. What manner of myth are you?"

"Are you King Hilvar?"

The draug laughed. "What is left of him."

Nels looked at the wealth surrounding them. If this spirit was the ghost of Hilvar, then this room had to be his treasury. "What is this place? I thought your treasure was stolen?"

Hilvar frowned. "No hand but mine has ever touched this treasure. Is that what you have come for? I will gladly share it with you!" The draug pinched a coin and flipped it at Nels, only for it to soar right through him. The coin clinked onto a larger pile. "That is, if you allow me the use of her body first . . ."

19

HILVAR'S TREASURE

The draug scooted closer to the open chest as he stared at Nels.

Nels stared back, disliking what Hilvar said about wanting to *use* Tyra's body. What could he possibly mean? They came only for one thing, and a deceased king was not about to stop them.

"Well," the ghost blared. "Are you going to answer or just gawk at me all night?"

"Listen — we didn't come for your treasure."

"Is that so?" Hilvar rubbed his neatly trimmed beard. "Why have you come?"

"For the Needle of Gailner," Nels said.

Hilvar let out a laugh. "Who hasn't sought that?"

Knowing that this draug knew of the Needle brought a measure of relief to Nels, assuring him that their journey to Westmine wasn't a complete waste of time. "You know where it is, then?" he asked, carefully choosing his words. "We need to know; please tell us."

Pinching his thumb and forefinger close together, Hilvar glanced up. "I was *this* close to the Needle." He dipped his hand into the chest beside him and scooped up a palm of gold coins. "Instead of finding it" — he allowed the coins to slip from his hand — "you can guess what happened."

Nels didn't have to; Hilvar was a draug, after all. The specter raised another handful of money and sneered at it. There was an intense hatred in his eyes; frustration lined his face.

"Your Majesty," Nels said. "All we're here for, all we want from you, is to find —"

"You've already established that!" Hilvar barked. "What need have you for this relic?"

"If I tell you, will you promise to tell me where it is?"

The draug glowered at him. "A bold phantom, you are. Headstrong! Abrasive! If we were alive at this moment, I would toss you in the dungeons for your insolence!"

"If we were alive," Nels countered, "I wouldn't dream of fighting you."

The draug gave him another short laugh. "Death changes everything — well put, lad. Tell me how you have come to be here, and, if you entertain, I may bestow all that you wish to know."

Jumping at the offer, Nels recalled everything he could to the dead king: his death, the loom, and their search for the Needle. After Nels recounted their scuffle with the bear, the ghost held up a hand. "You mean to tell me that with this Needle, you will have a second chance to live?"

The envious stare coming from the draug cut through Nels like a winter's chill. There was no way to beat around it, so he faced the man and nodded.

Hilvar frowned. "A second chance." He closed his eyes, tight at first, before he opened them with a sigh. Remorse weighed down his voice. "A worthy cause." He stood and waved his hand, motioning for Nels to come. "I will show you where my search for the Needle of Gailner began."

Accompanying Hilvar around a pile of emeralds, Nels saw more wealth than he could have ever imagined, a treasure without end. Precious metals and gems caught his eye, including many whose names he didn't know. Then, as they both rounded an enormous pile of gold, Hilvar crossed through a granite wall. Nels followed, hoping the king hadn't given him the slip.

A black blur clouded Nels's vision until he emerged from the wall. It was too dark to see anything until the draug snapped his fingers. Small fires burst from various torches, the same way Gleesel had lit her candles. A circular chamber came into view, its walls lined with ancient stone.

"How did you summon fire?" Nels asked.

"Magic lives in the walls." Hilvar snapped his fingers again. The lights went out. "Try it."

The moment Nels clicked his fingers, the light returned. He could hardly believe it: this place had magic that could react to the actions of a ghost! Amazed by this discovery, Nels used the new light to look around. He saw no treasure in the room, but there were tables and shelves that held the remains of pottery, glass bottles, and mechanisms with complex gears and pulleys. The mechanisms were in shambles, decayed and layered with dust, as if abandoned for centuries.

In the center of the room was a freestanding arch of dark stone. Directly beneath it sat a decrepit loom. It resembled the one Bosh used, only larger.

"What is this place?" Nels asked.

Hilvar opened his arms. "This is Gailner's chamber — the birthplace of Fabrication."

Before Nels could let this revelation sink in, Hilvar led him to the arch. As they got closer, Nels noticed a heap of clothes and a pair of black leather boots leaning against one side of the arch. A bony grin bared its teeth from under a tattered hood.

Nels pointed at the corpse. "That's not you, is it?"

"He was the only man besides me who came close to finding the Needle." Hilvar walked to the dried body and leaned against the arch. "Until I killed him, that is."

"Killed him?" Nels stepped back as he said this. He had never stopped to think about how dangerous a draug could be, or that a ghost could take the life of a mortal. "*You* killed him?"

"Why do you stare at me like I'm some monster? It was not my intent!" Hilvar bellowed. "I was merely going to *borrow* him. I didn't expect him to be such a powerful conjurer."

"Conjurer?" Nels's thoughts turned to Gleesel's father, the man who had disappeared. He approached the body. On its skeletal hand was a ring similar to Tyra's. "Oyren?"

"Was that his name?" Hilvar sighed. "Well, now I know. He resisted with such fervor!"

Nels studied the loom some more. "What do you know about this loom and arch?"

Hilvar turned, careful not to step through Oyren's bones. "This arch is a Weaver's Gate. It was created for a unified purpose." Hilvar pointed at three people engraved on the face of the arch. The people had their arms outstretched, and each held an item in their hands. "To summon the gate's power, three sorcerers — one from each of the three magics — must stand in front of the gate while holding a tool of their respective powers."

Nels stooped down and raised Oyren's hand for a better look at his ring.

"Have you no respect for the dead?" Hilvar asked.

Oyren's body fell to the side, causing a chalky dust to scatter. The sound of his rattling ribs traveled up the chamber.

Nels looked down at Oyren. Seeing the dead conjurer reminded him of the cryptic passage that Oyren had written inside the shadowed book. "The Weaver's Gate," Nels repeated quietly.

Hilvar nodded. "It was Gailner's greatest accomplishment before his Needle."

"It doesn't look anything like a gate."

"It's one of three. The others are long since lost."

Nels took Oyren's ring as he stood. "What does a Weaver's Gate do, exactly?"

"I will tell you on the way up; it is a long walk."

Nels nodded. Based on how deep they had fallen, Nels could only imagine.

"Let us leave," Hilvar said. "An untidy floor is no place for your friend."

Nels smiled, surprised that the draug shared his concern. He glanced at Oyren the Conjurer one last time before the torches went out with the draug's exit. Nels approached the wall, ready to pass through it, but instead he bounced back — as if he were solid. He looked at the ring in his hand. To hold it, he had had to become tangible. Doing so would not let him pass. Nels returned the ring to Oyren's lap and proceeded through the wall without hindrance.

On the other side, he found himself in one of dozens of prison cells.

"Time has a way of keeping some tales but casting others aside," Hilvar said as he headed up a spiral stairwell. "Have you never heard of the man who made the Weaver's Gates?"

"I know Gailner made the Needle," Nels said, following him. "But that's all."

As they ascended, Hilvar spoke of a time unlike any Nels had heard of, and of lands that he had never known. A terrible conflict once kept the world divided. Those caught in the middle were trampled underfoot, but one man — called Gailner — sought peace. Gailner formed and led an alliance of three sorcerers — himself and one sorcerer from each of the other two magical traditions. Together, the three unified sorcerers discovered a realm of endless truth where they learned how to unify the nations. They forged three Weaver's Gates — one for each land — to establish lasting friendship and peace among the nations. But they had no idea the damage that the Gates would inadvertently cause. Such powerful magic linking three separate points in the world stretched the Great Tapestry beyond its limits; a tear opened in reality itself. Because of this tear, a great rendt nearly devoured the world.

To correct their misuse of magic, Gailner created the Needle, a powerful tool with the ability to mend the torn fabric of reality. But Gailner soon realized the danger the Needle possessed. In addition to mending the fabric of reality, it had the power to destroy it forever. This led Gailner to create a secret fourth gate, where he entered and vanished with his Needle, never to return.

"Without Gailner, the sorcerers' alliance dissolved," Hilvar said. "The nations remained at peace for a time. Other sorcerers tried to form a new alliance, but they failed. I have no knowledge about the state of the world as it is now."

"Incredible," Nels said. "Did you know Gailner?"

The draug let out a boisterous laugh. "His time was six centuries before mine!"

Nels cursed his naivety. "Sorry. You just seem to know so much."

"Books, my lad; my library is filled with them, some of them written by Gailner himself. It is amazing how much reading one can do in four hundred years."

"I met another ghost," Nels said, thinking of King Yalva. "He said a ghost can bind itself to what it cared for most in life. Are you here because you bound yourself to your treasure?"

"No," Hilvar grumbled. "I *thought* they were my treasures, but no cavern of gold can fill the emptiness inside of me. If I had treasured what mattered, I would not have lost my *true* treasure."

"The Vagas didn't steal your treasure, then?"

"My treasure *was* a Vaga . . . and she stole herself from me."

Nels couldn't help but think of the woman from the painting upstairs.

"No jewel in the world was greater than she, a fair maiden of the forest. My father, ruling before me, had already stripped the Vagas of their land, forcing them north to Mendarch."

Mendarch. The name struck a chord with Nels; Tyra's instructor had mentioned it.

"But when my father died," Hilvar continued, "I was free to do as I wished. I could think of no other woman to sit beside me. There were many who disagreed with our love. As king, I defied those who opposed our union. But over time, I grew obsessed with the many mines that dotted my kingdom. My treasures became more important to me." Hilvar sounded miserable, and he looked it. "I brought her inside these walls, only to ignore her. I left her alone, cut off from her people, surrounded only by those who rejected her — she wilted like a flower. The only way I can see her again is to cross into the next plane, but I am trapped in this valley. Only by giving up my kingdom and wealth can I be free."

Nels felt sorry for the old draug, but the solution to Hilvar's problem seemed easy enough. Nels certainly wouldn't mind lining his pockets a little, either. "Give your treasure to anyone?"

"I must bestow it to the rightful heir of my kingdom," Hilvar clarified.

Just like Tyra's grandfather, they both needed a worthy heir.

"Do you know who that is?" Nels asked.

"Yes." Hilvar smiled. "A child among the Vagas; they call her Mylan."

"How do you know she's the rightful heir? Do you know her?"

"I have spoken to her . . . through the mouths of others."

"Oh," Nels said. "*That's* why you want to use Tyra?"

"When I overheard that she was a princess, I *had* to. I have possessed countless intruders, but no matter how I try, I cannot bestow my throne, even with a willing host."

"Why would anyone be willing if it kills them?"

"If they do not resist me, the worst I can do is cause a deep sleep upon them after I leave the body."

Nels wondered: Had Fargut been one such host? The eccentric, pot-bellied man had spoken of Hilvar coming to take him.

"No one has proved a suitable vessel," the hopeless king continued. "However, none of them were of royal blood. I suspect possessing your princess will yield more success than a peddler."

"You're sure she'll make a difference?" Nels asked, continuing up the stairs.

"I have no way of knowing," Hilvar answered, "but it is my only hope."

Feeling uneasy about such a gamble, Nels wondered if they had enough time to settle this problem before his thimble's magic wore off. At sunrise, they would only have two days left to find the Needle and return to Avërand before the half-moon waned. It was unthinkable at this point.

"If she allows me," Hilvar said, "I will tell you where to find the Needle."

"I'll ask her," Nels said. After all, what choice did they have?

The smile on the old draug's face told Nels that it was precisely what he wanted to hear. "I envy you," he said. "You have a much better chance to reclaim your love than I."

Taken aback, Nels stared at him. "What love?"

Hilvar pointed up. "The love you have for your maiden."

"L-love?" Nels stammered. "That's . . . I mean . . . it's nothing like that —"

The draug shook his head slightly. "You bore me to the ground to protect her," he said. "Do not tell me you have no feelings for her. I know passion when I see it!"

"She's only helping me find the Needle. It was made my duty to protect her."

Hilvar grabbed Nels by the shoulder. "There is no sense of duty without love!"

No matter how Nels justified it, he couldn't refute the way he had felt when he saw Tyra ride into the festival. But that wasn't love — it was an attraction; nothing deeper. Wasn't it? The ghost of King Yalva had given him a charge to keep her safe, but Nels realized that wasn't the only reason he wanted to protect her. If Hilvar was right, then, deep down, Nels had fallen in love.

Hilvar let go of Nels's shoulder and tousled his hair. "I swear to you that no harm will come to her, so long as she agrees to help me. And then I will tell you where the Needle lies —"

Just then, Hilvar stopped, his face suddenly wrought with concern.

"What is it?" Nels asked.

The draug placed his hand on the wall. "Someone is coming, riding a horse."

Rasmus!?

Fearing the worst, Nels shot up the stairs to where Tyra had fallen.

Beams of sunlight streaked across the hall through the upper windows' broken panes of glass. Part of the roof was missing, exposing a clear sky above Tyra's head. She opened her eyes and stirred awake, not knowing how she wound up at the bottom of the stairs. Her head ached.

"Nels?" She sat up. "Where are you?" Tyra thought she heard laughter in the distance. "This isn't funny," she reprimanded. "Answer me!"

She went silent at the sound of her own name.

Someone was calling for her.

It came from outside.

Tyra stumbled to her feet and sprinted for the door. A pair of scavenging sparrows flapped away as she reached the entrance. Brooklet stood in the courtyard, nibbling on grasses among a few neglected rosebushes. The garden looked so different than it had at night; it wasn't as full or lush, and most of the plants were dead.

As Tyra neared Brooklet, the mare seemed skittish. Something was troubling her.

"Was that you I heard?" she asked the mare, stroking the long hairs on her white neck. Maybe it was just the wind carrying the horse's nicker. "Is that ghost bothering you again?"

"Tyra!" a voice cried from the front gate. "Is that you?"

She turned and saw Arek entering the courtyard.

20

THE MASTER THREADER

The favored knight of Avërand dismounted and emerged from the shadows, arms open wide.

Tyra sprinted across the weed-strewn path. The desire to be held by him had replaced her caution, but the closer she came to him, the more suspicious she felt. A terrible squall sounded from his horse. The stallion heaved from exhaustion and then fell to its side. The knight didn't flinch.

"Arek," Tyra said, slowing to a stop. "Your horse —"

"I know," he replied, glancing down at the poor animal. "Finding you safe is worth it."

The stallion looked up, its neck trembling, as if death were looming. The horse lowered its head, exhaled, and stopped moving. Brooklet stomped her hooves, startling Tyra from behind. She had done this once before, when Tyra nearly stepped on a coiled adder during a walk in the barley fields. This was Brooklet's way of warning Tyra that something was wrong.

If Arek loved anything more than Tyra, it was his horse.

He would never run it to death, not even for her.

Uncertain, but trusting her instincts, Tyra stepped back.

Arek tilted his head slightly, his sullen eyes curious. "Is something wrong?"

Tyra didn't know. The sight of Arek had filled her with elation, but to see the way he'd treated his beloved horse . . . It rattled her understanding of him.

And when she'd seen him on the pass, there had been two horses.

Where is his squire?

"Tyra?" Concern resounded in Arek's voice.

"You followed my handkerchief?" Tyra answered.

"Yes — not that I needed to," he said. "Why did you go off alone? You wanted my help to find some kind of a needle, right?" He stepped forward. "Now that I am here, I will help you."

Looking behind her, Tyra took another step back, wondering why the air felt so heavy and dark, contrary to the light morning. Arek smiled as he advanced another step. She'd listened to what the peasant had told her on their way here, about the man who assumed the faces of others, so Tyra couldn't contain her suspicion. Her ring would know for certain. "Where is your squire?"

The knight paused. "You knew he was with me?"

"I saw you when I was on top of the pass," Tyra said.

Arek smirked as he resumed his stride. "We should get you back to your father."

Tyra glanced at her ring. It didn't change. He had avoided her question completely — but why? She had to ask something more direct, something only the real Arek would know. "During our picnic, you wanted to ask me something," she said, trying to sound calm. "What was it?"

Without answering her, Arek took another step.

"You remember," Tyra said, "don't you?"

The knight raised his hand and flicked his finger. All of a sudden, Tyra's fears lifted like a fog in the sun. She was calm, enraptured by Arek's smile and the invitation of his strong arms. She couldn't help it — the thought of Arek holding her made Tyra blush. All she cared about was her love for Arek.

Involuntarily, she moved.

"Who told you about the Needle?" Arek asked, his voice cool and blunt.

"Ickabosh," she said, surprised by how fast the name flew from her mouth.

"I thought so," he said. "Did he send you here to find it?"

"He sent me to the mansion on the Westerly Pass."

Arek smiled. "And what did you find there?"

There was no way to explain it, but she knew something was wrong. Tyra was so happy, so light, but deep within, she was trying to turn away. Her instincts screamed for her to run.

She shivered as Arek reached behind his back.

"What have you discovered?" he asked. "What do you plan to use the Needle for?"

She had to resist him. Tyra tried to stop, but every time Arek flexed his fingers, she felt pulled from within, as if he forced the words out of her mouth. "I . . . need it . . . to save —"

Thump!

Arek dropped to the ground, knocked out by a cobblestone in the peasant's hand.

In an instant, Tyra's tranquil thoughts vanished, leaving her bogged down and confused.

Nels jumped over Arek, ran to Tyra, and seized her shoulders. "Did he hurt you?"

Tyra looked at the stone in his hand. "You hit him over the head again?"

"That's *not* Arek!" he said, more terrified than ever.

Tyra glanced at her ring; the stone stayed green.

The knight groaned as he stirred. Like threads in the wind, his skin unraveled. His hair followed. Something pulled at the fabric of his shirt, and then new layers of skin appeared. Cold eyes stared from a face that didn't belong to Arek. As he looked up, the man that had been Arek bared his teeth. The favored knight of Avërand had changed into someone else completely.

"We have to get out of here!" Nels cried. "Come on!"

Grabbing her by the hand, they ran to Brooklet and climbed onto her saddle.

"Run for the gate," he said. "Don't stop!"

Tyra kicked Brooklet's side and sent them off in a run. The wild growth throughout the courtyard narrowed their escape to only one way — the gate. The imposter jumped to his feet, the remains of Arek withering off his body like scattered lint caught in the breeze. He was about the age of her father; he had dark hair and he wore a thick cape and a fine suit paired with a violet vest. He had an air of refinement about him, like a noble, but with an unpleasant stare that chilled her.

The man, wielding a knife, blocked their escape.

"Good idea," Nels said.

Tyra turned to him. "I didn't say anything!"

"Keep going," he said, "no matter what. We'll be fine!"

Had Nels lost his mind? This man was no ordinary person. A simple stir of his fingers could control her feelings and draw from her lips answers that she couldn't afford to reveal. As they ran forward, the man raised his weapon, ready to strike. "Tell me where the Needle is!"

Tyra winced as the man brandished his blade and swung at them, but he suddenly stopped. His eyes filled with surprise as he let go of his knife. The imposter stepped aside, rigidly, as if doing so against his will. "I will hold him as long as I can," he said, in a completely different voice.

"Now's our chance," Nels cried. "Go!"

They bolted past the imposter, continued down the path, and soared through the gate. The empty city lay before them, but Tyra was too terrified to admire the sunlit edifices.

Who was that man? Why was he so intent on the Needle?

Her thoughts darkened. If this was Rasmus, where was Arek?

No stitch or potion or spell had ever stirred Rasmus's thread this way. Another entity had entangled its spirit with his. The words he spoke were not his own, the voice accented by the remnants of Westmine's past. Legends spoke of the ghost of King Hilvar, and he believed them; he had accepted what the diviners of Ilyden had taught him concerning the ethereal plane dividing life and death, where the souls of the dead cross after the passing of their lives.

Phantom or not, he couldn't lose the princess.

Release me, Hilvar. You and I have no quarrel.

The ghost threw his voice into Rasmus's mouth. "I will not let you kill her."

That is not my intention. Release me, or you will regret this.

Conjuring the magic deep within, Rasmus focused every strand of will from his thread and recited an ancient chant. The ghost resisted the craft, increasing his effort, but there was only enough room for one spirit to possess this body.

Mentally repeating archaic commands, Rasmus spread his focus throughout his chest until he was able to reach out and move his arms again. All he had to do was find the king's thread inside him and cast it out. Scratching at his chest, Rasmus found a solid pinch with his fingers. Then, with a slight tug, he slipped his fingers around Hilvar's thread, made a fist, and secured his grip.

The ghost struggled. "What manner of sorcerer are you?" he asked.

The strongest!

Twitching his forefinger, Rasmus applied as much strength into this thread as he could, removing the ghost from his body. Knowing the phantom would try to ensnare him again, he picked up his knife and flashed through the gate with a speed that rivaled lightning.

Once there, he closed his eyes and slammed his fists toward the ground. Stones fell from the ramparts as a loud crash rumbled the outer wall. The very foundation shuddered as Rasmus faced the gate and caught his breath, sneering at what he couldn't see. "I stitched your thread, Hilvar," Rasmus said. "You're tethered to this castle now and cannot leave."

A stone rose off the ground before it hurdled at him.

Rasmus brushed it aside without touching it. "I said you would regret this." The walls thundered, as if pounded on by great fists. The ghost couldn't stop him — so long as the *tethering stitch* held. If there was time for it, Rasmus wanted to learn more about this ghost, how he could move objects and possess the living, but that would have to wait. The princess was now just a small dot in the distance, halfway to the forest.

No matter; he had plenty of vigor left in his own thread — he could still cord to anything within his sight.

His arms outstretched, Rasmus formed another circle with his hands, put the circle to his eye, and searched for Tyra's mare.

Holding Tyra, Nels made sure no one was following them.

That was too close.

He didn't get a good look, but Nels knew the man by the cut of his cape. Good thing Nels had found them so quickly. Close as they were to knowing where the Needle was, their conversation with Hilvar would have to wait. At this pace, they would be out of the city soon. They had to find a safe glen to rest and wait for Rasmus to leave. Despite his tight grip, Tyra's body was shaking.

"Are you all right?" Nels asked. "Are you hurt?"

"That was Rasmus," she said, "wasn't it?"

He didn't want to answer her, but did anyway. "It was."

"Then," she asked hesitantly, "where's Arek?"

As they began to cross a bridge, Nels noticed a man on the other side, who fell to one knee as if in terrible pain. Nels wasn't sure who it was, but Rasmus couldn't have gotten ahead of them.

"Look! It's Arek!" Tyra cried. "He's alive!"

Before Nels could say anything, Brooklet tripped over something unseen that sent both him and the princess into the air. The mare squealed as she tumbled to a stop. Nels turned his back to the ground as fast as he could and let Tyra land on him. They dug into the earth together until they thumped against the trunk of a pine. Sticky needles fell around them.

Brooklet stayed on her side, writhing in pain, her leg broken.

Tyra moaned as Nels jumped to his feet. Tyra's knapsack — with the thimble inside it — had fallen off her when they tumbled through the air. Before he could grab it, the sound of footsteps made him turn. Rasmus emerged, his eyes fixed on Tyra. The Master Threader opened his arms, closed

240

his eyes, and slammed his fists toward the ground. The clearing fell silent. Brooklet stopped moving, her cries muted. Even Nels's feet stuck fast to the forest floor, just as he'd been frozen before Rasmus smashed him with the tree.

Nels struggled to move even an inch as the man approached the princess.

Tyra tried to sit up, but she couldn't budge. She could not move so much as a finger. Every muscle in her body was stiff. Her knapsack was on the ground to her side. Brooklet was in front of her, paralyzed on the ground. Nels stood still, his back to her. The only one who roamed freely about was the man who looked like Arek.

"I can't move," Nels said. "Run, Tyra, if you can!"

The imposter did not react. He could not hear the ghost.

"You're not Arek!" Tyra said. "Stop pretending to be him, Rasmus!"

The knight smirked, and his face and body changed once again into the fabricator. "You know of me? I thought they kept me a secret from you."

Tyra trembled. By *they*, she assumed he meant her parents. "You killed my grandfather!"

"Yes." His answer was blunt. "You say that as if it were a terrible crime." Rasmus stooped down, close to her. His eyes pried into hers. "I am not as wicked as you think, Princess. It had to be done." He retrieved her pouch and looked inside. "On Ickabosh's errand, are you?" His dark brow furrowed as he leaned even closer. "Tell me what you know about the Needle."

Tyra's heart thumped in her throat, her will faltering.

"Well?" Rasmus said. "Where is the Needle?"

"I . . . I don't know," Tyra whispered.

Rasmus rested on one knee, blocking her view of Nels. Tyra closed her eyes, hoping that she was not about to feel Rasmus's knife. She had to do something, but what?

"Look me in the eyes," Rasmus ordered. "Look!" Tyra opened her own. His cold blue eyes stared back. "I am cursed with knowledge, knowledge of how fragile our reality is, for it is in danger of undoing itself. With the Needle, I can mend what began years ago. I can *alter* reality, change it back to how it once was . . . the way it was meant to be." Rasmus took a deep breath, his nose grazing her hair. His dark blue eyes opened wider as he pulled away. "This is why I seek the Needle, Your Highness. I have searched the world over for it, and if you do *not* know where it is, tell me — for the value of your life — why are you searching for it?"

"You wish to alter reality?" Tyra asked. "What are you talking about?"

"I wouldn't expect you to understand." The man adjusted his violet vest, acting calm, confident, and in control. "You have me all wrong, Princess. I don't wish to kill anyone, but I will do whatever it takes to keep the Great Tapestry from the rendt!" Rasmus gently grasped Tyra's chin with his fingers. "Do not hinder me, Tyra. Do what is easy; tell me everything you know."

"What have you done to Arek?" she asked, despite the murderer's clammy hand on her skin.

Rasmus laughed. "He was a hindrance, so I buried him." Tyra could barely see her hand, but her ring's stone was green. Rasmus reached behind his back and withdrew a knife. The blade, held expertly in his hand, glistened in the light. "Why do you seek the Needle? You had better tell me. Now!"

Rasmus flicked his finger at Tyra again. Her mind numbed. That same strange happiness from earlier buoyed her thoughts — a fake, contrived feeling. Knowing that her knight was gone brought forth tears, despite the effects of this magic. Her desire for life had lost its meaning.

"It's not for me," she said. "The Needle isn't for me."

Nels struggled to free himself. It was all he could do.

Rasmus groaned as he breathed again. "Who, then?"

Looking straight into his eyes, Tyra sneered. "It's for *you*!"

The man leaned back. "For *me*?"

"To stop you!" Hot tears ran down her face. "I will use it to stop you!"

In an instant, Rasmus's body unraveled once more. His skin and clothing whirled in the air like threads in the wind. They changed shape and color and wove back into a new person. He was no longer a man, but a woman, a young and beautiful woman — an exact likeness of Princess Tyra. Knowing that her defiance had sealed her fate, Tyra couldn't take another breath.

"You have outlived your usefulness," Rasmus said, using her voice, "but your beauty will not go to waste . . ."

21

MYLAN

Rasmus pitied the young princess writhing helplessly to avoid his hand. She was a lovely girl, but alas, she knew nothing about the Needle. And she was of no use to him now. He was sure the sobbing princess wished to take back what she had said, but it was much too late for that. Her eyes closed as he knelt down, raised his hand, and aimed for her heart.

Schhwaff!

A feathered shaft pierced his shoulder, knocking him back. It was an arrow, shot from the dense forest. Rasmus gritted his teeth against the rising pain. They weren't alone, and his *tacking stitch* hadn't reached far enough to paralyze the unknown archer — wherever he was.

Clutching his wounded arm, Rasmus returned to finish what he had started when a blow struck him in the face. The princess had escaped the dwindling tacking stitch. She had a bow in her clenched hand and she used it to whack the knife from his; she then struck his head. Rather than use up his strength, Rasmus wove back into himself and ran for the trees — just as another force sent him to the ground. Someone had tripped him; he couldn't see who had made him fall.

Has Hilvar escaped my tethering stitch?

The girl charged at him, but then she stopped.

"Let go of me, Nels!" she cried. "Let me go!"

That name . . . the son of Ulrich . . . It can't be!

Rasmus reached for Tyra's thread and *hooked* it around the pine behind her. He yanked hard, the pull forcing her to fly back. As she landed on her side, an unseen power slammed him in the jaw. He rolled, returned to his feet, and looked around but there was no one; at least, no one that *he* could see.

It's not possible — I killed him! I killed Ulrich's son!

Rasmus couldn't fight what his eyes and magic could not see, nor could he face those who were attacking him from afar. If he left the princess alive, he couldn't use her face to enter Castle Avërand — it would be too risky if the *real* Tyra arrived at the castle while he was there threaded *as* her. But Rasmus had to retreat from this attack; he would have to find another way into the castle.

"Never come back to Avërand, Princess Tyra!" Rasmus seized his cape, spun around, and vanished, leaving only dust and leaves as his voice faded. "If you return, you will *both* die!"

Nels relaxed his fists as Rasmus's voice diminished.

The rogue fabricator had left them, but that wasn't enough to settle his nerves. Even with ghostly powers, Nels had been unable to fully protect the princess — Rasmus was a true master of his trade. It was a good thing Tyra had nocked an arrow — she would have died without it. She stood and limped to him, her cheeks blotchy.

"How did you land that shot on him?" Nels asked. "I couldn't even move!"

Tyra stared at Nels, then looked at the ground where Rasmus once stood. "It was not mine."

A twig snapped. Pine needles crunched. Branches jostled around them. Nels turned toward the forest as several men emerged from its shadows. Their clothing blended with the greens and browns of the trees, and they carried sheaths and bows over their shoulders. Nels counted three . . . seven . . . thirteen. They all had dark hair, fair skin, and silvery eyes, a trait Nels had seen before. "I know where that arrow came from," he said.

Tyra looked at them, but said nothing. Brooklet raised her head and whinnied in pain. With grief written on her face, Tyra examined the mare's leg. "Not you, Brooklet . . ."

As the Vagas advanced, Tyra knelt down and buried her hands in her face. Nels took Tyra's dagger and wielded it at the incoming horde, but they didn't seem to care. More crunching came from behind as another group arrived from the east. The Vagas were coming from every direction, except for the path that led into the city. When they reached a charging distance, each of them came to a stop and waited. They stood silently, staring at the dagger in Nels's hand. To them, it was floating in thin air.

What are they waiting for?

From the north came one more Vaga. This one wasn't a man, but a child — a young girl. She entered the glen gracefully, with a leather satchel over her shoulder. She wore the same attire as her companions, only she had a skirt instead of trousers. Around her neck was a sapphire stone, speckled with golden dust. Her moonlike eyes glanced at Tyra and then stopped at Brooklet's leg.

She was the girl from the festival — the one Nels saved from a turnip.

The girl walked lithely to the injured mare, knelt by her side, and stroked her long mane. "Calm yourself, lady," she soothed. "Be calm." The mare flicked her ears back and gave the girl a small whine. "Spirit — bring me Her Highness's knapsack; I need her sewing kit."

Astounded but dutiful, Nels brought Tyra's knapsack to the girl.

"How does she know about the kit?" Nels asked Tyra. She said nothing.

The girl's eyes looked up and met his. "I am a diviner. The forest told me."

She heard me? Nels couldn't believe it. "Can you see me, too?"

"I hear your voice," she said, "but, no, I do not see you."

Impressed by her demeanor and moved by the serenity of her voice, Nels watched the girl rummage through the knapsack. She retrieved the sewing kit, paused, and said, "Oh, good — you have conjurer's medicine, too," and then also pulled out the flask of creamy, green goop that Gleesel had given Tyra.

The Vaga girl wasted no time in opening the sewing kit's small cedar lid and removing the lump of beeswax. The wax had healed Tyra last night; could it do the same for her mare?

The girl held the flask out for Nels. "Make her drink that," she instructed.

Nels poured the goop into the mare's mouth while the girl coated her hands with the wax and then massaged it into Brooklet's mangled knee. The mare gave a shrill cry as the girl's hands moved over and below the injury. Like the caressing hands of a potter, the girl molded Brooklet's limb into place. In no time, her leg looked normal again. The mare stood up slowly, with a slight limp, and leaned gently on her leg.

"Soon she will be ready to ride again," the girl said. "You are fortunate to have this wax."

There was something special about this girl. Nels hazarded a guess. "Are you Mylan?"

She smiled and nodded. "Hilvar told you?"

"He did. How did you know I saw him?"

Mylan raised her eyebrows and pointed to the city. "You came from his castle."

"Oh . . . right," Nels said with a laugh. "Thank you for healing Brooklet."

The girl gave a courteous bow. "You're welcome. Now I must see what can be done for *her*," she said, pointing at Tyra. She patted the mare's neck one last time before she turned and walked to the princess. "I may need you. Come with me, spirit."

Nels followed Mylan. Tyra had not moved. Her hands still covered her eyes. "We're safe," he said, gently touching Tyra's shoulder. She did not reply. "The Vagas have come and they're here to help. They just healed Brooklet — see? She's walking!"

"Get away from me."

Nels backed away.

"It's your fault!" Tyra's face flushed red. "Arek is dead because of *you!*"

Mylan reached into her satchel, opened her hand, and blew a chalky orange powder into Tyra's face. Tyra coughed until her eyelids slowly drooped closed. She leaned to her side; Nels caught her before she touched the ground. Every part of her was still now, except for her gentle breathing.

"Do not dismay," Mylan said. "You did nothing wrong."

"But what have *you* done to her?" Nels asked.

"I use this powder for my visions. It will help her sleep."

Nels couldn't speak. He just held Tyra, wondering what would happen to them. Death had never come so close to them as at that moment with Rasmus. And if what Rasmus said was true, Arek *was* dead.

"Mylan!" A man called the girl's name.

"Quick," the girl said, looking at the ground. "Lay her down."

Although he didn't want to let Tyra go, Nels did as Mylan instructed. The voice shouted again, closer this time. A moment later, a man entered the clearing and rested on the shoulder of a bowman. The man's beard was decorated with beads, which jostled when he spoke. "There you are," he said, breathing heavily before straightening himself up. "What are you doing here?"

"Acting against the council's will," Mylan answered. "I am sorry, Father."

"Roashil!" The man drew a deep, impatient breath. "When will you call me by my name?" He looked at the men and shook his head. Pine needles fell from his thick locks. "There is danger in this forest and you led our hunters to the heart of it? You may heed premonitions, but you must not answer them!"

The girl retained a respectful stance, but she didn't speak. Nels wanted to know what this man meant by *premonitions*. "I disagree, Father," Mylan said. "It felt right to intervene."

The man pointed at Tyra. "Who is this girl?"

"She is Princess Tyra, heir to the throne of Avërand."

Roashil's mouth dropped open as he bowed low to the forest floor. "Why are you all still standing?" he yelled to the others. "Show your respect to Her Highness!"

Mylan suppressed a small laugh. "She is *asleep*, Father ."

With a slightly embarrassed grunt, Roashil rose to his feet. "If we had known it was the *princess* who was in danger, we would have" — he stopped abruptly — "what is wrong with her?"

"She was in conflict, but I eased her with vision powder."

Roashil pointed at Brooklet. "Is that her horse?"

Mylan nodded.

"And the one who tried to kill her? Is he the one we suspected?"

"The Master Threader," Mylan said. "He is, just as we feared."

"Vigo," Roashil called. "Carry her back to our camp."

The largest of the Vagas stepped forward.

"No," Nels said. "I can't let him carry her."

Mylan raised her hand. "Wait." And then she whispered, "Why not?"

"I am charged with protecting her. I will do it."

He reached under Tyra and picked her up off the ground.

Roashil and the others pulled back and stared at the floating girl. Mylan, unfazed, grasped Brooklet's reins and coaxed the mare into following them.

"Great forces are at work," Roashil said. "Is Hilvar's ghost with us?"

"No, Father," Mylan answered, "but he spoke to them."

"Roashil . . ." the man insisted. "Call me Roashil!"

Nels walked beside Mylan as she led the Vagas north into the forest, unsure where the mysterious girl was taking them. He was curious as to why Roashil refused to let Mylan call him Father.

Nels was surprised by how calm he felt, considering Rasmus's attack, though he worried for Tyra. She had obviously been pushed past her breaking point. At least they were safe now. He hoped when she awoke that she would no longer be angry with him, but he knew she had every reason to be.

Arek — the man she had given her love to — was dead.

Tyra struggled to open her eyes. They flitted open and closed, barely able to focus on anything. She was still in the forest — the wind jostled the leaves high above her. Footsteps — many footsteps — marched on all sides of her, and birds chirped from the trees. As her vision sharpened, she saw that her head was resting on Nels's shoulder. He was carrying her. Before she could notice anything more, her eyes drooped closed and she drifted back out of consciousness.

Sunlight slipped onto Tyra's eyes through the loose seams of a tent.

Where am I?

She sat up. She was on a soft down mat lined with red silk sheets. The urge to doze off again began to sway her, so she shook her head repeatedly to force the sleepiness away. She looked around, feeling terribly wronged; her skin was bare — she had nothing on her body! Only a white sheet covered her, and her arms and hair were clean. Someone had given her a bath.

"She is awake," said a young female voice from behind her.

Tyra seized the sheet to cover herself and spun around. Kneeling at a table of woven fibers was a girl — a Vaga child. Nels sat across from the child. A tendril of white smoke rose from a stick of incense on the table. The colorful walls of the tent were like finely pressed tapestries; the ceiling swayed above her as the tent shifted in the slightest breeze.

The child approached Tyra's bed and bowed politely. "You are safe with us, Your Highness. Your dress was torn beyond repair, so we have some new clothes for you." The girl pointed to a red skirt that had been draped over the foot of the bed. The skirt had celestial symbols sewn into its pleats, and a matching vest and folded silk shirt lay nearby. The clothing was loud in appearance, but finely woven. "I will leave you, for now," the girl said. "When you are ready, you are invited to our celebration tonight."

The girl bowed again before she left.

Nels finally spoke. "You've been asleep all day."

Tyra's mind was too cloudy to acknowledge him.

Rasmus nearly killed me . . .

"Tyra?" Nels asked gently.

And Arek . . . Arek is dead . . .

"Hilvar knows where the Needle is," Nels said. "We have to go back —"

"What good is the Needle now?" she snapped. "It can only bring *you* back."

Nels looked at her with wounded eyes. "Tyra . . . I'm sorry . . . I'm very sorry."

"No you're not! Arek is gone. I can never go home because of you; all you think about is yourself!" Tyra's anger caused her cheeks to tingle. "I wish I had never met you!"

"If you never met me, then Rasmus would've killed *you* as well!"

Nels jumped up from his chair and stormed through the tent wall.

Shaken by his scolding, Tyra curled up and wept into a pillow.

22

THE ETHEREAL DANCE

Watching the Vagas go about their lives made Nels feel more at home in the strange land. Contrary to what he'd heard his whole life, the Vaga camp was not a small gathering of nomadic people; instead, it was a vibrant, thriving community of hundreds. Tents and wooden shelters occupied the forest floor without impeding on the plants and creatures that also lived there. In the last hour, he had seen dozens of Vagas, each hauling branches and logs to the center of the camp. Vigo stacked the wood high in preparation for an enormous bonfire. Smaller flames were already roasting venison and fowl on slowly rotating spits.

Nels tried to sniff the roasting meats; he inhaled through his nose, but all he could smell was the scent of stale beeswax. He spent the afternoon wandering about the Vagas' domain. The large pines were taller than castle turrets, their trunks wider than a nobleman's carriage. Apparently, the Vagas had taken great care of the forest and, in turn, it seemed to have taken care of them. They had an ample flow of water from a river to the north and worms from which they derived silky, abundant fibers for cloth. In addition, several Vagas hauled baskets of nuts and berries into the camp from diverse parts of the forest. Nels eventually found himself back outside the flap of Mylan's tent — the largest dwelling in the camp.

Tyra was still inside. Crying.

Nels kicked at the dirt outside the tent's door. The ground was too moist to make dust clouds, but he kept at it anyway. He heard Tyra sob occasionally, but he didn't move to check on her. Mylan had warned him that Tyra would struggle with this new reality and, thanks to Rasmus, Nels was afraid that she may never forgive him.

He didn't know what to do.

"You worry too much," Mylan said as she approached him.

She was so perceptive, even though he was invisible to her. The diviner's intuition reminded him of Bosh; somehow, they both knew things that ordinary people didn't. "How did you know I was standing here?" he asked.

The girl pointed at the ground. "Soil does not dig itself."

Nels stopped scuffing the dirt. "I'm glad you can hear me."

"You sound restless. You had an argument."

"Yeah," Nels confessed. "Nothing we haven't done before."

Mylan smiled. "Do not take her anger to heart. The only way she can restore the hope she once possessed is through the two greatest gifts of healing."

"What gifts are those?"

"Space and time. She will join us when she is ready."

Trusting in the girl's wisdom, Nels walked with Mylan to the heart of the Vagas' preparations. He was surprised to learn that Mylan was an accomplished diviner — a leader among her people. That was the reason why her father insisted that she call him Roashil — the Vagas thought it improper for a leader to favor one Vaga over another. The Vagas' strange culture was completely foreign to Nels, but he found himself drawn to their warmth and charisma.

"The sun is setting," Mylan said. "Every year on the midsummer eve, we give ourselves back to the forest, a thanks for providing us life. The forest enjoys our song and dance."

Nels looked at her. "How is it that you can hear me?"

The girl paused and turned; her eyes penetrated him. "You never knew your father. I never knew my mother. In our loss, we share a likeness. My sorrow resonates with yours."

Nels didn't understand what she meant, but he was grateful to confide in her regardless. "I'm sorry about your mother."

"And I for your father, but we ought to celebrate the lives they lived."

Nels nodded, accepting the comfort of her words. This young girl reminded him at times of Jilia — same height, same build — but the way Mylan carried herself was completely opposite.

Smiling, she looked to the celebration. "Tonight, you will —"

"Mylan!" They both saw Roashil as he ran toward her.

The girl bowed her head. "What is it, Father?"

Roashil shook his feather-adorned head as he panted to a stop. He was clearly irritated, but not enough to correct his daughter. "Not this year," he implored. "Please — must we cater to *him*?"

Nels looked past Roashil, wondering who he was talking about. "Who's *him*?"

"He is a part of what we celebrate," Mylan said. "It is only fitting."

"But all he does is eat and watch," her father answered.

"If one outsider can appreciate us, more will come to appreciate us," Mylan said. "If we are to seek favor from our neighbors in Averand, we must not turn away our only friends."

Nels had learned from Mylan that her people had tried to earn the acceptance of Averand for most of a century. Now that King Hilvar wanted the Vagas to have his land, Nels understood why. If the kingdom of Westmine was restored, they would be neighbors with Avërand.

Roashil smiled. "You are even more insightful than our elders." He placed a kind hand on her head. "Never has a diviner like you lived among us; I am proud to be your father."

Mylan returned the smile. "Thank you, Roashil."

He laughed. "You will never leave me alone, will you?"

"Oye, there!" A pot-bellied figure shuffled toward them. It was Fargut, carrying a large clay jug of honey. "Be bring'n the bee barf! Happy to be see'n the dance'n about soon!"

Mylan laughed and so did Nels, surprised by how happy he was to see the eccentric man.

Rasmus collapsed as he neared the summit of Westerly Pass.

Moments ago, the sun had set behind him, cloaking the sky with a violet that revealed the more prominent stars. Cording to the top of the pass had worn him out. He clutched the arrow in his hand — he'd pulled it from his shoulder before beginning his ascent. The pain was of no concern to him. He obsessed, instead, about Ulrich's son thwarting his plan.

Miserable boy! How did he get involved with the princess?

"Ickabosh!" he whispered. "You basted their threads together, didn't you?"

Only his old mentor was capable of a stitch like that.

But what does the princess really want the Needle of Gailner for?

The Needle couldn't bring back the dead, so it was useless to her new, invisible friend.

Unless . . .

The thought chilled him. What if the boy wasn't actually *dead*? The Needle *could* weave together an unwoven soul. The old tailor must have hidden the boy's body somewhere. Rasmus cursed. By the blood of his wound, he would stop at nothing to prevent the princess from saving the boy; he could not allow the son of Ulrich to live.

"This way!" someone shouted. "It came from over here!"

Rasmus jumped as a few steps drew close. A dozen more followed. He couldn't afford to be discovered, not now, and not like this. He threaded back into the form of the knight he had slain.

"Sir Arek?" Canis said. "What's happened to you?"

The false Arek turned to the approaching knights, holding up the arrow in his bloodied hand. "Ambushed — by a horde of Vagas. They have the princess!"

"Help him up," Canis ordered.

Many men were with Canis. These same knights had searched for Tyra while wearing nothing more than vests and trousers. But now they were in full armor — dressed for a fight. Were they onto him? Did they know that Rasmus was back?

Two sturdy knights helped him to his feet. "Where's your squire, Sir Arek?"

He faked a frown. "I was about to ask you the same. He . . . deserted me . . . when the Vagas attacked. He could be anywhere in that valley."

As they reached the meadow, Rasmus was truly amazed by the number of men who had gathered on the Westerly Pass. There had to be a hundred, if not more. "What is going on, Sir Canis?"

"Your squire is dead."

They found the boy's body. "What?!"

"We found him after we returned to the castle — *after* you and your squire continued the search without us," Canis said. "The Alvil you and I were traveling with was an imposter."

"But — how — this is —" Arek feigned utter disbelief.

"We're sorry for doubting you, Arek."

Arek tightened his fists for show. "If I had known."

"It's Rasmus," said another of the knights. "He's returned."

Canis nodded. "And now he's after our princess."

"I saw her," Arek said. "Before the Vagas nearly killed me."

"So you left her with them?" One of the younger men had spoken up. He was armed with little more than a head of red hair. "You — the favored knight — ran away from *them* when the princess was in danger?"

"Quiet, Wallin!" Canis ordered. "He's done the right thing, coming to us." He leaned in close to Arek's ear. "Don't mind this untrained lot. We felt it best to gather a few volunteers. If Rasmus has come back, we need every able-bodied man if we stand a chance of stopping him."

Arek said nothing. If Lennart had sent these men to reclaim the princess *and* stop him, then their absence would make the castle vulnerable. He could alter his plan. "That explains why Alvil behaved so strangely," Arek said. "He was in league with the Vagas!" Arek turned to the men waiting for his command. "I need a horse. I must go back and inform the king!"

They collected a stallion without questioning him further. The knights cast angry looks to the Valley of Westmine. The false Arek smiled; he had put their prejudice to good use. As he mounted his new horse, he announced profoundly, "Do what you must. The Vagas will not give up without a fight. I will return once I have spoken with the king."

"Be on your guard," Canis warned. "Rasmus could be anywhere — or anyone."

The knights of Avërand and their untrained peasants marched west as Arek spurred his horse to the east. That had been a close one. If that lot had suspected him, he would have been done for, even though he had enough magic left in his thread to handle many of them. The ground was dark, making it hard to navigate past the Westerly Mansion and the mound where he had left the real Arek to rot.

It was a relief to see the shallow grave undisturbed.

Arek stopped at the cliff, raised his hands, and formed another circle with his fingers. He pointed them at Castle Avërand, which from here was just at a splotch of light in the distance. His arms shook, as did his breath. "No," he whispered. He had to accept his limits. "Cording that far will tear me apart."

He pointed to the base of the mountain instead, and was gone.

The sun had set, but the moon had yet to rise.

The Vagas celebrated the night with fervor. Everyone came fashionably dressed, wearing extravagant blends of red, white, and gold. They danced around a dozen fires, each flickering above the heads of even tallest Vagas. The camp was bright, and the tall flames cast long shadows into the forest. Fargut was clearly enjoying himself, clapping to the beat of tambourines between sips of strong cider.

When they weren't dancing, everyone drank, enjoyed the feast, and told stories — many of them new to Nels. They were a happy people — genuinely happy.

And Tyra was missing everything. His anger toward her had faded. He recognized the amount of shock and loss she'd been forced to confront in a very short time.

Mylan was sitting beside Nels, enjoying her people's talents. She clapped whenever it was warranted — which was often — but between cheers, she told Nels more about her people's reason for the celebration. Midsummer was the height of life for the Vagas, and each of their dances carried a special meaning. Their music and dancing stirred his spirit, just as it had when he was alive — at the Cobblestown festival. In their celebration of life, the Vagas held nothing back.

Right now, only couples twirled in the circle.

"The courtship dance," Mylan said. "For those who have found love."

It was a nice thought. "I should check on Tyra," Nels said.

"No need," Mylan replied. "She will find her way."

Nels wanted to believe her. But he also wanted to make sure Tyra was all right, even if he was the last person the princess wanted to see. He was about to stand and go to her anyway, despite Mylan's advice, when the music changed.

New dancers entered the circle, lighting long yellow candles as they stepped within the perimeter. Each participant lit the candle of the person behind him or her.

"The knowledge dance," Mylan explained. "A light in the darkness will guide one through."

All the dancers held the candles in their left hands. The women used their right hands to hold up their skirts, and the men pressed their closed fists into their sides. They spun slowly and placed their steps with perfect grace. Nels had never seen such a beautiful waltz.

"Why do they move so slowly?" he asked.

A warm smile sprang onto Mylan's face. "Move too fast and your light will go out," she said. "What will you learn if you rush through life?"

Knowledge. Nels thought about her words through the remainder of the dance. This young girl knew so much — probably even more than she let on. He remembered when they had met at the festival, and how she had withdrawn from him. She'd seemed frightened of him.

"Do you remember me from the festival, in Cobblestown?" Nels asked.

She laughed. "Yes. Should I eat another turnip, it will be too soon."

"When you said, 'you are not supposed to be here,' what did you mean?"

The girl looked away uncomfortably without answering the question. Nels was about to ask again when Mylan's eyes darted over his shoulder. "Welcome, Your Highness!"

Nels turned around. Tyra stood behind them, watching the dance with a glazed look on her face, the glow of the fire shining in her swollen eyes. She had cried for hours. Nels wanted to say something, but Tyra's sad beauty left him speechless.

She wore a long red skirt, a matching blouse that emphasized her bare shoulders, and a leather bodice that had a small pocket on the side. Every seam was sewn with gold thread, and flowers and leafy stems were embroidered throughout in painstaking detail. Were it not for her blue eyes and yellow hair, she would have looked exactly like one of the Vagas. The only item she wore from her old wardrobe was Sibylla's iron ring.

"Where is my mare?" she asked.

It was a good question. Nels hadn't thought of Brooklet since that afternoon.

"She is resting," Mylan answered. "Are *you* rested, Your Highness?"

The princess didn't answer. The music came to a stop, bringing the knowledge dance to an end. Tyra's eyes stared blankly at the Vagas as they clapped for the carefully bowing dancers with their still-lit candles. The musicians set down their instruments and helped themselves to what they could find on passing plates. With a grateful nod, Mylan accepted a helping of flatbread. Tyra let the plate pass by her untouched; she seemed oblivious to her surroundings.

"Be with me," Mylan said to Tyra, inviting the princess to sit by her side.

Without looking at anyone, Tyra complied.

"I hope you like your dress," Mylan continued. "We do not have textiles or looms as advanced as yours, but it is our very best. It is our gift for your return home."

"Home," Tyra said mournfully. "I can't go home."

Nels stared at her, saddened by the emptiness in her voice.

"You are welcome to stay with us as long as you like," Mylan said. "If you decide to stay, our eligible young men will certainly take notice, as beautiful as you are."

Another plate — this one loaded with drumsticks — came their way. Tyra turned it down.

"You should eat something," Nels said. "You haven't eaten all day."

"I don't want to."

"You'll starve."

"So what?"

Mylan held out her hands and took hold of Tyra's palm. The Vaga leader closed her eyes and drew a long, steady breath. A cool breeze followed, as if called by the breath, leaning the fire's flame to the south. "It is easy for sorrow to consume our feelings. You suffer, Princess of Averand, because

262

you hold more than a memory. You wish to solemnize your heartache. You are not alone."

Tyra raised her eyes. Nels did the same.

A few Vagas had returned to the dance and waited for the fiddlers to start a new melody. The women held the hems of their skirts with one hand and extended their other hands; the men formed a similar pose with one arm behind their backs. None had a partner.

"The ethereal dance," Mylan said. "We diviners believe in an unreachable plane — called the ethereal — where we all must cross to when we die. This dance allows our hearts to ease the burden of loss. That child over there" — she pointed to one side of the circle — "lost her brother to a fever last winter. And that man over there buried his wife many years ago." Mylan released Tyra's hand and stood. "If you would pardon me a moment, I wish to dance with my mother."

With that, Mylan left them and entered the dance.

Nels observed the girl, her face calm compared to those who cried. He was just realizing that the crying dancers weren't sad, they were joyful, when a sharp sob drew his attention away. The firelight glistened in Tyra's tearful eyes. Her tears were not ones of joy.

Nels didn't know what to say after all they had been through, but he decided to try anyway. "You're doing okay," he said, reaching for anything that might help. As expected, she did not respond to him. "When I died, my mother was much worse," he continued. "After a while, she just didn't have any more tears left to cry."

"It's my fault, Nels. I left a handkerchief for him to track us."

Instead of being upset at her confession, Nels accepted it. She had never sounded so sincere. "No," he said, "It's not your fault. I should have told you sooner that we were in danger. You had no idea."

She looked at Nels with regret in her eyes. "You were right. Arek wanted the throne for himself, and in my heart, I knew it. But I *wanted* him to have it — so *I* wouldn't have to rule. I'm a coward, just like my father!" She raised her hands to her face. "I'm afraid to return to Avërand."

"You're not your father, Tyra. You're brave. Your parents need you, your kingdom needs you, and" — Nels reached for her hand and linked his fingers with hers — "*I* need you."

Tyra glanced down. Her fingers slid through his hand as she stood. "I can't."

Feeling useless, Nels watched as Tyra joined the dance.

It was the fire that lured Tyra into the dance.

Its heat caressed her shoulders and its light threw shadows on her face. This was her home now, this wilderness with the Vagas. They were nothing like her subjects had made them out to be; they were kind and generous. Though she still wished this were all a dream, she was slowly coming to terms with reality — her reality.

The Vagas moved around her like phantoms, dancing with memories of the dead. It was a ludicrous idea, but for Arek, it was all she could do. Tyra looked at the women, copied their stance, and imagined Arek's hand cupping her waist. She stepped back, mimicking their steps. The ground was free from obstacles, and the other dancers provided her with plenty of space, but her balance swayed and she fell out of sync when she tried to imagine her handsome knight. No matter how hard she tried, his presence would not take hold in her mind.

As Tyra danced, she asked a question that she'd never thought — or dared — to ask.

Did I really love him?

Now that he was gone, there was no way for her to know if she could tolerate his blatant imperfections, his vanity, or his arrogance. She'd cared about him because she knew, when the time came, she could easily shift her responsibilities to Arek. He would have welcomed it. It was convenient . . . for them both. But that was not love; it was nothing short of selfish.

No. She never truly loved Arek. Being threatened by Rasmus made her realize just how pathetic she was. She didn't cry as much for her knight as she did for her parents and her kingdom. They were in danger, but she wanted to stay here, hidden and safe. Exhausted from grief, Tyra stopped her dance and stood still. The shame of her cowardice caused her legs to shake.

Someone took her by the hand, making her look up. Nels was standing by her side, tall and confident. Something in his eyes — something new — strengthened her. Whatever it was, it gave her courage and made her feel safe. Instead of pulling away, she returned his stare and tried to return his grasp.

"You're rather close," she said.

Nels placed his free hand on her back. "Not close enough."

With the rising tempo, they joined the dance.

He stepped forward, and she stepped back; she was no longer unbalanced and out of sync. The Vagas saw this and cheered. Even Fargut gave a loud holler, a shred of pheasant dangling from his beard. A smile found its way to Tyra's face as she locked her eyes with Nels's. Of all the men Tyra had known, he was the most selfless and the most honest. His eyes, shining in the firelight, had never been this close. She wanted to run her fingers through his hair, just to feel *him*.

She leaned forward and tried to rest her head on his chest. She felt nothing there, but she kept her head in place anyway. There was no warmth, not even the beating of his heart, but that didn't stop her from imagining what it would sound like. There was no one else like him in the world — and soon, he would be gone. He was on the edge of the ethereal.

But with the Needle, she could change that. The thought of seeing him alive — really *alive* — summoned courage from within her.

When Tyra raised her head from his intangible chest, she had made her choice.

I have to bring him back.

The music reached its climax and then came to a halt. The dancers applauded the musicians, who all took a bow. Roashil was among them, holding a fiddle. Tyra stayed close to Nels, his hand still on her back, until their eyes met again. For the first time since they'd met, she wanted to know what his hands felt like. Alive. Holding her.

"I never thought a peasant could dance so well," she said.

Nels smiled and laughed. "I never thought a princess would dance with one."

Mylan joined them. "You danced well. A ghost partner must make a difference."

"Are you Mylan?" Tyra waited for the girl to nod. "I must apologize to you."

The girl shook her head. "No need. We are at peace with your misunderstanding."

Grateful for the forgiveness, Tyra clasped hands with Mylan. "What matters now is finding the Needle."

"What about Rasmus?" Nels asked. "He said he'd kill us if we go back."

"We'll use the Needle to stop him," Tyra uttered.

"Assuming we find it and learn how to use it," Nels said.

"We'll have to. It's the only way we can stop him."

"You're right." Nels looked into her eyes again. This time, Tyra welcomed it. "And I'm not ready to die just yet."

Tyra smiled. "Then we must find Hilvar."

"Does Hilvar know where your Needle is?" Mylan asked.

"Yes, but until he gives his land to you and your people, he won't tell us." Nels's eyes returned to Tyra's. "He thinks he can do this through *you* — by possessing you."

Tyra swallowed. The thought of *allowing* the spirit to enter her body again; it made her shiver. But if they had any hope of stopping Rasmus, or saving Nels, she was willing to do what she had to. "I'm ready to speak with him," Tyra said. "How do we find him?"

"There is no need," Nels said, looking at Mylan.

The girl nodded. "Hilvar is already with us."

"He is? How do you know?" Tyra asked.

Mylan smiled. "The scent of a draug is unmistakable."

Before Tyra could react, a cold sensation overtook her, just like when she stood on the landing in Westmine Castle. She had no control of her arms, her body, or even her voice. This time, she didn't feel angry or threatened. Without fighting back, she relaxed and allowed the ghost of King Hilvar to use her however he needed to.

"Mylan." Tyra was surprised by her voice — strong and deep. Compelled to step forward, the draug raised her arms and laid her hands on Mylan's shoulders. "Centuries ago, my father wronged your people. I wronged the love of my life. Only by bestowing this valley and all of my riches to you — my heir — can I leave this plane and join my love. Will you accept my kingdom?"

Mylan reached for Tyra's hands and gently lifted them off her shoulders. She brought their joined hands down, continued to hold them, and smiled. "I will, mighty Hilvar."

After the ghost made Tyra bow, Hilvar turned to Nels. "Now I am free." Tyra's hands found their way onto Nels's shoulders now, clasping them firmly. Strangely, Tyra could feel him. "West of my castle, there is a black peak in a barren land. Sealed in a cavern beneath the peak, you will find what you seek. Only a living soul may access the Needle's resting place. If . . . if you should find my remains, please dispose of me."

With that, the ghostly presence left her. Tyra's knees felt weak, as if the ground had fallen away beneath her. Nels caught her before she fell. She wanted to sleep, and she nearly did, until Mylan approached with a powder in her hand. One sniff of it and Tyra was wide-awake.

"It is done," Mylan said joyfully. "Hilvar is at peace, and my people will have a home."

Mustering a smile, Tyra found the strength to stand. Nothing felt impossible now. "There's no time to waste," she said. "We must find this black peak! Where do we start?"

"Go'n to Black Peak, you say'n?" Fargut approached from behind. He put on his lantern hat and rubbed a few traces of food from his fingers — leaving plenty of scraps still in his beard.

This man knew the valley better than anyone.

"Can I ask for your help, Fargut?" Tyra asked.

"Oye?"

"Can you take us to the black peak?"

"Desolate land, be'n there. You sure'n about go'n?"

"Yes," Tyra said. "I will even make it worth your while."

The man's fleshy lips puckered to the side. "My while?"

"Do you know the town of Harvestport in Avërand?"

"Oye!" Fargut held up three fingers. "Be'n there twice!"

"In return for guiding us, the next time you visit my

kingdom, you and I will go to Harvestport together," Tyra promised. "You can take anything that you can carry!"

The man let his hands rest on his full belly as he rocked on his heels.

"Assisting our friends will repay our kindness to you," Mylan chimed in.

Fargut let out a small burp, and then he swallowed. "Be a fair trade'n. Pack'n wares! We're leave'n!" He turned around, hiccupped, and sloshed to the other side of the celebration.

"Trading," Mylan sighed. "That is how we deal with him all the time." She looked Tyra in the eyes. "I am pleased you feel restored, Princess. If you are to reach the peak by noon tomorrow, you had best leave now."

Tyra appreciated the advice. "Will you have my horse ready for us to leave?"

Mylan shook her head. "She is lucky to walk. Your bees-wax and flask of conjurer's medicine saved her leg, but we have other remedies to give her before she can ride. Once you find your Needle and return, she should be ready to carry you back to Averand — and we will be ready to escort you home."

"You needn't trouble yourself. This isn't your errand."

"It is not, but in doing so — as the new queen of Westmine — perhaps I can lay to rest the rumors about us." The young queen bowed as she removed her sapphire neck-lace. "I feel that you may need this." She placed it in Tyra's hand. "When you return it, please tell me why."

With that, Mylan left them. Tyra waited with Nels by the edge of the celebration. She could barely feel the heat from their fires. She took the sapphire and looped the band around her neck, eager to pick up where their journey had left off.

"Thank you," Nels said.

She turned. The smile on his face was perfect. "For what?"

"For being the princess that everyone knows you to be."

"No. I should thank *you* for acting like the knight that you are," Tyra said. "Let's find the Needle."

"Right," Nels said. "And when we do —" A repulsed look suddenly replaced his smile. He sniffed once, and then twice, as if he were a hound.

Tyra sniffed. All she smelled was the fire. "What's wrong?"

Nels looked around. "I can't smell beeswax anymore."

"What *do* you smell?"

"Hay . . . and horses?" He paused. "I'm in a stable!"

His eyes widened as fear spread across his face. Someone had moved his body.

Was it Bosh? Or someone else?

Tyra's thoughts turned to the worst. She couldn't let Rasmus find Nels. "Come on," she said, reaching for his hand. "We have to leave this place right now!"

The false Arek rode past the city gate, his bloodied shoulder smarting. He had tossed his thread across the countryside, cording over field and plain whenever he had the strength for it. When he entered the city, some of the peasants asked if he had found the princess. He ignored them. Now that he was inside, he had only enough time for one last ruse before he needed to rest.

He lumbered up the stairs of the main hall, sneered as he charged past the royal portrait, and barged into the throne room, startling a few noblemen who were conversing with the king.

Lennart raised his head, immediately noticing the wound. "What has happened?!"

Out of breath, Arek fell to his knees. "I need water." He wasn't pretending.

The king summoned a courtier with a chalice. Arek seized the cup and drank; he hadn't realized how thirsty he was. A pair of physicians entered and began cleaning his wound.

"Who harmed you?" Lennart asked. "Where is my daughter?"

"The Vagas have her," the false Arek answered. "This arrow is theirs."

The king tucked his chin and crossed his arms. "It is worse than I thought."

"Canis told me everything," Arek added. "The imposter is with the Vagas."

"This is no longer speculation, Your Majesty," said a nobleman. "What are we to do?"

"I sent my finest knights," Lennart said. "Then again, that may not be enough." The king raised his head. His eyes searched the room, pausing only at those who stared back. "Send the rest. Send them all. Have them join with the ranks of Canis. Leave only the reserves behind!"

"But, Sire," implored another nobleman. "Suppose the intruder comes back?"

Arek took another long swig to cover his nerves.

He was so close to Lennart — closer than he had been in years.

"I am nothing unless my daughter is safe," Lennart said. "Send the order. And leave us!"

Arek raised his head. *Us?*

Everyone left, including the physicians who had applied a stiff bandage to the false Arek's shoulder — not even they could tell the difference between real and fabricated skin. What he would give for a touch of beeswax right now, just to alleviate some of the pain!

"I know Tyra is fond of you, that she is close to you," Lennart said as the throne room doors closed. "If you save her, I will grant you her hand. Tell me what you know."

The king stood over Arek, who couldn't believe his good fortune. No one was watching; no one was near. No one saw Arek smile as he drew his knife.

Rasmus couldn't have arranged a more perfect reunion.

23

THE WEAVER'S GATE

The sun moved toward the west, having traveled far since they'd left the Vagas' camp. The land was dry and hilly, with only a few trees scattered about. Rocks and hardy bushes dominated this region — a more desolate place than Nels liked.

As he'd promised, Fargut was their guide. He asked for a rest every now and then, but Tyra kept going. She refused to stop. Nels couldn't help but wonder why she'd become obsessed with finding the Needle. Ever since their dance, since he held her close, she had changed — a change that he liked.

When the peak came into view, Tyra took the lead. Fragments of black rocks were scattered around their feet as they marched. Nels encouraged her to slow down, but she stubbornly maintained her pace.

"Sit us down!" Fargut bellowed, about to plop down at the trail's end.

"We must find the entrance," Tyra said. "We still have a lot of ground to cover."

Fargut, out of breath, wheezed as the three travelers climbed a narrow path that wrapped around the strange mountain. Nels had never seen anything like it; the peak's curves were perfectly round, and there were crunchy, glass-like rocks under their feet. Sweat covered Tyra's forehead. Her legs shook.

"I have never seen . . . a real volcano . . . until now," she said, breathing hard.

"Gailner picked a good place," Nels said. "I'd never think to come here."

Tyra heaved a laugh. "I'm sure . . . that's why . . . he chose . . . this place."

She was obviously tired. "Please slow down," Nels begged as he retrieved her waterskin and handed it to her. "You won't have any strength to go back."

"We may be too late already." She looked up, drank from the skin, and wiped her mouth dry with the sleeve of her new shirt. "I have a promise to keep."

By the time they had rounded the other side of the peak, they had climbed high enough to see far into the fissured lands of the southeast, where the Westerly Mountains stretched to the sea. If they had a boat, they could sail around the peninsula, head east, and reach Avërand in a day. If Nels could fly and carry Tyra all at once, they could go over the mountain and be at the castle in a matter of hours. But no matter how often he'd tried, Nels couldn't figure out how to simultaneously fly *and* hold things.

Fargut turned a bend and collapsed into a shallow alcove. "Find'n it," he said, pointing at a thick man-made wall of stone. "Good luck get'n in. I couldn't."

Layers of dense masonry had sealed the entrance from top to bottom. Rusted shovels and broken pickaxes littered the threshold. It was clear that many prospectors had been here and — given the wall's pristine condition — it appeared that none of them had succeeded in entering. Tyra traced her finger along the grout lines; for the first time this day, she looked doubtful.

"We never asked Hilvar how to get in, did we?" she asked.

Nels shook his head. "He seemed confident that we would, though."

"There be'n no way in," Fargut said. "I pick'n for days, and not once make'n a chip."

Reaching for the nearest discarded tool, Tyra swung at the wall with all her might.

Clang!

The pickax left no mark — not a single scratch. She tried again, harder. This time, the now-crooked tool bounced back with a spark. Nels reached out and stopped her. "You know," he said, smiling, "I can walk through walls."

Tyra blew a strand of hair away from her face and gestured at the wall. "After you . . ."

Nels stepped into the wall. Light turned to darkness. He couldn't see a thing, nor could he tell if he was past the barrier and inside the dark mountain, or if he was still merged with the stone.

He felt his way around, trying to focus his eyes. Suddenly, he kicked something. He reached out and grasped some kind of pole. It seemed loose, so he pulled on it. A sharp click resonated from within the walls, then he heard a low rumble. As the wall began to sink into the earth, daylight spilled into the cave, drawing air into the cavern like a breath.

Fargut dashed up, astonished. "How'n you do that?"

Tyra entered as the wall became level with the ground. "I would like to know, too."

Nels pointed at the lever. "A mechanism, like the one I saw in Hilvar's castle."

Tyra glanced at it. "It looks like a crochet hook. How do *non-ghosts* enter this place?"

The lever did resemble a crochet hook — and Bosh's walking stick. "Maybe only fabricators can enter," Nels said.

275

"Maybe they use their thread to pull the lever from the other side?"

"We can ask Bosh later." Tyra gazed deep into the cave. "It's very dark in there."

"Not'n problem!" Fargut removed his lantern hat. He sparked up a wick, adjusted a few mirrors, and in no time had a little flame shining bright from atop his head. Nels looked at the long shadow that Tyra cast on the undisturbed ground. "Walk'n close," Fargut said. "Be'n dangerous, caves."

They walked carefully, listening to the air as it howled through the tunnel.

"We're almost there," said Tyra, a glint of lantern light in her eyes.

Nels smiled and took hold of her hand.

Hot, dry air flew up from the chasm below. It brought with it a smell of molten iron and sulfur that reminded Tyra of boiled eggs, making her gag. Tyra leaned over the side of the precipice and peered down the shaft, holding tight to Nels's hand. She could see nothing but a black abyss. She glanced back at the speck of light where they had entered; it was a straight walk with no forks or any intricate passageways. The chasm didn't have a staircase or a ladder, nor was there a rope that dangled to the bottom. There was nowhere to go but down.

But how do we reach the bottom?

She turned to Nels. "What now?"

Nels let go of her hand. "I'll have a look. Maybe I have to pull another lever down there."

He stepped off the edge and fell into the darkness. Fargut gave a short grunt. He looked around, found a sizable rock, and let it fall over the side. They listened . . . and listened . . . and listened. Seconds later, Nels floated back up, arriving just as they heard the echo of the rock bursting below.

"That could've hit me," Nels teased.

Tyra smiled nervously. "How do we go down there?" she asked, glancing at Nels. "Can you fly me down?"

"It doesn't work that way," he said. "I can only carry things when I'm on the ground."

"Oh," Tyra said. She had never considered that before. "Do you have any rope, Fargut?"

"Not enough'n," he answered. "Still have'n sew'n kit?"

"I do," she said, "but what good will it do here?"

Fargut held out his hand, waiting to receive the kit. Tyra searched through her knapsack and retrieved the little box of cedar wood. Fargut opened the lid and passed over the seam ripper and the vial of black dye. He picked up the spool of thread and set it on the ground next to them. Next, he delicately pinched the brass thimble with his thick fingers, picked it up, and handed it to Tyra.

"Best be carry'n," he said. "Thimble magic protect'n you."

She took the thimble from him and placed it in the pocket of her leather bodice.

"Here." Fargut unraveled the spool of thread. "I be lower'n you down."

"Down?" Was he serious? "You're going to lower me down with *thread*?"

"Yep! Take'n end. I'll unravel'n some. See your knife? Hold your end tight."

Tyra gave Fargut her dagger, found the loose end of the clear thread, and took hold of it. She unraveled a good yard of the thread and waited to see what the man would do next.

What exactly did he have in mind? He held the dagger tightly and placed the edge on the translucent thread. He pressed down, hard, but it didn't sever — it wouldn't cut. The thread resisted her sharp blade.

"Just when you've seen everything," Nels said.

"Invincible!" Fargut returned the dagger. "Tie'n end under arms. I stay'n and you lower'n."

Tyra agreed with Nels; this magic was astounding. "What is that vial?" she asked.

Fargut squinted as he held the vial up over his head. "For dye'n another threads." Fargut unraveled the spool some more, revealing more silky clear thread. "Good for make'n threads seen, reveal what fabricators hide'n under sleeves. Remove'n illusions, be'n marked by it."

Fargut placed the vial back inside the kit.

"That could be useful." Tyra cleared her throat. "Is there enough thread?"

The man looked over the side again. "Always enough'n for job."

Tyra asked Nels to take the end of the thread and fasten a secure knot under her arms. He did so, but looked skeptical. He had fair reason to be; it was terribly disconcerting to think of Fargut lowering her deep into a dark chasm with only a thin thread to support her. Fargut held the spool of thread in one hand, then unraveled several yards of thread with the other.

"I'll hold'n this while you go'n down," he said.

Tyra sat on the edge of the chasm. Fargut lifted her up by the thread under her arms and dangled her just past the edge, over the blackness.

"You will wait for us after we get to the bottom," Tyra said, looking up at the potbellied man. "Won't you?"

Fargut nodded solemnly and began to lower her into the darkness.

278

Closing her eyes with a sigh, Tyra tried to relax so there wouldn't be unnecessary movements to cause Fargut extra strain. She'd even left her knapsack above to lessen the load on the man. The lantern light dimmed the farther she descended. The smell of molten iron grew more potent with each passing second. She was grateful to have Nels floating by her side.

"How much farther before we reach the bottom, do you think?" she asked.

"A ways off, but there's another tunnel down there. An *orange* tunnel."

"Lovely. You don't suppose we'll need Fargut's lantern?"

"I hope not," he answered. "I'll walk ahead in case you —"

Tyra didn't hear that last part. She'd entered into a free fall. She scratched at the chasm's wall and tried to scream, but there was no air in her lungs. Suddenly, she jerked to a stop, bouncing a little from the abrupt change in momentum. The thin thread under her arms felt sharp, and she was surprised that it hadn't cut into her.

Thank goodness for the thimble!

Finally catching her breath, Tyra looked down and found herself dangling mere inches above the ground.

"Are you hurt?" Nels asked.

Something dripped on Tyra's hand as Fargut's voice reached them. "Girly alive?"

"Yes," she said, but not loud enough. She cleared her throat. "Yes, I am fine!"

"M'sorry! Lost'n my grip! Hand hurt'n! Thread cut it when I caught'n ya! Have you beeswax?"

Tyra felt sick, knowing it was his blood that she'd felt on her hand. "We're fine!" she shouted as she rubbed her hand on the side of her skirt. "Take as much wax as you need! Is there much thread left?"

After a slight pause, they heard him shout back. "Nope! Unravel'n all of it — and you be'n out of beeswax."

Looking over her shoulder, Tyra saw a faint orange light in the distance. The light was much dimmer than a lantern but more consistent. Wiping the sweat from her face, she found the chasm floor with her toes and pushed the thread down her body, stepping out of the loop.

She left the thread hanging there. "We're moving on! We'll be back soon!" she called up the chasm, hoping that Fargut's hand would be okay. She then looked around, searching for Nels.

He was leaning against the wall, his hands on his knees.

"What about you?" she asked. "Are you all right?"

He glanced at her and straightened up. "I will be — after we find the Needle."

"Right." Tyra nodded resolutely. "What do you suppose is down here?"

"I don't know." He turned toward the orange light emanating from the tunnel. "Stay close to me."

"Don't worry," she said, coming to his side. "We'll find it."

As he smiled, she wished in silence that she was right.

Before entering the tunnel, Nels was surprised that he felt lightheaded and short of breath, which he had never experienced as a ghost. He didn't say anything to Tyra. He didn't know what to say. Perhaps the magic in his thimble was beginning to wear off. He couldn't smell the protective beeswax anymore, just the stink of horse droppings and damp alfalfa. Knowing his body had been removed from Bosh's cellar made Nels even more anxious — especially with the threat of Rasmus's return to Avërand.

They were under the earth now, nearing the source of light.

"It's warm down here," Tyra said. "A little *too* warm."

Nels noticed her flushed face. "Just a little farther."

Tyra gasped the moment they reached the orange light. The tunnel had given way to a cavern that was bisected by a river of liquid fire. Yellow blotches rose like scalding bubbles, plopping and popping with a deep gurgle. Dark red patches sunk beneath the surface. On the other side of the river was another tunnel.

Tyra threw her arms in the air. "There's no bridge. How do we get across?"

Nels approached the edge of the fiery flow. "Wait here."

He jumped into the air and floated over the molten rock. A pile of skeletal remains within a charred suit of armor sat on the river's far bank. In the skeleton's slightly curled hand was a partially melted brass thimble.

"Hilvar," Nels said. "Not even a thimble could help you here."

The tunnel's entrance was blocked by a large stone wall. Nels stepped into the wall — and bounced right back. He tried again, but he could not pass through. He examined the wall's surface. There was an engraving of a person, very much like the figures carved into the arch in the Fabrication chamber beneath Westmine Castle. But this person was alone, life-sized, and held three objects in its outstretched hands. Nels couldn't tell what the objects were — time had faded the details of the engraving.

On the engraved person's chest there was a slightly recessed handprint. Nels reached out and placed his hand into the print. Nothing happened. He pushed. Still, nothing.

Just then, Nels remembered what Hilvar had said:

Only a living soul may access the Needle's resting place.

That's why he couldn't walk through the wall; Tyra would have to open the door. Frustrated by his discovery, Nels floated back over the molten river and told Tyra of Hilvar's remains and the door.

Tyra stared across the burning river. "Is Hilvar's body *really* over there?"

Nels sighed. He was out of ideas. "What's left of him."

"I was hoping this would protect me," she said, clutching her thimble.

"I wouldn't trust it fully," Nels said, looking again at Hilvar's remains. "I can't get through the barrier, and I don't know how to get you over there. We'll have to find another way."

"If you can't fly me across," she said, "then you'll have to carry me."

Nels spun around. "What?"

"The fire will not hurt you. I have this thimble, and you are tall enough."

She could not be serious. "What if I drop you?"

"There's no other way," she said. "You won't drop me."

"It's too dangerous. I won't carry you into harm's way!"

"Nels" — her eyes shone from the fiery river — "carry me."

Her bravery dissolved Nels's reservations. She was right; it was the only way and they had no time to argue. To claim the Needle, they had to reach the other side — together. Tyra let out a gasp as Nels reached below her, wrapped her skirt around her legs, and raised her high into his arms.

"No matter what happens, don't let go of that thimble," he warned.

She nodded and wrapped her arms around his shoulders. Nels entered the river and started to cross. He took three steps, and the molten river came up to his knees. Six steps later it was just under his waist. Tyra's skirt began to scorch.

Sweat flowed from her pores. "This is *really* hot!"

Nels trudged on, holding her body up as high as he could. If they did not reach the other side soon, she would roast. Midway across, his vision began to blur, and his head started to ache.

"Hot!" Tyra cried again. "Hurry, Nels — ouch!"

His concentration waned, and Tyra began to slip through his arms. Gathering the last of his focus and strength, Nels flung her across the burning river. Tyra let out a scream as the hem of her skirt caught fire, and she landed on the charred bank. Nels ran the rest of the way and swatted at the flames.

"What was *that*?" Tyra sounded furious. "Why did you throw me?"

"I had no choice. You were slipping through me," he said.

"Slipping *through*? But that means your thimble is" — she stood and looked at the corpse beside them. Everything from the torso down was missing — "running out of magic."

"We'd better hurry, then." Remembering Hilvar's request, Nels pressed his hands onto the armor. "Thank you," he whispered to the king's remains. Then he gently pushed them into the river.

They vanished quickly, with the half-melted thimble sinking last.

As she and Nels left the charred bank, Tyra felt grateful for the respect he had shown Hilvar. She never saw Hilvar's ghost, but she'd felt him both times when he possessed her. She shook the thought from her mind — their business with the ghost was finished, but their reason for coming was still in front of them. They had to find the Needle, and they had no way of knowing how much farther they had to go.

"All you have to do is touch this, I think," Nels said, placing his hand on the recessed print engraved on the wall. "Try it."

Tyra reached out and placed her hand over his. Something clicked deep within the wall, and a rumbling began beneath their feet. The wall shifted and lowered into the ground, just as it had at the cave's entrance. A cool breeze rushed out of the newly exposed passage; she basked in the refreshing change in temperature.

They glanced at each other before they both walked inside.

The passage wound to and fro for several feet. As they rounded the final bend, they saw dozens of candles, all lit, surrounding the perimeter of a smaller cavern. More candles sat on various protrusions along the walls. Three life-sized statues surrounded a pool of shallow water where a dark stone arch hung over a loom forged entirely of metal. The three statues had their arms out, palms open, like pedestals. Tyra and Nels walked in front of them. The statues' gem eyes gleamed. It was like nothing they'd ever seen, but there was no Needle here. They had reached another dead end.

"What is this place?" Tyra asked. "Who lit these candles?"

Nels snapped his fingers and paused, waiting.

Nothing happened. "What are you doing?" Tyra asked.

Nels pointed at the statue of a young girl to their left. "Diviner!" He then turned to the statue of a bald man to their right. "Conjurer!" And finally, he acknowledged the bearded man in the center. "Fabricator!"

If there was a connection, Tyra failed to see it.

"The three magical traditions in the sorcerers' alliance!" Nels said.

Tyra rubbed her temple. "What are you talking about?"

"This loom and this arch — it's a Weaver's Gate!"

"Gate?" Tyra asked. "*What's* a Weaver's Gate?"

Nels held out his hand. "Can I see your ring?"

She pulled it off her finger and handed it to him. He walked to the conjurer's statue, placed the ring into its upturned hands, and quickly stepped back. Its gem eyes began to glow.

"Mylan's necklace," he said. "Hurry!"

Tyra removed it from her neck and watched him place it in the diviner statue's hands. Like the conjurer statue, its eyes also began to shine. Finally understanding the pattern, Tyra seized her thimble and put it in the fabricator's hands. Light streamed from its eyes.

The water beneath the loom churned and rose into the loom's empty shed, forming a clear wall.

"Whoa," Nels said. "Bosh's loom never did this . . ."

As the water climbed higher, it revealed Nels's reflection, but it didn't show Tyra's. She was standing next to Nels, but in the water, she was invisible. "Why can't I see myself?" she asked.

"I don't know." Nels poked the liquid mirror with his finger. Water dripped down his hand and forearm. He pulled back in surprise. "Did you see that? I felt it." He paused. "*How* can I feel it?"

When Tyra touched the reflective surface, she felt nothing — and her finger was dry.

Nels stepped back and dived headfirst into his reflection inside the loom. He came right back out and laughed; he was thoroughly soaked. "Can you believe this?"

Tyra laughed, too. "This is certainly the strangest gate I've ever seen. Let me try."

She plunged into the water — and the cavern vanished.

To her surprise, Tyra stood perfectly dry in a hall that stretched on forever. More candles than she could count —

thousands of them — lined the stone floor, and hundreds of tall columns stretched high above her head and far into the horizon on both sides. There were no walls or doors here, only a vast open space. Instead of a ceiling, more candles shone above her head, like stars against a black sky. The floor was made of a transparent, refined crystal, showing more open space below. This strange place resembled the halls and passages of Castle Avërand, but in an infinite and grander scale. Directly in front of her, a very old man — he was ancient, really — stared at her from beneath a dark cowl. The look in his eyes as he opened his arms wide sent a chill down her spine.

He smiled at her. "Greetings, Princess Tyra, and welcome to the Grand Hall." He spoke with a deep, booming voice. Many of the smaller flames flickered on their wicks. "I have been waiting for you."

24

THE WHISPERING LIGHTS

Tyra's first impulse was to run back to the loom from where she'd come. But before she could move, the watery reflection fell with a splash, back into a puddle on the ground. The old man continued smiling as he watched her intently, but he didn't move from his position in front of the loom. She inhaled deeply, wondering what she'd gotten herself into. Finally, the man moved to the side of the metal loom and pressed his hand firmly on its frame.

"You have just arrived," he said. "Leave now and you will never obtain what you seek."

Tyra backed away. She had no idea where she was or what had happened to Nels. Between the floating candles above her head and the crystal floor that looked just as much like the night sky, she had no way of knowing which way was up and which way was down. She was frightened and a little dizzy.

"Who are you?" she asked, her voice quivering.

"*What* are you," he said. "*That* should be your question."

Tyra swallowed; her nerves made her tongue dry. "I don't understand."

"Pardon my vagueness," the man continued. His strong voice belied his obvious age. "I have had no living company for so long. My ability to converse is a little unpracticed." He slowly started to walk to her. "I was a fabricator many years ago, even before your grandfather's time."

Tyra studied his wrinkled face and his old-fashioned attire. "Are you *not* alive?"

"I am but a shadow of life, Your Highness. Threadbare was my name."

"May I call you that?" she asked.

"It would delight me! No one has called me by that name in over forty of your years." Threadbare stood immediately before her now, his clear-blue eyes like blocks of ice. He wasn't much taller than Tyra — age had withered and shrunken him — but his eyes were brighter and livelier than any she had ever seen. "Have you ever stood at the edge of still water?" he asked.

Tyra didn't understand where this was going, but she nodded anyway.

"Beneath the water is a very different world from yours, a place where you could not live for long. Some creatures thrive there, but they, too, would die if left stranded on your banks, outside their world." Threadbare swept his arm in a wide arc. "We are within the line that divides such worlds; everything begins and ends here."

His cryptic answer puzzled Tyra. Mylan had spoken of such a place, of a line between the real and the ethereal worlds. Had she been referring to this hall?

"You are a fortunate girl," Threadbare continued. "You are among a select few from your world who have entered this place — the third, to be precise. May I ask how it appears to you?" As thoroughly as she could, Tyra described to him everything she saw, from the infinite line of columns, to the candles overhead and the transparent crystal floor. Threadbare smiled. "Just as I saw it when I first entered. Follow me."

"Where?"

"To many places, Your Highness," he said. "You have much to see."

She saw small lights ahead in the darkness.

Threadbare bowed his head and they started walking down the hall. Tyra was afraid to follow him. What if she lost her way or could not find the loom again? How would she return to Nels? He was alone in that cave. If he had been the one to vanish without a trace, she would have been panicked. She could only imagine how worried he must be.

Still, this man's name was familiar, and he had done nothing to deserve distrust. She followed him, still amazed by the space they were in. Her skirt fanned a slight draft as she passed, causing the little candle flames to flicker. And as they did, she heard voices — tiny ones, scarcely distinguishable to her ears. She tried to eavesdrop on them, but she couldn't make out the words. She leaned closer, but it made no difference.

"Do the candles speak?" she asked.

"The candles?" Threadbare said. "Oh, yes, the *flames* — they indeed whisper. They are the echoes of inspiration, the resonance of those who made contributions to the Grand Hall."

"Why can't I make out their whisperings?"

"You are alive. You see, when someone dies, they pass through this place, and their knowledge is pressed into the fabric of this Grand Hall — most of which has come from beyond your world."

Tyra stopped in her tracks. "*Beyond* my world?"

"Life *is* reality. Without life, there is only emptiness." Threadbare smiled. "Where there is life, there are endless realities — and worlds of every possibility. Your world is not the only one."

The candles surrounding them had given way to many looms. As far as Tyra could see, there were rows and rows of looms, all weaving by themselves, unattended. The sound of pressing reeds and shifting fabric grew louder and louder the farther they walked. Some of the looms produced narrow tapestries; others created wide ones. Some tapestries stretched on forever, featuring embroidery, crewelwork — all the sewing arts. The massive tapestries showed more landscapes and peoples than she ever could have imagined; the diversity was breathtaking.

"There's more than *one* Great Tapestry?" Tyra asked.

Threadbare winked at her.

She took that as a yes.

Tyra could not comprehend the extent of this place nor what it contained; the ramifications of what she was seeing were dizzying. They approached one loom as it began a colorful pattern; its tapestry was no more than a few yards long, the fabric coarse and primitive, showing grasses and striped barks. Curious about its texture, she reached out and delicately touched the fabric as she passed. Quick as a wink, she stood in a vibrant land of countless trees and ferns. The air was humid — and the creatures were terrifying. Right in front of her, one beast shook the ground as it used its enormous legs to charge at another creature that appeared less fierce. The two animals — if that's what they even were — struggled for a moment until the aggressive one feasted on the other.

A hand grabbed her shoulder and yanked her back to the Grand Hall. Her finger left the tapestry. The jungle and its strange creatures were now threads, their images woven in the fabric. She turned around and caught the glare of Threadbare's disapproving eyes. "I advise against touching the Tapestries, Princess. You may encounter what has only existed in nightmares."

Tyra inhaled sharply. "I have never seen animals like that before!"

"No one has — no one from *your* world, anyway."

"Those monsters live in another world?"

"*Lived*. You only saw a moment in time from *that* world." Threadbare picked up Tyra's hand, took her finger, and brushed it across the surface of another tapestry. Flashes came to her: glimpses of people and of nations, both great and small; some flashes resembled her world, and others did not. Metal birds flew without flapping their wings. She saw great celebrations and horrific wars. Then it stopped. "Knowledge is a cherished gift," Threadbare explained, "but if people are not prepared to receive the knowledge, it will devastate them."

Nothing could have prepared Tyra for any of this. She could see into another world, at any point in time, just by touching a thread in a pattern on a tapestry. All knowledge was at her fingertips — literally.

Which tapestry was *her* world? Although tempted to ask, she remained quiet and listened to Threadbare. She understood how he'd come to be so wise.

"Come," Threadbare said. "We are nearly there."

They walked on, passing loom after loom, each one weaving a tapestry. There really were more worlds than she could count.

The ancient man and the princess entered an area that had no looms at all. Finished tapestries of all shapes, sizes, and colors lined an endless, majestic wall. There were hundreds of them — maybe even thousands.

"These are the realities that have come and gone," Threadbare said. "Each began with a conscious thought, and each ended when there was nothing left to sustain them. Some did not last for long. Others have flourished, sometimes for millennia that I cannot account for."

"Incredible! How can a place like this exist?"

Threadbare turned and smiled at her. "Does it?"

Tyra stared at her feet. She hoped it did. It felt strange to be in a place that was neither here nor there.

"I have waited a long time for you," Threadbare said solemnly. "Your pattern indicated that you would come, but I feared you would be too late. Your reality needs the Needle."

"Wait," Tyra said. "You know that I'm here for that?"

Threadbare raised an eyebrow. "Your pattern is clear, Princess. Your desire for the Needle is pure, so the Lights may approve your request. But the Needle cannot save Nels."

Tyra's heart caught in her chest. "It can't save him?"

"Indeed not, but you can save Nels on your own."

She glared at him. "I would have done so already if I could."

"I know. You tried but it did not work, did it?"

"No," she said, shamed by her failure. "No, it didn't."

Threadbare smiled. "Now that you love him, it will."

Tyra never would have used that word in regards to Nels, yet she knew she had grown fond of him. The more she thought about Nels, the more she realized how much she genuinely cared.

"I love him?" she said, surprised. "I *do* love him."

Threadbare nodded. "And he loves you in return." Threadbare put his arm around Tyra's shoulders and steered her farther into the Hall. "With your feelings and your basted thread, you can restore him — and you may weave more than his body and soul."

Tyra blushed. "Basted thread?"

"Ickabosh basted your thread with Nels's, in the hope that — no matter the outcome, no matter the length of any

292

separation — you would always find each other . . . even in death." Threadbare cleared his throat. "Everyone is equal in death, Princess. Nels lives because of his thimble. You see him because your thread is basted to his. You have been prepared for a seam that only the two of you can sew through a union of your souls — a kiss, if you will. If you both had possessed genuine love when you kissed in Ickabosh's chamber, Nels's spirit would have woven back into his body and your seam to him would have been sewn." Threadbare paused. "You see, Princess, fabricators can baste your thread to another's, but sewing a seam . . . weaving your hearts together . . ." The ancient man smiled. "That choice must be entirely your own."

Tyra's head swam. She felt lightheaded. No wonder her heart had leaped when she first saw Nels at the festival! Tyra's eyes moistened, her emotions overpowering her resolve. In a week's time, her perception of his worth had changed into something genuine. "Are you sure Nels feels the same for me?"

Threadbare laughed. "Look at what you have accomplished together. Think of what you have sacrificed — together. A common goal can eradicate the deepest prejudice."

"Then if love is all I need, let me go back to him."

"You will, but you must take the Needle with you."

She wiped her eyes. "You said I don't need it. It can't save him."

"It's not for Nels," he said. "It's for something else."

"Rasmus," she remembered. "I have to save my kingdom."

"You do not need it for that, either. The reality of your world needs it."

"What do you mean?"

The man pointed over Tyra's shoulder. "See for yourself."

She turned and gasped. The way they had come had changed into an endless void. Empty space extended all around them. Tyra gritted her teeth and ignored her perception, stepping out into the void, onto a floor that she couldn't see. New lights appeared around her. Some of the lights formed bright circles and spun like flaming pinwheels. With each new step, more lights appeared — above, below, and behind her. Threadbare followed as she moved on toward a stretch of bright lights.

Directly in front of her was a shiny metal column, like polished steel. Behind it stood another loom, identical to the one she had stepped through to get to the Grand Hall. Candles of all shapes and sizes surrounded this loom, each of them whispering in indistinct voices.

Threadbare touched her arm. "Allow me." He moved in front of her and raised his arms. "Lights of the worlds and ages past, the answer to our problem has come. Will you lend this child the Needle so that my patch may be sewn?"

The candles flickered, as if they'd been billowed by a sudden wind.

Tyra felt no wind.

"I know she is not a fabricator," Threadbare continued, "but my patch may give at any time. You know what will happen then. Let her take the Needle; she can deliver it to my apprentice."

Tyra tugged Threadbare's cloak. "Do you understand what they are saying?" she whispered.

"I am to this realm what Nels is to yours," he said, careful not to speak above a whisper, either. "The Lights are what remain of those who die as they pass through this plane. Their knowledge shines forever, even after they enter the next life. The living cannot perceive them."

She let go of his cloak. If the living could not hear the Lights . . . "What are you?" she asked.

The man smiled and shrugged. "I do not know."

One of the candles — one of the Lights — waved them forward. It was the tallest among them. Threadbare turned to it. "It is good to hear your voice, Master Gailner."

Gailner? Tyra held her breath. It was the fabricator who created the Needle.

"Please consider," Threadbare said. "I did what I could, but the rendt —"

The tall flame moved fiercely, and so did the others.

Threadbare did not finish what he was trying to say.

Rendt? Tyra had heard Rasmus speak of this. The Lights flared brighter, their wicks glowing hot, then burned steadily again.

"They have agreed to let you take the Needle," Threadbare said, "and I apologize."

She looked into his disparaging eyes. "Apologize for what?"

The man sighed. "For the burden you are about to bear."

Tyra shivered. "What do you mean?"

"I cannot say," Threadbare answered. "Every tapestry here is woven by the living. There is no reality without consciousness. The pattern is woven based on the living's actions. Your pattern indicates several possible outcomes. If you leave with the Needle, most of them will be unfavorable."

"Like what?" Tyra asked. She had to know.

"I . . ." He glanced at the candles. "I am forbidden to say."

"Then I will go without; I don't need it."

"The Needle is for another purpose. You must deliver it."

"How can I deliver it if I do not know what it's for?"

Threadbare pointed behind her. "Touch and see."

Tyra spun around. The metal column was now behind her. An elongated opal in a thin metal frame sat on top of the column. The opal was the largest she'd ever seen, a gem both clear and colorful. Tyra walked to the column and touched her finger to the surface of the gem.

Like her vision of the jungle moments ago, the Grand Hall became another place. Dark clouds swirled in a red sky. The ground shook. The earth rolled under her feet, as if it were about to crumble and fall away. Cries reached her ears. A great dark void hovered over a flattened city. Debris and people were being pulled from all directions into the vacuum. The people held fast to anything they could grab, but the void's pull was too great. The victims screamed as they vanished into nothingness.

Within the chaos, Tyra could see Threadbare standing before the void, resisting its pull. He tried to access a sewing kit, but it slipped from his grasp and flew away, sucked into the abyss.

"Time," he said. "That is all I can give . . ."

Threadbare pinched his fingers at the air as he flew into the heart of the devouring hole. A blinding light forced Tyra to shield her eyes. The ground settled, and the cries stopped. Rocks and branches fell. Particles of dust and articles of shredded cloth floated to the ground.

Threadbare was gone, as was the great city and the void that had taken it.

In the midst of the devastation sat a small child. Crying.

Tyra felt a hand on her shoulder. The devastated land became the Grand Hall once more. "Those people!" she said. "What did I see? What happened to you?"

Threadbare breathed deeply. "The fabric of reality was thin in Mendarch," he said. "There was no time to find the Needle. Without my intervention, the rendt would have ripped our world apart." Threadbare turned from her, frowning as he closed his eyes. "Unless the tear is mended, it will reopen and the rendt will come again." Threadbare reopened his eyes. "The Needle was made to mend such tears. But with it, you can also alter the laws that bind the fabric of reality. You can achieve whatever you can imagine — so long as you possess the Needle."

"Achieve anything?" she asked. "I just have to wish it?"

Threadbare held out his arm and motioned her away from the Lights. "It's not that simple or easy, Princess. Reality is not a game. Like all needles, the Needle of Gailner requires a thread if anything is to be mended." The man held Tyra by her shoulders again. "Threads are only as strong as you can spin them. Trust in your heart, and you will spin a thread that no one can sever." Threadbare sighed as he released his hold. "To keep the rendt at bay, I had to use my *own* thread as a patch. Doing this served as only a temporary fix. You must take the Needle to your world. Have your strongest fabricator seam the tear before my patch gives way. You have time to save your friend, but do not delay. You have to save your reality. Do you understand?"

"I do," Tyra said, suppressing her uncertainty. "I need to go home."

Threadbare turned back to the opal on the metal column. "Take it."

While they watched, the opal levitated, rising straight up from its pedestal and into the air. Extending beneath the gem was a long, thin piece of metal. It was the Needle, and the oval opal was its eye, reflecting a wealth of vibrant colors from the flickering candlelight. Tyra reached out to the floating Needle and grabbed it with both hands. "This is a *big* needle."

"More beautiful than I imagined," Threadbare added. "If only I had obtained it in my lifetime, you would not have to take it now. You must promise me something."

Tyra was eager to leave, but she stopped and listened.

"Once the tear is mended, return the Needle here. Only then can I leave this place." Threadbare patted his chest with a thump and did the same over his abdomen. His hand went through his stomach, as if he were a ghost. "In your hand is the power to mend your reality — and mine. Now go."

The man pointed. The loom among the Lights sparkled as a wall of water rose into its shed. Tyra stepped toward the loom. Before she entered, she wanted to know. "Who was the child I saw after you closed the rendt?"

Threadbare released a massive sigh and shook his head, as if he were hesitant to answer. "About Nels," he said cautiously. "There is something you deserve to know."

The water splashed as the hem of Tyra's dress left the Weaver's Gate. Nels threw his arms up, frustrated. Like him, she had returned the moment she dived into the reflective water. He had no idea what the loom was for or how to use it. Just then, he noticed something in Tyra's hand — a rod of metal, pointed at the tip. It was a needle — a *large* needle.

Colors sparkled from an opal at its end. "Is that —? How did you get that?"

She looked up at him with a blend of relief and confusion.

"What's wrong?" he asked.

Tyra placed a hand over his heart. "I was gone for so long," she said. "Were you not worried?"

"What do you mean? You jumped in and came right back, just like I did."

"I never left?" Tyra stepped back, grasping the Needle with both hands.

Nels stared at the object and repeated himself. "How did you —"

"There's no time to explain. Come on!" Tyra turned and ran for the exit.

Before he chased after her, Nels reclaimed Mylan's necklace, Gleesel's ring, and Bosh's thimble. When he reached Tyra, she was standing a few feet from the molten river's bank, holding the Needle at her waist. Nels looked across the fire as he handed Tyra the reclaimed items.

"I'll be careful this time," he said.

Before he could pick her up, Tyra raised the Needle near her face and looked into the opal — through the Needle's eye. She vanished and instantly reappeared on the other side of the cavern.

Nels stared at her. "How did you —"

"There's no time!" she cried, clutching her chest and gasping a little. "Come on!"

Nels flew over the river and into the tunnel, the passage no longer dominated by shadow. Tyra was holding the Needle above her head, like a bright torch. A strong light illuminated from its eye. When they reached the chasm, Tyra raised the Needle high with both hands. Holding it tight, she floated with it as it ascended the chasm. Nels was amazed. Not only had she found the Needle — she knew how to use it.

They reached the top and saw the mountain's open entrance. Fargut was against the far wall, a blood-soaked cloth wrapped around his hand.

"Let me look at your hand," Tyra said quickly.

"No wound for lady's eyes to be see'n!"

"Let me look at it," she insisted.

Fargut removed his makeshift bandage. Half of his palm was sliced through.

"He grabbed the thread when you fell," Nels said.

Without another word, Tyra raised the Needle over Fargut's hand. The bleeding stopped. The incision fused and the wound healed. Fargut pulled his hand back and turned it over, looking at both sides. He flexed his fingers. "Deceived mine eyes be! Lost mine hand, I'd thought. That trinket you'd be seek'n?" He grazed his finger along the Needle's side. "Biggest needle'n I'd ever see'n!"

"Sorry, Fargut," Tyra said. "We must leave you. May I have my kit back?"

He handed her the cedar box. "Happy help'n. Be see'n you at Harvestport!"

Nels watched their exchange. The confidence in Tyra astounded him. A satisfied look spread over her face, but when she turned to Nels, her expression changed. She seemed worried — a hint of reservation, perhaps, or maybe a speck of fear? He wanted to ask if something was wrong, but she had already sprinted gracefully for the exit.

He waited a moment, basking in her glory, when she looked back quizzically.

"Come on, slowpoke!" she cried. "Let's get you woven!"

She didn't have to explain her haste. Nels raised his hand and looked at his transparent fingertips. If the half-moon was tonight, the rest of him would disappear in a matter of hours. Even if they made it to Castle Avërand with the Needle in time, what would they do about Rasmus? If they stopped him — *and* if she restored Nels — what would become of the two of them?

Nels ran outside with her, eager to find out.

25

BROOKLET'S FLIGHT

The sun hung low in the sky as they journeyed to Westmine City. Sweat trickled down the sides of Tyra's face, and her legs began to wobble, but she forced herself to keep pace. They had two hours left before nightfall. She was grateful that their return from the dismal peak passed by faster than their journey to it, but they still had a long way to go.

They had two hours left before dusk.

We have to make it. I won't let him die!

Tyra hadn't said much since they'd left Fargut inside the cave. Neither had Nels. She couldn't blame him. Parts of him were fading in and out of existence before her eyes. She was worried. At their current rate of travel, they would reach the castle in another two days. Any hope of making it in time relied on Brooklet; it was a lot to ask of her, but they had to try.

Tyra snagged her toe on a protruding pine root. The Needle flew from her hands and rang against the pine's trunk as she fell to the ground. She sat up before Nels could react. But every muscle in her body complained when she even *thought* about standing.

"Don't take this the wrong way," Nels said, "but you don't look so good."

He retrieved the Needle and walked back to where she sat. She looked at him, not sure what to think. She wanted him to live. She wanted to embrace him, and be with him, even if the truth about Nels — and the child she'd seen — was impossible to forget. "Never mind me," she said. "How are you holding up?"

Nels looked at his limbs. "For a second, I thought I'd lost my leg."

"Then we can't rest," she said. "Help me up."

"In a moment," Nels said. "We can spare a moment."

"No, we can't!" she cried. "Carry me again!"

"Are you sure?"

"It's the only way to mend you in time!"

A smile surfaced on his face. "You never give up, do you?" Nels reached down and picked her up in his arms. Like before, she rested her head on his shoulder. "Hold tight," he said.

She did, as tight as she could, before he sprinted north. The rush made Tyra feel like a seedling caught on a breeze. It took all her will to stay awake, her thoughts drifting to the day when she first saw Nels at the Cobblestown festival, and the way she felt when their eyes locked. Those fantasies ended when her body tumbled to the ground and a surprised shriek escaped her mouth.

Nels turned back, his torso reappearing. "I'm not very stable anymore."

"We have to keep going," Tyra insisted. "It doesn't matter if I fall."

Hesitantly, Nels hoisted her onto his back and took off.

Tyra passed through Nels's body a couple of times more, but he was able to shorten their return to the Vagas' camp considerably. The sun touched the edge of the horizon when they arrived. Nels set Tyra on her feet. Something was wrong here: There was no evening fire and the forest around the camp was unusually quiet. Tyra seemed well enough to walk, but she looked as concerned about the empty camp as Nels felt. They entered the vacant clearing where they had shared their dance.

"Where is everyone?" Tyra asked.

Nels had no idea. The place was deserted, half of the tents undone or lying in loose and tangled heaps. Not even the dogs ran about. The Vagas were simply gone — except for a horse's neigh that blared down the thoroughfare. Tyra limped toward it, breaking into a slow run. Someone had tied Brooklet to a felled tree, next to a few other steeds. "There you are," Tyra said as she stroked the mare's neck. "Let's untie you." She pried at the strap, but the knot was too secure for her weak, shaky fingers. She set the Needle at her feet and reached for her dagger. She was about to cut the line when the unsheathing of swords sounded behind them.

"Drop your weapon, thief!"

Tyra let her dagger slip to the ground as she and Nels turned. Three young men had closed in on them, their swords held high and ready — squires from Avërand! Nels recognized Davin, and he paused at one of the others, completely surprised to see his old friend dressed as a squire.

"Wallin?"

Aside from the hostility on his face, Nels was happy to see his sparring companion.

"Turn around," ordered the squire Nels didn't know. He had dark, matted hair and cool teal eyes. "You're not stealing the Princess's horse."

Tyra remained facing them. "How can I steal what is mine?"

303

"Hold off," Wallin said, lowering his weapon. "She does look like the princess."

"I *am* the princess, and I doubt my father would like to hear of this!" Tyra was growing impatient.

The squires exchanged quick glances and, in unison, knelt. "Forgive us, Your Highness!" Davin said. "We thought you were one of them, dressed like them and all."

"That's better," Tyra said. "What are your names?"

The unknown squire looked at the others before speaking for them all. "Um . . . this runt is Davin, Wallin's the tall one, and I'm Taner."

Tyra leaned toward Nels and whispered out the side of her mouth, "Can we trust them?"

He glanced at her ring. "They're telling the truth."

"Very well," she said. "What are you doing in this camp?"

"Guarding it," Taner said. "The others went after the Vagas."

"That's right," Davin said. "Your father sent us here."

"He sent most of the knights," Wallin added, "after they found Alvil dead."

Nels clenched his fists.

Retrieving her dagger from the ground, Tyra moved to pick up the Needle. "If it had not been for the Vagas, Rasmus would have killed me."

"What?" Wallin said. "The Vagas *saved* you?"

"You don't have to kneel anymore. Stand up."

The squires obeyed and sheathed their swords as they stood. Davin looked unsure. "That's not what Sir Arek said. He said the Vagas kidnapped you."

"And Rasmus is working with them," Taner added.

Tyra's eyes glistened. "When did he tell you that?"

"Last night," Wallin said. "On the Westerly Pass."

Nels knew what Tyra was thinking long before she looked over at him. These three had been misled. "Did he have a wound in his shoulder," Tyra asked, "from an arrow?"

Wallin opened his mouth. "Did you see him get attacked?"

"*Rasmus* was attacked. The Arek you saw was an imposter. Rasmus killed Arek *before* last night."

Davin pointed at Tyra. "How do we know she's *really* the princess?"

Nels could not blame them for questioning Tyra. They knew that Rasmus could be anyone. In unison, they removed their swords again and advanced toward Tyra, more cautious than before.

"What are you doing?" she cried. "Be still!"

"Look at what she's holding," Davin said. "A giant needle?"

"Yeah," Taner agreed. "Only a fabricator would carry something like that."

"That sinks it, then," Wallin said. "Put down your . . . your . . . *thing*, sorcerer!"

Tyra insisted that she was not Rasmus, but they would not listen. Each of them raised an arm to restrain her, but Nels leaped forward and took down both Davin and Taner together. They slid backward as Nels tripped and pinned Wallin. He gave his old friend no room to wriggle free.

"This hold!" Wallin's eyes looked around frantically. "Nels?"

The other two squires jumped back to their feet and charged for Tyra. She raised the Needle and the squires stopped, frozen in place. She paused for a breath. "They believe *me* to be Rasmus?"

"They will *now*," Nels said. "How did you do that?"

Tyra pointed the Needle at Wallin. "You know this one?"

Nels nodded adamantly. "He's one of my best friends."

"Who — who are you talking to?" Wallin cried.

"Listen," Tyra ordered. "We haven't much time. Lend me your sheath."

Without a word, Wallin tapped the ground, signaling his defeat. Nels climbed off. Wallin sat up and stared at Tyra as he removed his sheath and handed it to her. She buckled it around her waist and placed the Needle inside. Wallin glanced at his immobile companions. "What did you do to them?"

"Ride for the knights. Have them return to the castle immediately. I will ride ahead." Tyra severed Brooklet's tether and mounted her saddle. Everything was still there, including her quiver and bow. "I will explain everything at the castle — you must convince them to follow!"

"Nels is a ghost," Wallin said suddenly. "He's here, isn't he?"

Impressed by his friend, Nels jabbed him hard in the shoulder.

"Yeow!" Wallin jumped to the side, rubbing his arm.

Tyra shook her head, smiling at Nels.

"Jilia wasn't lying!" Wallin said. "You told his mother —"

"Go!" Tyra put Brooklet into a gallop, leaving them behind.

The other squires stirred from their paralysis, thoroughly upset. "Where'd she go?" Taner asked, searching wildly. "There goes our chance. How could we let that sorcerer get away?"

"She's not Rasmus," Wallin said. "Let's get going."

"Wh-where are we going?" Davin stammered.

"We have to find Sir Canis and go back!"

"Why?" Taner asked. "What for?"

Wallin mounted a horse. "Rasmus is at the castle!"

The other two climbed onto their horses, and all three rode off to the north. Nels couldn't help but feel pride in his friend. Rarely had Wallin acted so responsibly; it was as if he truly understood what was at stake. Nels's body faded in and out, but his smile remained strong as he thrust into the air to catch up with Brooklet.

Darkness crept across the sky as they neared the top of Westerly Pass.

It was steep, so Tyra dismounted and climbed, careful of the ledges as she guided Brooklet. The mare shook, on the brink of exhaustion — like Arek's horse before it had surrendered its life. She hated to inflict suffering like that on her mount, but they had so much ground to cover and so little time.

Nels trailed behind, fading and reappearing often.

"Just a little more," Tyra urged them both. "Gleesel will help us."

If Nels said anything in reply, she did not hear him. Her heart pounded in her ears. She could not stop thinking about the three squires and their story. If her father had sent most of the knights after the Vagas, then the castle was vulnerable. Rasmus could easily pose as someone else, slip inside, and — with fewer eyes watching — spring at the chance to slaughter her parents.

Tyra almost cheered when they reached level ground and started toward Gleesel's mansion. They had to find a way back to the castle without killing Brooklet. *No one* was going to die. They reached the path that led through the small meadow, and Tyra leaped from her horse. She sprinted for the stairs and knocked on the door.

"Gleesel?" No one answered. She knocked again. "Please open! It's Tyra!" She heard nothing, except for the sound of Brooklet breathing too hard behind her.

"Where is she?" Nels asked. "I thought she couldn't leave the house."

"As a human," Tyra reminded him. "Do you see a goat anywhere?"

Nels shook his head. "Maybe she hid from the knights?"

"Wait . . . Something here might know where she is."

Nels raised an eyebrow. "Some*thing*?"

Tyra shoved at the mansion door and it creaked open. It was dark and dusty, just like their first arrival here, but Tyra did not let that stop her from running to the stony posts at the bottom of the stairs. "Is Gleesel here?" she asked the gargoyles. Neither statue moved. "Do you know where she is?" Still nothing. There was no magic in them. Her plan unsuccessful, Tyra returned to the porch, where she sat on the top step and held her head in her hands. They had traveled so far and worked so hard, but it wasn't enough. They would never reach home before the moon appeared.

Tyra had to face the truth. She had failed.

"I know what you're thinking," Nels said. "We did our best. It's not your fault."

She looked up at him. Sadness, longing, and pain cut through her. With so many emotions swirling inside her chest, she was beginning to feel mad. *Mad* . . . Tyra sat up. The thought made her pause. It gave her an idea. She had no *rational* way of getting home in time, but she could try something *mad*. She had nothing to lose.

Tyra unsheathed the Needle and jumped onto Brooklet.

Nels's furrowed his brow. "Okay," he said. "Maybe I *don't* know what you're thinking . . ."

"Climb up here," she said. "Hurry!"

"Brooklet will die if you ride her any farther."

"*You* will die if we argue!" Tyra reached out her hand. "Trust me." With a skeptical look on his face, Nels took her hand, floated up, and sat behind her. "A little farther, girl," Tyra cooed to the mare. "I will take care of the rest."

"Just how are you planning to do that?" Nels asked.

Without facing him, she raised the Needle.

"How did you learn to use that thing, anyway?"

"I'm not sure how to explain it — and we have to hurry now, anyway," Tyra said. They trotted down the path until they reached the view of her kingdom. She could see lights from a few villages, and then the castle beyond. Remembering what Threadbare had told her, she secured her bow over her shoulder and closed her eyes as she raised the Needle high. "Hold me," she commanded.

"I hope you know what you're doing."

She nodded slightly and opened her eyes. "So do I."

With Nels's arms wrapped around her waist, she held the Needle's eye up to her own, looked through the translucent gem, and spotted her castle. She hoped it wasn't farther than she could handle, otherwise this would kill her, but to save Nels, Tyra had to test the strength of her thread. She had no choice. She was ready. Tyra concentrated, looked at the castle through the Needle's eye, and imagined all of them — Nels, Brooklet, and her — standing before the castle gates.

A sharp rush penetrated Tyra, the same feeling that seized her when she'd crossed the fiery river. The sensation was more intense this time — agonizing, as if something pulled every muscle in her body to the point of tearing. Her stomach burned with the pain that had originated in her heart, and just when she was about to be sick, she felt herself slip off her saddle.

She crashed at the feet of a startled castle guard.

"What the —" the guard cried. Another ran to join him. "Where did *you* come from?"

Tyra raised her head, the Needle still in her hand. "We did it!" Excited, she looked behind her. "We did it, Nels —" He wasn't there. He wasn't sitting on Brooklet's saddle, either.

A pair of sharp spears pointed at her. "Who are you?" one of the guards asked. Tyra stared into their surprised faces as they stepped back. "Princess?!"

Brooklet released a weak moan and hung her head low.

Tyra sprinted for the gate. "Take care of her!" she yelled back.

She was within the castle walls before the startled guards could question her. Faint light filled the main hall, and a few candles blew out as she opened the door. She paused at the threshold, breathing hard as she ignored the servants' excited yells about her return. She made her way to the stairs that led to Bosh's chamber and descended; she had to find the tailor. There was no one else she could trust, no one else that could help her weave Nels back to life. She hoped it was Bosh who had moved Nels's body. And she hoped his ghost was okay . . . wherever he was.

She could hardly believe what she'd done. Her thread was stronger than she'd thought.

Thank you, Threadbare. You knew I could do this.

The bottom of the stairs came faster than she remembered, but Bosh's open door caused her to pause. It was dark inside. Tyra used the Needle to cast a light into the chamber. The place was a mess.

"Hello?" she called, and stepped inside. "Are you here, Ickabosh?"

No one answered. It didn't take her long to realize that something was wrong. Overturned furniture and other materials were scattered throughout the room. Even the squirrel cage was damaged on the floor, the critter no longer inside. Tyra hoped she wasn't too late.

Sheathing the Needle, she turned and ran back up the stairs.

Where could he be?

She searched the castle high and low, through kitchens and halls, bedchambers and libraries, but there was no sign of either Bosh or Nels. She paused for breath in the dining hall and thought of one other place she had yet to look — the courtyard. Tyra ran down a hall filled with suited armor and barged onto the polished granite landing. As she started down the stairs to the grand terrace, someone was ascending the lower staircase from the courtyard. He was holding a large crochet hook.

"Ickabosh!"

The man stopped when he reached the terrace. "Who is that?"

"It's me, Tyra!" she cried, running down the stairs.

A glint of surprise flashed in his eyes. "Stop!" He raised his arm and brandished his hook. His old face looked terribly grim. "How do I know you are the *real* princess?"

She came to a stop a few feet away from him. "You know Rasmus is here?"

"Answer me first: What did I have you search for on the Westerly Pass?"

The man was testing her — a good idea. "A shadowed book."

Bosh lowered his arms and smiled wide. "Welcome home, Princess."

"Not so fast!" She pulled out her dagger. "How do I know *you're* not Rasmus?"

"Is that a conjurer's ring?" he asked, pointing to her hand. "My name is Ickabosh."

Tyra looked at the stone. Green — he was telling the truth. Tyra wrapped her arms around the old man. "I'm so glad to see you!" Then she turned serious. "Where is Nels's body? Did you move him?"

"Yes." The tailor pointed at the sheath around her waist. "Is that a sword?"

"Not at all," Tyra smiled. She proudly pulled out the Needle. "See?"

He looked it over carefully. "Incredible," he murmured. "I imagined it smaller . . ."

"I think we all did!" Just then, a brisk wind picked up and the stars overhead became shadowed by a thick thunder-cloud. Tyra couldn't believe it; the last thing they needed was a summer storm. "I used it to come back from the Westerly Mountains," she continued, "but Nels is still —"

"That can wait," Bosh said. "Until then, let me get acquainted with the Needle."

Bosh held out his hands, and Tyra carefully placed the Needle in them. The tailor examined the legendary object, turning it over in his hands.

"Oh. Rasmus has disguised himself as Sir Arek," Tyra warned. "He murdered Arek, too."

"Moth holes!" Bosh glanced at her with an alarmed expression. "Sir Arek arrived here last night!"

"Then we have to find him," Tyra said. "I will inform the guard!"

She was about to step forward when something stopped her from leaving, locking her limbs in place. A dull throb spread through her body. Tyra panicked as she glanced down, away from Bosh's smiling face — which had begun to unravel like a spool of fleshy thread.

The Needle had pierced her chest.

26

EVEN IN DEATH

Nels soared across the sky as fast as he could.

He had been holding on to Tyra as she'd instructed when his body began to fade again. His arms had gone through her stomach, and she and Brooklet vanished. He realized immediately that Tyra had used the Needle to return to the castle.

The forest below him flew by in a blur as he crossed terrain that he had known his entire life: over Kettlescreek, Cobblestown, and his own cottage. A thin wisp of smoke curled from its chimney, making him think of his mother. He hoped he would see her soon, but he had to hurry; he was more transparent than ever.

Pushing himself to his limit, Nels darted for the castle. As he approached Hillshaven, distant thunder met his ears; a storm was on its way. Nels slowed and hovered over the castle. The people were running around the grounds like a disturbed colony of ants. Men lit torches and sounded alarms as a pair of guards led Brooklet into the courtyard. *Brooklet* — Tyra had made it back!

A lightning flash revealed a pair of shadows on the castle's grand terrace. Two people were there; one of them wore a red dress. As Nels watched, the girl fell back, landing with her arms splayed above her head. The other was a man in a dark cape — Rasmus held the Needle in his hand.

"Tyra!" Nels cried. "No!"

He plunged to the terrace and landed between Tyra and Rasmus. Tyra convulsed. She coughed, her lungs straining for air. Blood spread over her chest and seeped through her blouse.

Nels tried to shield her from Rasmus, but the man passed right through him and stood over Tyra. He smiled, one side of his mouth curling. "Never trust a conjurer's ring around a Master Threader. Illusions of that size are easy to stitch."

Nels sprang at Rasmus, ready to pummel the villain, but his fists had no effect. He tried to grab him, kick him, trip him — but it was no use. Nels could no longer interact with the real world.

Rasmus reached into his pocket and cleaned the Needle with a handkerchief — the one Tyra had left as a clue in the woods. "It's a shame that you had to die, Princess. You would have made an excellent slave, but I am grateful to you for bringing *this* to me." Crouching near her head, Rasmus closed her eyes with his fingers. "At last, the Needle is mine. And with it, I will finally mend the Great Tapestry and reclaim my part of it." Back on his feet, Rasmus ascended the upper staircase and walked away, his head high as he entered the hall of armor.

Helplessly, Nels watched as Rasmus left and then collapsed at Tyra's side. He tried to caress her, move her, lift her eyelids, but he could do nothing. She wouldn't move. Her skin turned pale, and then it turned blue. He was charged with protecting her and now she was dead. He'd failed her.

All Nels could do now was disappear from the world.

"Nels?"

It was Tyra, but her voice didn't come from her mouth. Her ghost moved freely to him. Inside the palm of her body's hand lay a brass thimble. Like Nels, she was unwoven, a loose thread in the Great Tapestry. Her ghostly hair didn't move with the wind. "I'm so sorry, Nels. I thought he was Bosh, but it was another illusion," she said sadly. "I held on to the thimble like you told me to, but it didn't protect me from the Needle."

"It's over." Nels glanced down and sighed. "It's too late."

"You can't give up on me, Nels. You can still stop him!"

Tired of fighting what he could never defeat, Nels raised his hands in front of her face. As his arms faded, Tyra slumped by his side — and her body — on the stairs. His clothing lost its pigmentation. The tips of his fingers vanished. His legs went next. The transparency spread to his chest, too. Where had they gone wrong? This wasn't supposed to happen. "I'm sorry, Tyra," Nels said, his voice like an echo. "I never meant for this to —"

Tyra wrapped her arms around him and held him. "It's not your fault."

Nels leaned into her embrace, waiting for his end to come. Even under the blanket of death, she comforted him. He held her close, in a way that he'd never held another person.

Tyra's grasp tightened around his shoulders. "Your arms! I can feel your arms!"

Now that she'd mentioned it, he could sense her touch, too! Her skin, so soft and warm, rubbed against what remained of his. "That's right — ghosts can touch each other."

"Even in death . . ." Tyra said, looking deeply into his eyes.

Nels returned her stare. "That's what Bosh told me."

"We're even in death; our threads are still basted!"

"And that means —"

He never finished. Tyra had pressed her lips to his. Her perfect smile was the last thing Nels saw before his weightless spirit disappeared from the terrace.

A pair of horses snorted when Nels sat up from the strewn pile of hay. He drew in a long, deep breath. Someone *had* taken his body to the stables and buried him in a haystack. He'd been cleaned of the beeswax that once coated his frame — no wonder he'd stopped smelling it — and his body was no longer wrapped in gauze. A dull ache spread throughout his muscles; his every limb had fallen asleep. Nels didn't mind — he was alive. Even in death, their kiss had worked.

What about Tyra?

He stepped forward, stumbled, and heard a soft ringing on the stone floor. His brass thimble rolled toward the exit, as if urging him to keep moving. His stomach churned, and he dry heaved. He was thirsty, and he had no clothes. Nels moved to a vacant stall and found his trousers, shirt, and green vest, all washed and folded. He picked up his clothes and dressed.

It was slow going with his stiff joints, but he forced himself to move and stretch. He had to get back to the grand terrace. He picked up his thimble and limped out the stable doors. Torchlight filled the grounds with an orange glow. The summer thunderstorm had gathered closer — and it looked to be a violent one.

Nels ran to the castle courtyard, where a set of stairs led to the terrace. It was a steep climb, a nearly impossible feat in his condition. His first instinct was to jump and soar into the sky, but he couldn't fly anymore. Adjusting to his body was going to be harder than he'd expected.

An elderly stable hand was leading Brooklet to her stall. "You're worn ragged, girl," he said to the mare. "Makes me wonder what the princess was doing out there."

Nels ran over and blocked their way.

"Hey! What are you doing, boy?"

"Rasmus! He's in the castle," Nels said. "And he's hurt Tyra!"

"How do you know?" the stable hand asked. "And who are you?"

Nels doubled over, his heart racing. His body couldn't keep up.

"Wait here. I'll see if I can fetch the guard." The man hurried off to the main gate.

Nels straightened up and looked Brooklet in the eye. She was tired, but more alert than before. Nels touched her long face and, this time, she didn't pull back. "You know me," he whispered. "Take me to her." Summoning his strength, Nels mounted the mare, settling comfortably into the saddle.

Brooklet whinnied and took off. When she reached the grand terrace's lower stairs, they quickly ascended. Seconds later, Brooklet's hooves clomped onto the terrace and came to a stop. Nels jumped down. The wind gusted and lightning flashed. A few of the torches blew out.

As thunder cut through the air, a raindrop fell on his cheek.

Tyra was in the middle of the grand terrace. Unmoved.

He ran to her and knelt by her side. The rain became more intense and began to dilute the puddle of blood that had pooled beneath her. Nels looked around. "Tyra? Tyra! Where are you?" When he heard no answer, Nels stroked the hair from Tyra's face and scooped her up into his arms. Brooklet ambled over and lowered her head, whickering as she nudged Tyra's shoulder. Tears filled Nels's eyes. "Tyra . . ."

Tears dropped from his lashes and blended with the cold rain.

Their kiss had brought him back; they had sewn their seam. Nels was alive, but . . . why wasn't she?

317

"Don't *you* give up," Nels begged. "You never give up, remember?" He held her as tight as he could and pressed his forehead against hers. "I should have told you before. I love you, Tyra."

Tilting her head back, he kissed her lips, hoping for a miracle.

Nothing changed.

The rain formed a pool in her cupped hand, filling her thimble with water. She couldn't be gone — she *couldn't* be! When they kissed, it should have woven her back, just as he had.

And then it hit him.

What if she is? What if she's in there, right now?

For all he knew, Tyra was trapped inside her unconscious body.

Nels put his cheek to her face, hoping he'd feel breath. Nothing. He listened for any sounds of life. All he heard was a man shouting; the stable hand had returned to the courtyard and was nearing the steps to the terrace. Nels looked down at Tyra. He didn't want to leave her, especially if she was alive in there . . . somewhere. But staying here with her wasn't going to help her, either. It wouldn't bring her justice, it wouldn't stop Rasmus, and it definitely wouldn't heal her.

But the Needle would.

He kissed Tyra's lips one last time before he reached inside her knapsack, grabbing her dagger and sewing kit. He considered taking the thimble from her hand, but he didn't.

She needed its protection, now more than ever.

Nels returned to his feet and followed after Rasmus, into the heart of the castle.

27

ALTERATION

The upper floor of the castle was a maze of hallways and chambers. Nels wished he could still pass through walls. His stiff body ached and it continued to feel limp and useless.

Even if he managed to find Rasmus in the castle, what could he do in this weakened state to stop him?

How do I take the Needle from such a powerful man?

Nels was in no condition to fight, but he had to get the Needle. It was Tyra's only hope . . . if any hope for her remained.

He leaned against a doorframe and opened the sewing kit's cedar box. A raindrop fell on the velvet lining. He eyed what was left of the kit's contents: the seam ripper and the vial of black dye.

Black dye . . .

At Black Peak, Fargut had said something about the black dye: it could reveal fabricator's threads and remove their illusions. Nels shoved the seam ripper into his pocket, clutched the vial of black dye in one hand, and held Tyra's dagger in the other. He bolted down the hall as fast as his battered body would let him. He came to a stop at the balcony overlooking the main hall.

A crowd of the residing nobility had gathered below. Nels didn't understand what they were doing until King

Lennart appeared at the hall's far end — holding the Needle in his hand.

"Rasmus . . ." Nels's voice was too weak to be heard. Every noble hushed as the false king entered, followed by two of his guards. Nels limped to the balcony's staircase and leaned on its banister. He started slowly down the stairs, his limp feet dragging down onto each step. When he reached the bottom, he inhaled deeply. "Rasmus!" This time, his voice echoed throughout the hall. Lennart spun around. His eyes grew wide and then narrowed.

The false king pointed at Nels. "Take him!" he commanded to his guards.

The gathered nobility began to whisper and murmur. A few who recognized him gasped — he realized that, to them, he was back from the dead.

Knowing that he was too weak to fight, Nels let the king's guards seize him. Nels wanted to be close to Rasmus; only then could he use the black dye to reveal the truth. Besides, the fabricator would not kill Nels — not here, not in front of witnesses. The guards forced the dagger from Nels's hand. The seam ripper remained in his pocket and he surreptitiously palmed the small vial of dye.

All he needed now was an opportunity.

"Bring him to me," Lennart said, "and hand me his weapon."

The guards kicked Nels behind the knee, forcing him to kneel before the impostor. The whisperings grew louder as Tyra's dagger was delivered to Lennart's awaiting hand. The king stared at Nels and smiled. "You chose a poor disguise in which to kill me, Master Threader."

The guards tightened their grips. The observing nobles backed into the walls. All Nels could do was glare at the imposter, waiting to make his move. He was close enough. If only he could free his arms. But the guards held him tight. Being unwoven had taken its toll.

"I sentence you to death," Lennart said, touching the dagger's tip to Nels's neck.

Schhwaff!

The dagger fell from Lennart's grip — an arrow lodged in his forearm. The crowd gasped and the guards spun around. Nels scrambled to turn his head, and when he did he was filled with shock and relief. Tyra stood on the balcony, weakly holding a bow in her hand. The torso of her dress was stained with blood. She smiled, and then she collapsed in a heap at the top of the stairs.

Feeling the guards' hold on him relax, Nels shoved them away and, as hard as he could, threw the vial of black dye at Lennart. The glass shattered against the king's forehead, the dye smearing across his face. Nels reached into his pocket, unsheathed the ripper, and stabbed Lennart's fist. As the Needle fell to the floor with a clang, the false king cursed. His face and clothing began to unravel, like a spool of fleshy thread.

Rasmus, his true form exposed for all to see, stood where the king had once been. As the nobles screamed and ran from the room, Nels scrambled to the Needle and grabbed it.

"The lad's right! Arrest the imposter!" one of the guards cried out.

The guards charged. Rasmus closed his eyes and slammed his fists toward the ground. The guards stopped, frozen in their positions. No one could move, except for Rasmus — and this time, Nels.

The Needle protected him from the fabricator's magic.

I have to get the Needle to Tyra!

Nels ran for the balcony steps as fast as he could when Rasmus flashed to the middle of the staircase and blocked

Nels from ascending. The Master Threader yanked the arrow from his arm and held the wound tightly. Blood dripped from the incision, just like the black dye dripped down his face.

Nels held the Needle with both hands. If only he knew how to use it!

"I watched you die," Rasmus said, pointing at Nels. "Only the Needle could bring you back, but I took it before *she* could use it. How are you alive now?"

Nels kept the Needle pointed at the fabricator and said nothing.

Rasmus drew a knife from behind his back. "You would keep silent to my question, boy?"

"What good is my answer? You'll kill me anyway."

Rasmus shook his head and snickered. "How right you are."

Nels jabbed the Needle at Rasmus, but the villain dodged to the side and lunged at him with the knife. Nels raised the Needle and deflected the blow — if only he could use the fabrication tool as more than a sword. Remembering what Tyra had shown him about swordplay, Nels held his ground.

"Why did you kill my father?" Nels asked.

Rasmus laughed. "You wouldn't understand. My design was perfect, but Ulrich came and he altered everything. My status, my favor, my friends, my lovers — your father eclipsed them all!"

The fabricator pushed his palms out, grabbed the air, and pulled his fists across his chest. The banisters on either side of the staircase tore from their moldings and flew at Nels. He dodged them — just barely — and they crashed together, sending splinters of wood around the room.

"Everyone is a thread in the Great Tapestry — but what *kind* of thread?" Rasmus asked. "And from where has it come? You do not know that your father was a *foreign* thread, not meant for our reality, not of our world. He would have caused the rendt and destroyed everything!"

Rasmus reached behind his back for another knife. "You share the blood of your father, so you also threaten the fate of this world!" Rasmus threw his arms back and cast both knives at the ceiling. Their tips dug deep into the wooden beams. Nels thoughts flashed back to the oak that had crushed him. If Rasmus had the means to yank the knives free, the beams would explode.

The fabricator reached for the ceiling and yanked his fists down. Chunks of plaster and heavy rubble rained into the hall as the beams shattered. The roof came crashing down, right over Nels. Unable to escape the collapse, Nels shielded himself by thrusting the Needle high above his head.

A light shot out from the Needle's opal eye. The ceiling's broken wood and fractured mortar slowed to a stop in midair and then reversed. The debris flew up and out of the now gaping hole in the roof. The storm outside invaded the hall as the rubble hammered onto the shingles above.

What did I just do?!

Nels fell to his knees, the Needle still in his hand. He felt so inexplicably drained. He wasn't sure what had just happened, but it was clear that whatever he'd done with the Needle had kept him from danger. The Needle's power came at a price, however; what little energy he'd had after being unwoven was completely gone now. He would have to be careful to not inadvertently call upon the Needle's power again. He could tell that he wouldn't survive it.

Rasmus stumbled back in shock, his eyes wide and angry. "I tire of your resilience, boy!" he snarled. "I spent half my life learning about the Needle's secrets. *You* are not strong enough to handle an object so powerful."

"Rasmus!"

The Master Threader flinched, looked up, and recoiled.

King Lennart stood at the door.

"How did you escape?" Rasmus cried. "I had you in chains!"

Lennart looked at Nels and winked. Nels had seen that mischievous wink before, but not from the king. "You should have killed me, like all of your other victims," the king said, "instead of imprisoning me." At that moment, Lennart's face and body uncoiled and strung in the air like loose threads. They quickly wove back into the old tailor, wearing his gray robe. "No chain can bind this fabricator!"

"It's not possible," Rasmus exclaimed. "I killed you!"

Rasmus stared at his former mentor as Bosh walked to Nels, his crochet hook pointed at the villain. The tailor gave Nels a welcoming smile, cupped by his weathered, old cheeks. "Good to have you back," he said, before his eyes shifted to the Needle in Nels's hand. "Hold on to that."

"This can't be happening!" Rasmus snarled again. "How are you still alive? I slit your throat!"

"Did you?" Bosh raised a hand to his neck. "Must have been the wrong throat."

"I've always hated your stale wit, old man. Answer me!"

"Patience, Rasmus," Bosh said. "Because you refused the basic truth of fabrication, I was never able to teach you that true power was always within you. It was that power that kept Nels and Tyra from death."

Rasmus looked at the Needle in Nels's hands. "The power to change reality?"

"The power to design fate. Unfortunately, you care only for yours." Holding his hook steady, Bosh approached the stairs. "As I was bringing the boy's body here after you crushed him, I happened upon a sick creature preparing to die by the side of the road. Knowing you would come for my life, I performed an *alteration*. I allowed the beast a chance to die a more noble death than along the side of the road."

Nels could think of only one such creature. "The squirrel?"

"A *squirrel*?" Rasmus scoffed. "I slit and buried a rodent?"

"Larger than usual, but yes," Bosh said. "I altered the creature into a likeness of myself, took the king's place, and hid the king and queen where you would not find them. You are a fool to think I would sit serenely all these years without preparing for your return — I watched your pattern. You have tampered with the Great Tapestry long enough, Rasmus," Bosh continued. "You will account for all the threads you have severed. You will suffer the repercussions."

"You call me a fool?" Rasmus laughed. "You, who brought destruction upon us? I know the pattern well. If that boy lives, our world will rendt!"

"And what if this boy is keeping our world together?"

Nels had never heard the tailor sound so serious. The exchange of their words confused him. How could *his* life tear the world?

"For fifteen years, Ulrich lived in this castle," Bosh said. "Add sixteen more since the night you killed him. Has the fabric of reality changed? Are the laws of nature not intact? You never wanted to preserve the Great Tapestry. You always wished to recover the life you think you lost. You suffer from pride, jealousy, and a broken heart that *you* refuse to mend, so you allowed murder to become your answer!" Bosh extended his hands, his crochet hook raised like a weapon. "An unintended thread in the Great Tapestry — like Nels — can stop those who are bent on tearing it apart — like you!"

Rasmus fell silent.

"Sew your seam, Rasmus," Bosh invited. "End this madness."

"I intend to," Rasmus replied, "once I undo your meddling!"

Rasmus raised one arm and pointed at the rain pouring in from the hole in the roof. Hundreds of droplets froze into needlelike icicles. Each one darted at Bosh as if fired from a bow. The tailor whirled his hook like a scythe, and every icy pin melted into one giant ball of boiling water, still heading for Bosh. He then struck the boiling orb with his hook and catapulted it back toward Rasmus. The rogue fabricator ducked, and steam rose from the floor where the orb splashed.

Nels had the Needle, but he didn't know what to do. Its jeweled eye caught his attention — something wispy and gray rested within. He held the eye up to his own and looked through it. Threads — thousands of iridescent threads — were strung across the main hall. Everything in the room was connected together by shimmering fibers. Bosh and Rasmus had seized and were manipulating many of them, using the threads to control the surrounding objects. Like a real tapestry, Nels could see how every single thread was connected to the scene. Everything about his world was interwoven as one.

The brightest of these threads ran from him — from his heart — up the stairs to where Tyra lay.

Their connection — their love — was strong.

Nels limped for the stairs. The stone busts on either side of the staircase burst, sending marble fragments flying through the air. The blast threw Nels onto the floor. His ears rang and his eyes filled with dust. His face stung and blood dripped from a cut on his chin.

A great crash made Nels turn and face the door. Bosh and Rasmus were on opposite sides, circling the hall while they stared each other down. Each had one arm extended, grasping at the invisible threads of various objects around the room. Bosh's temple had a deep, red gash, and blood fell from

Rasmus's nose. For a magical art dedicated to mending, Nels found it ironic that fabrication was capable of causing as much devastation as a legion of knights.

Bosh's outstretched hand reached toward a vase sitting atop a large stone pedestal on the far end of the hall. The vase flew through the air toward Rasmus, who raised his other hand and made a swatting motion, causing the vase to shatter against the wall.

Rasmus glanced over at Nels. He reached for the stone pedestal that once held the vase and hurled it at the boy with incredible speed.

"Stand back, Nels!" Bosh turned to deflect the heavy pedestal, but Nels could see that this was a mistake. With Bosh distracted, Rasmus closed his eyes and slammed his fists downward.

Bosh froze in place.

Rasmus's jaw clenched. "Now, I will take that Needle!" In an instant, he reached his hand out toward Tyra's dagger, which was still on the floor where he had dropped it. The dagger sailed through the air and struck the Needle with such force that it flew out of Nels's hand.

Rasmus instantly appeared in front of Nels. He shoved his hand onto Nels's face and pushed him to the floor. He straddled Nels's torso and pinned him to the ground.

Nels struggled, flexing and straining — he couldn't wrestle free!

Rasmus wrapped one of his hands around Nels's throat and then stretched out the other to pick up the Needle. Nels tried to pull himself free from the rogue's grasp, but he couldn't breathe. Like a rolling fog, his vision was beginning to cloud. The light from the Needle's eye shone as the shaft found its way to the Master Threader's hand. Rasmus placed the Needle's tip over Nels's heart.

"I killed you once," he snarled. "And this time, you will stay dead!"

Nels looked away, hoping that his second death would be painless — but nothing happened. He glanced back at Rasmus. The fabricator's eyes bulged; the color had drained from his face.

The tip of a sword had impaled Rasmus from behind.

Gathering the last of his strength, Nels struck the Needle from Rasmus's hand. It fell to the ground and its light extinguished. Rasmus twitched, clawing at the blade protruding from his body. He slumped to his side and released his breath. A pool of blood spread beneath him.

"Stab *me* in the back, will you?" cried the favored knight of Avërand.

Nels couldn't believe it; Arek was alive!

Wriggling himself out from under the dead man, Nels sat up and gulped down as much air as he could, as if his strangled throat were on fire. Seconds later, Bosh and the two guards began to move again. The battle was over.

With his death, Rasmus's magic had released its hold.

Tyra . . .

Nels grabbed the Needle from where it had fallen and hurried up the stairs, but when he reached the landing where Tyra had fallen, Bosh had vanished from the main hall and reappeared next to both of them.

"Wait," the tailor said. "You have worn your thread far too thin. Please, allow me."

Knowing that time wasn't on their side, Nels placed the Needle in Bosh's hand. The old man held it over the open wound on Tyra's chest. Its eye glowed. Tyra's flesh began to mend before their eyes. The wound closed and her pale skin began to return to normal. Her bodice and dress remained a bloody mess, but her eyes flickered, and she uttered a weak moan.

"Tyra?" Nels cupped the back of her head with his hand. "Are you okay?"

She moaned again and their eyes met. She reached out her hand and touched the side of his face. A joyous smile spread clear across her tearstained cheeks. "You're . . . woven."

Her eyes closed, and she fell unconscious.

"Her thread is also very weak," Bosh said. "You've both been through too much."

"Tyra!" Arek ran up the stairs and pushed Nels aside. The favored knight glared at him. "What are you doing here? I thought you were dead!"

"I thought you were dead, too," Nels replied.

Arek blinked, as though he were confused.

"We must take the princess to her room," Bosh said. "I will send for her mother and father."

Nels was about to stand and cradle Tyra when Arek stepped in front of him. The knight's large frame blocked Nels completely. "Thanks," Arek said. "*I* will carry her." He slipped his arms under Tyra's body and walked toward the castle's upper floors.

Nels had begun to follow Arek when a hand clasped his shoulder. Holding the Needle at its middle, the old tailor kept Nels back as Arek and Tyra disappeared down the hall.

"I have to make sure she's all right," Nels said.

"That would be unwise." Bosh placed a second hand on Nels's shoulders. He led the boy to the stairs, and descended with him. They approached Rasmus's body, sprawled on the floor. Guards stood on either side of him, their spears ready to strike if there was the slightest twitch. "Tyra's thread is worn even thinner than yours. I fear the smallest excitement could

329

sever it. If I could keep the favored knight away from her, I would. But for now, having the two of you wrestling at her bedside will only do her harm."

"Please," Nels said, "just for tonight."

"There is nothing more you can do here," Bosh said, "but there is much that you can do for your mother. She deserves to see you right now. Go home and rest." Bosh leaned close. "You may not realize it, but you followed in your father's footsteps, standing up against Rasmus as you did. Averand is in your debt. Be proud of that." They walked away from the Master Threader's body and headed for the hall's exit. "I will send you word when Tyra is well."

The promise comforted Nels, even if he was tempted to stay anyway. The hole in the roof allowed light from the waning half-moon to enter the hall. "What will become of the Needle?"

"I can assure you that it will be safe with me."

"Ickabosh?" A woman rushed forward from the open doorway.

Bosh spun right around. "Gleesel! Is that really you?"

Surprised to see her himself, Nels backed away, allowing the old woman to wrap her arms around the old tailor. "Oh, Ickabosh! I have so much to tell you, I don't know where to begin —"

"Neither do I!" Bosh exclaimed. "What are you doing here?"

Nels couldn't help but interrupt. "Why aren't you a goat?"

Bosh looked at Nels with an appalled face. "A goat?"

Gleesel laughed as she stepped back; her attention fell on Nels. "Only Princess Tyra and her ghost would know about that. It's nice to finally see and hear you, Nels. Thanks to the shadowed book — and you — I was able to lift my curse. And after I saw that horrible fabricator leave that knight to die, I removed him from the ground and cared for him. I used healing spells until he was strong enough to return to Averand" — she glanced at Rasmus's body — "and just in time, I see!"

Bosh stood speechless, his eyes never leaving the old woman.

Gleesel smiled, returning his gaze. "I'm so happy to see you."

Grateful to see the two old sorcerers reunited, Nels turned to go home. The waning moonlight spilled through the clouds and guided his way along the path through the fields. Nels took a deep breath, welcoming the cool night air. Tyra would be well soon, and then they would be together.

Like a ghost, Nels walked away from the castle without anyone noticing.

The first rays of sunlight grazed the highest peak of the Westerly Mountains as Nels snuck along the outskirts of Cobblestown. He wanted to remain hidden. If the villagers saw him, their questions would keep him from returning home. If anyone was going to see him alive first, it would be his mother.

There were not many early risers among the villagers, so his journey to the white oaks was an easy tread — until a company of knights charged through the village.

Wallin rode among them.

No, he was *leading* them.

They had missed the fight, but Nels was glad to see the men return. He hoped the Vagas were safe; he would have to visit Mylan soon, to thank her for all she and her people had done. Thinking of her ruling Westmine made Nels smile. It was a happy thought, but Nels couldn't stop worrying about Tyra.

As he walked among the white oak trees, every muscle in his body wanted to stop and rest. But he was grateful he had a body again to experience physical pain. He welcomed hunger, the thirst for water, and the smell of bluebells — so much sweeter than the beeswax that once overwhelmed his nose.

Moments later, Nels arrived at his cottage in the clearing. Smoke rose from the chimney. Mother always had an early start. Someone had painted the barn, and the fence had never looked better. Nels could not picture his mother doing all this work on her own — even with Jilia's help. The whole town must have pitched in. It comforted Nels to think that his mother had been well cared for during the difficult time. Nels let out a laugh as he passed his grave and approached the door. He stopped when he heard whining on the other side of it.

"It's scratchy!" Jilia protested. "I *really* don't like wearing this material!"

A smile crept over Nels's face as he pushed the door open.

His mother sat on a stool next to Jilia, who was wearing a half-finished dress. The girl seemed a little taller, though Nels knew that was unlikely, and her hair had been cleaned up some. Without the rough edges, she was quite pretty. As they turned to the door, their jaws fell open. The look in their eyes brought tears to his own.

"Nels!" Mother cried. "Is . . . is it *really* you . . . ?"

Her voice made his tears flow. "I'm home, Mother."

Jilia gasped, jumped off the stool, and threw her arms around him. "You're alive!" she cried. Tears drenched his green vest. "I can't believe it! Oh, Nels! You're alive!"

His mother rushed in and embraced him, kissing him tenderly on the cheeks as she, too, cried onto his chest. "My son, my perfect son!" she said.

Nels held them both for a very long time.

28

THE PEASANT OF AVËRAND

Nels did not like the taste of dirt, but after all he had been through, he was glad to taste anything. "Do you give?" Wallin said, having pinned Nels outside the barn. "Do you?"

A part of Nels wanted to say *never* for old time's sake, but his body was still weak from his battle against Rasmus. Reaching out his hand, Nels tapped the ground. The unconquerable Knight of Cobblestown had finally lost.

Wallin wiped his brow as he leaned back. "You can't give up! I want a rematch!"

"Take the win, Wallin," Nels said, catching his breath. "You bested me."

"Get up, you quitter," Wallin demanded. "I want another go!"

"What're you doing?" Jilia ran over to the boys and groaned when Nels spat grime from his mouth. Rolling around in front of the barn had layered his body with dust. Accusation clouded Jilia's round face — a look that reminded Nels of a much younger, brown-haired version of his mother. Jilia's neat skirt completed the illusion. "I thought we were going to the village!" she said.

Wallin chuckled. "We were passing time while you were playing dress up."

Jilia's hands curled into fists, her cheeks red. "Watch it . . ."

Nels reached for Wallin's hand. "Help me up, will you?"

Wallin clasped his hand around Nels's wrist and pulled his old friend up. Wallin looked down at his hand and flexed his fingers. Nels sensed the confusion, the need for reassurance; Wallin had acted this way ever since Nels returned from the grave.

"You owe me a rematch," Wallin said.

"Count on it. Just let me take care of my errands first," Nels replied.

Turning to the barn, Wallin retrieved a leather vest from a sawhorse. Beside it was a long sheathed sword. He looped a new leather scabbard through a strap and let it rest against his thigh. Nels's return was not the only amazing story that had spread throughout the countryside. Those who knew about Rasmus had cheered at the news of his death, and they celebrated Sir Arek for killing him. Others found joy in the princess's safe return, and for her returned sanity. The people of Cobblestown showered Wallin with praise for helping the knights in a time of need; the knights had rewarded him, too, officially making him a squire.

Once Wallin had assembled his gear, they headed into the woods for Cobblestown.

"When do you begin training?" Nels asked.

"Today," Wallin said, without a shred of excitement. "I'll stop at home first."

Jilia glanced at him. "You don't seem happy about it."

"You wouldn't be, either," Wallin said, "if you had to serve under that pompous *Sir* Arek." He let out a sigh. "*You* wanted this more than anyone, Nels. You should be the one —"

"You've proven yourself," Nels said. "We both have."

Wallin smirked. "I'm glad you're okay, but you wrestle like you're only half alive."

Nels crossed his arms as Jilia raised a fist. If Wallin only knew.

"Give him a chance!" Jilia cried. "He's still recovering."

"I'm his friend, too, you little imp-sprout. Don't hit me for being honest." Wallin adjusted the collar of his new vest. "We bury him and then he dawdles back like nothing happened?" The new squire locked his eyes on Nels's. "I don't buy that, but I can keep a secret."

Nels understood what Wallin meant. He knew Wallin couldn't deny the wrestling match they'd shared at the Vagas' camp. It was noble of him to keep their encounter a secret. Jilia, on the other hand, was oblivious. She kept staring at Nels, her eyes darting away when he caught her looking.

They had reached the quarry when a whinny caught their attention. Lars the blacksmith's horse and wagon approached the summit. The blacksmith was trim and wore a black vest similar to one of Nels's. It was obvious that Mother had made it for Lars. They'd seen a lot of each other since Nels's death. "Afternoon," Lars greeted, pulling the wagon to a stop. "How are you today?"

"Feeling better," Nels said. "Still have a lot on my mind."

"I'm sure you'll mull it out soon. How is your mother?"

"She's been waiting for you all morning," Jilia said. "You're late!"

Lars winked at her. "I must tread lightly. Thanks, Jil."

Nels couldn't contain his laughter. Neither could the others. Lars tapped his horse with the end of his whip and the wagon rolled to the white oaks as Nels and his friends descended toward the village. Nels was grateful that he already felt well enough to fetch the usual supplies that his mother needed. Jilia's dress hindered her stride as they walked.

The castle in the distance seemed to touch the clouds. Nels breathed deeply, his journey with the princess still fresh on his mind. A day and a half had passed since that night and he'd still had no word from the tailor or Tyra. If he had to wait much longer — the very thought drove him mad.

What could be taking so long?

The three paused before they entered the village. "Ready for this?" Jilia asked.

Nels nodded. "I have to go in there at some point."

"Maybe I'll tag along for a while before I go home," Wallin said.

Once they'd entered, a few villagers smiled in passing, but most stared at Nels in shock. Others tried to ignore him or called for their children to come inside. Even a few of the girls who used to smile at Nels shied away from his glance. It made sense — they'd held a funeral and buried him. Those who didn't see his return from the grave as a miracle must have thought it a curse. He sighed. He couldn't blame them.

As they neared the textile shop, Nels heard Tyra's name mentioned from one villager to another. "Have you heard the news?" Hilga asked them. "Princess Tyra is set to marry Sir Arek! I had a feeling they would, as close as they were during the festival and all!"

Nels's heart jumped to his throat. He couldn't believe what he'd heard, not after what he and Tyra had been through together. Doubt set in. Something wasn't right. He knew there was something genuine behind their kiss, and he was sure that Tyra knew it, too. Love was the only way they could have come back from death — they *both* had to love each other.

Then why would she agree to marry Arek after all that? Abandoning his errands, Nels turned down the road toward Hillshaven.

"Uh, Nels?" Jilia asked. "The shop's right here. Where're you going?"

Nels didn't stop. He couldn't wait for Bosh any longer.

"Wait up!" Wallin called from behind.

No. I have to see Tyra — now.

It was midafternoon by the time they entered the city gates. Nels headed for the castle, his stiff legs still keeping him from a full run. Both Wallin and Jilia clearly wanted to know what he was up to, but he wouldn't speak. He couldn't be bothered with anything else.

Nels walked through the castle into the main hall. A few servants paused as they were cleaning up the rubble and asked if they could be of assistance. Nels ignored them, climbed the stairs, and turned down the corridor that led to Tyra's chamber.

"What're you doing?" Wallin said. "We're not allowed to go this far."

"How do you know your way around so well?" Jilia added.

At the entrance of the east wing, guards blocked Nels from continuing. "I'm here to see Tyra," he said. "Let me pass."

"You'll end up in the stocks if you keep this up," Wallin warned.

Down the hall, Nels saw Arek leaving Tyra's bedchamber. Nels stepped forward, pushing his weight against the guards' crossed spears. The guards shoved back, sending Nels to the floor.

Both Wallin and Jilia gasped, the looks on their faces confirming that they thought Nels had lost his mind. Maybe he had. So be it. One way or another, he was going to find a way to Tyra.

Arek made his way toward them, cracking his knuckles as he walked. "What is this?" The favored knight looked down at Nels. "You?" He frowned hard. "What is *your* business here?"

Nels returned to his feet. "My business isn't with you, Arek. Let me pass."

The commotion had gathered the attention of a few servants and nobles; many gawked at Nels and his lack of propriety. Arek smiled thinly. "You are not permitted to see my betrothed."

"*Your* betrothed?" Nels scoffed. "I'd like to hear that from Tyra herself, thanks."

Nels stepped forward, about to force his way past, when the knight grabbed his shoulder and flung him back again. As he hit the ground, Nels heard the onlookers whispering to each other, asking who he was and what he was doing there.

Why would a peasant come to see the princess?

"Do not think I will allow you near her," Arek said coldly. "You are neither welcome nor wanted here." He nodded at the nearby guards, who reached down and lifted Nels by his arms. "Lock him in the stocks for a few hours. That should knock some sense into him."

It would take more than stocks to silence Nels. "Tyra doesn't love you! She knows you only want to marry her for the throne." Nels watched Arek's face turn pale as the onlookers paused, holding their breath at the sudden accusation. "No matter how many coins you slip, and no matter how many lies you tell, Tyra will never marry you!"

Like a rat caught in a kitchen, the knight glanced around nervously at the onlookers, who looked back at him with questioning stares. "Enough of your insolence," Arek said. "Make it a few *days* in the stocks. That will teach you your place, *peasant*!"

Not without a fight!

Yanking his arm free, Nels flung his fist into the knight's jaw.

Arek reeled back, his hand flying to his mouth. A chorus of gasps echoed down the corridor as pain began to set within Nels's knuckles. Arek's jaw was as strong as it looked. Wallin stood speechless and Jilia had tears in her eyes. She had never looked so disappointed. While the knight nursed his face, the guards grabbed Nels again, so tightly that his arms tingled from a lack of blood flow.

Arek towered over Nels. "I will have your head on a block before this day is through." Arek turned to the side and spat blood onto the floor. "Take this filth to the dungeons."

The dungeons — the one place in the castle that Nels hadn't seen yet.

"No!" Jilia cried. "He didn't mean it. Please don't take him away!"

"Don't worry," Wallin said, his hand on Jilia's shoulder. "I'll —"

"Wallin!" Arek shouted. "How could you let these peasants enter the castle? Get her out of here!"

Jilia's sobs faded away as the guards dragged Nels underground. The torch-lit corridors reminded Nels of Bosh's own underground chambers. Where was Bosh, anyway? The tailor had promised to send word when Tyra was well.

Nels laughed at himself. It no longer mattered. He had picked a fight that he knew he couldn't win. It was unlikely the king would have Nels executed for such an offense, but whatever the punishment, it would undoubtedly be severe.

You've really done it this time, Nels. . . .

The guards threw him into an empty cell and slammed the iron door. Nels grabbed the cold metal and tested the bars; he was alone with a single torch for light. With no cot or chair, Nels sat on the floor, his back against the stone wall.

This was but a momentary setback, he tried to convince himself. Nothing would stop him from finding Tyra.

In hindsight, a little patience would have done him well. Finding a different way to Tyra would have been no trouble. Nels hoped she would see through Arek's fraud — whatever tricks he'd played on her. Nels sat for what felt like hours and listened to the quiet. His thoughts returned to the kiss that had brought him back to life. Would he ever know that feeling again?

Nels heard a door open down the passage, followed by hurried steps and rattling keys. Someone was coming for him. "I can't believe you would stoop this low," Tyra said. "Where is he?"

"He was acting like a madman," Arek answered. "Look what he did to me!"

"He did *that*?" She paused, a smile in her voice. "Looks like he saved me the trouble."

Nels stood and faced the bars as Tyra entered his view. Their eyes met at once. She was wearing her nightgown, despite the midday hour. She looked tired. Mylan's sapphire stone hung around her neck, and she wore the conjurer's ring on her hand.

Arek followed her, his face full of frustration. "This is a mistake, Tyra."

"The only mistake is what *you've* done. How dare you send a knight of Averand here!"

"Knight of Averand?" Arek scoffed. "He is no knight. He is a peasant, nothing more —"

"He is a knight to *me*! Hand me the keys."

"My love . . ." Arek said, his anger rising. "What has become of you?"

"The keys, Sir Arek . . ." she demanded. Exhaling through his nose, the knight placed the keys into her hand. "You may leave us. Nels will accompany me back to my chamber."

Arek's final, infuriated glare sent a chill down Nels's back. The knight turned down the passage and left him alone with Tyra. Although she looked alert, Nels could tell from her stance that she was still recovering from their ordeal. Her thread was not yet at its full strength again — just like his. Nels cleared his throat. He had no idea what to say, but he was relieved to see that Tyra seemed excited to see him.

She shook her head. "I'm not surprised to see you down here."

Nels smiled back. "*I'm* surprised to see *you* here."

"I know," she replied. "Come to think of it, I've never been down here until now."

A rat scampered across the far corner of the cell.

"It's cozy," Nels said.

Tyra reached for her heart, as if she were in pain.

"How's your wound?" he asked.

Her hand lingered over her chest. "It stings, sometimes."

"Bosh said he'd send for me when you were well, but I'd heard nothing."

"He had to rush to Mendarch to . . . fix something . . ."

"Fix something? In Mendarch?" Nels couldn't imagine what would take Bosh to that distant land. Then again, who knew where a fabricator's help was required? "Did someone bury Rasmus?"

"Burned," Tyra answered. "Bosh was very thorough."

This relieved Nels. Nothing was more final than ash.

"Why are you so full of questions all of a sudden?" Tyra asked.

Nels glanced around. "That's really all I can do in here."

"Oh! Right! I'm such a half-wit!" Tyra searched the keys, trying to find the right match. "You were right about Arek. I didn't want to believe what you said, but —" She pointed at her ring. "What a louse! While I've been too weak to leave my chamber, he spread rumors about me being engaged to him." The third key did the trick and she wasted no time opening the door.

Nels rushed from the cell and embraced his princess.

Tyra settled into his arms. "I meant what I said to Arek," she said. "You've proven yourself a knight to me, and my father has agreed to accept you into Avërand's ranks — just as you wanted!"

In the past, those words would have thrilled Nels. "Thank you . . . but I can't."

Tyra gasped in surprise. "I thought you wanted to make a difference."

"You taught me that I don't have to be a knight to do that. I've wanted to make a difference my whole life, but I never saw the difference that I could make — just by being who I am."

She tightened her embrace. A single tear graced her cheek. "That's all I want," she said. "I love you, Nels!" She held his neck and their lips touched — longer than any kiss they had shared before.

As they parted, Nels whispered into her ear. "You're rather close . . ."

Tyra smiled. A new desire burned in her eyes. "Not close enough."

Needing no further encouragement, Nels smiled back as they kissed again.

EPILOGUE

A PROMISING SEAMSTRESS

Jilia sat in the town square, her mood a tangled mess.

Most of the wedding party had returned home by now. The guests had carried on for hours after the newlywed couple left for the Valley of Westmine, a political retreat some had called it — not that Jilia cared. The castle's grand terrace was a wreck. Jilia wanted to leave, but her ride was with Lars, and he wouldn't leave without Norell, who was busy chatting with the few guests who still lingered. The dress Norell wore — she'd sewn it herself, of course — made her look like a noblewoman.

All evening, Jilia had suppressed her quivering lip.

Why would you marry her, Nels?

Jilia couldn't stop thinking about Nels, happily married to the last person she expected him to marry. She tried to distract herself by focusing on the potbellied guest who wore a lantern on his head, or the unexpected entertainment the Vagas had provided, and the strange wisdom of Mylan, the new Queen of Westmine. It was no use; her thoughts never strayed long from Nels. Sir Arek was the only person at the wedding who appeared as frustrated as she was. He'd had too much to drink, and he scowled at the newlyweds whenever he thought no one was looking.

Jilia let out a sigh. She had always liked Nels, but it was only a matter of time before some pretty strumpet his own age took him away from her. The day wasn't a complete waste, however: Tyra's gown — Jilia's own seamstress work — was the most talked about topic at the party. The king had visited Norell personally to ask if she would fashion a dress for his daughter. Norell asked Jilia to sew a hem, and before she knew, she had finished most of the dress in no time.

From that day on, Norell kept telling Jilia, "You have a gift."

The girl tapped the rim of her glass and listened to it hum.

"Excuse me, miss. Did you make the gown the princess wore today?"

Jilia looked up, startled out of her thoughts. She had seen this old man once before; months ago, he had accompanied Nels to the festival.

"I helped," she said curtly. "Why do you want to know?"

"I was impressed to hear that in just a few days you sewed what should normally have taken a month."

Jilia rolled her eyes and laid her head down on her arms. "It's not that hard, really."

"Harder for some than others, but there are those who have a knack — a natural ability," the old man said. "And I have no doubt that you will make a promising seamstress one day."

He searched his pocket and held out a small object. Jilia lifted her head and took the brass thimble from his palm. It surprised her how cool the metal felt in her hand. She looked up at the old man.

His smile reached his ears. "Would you like to learn more?"

Michael Jensen spent ten years developing the concept behind *Woven* before he met coauthor David Powers King, who expanded on Michael's vision and made it a reality. A graduate of Brigham Young University's prestigious music, dance, and theater program, Michael taught voice at BYU before establishing his own vocal instruction studio. In addition to being an imaginative storyteller, Michael is an accomplished composer and vocalist. He lives in Salt Lake City with his husband and their four dogs.

David Powers King was born in beautiful downtown Burbank, California, where his love for film inspired him to become a writer. An avid fan of science fiction and fantasy, David also has a soft spot for zombies and the paranormal. He now lives in the mountain West with his wife and their three children.